The View from Alameda Island

ROBYN CARR

The View from Alameda Island

mira

mira

ISBN-13: 978-0-7783-6895-3

The View from Alameda Island

For questions and comments about the quality of this book, please contact us at CustomerService@Harlequin.com.

BookClubbish.com

Printed in U.S.A.

For Phyllis and Eric Preston, with affection.

The View from Alameda Island

CHAPTER ONE

Today was Lauren Delaney's twenty-fourth wedding anniversary and there wouldn't be a twenty-fifth. To many it appeared Lauren had a perfect life but the truth was something she kept to herself. She had just been to see her lawyer and now she needed a little time to think. She headed for one of her favorite places. She needed the solace of a beautiful garden.

Divine Redeemer Catholic Church was an old church that had survived all of the earthquakes since the big one—the San Francisco earthquake of 1906. Lauren had only been inside the building a couple of times, but never for mass. Her mother had been Catholic, but she hadn't been active. The church had a beautiful garden where parishioners often walked and there were several benches where you could sit and pray or meditate. Lauren was on her way home to Mill Valley from her job at Merriweather Foods and she stopped there, something she did frequently. There were no brochures explaining the genesis of the garden or even the fact that the church sat on such a generous plot of land for Northern California, but she'd happened upon an old priest once and he'd told her one of the priests in the early 1900s was a fanatic about growing things. Even though he'd been dead for decades, the church kept the garden going. They even preserved a large garden behind the beautiful flowers for fruits and vegetables, which they donated to food banks or used to feed hungry people in poorer parishes.

Divine Redeemer's parish just outside of Mill Valley, California, didn't have many hungry people. It was an upper-class area. It was where she lived.

She was very well off. Richer than she'd ever imagined by her family's standards, yet her husband ranted about his low pay. He was a prosperous surgeon raking in over a million a year but he didn't have a yacht or a plane, which irked him. He spent a great deal of time managing and complaining about his finances.

She would be leaving him as soon as she could finalize the details. She had spent an hour with her attorney, Erica Slade, today. Erica had asked, "So, is this going to be it, Lauren?"

"The marriage was over many years ago," Lauren said. "All that's left is for me to tell him I'm leaving. I'm getting my ducks in a row."

They would be spending the evening at a charity auction and dinner. For that she was so grateful. There would be no staring at each other over a starched white tablecloth searching for things to say, no watching Brad check his phone and text all through the meal. As he was fond of reminding her, he was an important man. He was in demand. She was nothing.

If she ever received a call or text, it was from one of her daughters or her sister. But if they knew she was out, they wouldn't expect a response. Except maybe her eldest daughter, Lacey. She had inherited her father's lack of boundaries and sense of entitlement—it was all about her. Her younger daughter, Cassie, had, perhaps unfortunately, inherited Lauren's cautious and reticent nature. Lauren and Cassie didn't like conflict, didn't step on toes.

"When are you going to stand up for yourself, Lauren?" Brad had been known to say to her. "You're so spineless." Of course, he meant she should stand up to anyone but him.

Oh, wouldn't Brad be surprised when she finally did. And he'd be angry. She knew people would inevitably ask, *Why now? After twenty-four years?* Because it had been twenty-four *hard* years. It had been hard since the beginning. Not every minute of it, of course. But overall, her marriage to Brad had never been a good situation. She spent the first several years thinking she could somehow make it better, the next several years thinking she probably didn't have it so bad since he was *only* emotionally and verbally abusive, and the last ten years thinking she couldn't wait to escape once her daughters were safely raised. Because, the truth was he was only going to get more cantankerous and abusive with age.

The first time she'd seriously considered leaving him, the girls were small. "I'll get custody," he said. "I'll fight for it. I'll prove you're unfit. I have the money to do it, you don't." She'd almost done it when the girls were in junior high. He'd been unfaithful and she was sure it hadn't been the first time he'd strayed, just the first time he'd been caught. She'd taken the girls to her sister's cramped little house where the three of them shared a bedroom and the girls begged to go home. She returned and demanded marriage counseling. He admitted to a meaningless fling or two because his wife, he said, was not at all enthusiastic about sex anymore. And the counselor cautioned her about throwing away the father of her children, explained that the repercussions could be very long-term. She found another counselor and it happened again—the counselor sympathized with Brad. Only Lauren could see that Brad was a manipulator who could turn on the charm when it suited him.

Rather than trying yet another counselor, Brad took the family on a luxurious vacation to Europe. He pampered the girls and ultimately Lauren gave the marriage yet another chance. Then a couple of years later he gave her chlamydia and blamed her. "Don't be ridiculous, Lauren. You picked it up somewhere and gave it to me! Don't even bother to deny it."

She'd told him she wanted a divorce and he had said, "Fine. You'll pay the price. I'm not going to make it easy for you."

Knowing what was at stake, she moved into the guest room instead.

Days became weeks, weeks became months. They went back to marriage counseling. In no time at all Lauren suspected their marriage counselor had an agenda and favored Brad. She helped him make excuses, covered for him, pushed Lauren to admit to her manipulative nature. Lauren suspected him of sleeping with the counselor. He told her she'd become sick with paranoia.

By the time Lacey was in college and Cassie was applying to colleges, Brad was worse than ever. Controlling, domineering, secretive, verbally abusive, argumentative. God, why didn't he want her to just leave? Clearly, he hated her.

But he told her if she left him he wouldn't pay college tuition. "No judge can make me. I can be stuck with some alimony but not support payments. And not tuition. When they're over eighteen they're on their own. So go then," he'd said. "You'll be responsible for cutting them off."

The last few years had been so lonely. She had spent a lot of time worrying that by staying with a man like Brad she had taught her daughters a dreadful lesson. She'd done her best with them but she couldn't make them un-see how their own mother had lived her life.

She'd taken a few hours from work to meet with the lawyer, laying out plans, creating her list and checking things off. The lawyer had said, "He's had you running scared for years. We have laws in this state. He can't cut you off and freeze you out. I'm not saying it will be easy or painless, but you will not starve and your share of the marital assets will be delivered."

It was time. She was finally ready to go.

Lauren inhaled the smell of spring flowers. This was one of the best times of year in Northern California, the Bay Area and inland, when everything was coming to life. The vineyards were greening up and the fruit trees were blossoming. She loved flowers; her grandmother had been a ferocious gardener, turning her entire yard into a garden. Flowers soothed her. She needed a garden right now.

Lauren heard the squeaking of wheels and looked up to see a man pushing a wheelbarrow along the path. He stopped not too far from her. He had a trowel, shovel and six plants in the wheelbarrow. He gave her a nod, and went about the business of replacing a couple of plants. Then he sat back on his heels, looked at her and smiled. "Better?" he asked.

"Beautiful," she said with a smile.

"Is this your first time in this garden?" he asked.

"No, I've been here a number of times," Lauren said. "Are you the gardener?"

"No," he said with a laugh. "Well, yes, I guess I am if I garden. But I'm just helping out today. I noticed a few things needed to be done…"

"Oh, is this your church?"

"Not this one, a smaller church south of here. I'm afraid I've fallen away…"

"And yet you still help out the parish? You're dedicated."

"I admire this garden," he said. He rotated and sat, drawing up his knees. "Why do you come here?"

"I love gardens," she said. "Flowers in general make me happy."

"You live in the right part of the country, then. Do you keep a garden?"

"No," she said, laughing uncomfortably. "My husband has very specific ideas about how the landscaping should look."

"So he does it?"

Get dirt under his nails? Hah! "Not at all. He hires the people who do it and gives them very firm orders. I don't find our garden nearly as beautiful as this."

"I guess you have nothing to say about it, then," he said.

"Not if it's going to create conflict," Lauren said. "But it's kind of a secret hobby of mine to find and visit gardens. Beautiful gardens. My grandmother was a master gardener— both her front and backyard were filled with flowers, fruits and vegetables. She even grew artichokes and asparagus. It was incredible. There was no real design—it was like a glorious jungle."

"When you were young?"

"And when I was older, too. My children loved it."

"Did your mother garden?" he asked.

"Very little—she was a hardworking woman. But after my grandparents passed away, she lived in their house and inherited the garden. I'm afraid she let it go."

"It's a hereditary thing, don't you think?" he asked. "Growing up, our whole family worked in the garden. Big garden, too. Necessary garden. My mother canned and we had vegetables all winter. Now she freezes more than cans and her kids rob her blind. I think she does it as much for all of us as herself."

"I would love that so much," Lauren said. Then she wondered how the residents of Mill Valley would react to seeing her out in the yard in her overalls, hoeing and spreading fresh, stinky fertilizer. It made her laugh to herself.

"Funny?" he asked.

"I work for a food processor. Merriweather. And they don't let me near the gardens, which are primarily research gardens."

"So, what do you do?" he asked.

"I cook," she said. "Product development. Testing and recipes. We test the products regularly and have excellent consumer outreach. We want to show people how to use our products."

"Are you a nutritionist?" he asked.

"No, but I think I'm becoming one. I studied chemistry. But what I do is not chemistry. In fact, it's been so long..."

He frowned. "Processed foods. A lot of additives," he said. "Preservatives."

"We stand by their safety and it's a demanding, fast-paced world. People don't have time to grow their food, store it, make it, serve it." His cell phone rang and he pulled it from his pocket. "See what I mean?" she said, his phone evidence of the pace of modern life.

But he didn't even look at it. He switched it off. "What, besides flowers, makes you happy?" he asked.

"I like my job. Most of the time. Really, ninety percent of the time. I work with good people. I love to cook."

"All these domestic pursuits. You must have a very happy husband."

She almost said nothing makes Brad happy, but instead she said, "He cooks, too—and thinks he's better at it than I am. He's not, by the way."

"So if you weren't a chemist cooking for a food company, what would you be? A caterer?"

"No, I don't think so," she said. "I think trying to please a client who can afford catering seems too challenging to me. I once thought I wanted to teach home economics but there is no more home ec."

"Sure there is," he said, frowning. "Really?"

She shook her head. "A nine or twelve-week course, and it's not what it once was. We used to learn to sew and bake. Now there's clothing design as an elective. Some schools offer cooking for students who'd like to be chefs. It's not the same thing."

"I guess if you want homemaking tips, there's the internet," he said.

"That's some of what I do," she said. "Video cooking demonstrations."

"Is it fun?"

She nodded after thinking about it for a moment.

"Maybe I should do video gardening demos."

"What makes you happy?" she surprised herself by asking.

"Just about anything," he said with a laugh. "Digging in the ground. Shooting hoops with my boys when they're around. Fishing. I love to fish. Quiet. I love quiet. I love art and design. There's this book—it's been a long time since I read it—it's about the psychology of happiness. It's the results of a study. The premise that initiated the study was what makes one person able to be happy while another person just can't be happy no matter what. Take two men—one is a survivor of the Holocaust and goes on to live a happy, productive life while the other goes through a divorce and he can hardly get off the couch or drag himself to work for over a decade. What's the difference between them? How can one person generate happiness for himself while the other can't?"

"Depression?" she asked.

"Not always," he said. "The study pointed out a lot of factors, some we have no control over and some are learned behaviors. Interesting. It's not just a choice but I'm a happy guy." He grinned at her.

She noticed, suddenly, how good-looking this man was. He looked like he was in his forties, a tiny amount of gray threading his dark brown hair at his temples. His eyes were dark blue. His hands were large and clean for a gardener. "Now what makes a volunteer gardener decide to read psychology?" she asked.

He chuckled. "Well, I read a lot. I like to read. I think I got that from my father. I can zone out everything except what's happening in my head. Apparently I go deaf. Or so I've been told. By my wife."

"Hyper focus," she said. "Plus, men don't listen to their wives."

"That's what I hear," he said. "I'm married to an unhappy woman so I found this book that was supposed to explain why some schmucks like me are so easy to make happy and some people just have the hardest damn time."

"How'd you find the book?"

"I like to hang out in bookstores…"

"So do we," she said. "It's one of the few things we both enjoy. Other than that, I don't think my husband and I have much in common."

"That's not a requirement," he said. "I have these friends, Jude and Germain, they are different as night and day." He got to his feet and brushed off the seat of his pants. "They have nothing in common. But they have such a good time together. They laugh all the time. They have four kids so it's compromise all the time and they make it look so easy."

She frowned. "Which one's the girl? Oh! Maybe they're same sex…?"

"Germain is a woman and Jude's a man," he said, laughing. "I have another set of friends, both men, married to each other. We call them the Bickersons. They argue continuously."

"Thus, answering the question about gender…"

"I have to go," he said. "But… My name is Beau."

"Lauren," she said.

"It was fun talking to you, Lauren. So, when do you think you might need to spend time with the flowers next?"

"Tuesday?" she said, posing it as a question.

He smiled. "Tuesday is good. I hope you enjoy the rest of your week."

"Thanks. Same to you." She walked down the path toward her car in the parking lot. He steered his wheelbarrow down the path toward the garden shed.

Lauren made a U-turn, heading back toward him. "Beau!" she called. He turned to face her. "Um… Let me rethink that. I don't know when I'll be back here but it's not a good idea, you know. We're both married."

"It's just conversation, Lauren," he said.

He's probably a psychopath, she thought, *because he looks so innocent, so decent.* "Yeah, not a good idea," she said, shaking her head. "But I enjoyed talking to you."

"Okay," he said. "I'm sorry, but I understand. Have a great week."

"You, too," she said.

She walked purposefully to her car and she even looked around. He was in the garden shed on the other side of the gardens. She could hear him putting things away. He wasn't looking to see what she was driving or what her license plate number was. He was a perfectly nice, friendly guy who probably picked up lonely women on a regular basis. Then murdered them and chopped them in little pieces and used them for fertilizer.

She sighed. Sometimes she felt so ridiculous. But she was going to go to the bookstore to look for that book.

Lauren was in a much better mood than usual that evening. In fact, when Brad came home in a state—something about the hospital screwing up his surgery schedule and flipping a couple of his patients without consulting him—she found herself strangely unaffected.

"Are you listening, Lauren?" Brad asked.

"Huh? Oh yes, sorry. Did you get it straightened out?"

"No! I'll be on the phone tonight. Why do you think I'm so *irritated*? Do you have any idea what my time is worth?"

"Now that you mention it, I don't..."

"Isn't it lucky for you that you have a husband who is willing to take care of details like that..."

"Oh," she said. "Lovely."

"It might be nice if you said something intelligent for a change."

"It's the odd night when you're not taking calls," she said. "Were you hoping for a night off?"

"Obviously! Why do you imagine I brought it up? I've told them a thousand times not to get involved with my schedule. They're going to cause patients unnecessary anxiety, not to mention what they do to me! But they think I'm at their beck and call, that I serve at their pleasure, when I'm the money-making commodity. Even when I very carefully explain exactly how they should manage the schedule, can they figure it out? I'm paying a PA, a very overqualified PA to schedule for me, my clinics and my surgeries, and the hospital brings in this high school graduate who took a six-week course and gives her authority over *my* schedule..."

Lauren listened absently and fixed him a bourbon, watered, because they had to go to that fund-raiser tonight. She poured herself a glass of burgundy. This was her job, to listen and let him rant, to nod and occasionally say, *That must make you so angry.* While she did that, he paced or sat at the breakfast bar and she unwrapped some cheese and crackers and grapes for him to snack on.

But while all this was going on she was thinking about the man with the easy smile, the tiny bit of gray, the dark blue eyes. And she fantasized how nice it would be to have someone come home and not be a complete asshole.

"We might think about getting ready for the dinner," she said. "I'd like to look at the auction items."

"I know, I know," he said. "I bought a table. We shouldn't be too late."

Of course people would expect him to be late, to rush in at the last minute. "I'm ready. Do you need a shower?"

"I'll be down in five minutes," he said, leaving and taking his bourbon with him.

"Happy anniversary," she said to his departing back.

"Hmph," he said, giving a dismissive wave of his hand. "Nice anniversary," he grumbled. "My schedule is all fucked up."

The charity event was for the local Andrew Emerson Foundation supporting underprivileged children. They came to be known as Andy's kids. Tonight's event would raise money to provide scholarships for the children of fallen heroes. Professional athletes, businesses, the Chamber of Commerce, hospitals, veterans' groups and unions from San Francisco and Oakland supported the charity with fund-raising events such as this dinner and auction. Andy Emerson was a billionaire software developer in San Francisco; he was politically influential and admired by people like Brad. Brad never missed an event and claimed Andy as a friend. Brad was a fixture at the golf tournaments and donated generously. The children of military men and women and first responders disabled or killed in the line of duty could apply for the scholarships generated tonight. To be fair, Lauren had a great deal of respect for the foundation and all that it provided. She also happened to like Andy and Sylvie Emerson, though she was not so presumptuous as to claim them as friends. This event was a very popular, well-organized dinner that would raise tens of thousands of dollars.

Brad and Lauren attended this and many other similar

events; Brad's office and clinic staff were invited and he usually paid for a table. This was one of the few times during the year that Lauren visited with Brad's colleagues. And while Brad might be primarily fond of Andy's assets, Lauren thought the seventy-five-year-old Emerson and his wife of almost fifty years, Sylvie, were very nice people. It's not as though Brad and Lauren were invited over to dinner or out for a spin on the yacht—the Emersons were very busy, involved people. However, it was not unusual for Brad to get a call from some member of the Emerson family or a family friend with questions about an upcoming medical procedure or maybe looking for a recommendation of a good doctor.

Just as she was thinking about them, Sylvie Emerson broke away from the men she was chatting with and moved over to Lauren. She gave her one of those cheek presses. "I'm so happy to see you," Sylvie said. "I think it's been a year."

"I saw you at Christmastime in the city," Lauren reminded her. "You're looking wonderful, Sylvie. I don't know how you do it."

"Thank you. It took a lot of paste and paint. But you're aglow. How are the girls?"

"Thriving. Lacey is doing her post-grad study at Stanford so we see her fairly often. Cassidy graduates in about six weeks."

"UC Berkeley, isn't it?" Sylvie asked. "What's her field?"

Lauren chuckled. "Pre-law. She's scored beautifully on the LSAT and is bound for Harvard."

"Oh my God. Are you thrilled for her?"

"I don't know yet," Lauren said. "Don't you have to be a real tiger to take on law? Cassie seems so gentle-natured to me."

Sylvie patted her arm. "There is a special place within the legal system for someone like her. I don't know where, but she'll find it. And no one chose medicine?"

Lauren shook her head. "I'm a little surprised about that,

since I have a science major as well. Though it's been so long ago now that—"

She was distracted by a man who had been pressing his way through the crowd with two drinks and suddenly stopped. "Lauren?" he said. Then he smiled and those dark blue eyes twinkled. "I'll be damned."

"Beau?" she asked. "What in the world are you doing here?"

"Same as you, I suppose," he said. Then he looked at Sylvie and said, "Hi, I'm Beau Magellan. I just recently ran into Lauren at church."

Lauren laughed at that. "Not exactly, but close enough. Beau, this is Sylvie Emerson, your hostess tonight."

"Oh!" he said, sloshing the drinks. "Oh jeez," he mumbled. Finally, laughing, Lauren took his drinks so he could shake Sylvie's hand…after wiping his hands on his trousers. "It's a pleasure, Mrs. Emerson. I'm personally indebted to you!"

"How so, Mr. Magellan?"

"My sons have a friend whose dad was killed on the job, Oakland police, and she received a scholarship. Now I'm a big supporter of the cause."

"Magellan," Sylvie said. "Why does that sound familiar?"

"I have no idea," he said, chuckling. "I'm sure our paths wouldn't have crossed. Magellan Design is my company. It's not a big company…"

She snapped her fingers. "You designed a rooftop garden for my friend, Lois Brumfield in Sausalito!"

He beamed. "I did. I'm very proud of that, too—it's incredible."

Sylvie looked at Lauren. "The Brumfields are getting up there… Aren't we all… And they have a single-story home in Sausalito. They didn't have any interest in a two-story anything, their knees are giving out. So they put the garden on the roof! And they have a lift! They sit up there any evening the weather will allow. It's gorgeous! They have gardeners tend their roof!" Sylvie laughed. "They have a patio on the ground floor as well, nice pool and all that. But that rooftop garden is like their secret space. And the house is angled just right so it's private. From there they have an amazing view."

"There's a hot tub," Beau said. "And a few potted trees in just the right places."

"Really, if the Brumfields had more friends, you'd be famous!"

"They have you," Beau said.

"Oh, I've known Lois since I was in college. She's outlasted most of my family!" Then she looked at Lauren. "Church?"

Lauren laughed. She put Beau's drinks on the table she stood beside. "I stopped to see the gardens at Divine Redeemer Catholic Church—they're beautiful. And they're right on my way home. Beau was replacing a few plants. I thought he was the groundskeeper." She made a face at him.

"I love the grounds and I've known the priest there for a long time," Beau said. "I gave them an updated design and got them a discount on plants."

"Do you have a card, Mr. Magellan?" Sylvie asked.

"I do," he said. He pulled one out of his inside jacket pocket. "And please, call me Beau."

"Thank you," she said, sliding it into her slender purse. "And of course, I'm Sylvie. Lauren, the weather is getting nice. If I give you a call, will you come to my house, have lunch in my garden? Just you and me?"

"I would love that," she said. "Please do call! I'll bring you a plant!"

"I'll call. Very nice meeting you, Beau. Excuse me please. I have to try to say hello to people."

And that fast she was gone.

Lauren looked at Beau. "What am I going to do with you? Met me at church, did you?"

"In a manner of speaking," he said. "Seeing you here is even more startling."

"We're big supporters," she said. "See that bald guy over there? With Andy? My husband."

"Hm," he said. "He's friends with the host? Andy Emerson?"

"He believes so," she said. "Like I said, big supporter. Do you play golf?"

"I know how," Beau said. "I don't know that you could say I play, in all honesty."

"That's right," she said, laughing. "You read psychology. And fish. And garden." She glanced at the drinks. "Should you get those drinks back to your table?"

"They weren't dehydrated last time I looked. They're signing up for auction items."

"It's possible we have friends in common," she said. "My brother-in-law is an Oakland cop. I remember a fatality a couple of years ago."

"Roger Stanton," Beau said. "Did you know him?"

She shook her head. "Did you know him?"

"No, but the boys know the kids. You'll have to ask your brother-in-law..."

"Oh, Chip knew him. Even though it's a big department, they're all friends. It was heartbreaking. I'm so glad his daughter is a recipient." She nodded toward the drinks. "You should probably get those drinks back to your wife..."

He shook his head. "She's not here tonight. I brought my boys, my brother and sister-in-law and a friend."

"But not your wife?" she asked.

"Pamela finds this sort of thing boring and the friend I brought is a guy. But I don't find things like this boring. So tell me, what are you doing Tuesday?"

"What are you doing?" she asked.

"I'm going to check on the plants, maybe hoe around a little bit. H-O-E," he specified, making her laugh. "I'm going to put some bunny deterrent around. See how things are doing. I like the plants to get a strong hold before summer. Do you think you'll want to be uplifted by flowers?"

"You're coming on to a married woman," she said.

"I apologize! I don't want to make you uncomfortable. I'll get out of your space," he said, picking up the drinks.

"I might check out the plants," she said. "Now that I'm pretty sure you're not a stalker or serial killer."

"Oh Jesus, do I give off that vibe?" he asked, sloshing the drinks over his hands again. "I'm going to have to work on my delivery!"

"You sure don't give off the waiter vibe," she said, lifting a napkin from the table to assist him.

Just then, Brad was at her side. "We're down in front, Lauren. Don't make me come looking for you."

"I know. Brad, this is Beau Magellan, a landscape designer. A friend of Sylvie's."

Brad's black eyebrows shot up. "Oh? Maybe we'll have you take a look at ours." He put out a hand to shake, once he heard there was an Emerson connection, but Beau's hands were full of drinks. They were wet besides.

"Oh. Sorry," Beau said, lifting his handfuls clumsily.

"Okay," Brad said with a laugh. "Another time. I'll save you a seat," he said to Lauren.

"Sure. Be right there." She looked back at Beau, a mischievous smile playing at her lips.

"You're a liar, Lauren," Beau said.

"I'm sorry." She laughed. "It was irresistible. I hope we run into each other again, Beau. Now if there's anything left in those glasses, get them to your table."

CHAPTER TWO

Lauren knew she'd be going to the church gardens on Tuesday after work even though she thought it could be foolhardy. Becoming attracted to a man was not a part of her plan. In fact, it could be a major inconvenience. But she liked him. She liked that he read a lot and wanted to talk about what he'd read. She enjoyed how flustered he was meeting Sylvie. She adored the way he sloshed the drinks he carried. And it moved her that he was there to support a scholarship recipient who'd lost her father.

Of course he was there. She saw his back moving through the plants and shrubs. He was pulling off dead leaves and dried flowers. And putting them in his pocket!

She noticed there were some things on the bench—the one she had occupied the last time. A bag containing something and two Starbucks cups. It made her smile. He shouldn't have known that Starbucks would make her happy.

She cleared her throat. He turned toward her with a smile, shoving a handful of dead leaves and buds in his pocket.

"Hi," he said. "I brought you a mocha with whipped cream."

Perfect! Of course. "That's very thoughtful," she said, just standing there, feeling awkward.

"And something else," he said, lifting the bag.

"Oh, why did you do that? You shouldn't be giving me things. You should sit and relax and enjoy the flowers. And you were tidying up."

"I'm always grooming plants. Maybe it's a nervous habit." He pulled a handful of dried leaves and small sticks from his pocket, dumping them in the trash can. He handed her the bag. Inside was a book. *Flow: The Psychology of Optimal Experience.*

"This is great!" she said. "I actually went looking for this book! But I didn't ask for it, just looked in the psychology section."

"I had to find it at the used bookstore..."

"Did it change your life?"

"No, but it was enlightening."

She sat down on the bench, looking through the book. He handed her a coffee and stood at the other end of the bench. "I guess it didn't make your wife any happier," she said.

"No," he answered with a laugh. "She has always wanted something more. Something else. Listen, full disclosure, my wife and I are separated. We've been living apart for six months. We're getting divorced."

"Ah," Lauren said. "And you're getting back in the game."

He looked stricken. "No! I mean, that has nothing to do with you! I'm not looking for anything. You're a complete surprise. I might've done this even if—" He shook his head, looking embarrassed. "You just seem like a very nice person, that's all. And you complimented my flowers. This divorce—it's long overdue. It's not our first separation. And no, I haven't been known to mess around on the side. I have a couple of sons. Stepsons, actually. I wanted to keep their lives stable for as long as possible. They're seventeen and twenty. I think they understand we should be divorced and that I'll always have a home for them. If they don't know they can count on me by now, they never will. I'm not going anyplace."

"And their mother?" she asked.

"She loves them, of course," he said. "Maybe because they're boys, they're closer to me. Or maybe it's because their mother is hard to please."

"Oh God," she said. "It is not a good thing that we have this in common."

"You're separated?"

"Not yet," she said, hesitantly. "I have a difficult situation. I'm not ready to talk about it. But can you tell me about yours? Unless it's too..." She shrugged.

He settled in, sitting on the bench with his coffee. "Okay, I'll give you the short version. I've been married twelve years. We lived together first. The boys were four and seven when we met. They have two different fathers. Disinterested fathers. Pamela wasn't married to either of them. They hardly came around and when they did, they took only their son, not his brother. That just didn't make any sense to me. They're adults. Don't they realize little boys would be upset by that? Feel left out? Have self-confidence issues? So if I knew one or the other was coming to get his son I tried to have something planned for the one left behind. It didn't take much— just a little extra time to throw the ball around or play a video game. Just attention, that's all."

"That's so...*nice*," she said.

"No it's not," he said, almost irritably. "It's what an adult should do. It just makes sense. Doesn't it?"

"What did their mother say? About one son being left behind?"

"She was in conflict with their fathers over lots of things, so it was one more thing. But that didn't matter to me. Mike and Drew were little kids. They had enough trouble, you know? The school was saying Drew had learning disabilities and they tried to pin ADHD on Mike because he was restless. He was restless because he was a boy with a lot of energy who was kind of bored with school. Pamela would get mad, which didn't seem to resolve anything so I started going to some of these meetings at the school with her and we worked out programs for them. Pretty soon I was going to the meetings alone." He stopped and ran a hand around the back of his neck. "On our good days, she was very grateful I was willing to take them on. On our bad days she accused me of thinking I was their father and she reminded me I had no authority."

"I'm sorry," Lauren said.

"Drew graduates with honors in a few weeks," he said with a smile. "So much for his learning disability. Mike's in college with a nice GPA. He's got a great girlfriend, plays baseball, has lots of friends. Wants to be an architect," he added with a proud but shy smile.

"When did you know?" she asked. He gave her a perplexed look. "When did you know the marriage wouldn't last?"

"Almost right away," he said. "Within a couple of years. But I wasn't giving up. The guys... They might have two different fathers but they were going to have one stepfather. We did fine. We managed. I might still be managing but Pamela wanted to leave and I didn't put up a fight. At all." He laughed uncomfortably. "Then she wanted to come back and I said, no."

"I guess you're done," Lauren said.

"My mother says I'm a peacekeeper. She didn't consider it a compliment."

"Shame on her," Lauren said. "We could use a little more compromise and cooperation in this world!"

"Spoken like a true peacekeeper," he said. "As military ord-nance, a Peacekeeper is a land-based ICBM. A nuclear mis-sile. Maybe all those people who take us for granted should look out."

"Indeed," she said, smiling in spite of herself.

Then they both burst into laughter.

"How long have you been friends with Sylvie Emerson?" Beau asked.

"I'm not so sure we're really friends," she said. "We know each other because of our husbands. I'm sure we like each other. We run into each other at fund-raisers and social events. We're friendly, that's all. My husband served on the founda-tion board of directors for a few years and got cozy with a lot of Andy's friends. It's not that he's passionate about the cause. He's passionate about being connected and about Andy's bil-lions and influence, though what he hopes to do with either is beyond me. That's why I run into Sylvie a lot—Brad hangs close. He would deny that, by the way. I'll be surprised if she calls me for that lunch date—she's very busy. But let me tell you something. What I know of the Emersons is they're both sincerely good, generous people. Sylvie has mentioned that of all the work their foundation is able to do, she's par-tial to the scholarship fund. She and her husband might not have identical priorities, I'm not well acquainted with Andy, but Sylvie has told me more than once—we have to feed and educate the next generation, that's the only way we leave the world better than we found it."

"I wonder if they even realize how great a gift that is—giving an education. I don't know about you, but my family wasn't exactly fixed to send me to college."

"Nor was mine," she said. "I grew up poor."

"What's poor?" he asked, raising an eyebrow.

"I have a younger sister, Beth. Three years younger. When she was a baby our father went out for the proverbial pack of cigarettes and never came home. My mom worked two jobs the whole time we were growing up. My grandparents were alive and lived nearby, thank God. They helped. They watched us so she could work and probably chipped in when rent was late or the car broke down."

He smiled. "I have a large extended family. The six of us—my mom, dad, brother, two sisters and I lived in an old garage my parents converted into a small house. My mom still lives in that house, but I don't know how long that's going to last—she's getting a little feeble. My dad was a janitor, my mom served lunch at the junior high and cleaned houses. We got jobs as soon as we were old enough. But my folks, under-educated themselves, pushed us to get decent grades even though they couldn't help us with homework. We did our best. We might've been competing with the cousins a little bit."

"Nothing like a little healthy competition," she said. "Did you know you were poor?"

"Sure, to some extent. But we had a big family on that land. A couple of aunts and uncles, grandparents, cousins. Sometimes it got crowded. But if the heat went out in winter there were plenty of people to keep warm with. Heat in summer—no relief." He drank a little of his coffee. "We didn't have any extras, but it wasn't a bad way to grow up. Thing about it was we might've been poor but we were never poor alone."

"Can I ask you a personal question?"

"You can always ask, Lauren..."

"How do you think your life's going to change, getting divorced? Does this begin a whole new adventure of some kind?"

"Adventure?" he asked. "God no. My life doesn't have to change. I love my life today. I have work that makes people happy, good friends, amazing family. I have enough predictability every day so that it's not very often that something throws me off balance. I sleep well. My blood pressure is good. I don't know if I could have a better life. I just don't want it to change *back*."

She was quiet for a long moment. Finally she said, "Life must have been difficult… Before…"

"That's a hard question," he said. "Difficult? There were days I thought it was hard. Unbearable, really. But those days passed. What didn't pass was irritation. Unbalance. Never knowing what would be coming at you today. But ask anyone—you're not allowed to bail out because your wife has mood swings. Or because she yelled and now and then threw a glass at me. Hey, she missed, and cleaned up the shattered glass. But she wasn't a drunk, she never came at me with a knife, didn't sleep around…not counting those separations, when the excuse was that we were separated. According to the rule book, if you're able to work it out…" He shrugged. "So I stopped asking myself if I could live like this because I *could*, but that was the problem. I started asking myself if I *wanted* to live my life like that. And the answer was no. Fortunately for me, Pamela needed a little time to think again, to determine what she wanted from life. She needed another separation. Our fourth in a thirteen-year relationship. It was the perfect time for me to say, me, too." He chuckled. "Her separation was very short after hearing that. Mine was not. I decided I was happier on my own. I think I could be a happy old bachelor." He grinned. "I wouldn't have a boring or lonely day in my life. I think the boys might look in on me sometimes, make sure I haven't broken a hip."

"How old are you?" she asked.

"Forty-five," he said.

She snorted. "I don't think you have to worry about that broken hip for a while yet."

"I'm just saying, my life right now is fine. More fine than it was wondering which Pamela was coming home to dinner. But being sick of living with a volatile, angry, unpredictable person is not moral grounds for divorce. For better or worse, right?"

Lauren identified with so much of what he said but her first thought was, it's so much easier for men. They're not expected to have to put up with moody, angry women but women are supposed to put up with difficult men. She really wanted to let loose and complain about what it was like to live with a controlling, angry man. A man who could keep an argument going for *days*. A man who cut the line of people waiting to purchase movie tickets, loudly accused maître d's of losing the reservation he never made, shortchanged maintenance workers on their bills because he assumed they wouldn't dare come after him because they were undocumented or spoke poor English. Once while they were vacationing in Turks and Caicos he found some lounge chairs by the pool that were desirable, but they had towels on them—someone had already claimed them. There were a couple of pool toys as well, indicating they belonged to children. He threw the towels and toys on the ground beside the chairs, claimed the chairs for himself and his family and when a young man with two small children appeared five minutes later, he briskly told him, "You can't save chairs with towels. You have to be using them."

Brad was a bully who thought he was better than everyone else.

But Lauren didn't say anything to Beau. Unless people really knew Brad, they would never understand. So she changed the subject and asked Beau to tell her about rooftop gardens.

"My specialty," he said happily.

After an hour of pleasant conversation she decided she'd better leave. He asked if he'd be seeing her the following Tuesday and she said, "Very doubtful. This isn't a good idea."

He chuckled softly. "Oh. I wouldn't want to put you in

an uncomfortable position," he said. "You didn't say it but I already know. You're in the same spot as me. Maybe not identical, but close enough. I sympathize. And if you want someone to talk to you know how to find me."

She nodded sadly. Of course he didn't know how to find her. And she didn't tell him.

Beth Shaughnessy was spending her Sunday cleaning up the remnants of the party she and her husband Chip had thrown the night before. Chip had a new smoker and had treated many of their friends to a barbecue. While she had made good progress in the kitchen and great room, the patio and grill were still a disaster. Chip, whose given name was Michael, pleaded a slight hangover and promised to get out there with the boys to clean up after they watched a little of the US Open on the big screen in his den. The last time she looked in on them, Chip was flipping between basketball and golf and women's beach volleyball.

When Beth's sister, Lauren, had called earlier and asked if she could get away for lunch, Beth had said she had chores. Lauren said she'd go to the gym for a while then head over to Beth's. She needed to talk.

When Lauren most needed Beth and the phone wasn't good enough, Beth suspected marital angst. When you were married to Brad Delaney, *angst* was the kindest word one could apply. It took several deep breaths for Beth to remind herself to be careful what she said. The only serious and alienating fight the sisters had ever had was over Beth's low opinion of Brad and her sister's marriage. Well, sort of. It was more Beth's strong opinion that Lauren should get out, no matter what it took. Yet Lauren had stayed on. And on. And on.

Beth had been only twenty when Lauren and Brad were engaged to be married. At first she thought Brad handsome and sexy, but soon her impression of him changed. She heard and saw things that just weren't right. More than once, she'd heard Brad call Lauren an idiot. She saw him squeeze her hand so tightly it caused Lauren to wince and pull away. She wasn't sure exactly what was wrong but she knew it wasn't right. Even at her tender, inexperienced age Beth had said, "Lauren, what are you doing?"

"I'm marrying a handsome and successful doctor!" Lauren had said, beaming with joy. Lauren was seeing all those things they'd never had growing up—financial security, a beautiful and spacious home, cars that didn't break down, dining out, vacations... But behind the brightness of her eyes, something else lurked. And of course they hadn't even gotten through the wedding without tears of anguish and serious doubts. As anyone close to the couple could see, Brad, ten years older than Lauren, was temperamental, self-centered, grumpy and an egomaniac. He had a widowed mother, Adele, who was just an older version of her son. Adele was a controlling and temperamental sourpuss who had very firm ideas about what exactly was good enough for her entitled only child. Except Adele didn't know how to be charming. While Lauren and Beth had grown up in relative poverty with their single mother, Honey Verona, Brad had grown up well-to-do.

Right before the wedding Honey said, "Lauren, don't do it. You must see he won't even try to make you happy."

"But everything is planned and his mother paid for it all!" Lauren protested.

"It doesn't matter," Honey said. "You can walk away. Let them sue us."

Lauren almost didn't marry him. It was a last-minute melodramatic moment when she said, "I can't. I'm just not sure." Beth almost threw a party. But then she and the other bridesmaids were banished from the room while Brad's mother took over, having a heart-to-heart with Lauren. Dame Delaney was a force to be reckoned with...

And the wedding proceeded.

Beth and Lauren were nothing alike and yet they were vital to each other. Beth was a professional photographer. She did a lot of weddings, anniversaries, parties, even funerals. She also shot bridges, fields, wildlife, flowers, children, elderly people, beaches, sunsets... Beth was an artist. But she photographed a lot of people and she had learned to recognize who they were in their eyes, their expressions, their body language, their smiles or frowns. She could read people.

She had read Brad right. He was an asshole.

Lauren was more scientific. More pragmatic. A plotter and planner.

Beth had been married to Chip for sixteen years. They weren't able to produce children on their own so they had adopted a couple. Ravon was thirteen; they'd had him since he was four. Stefano was nine; they'd had him since he was two. Both came through the foster care system. Chip was a cop and big-time sports enthusiast, particularly golf. He taught the boys to play and the three of them were doing something that involved a ball every free second. Beth lived in a kind of rough-and-tumble house with a husband in a high-risk profession; she was always fighting that testosterone poisoning that created messes wherever it passed.

But Beth was not wired to take the kind of shit Lauren put up with. She rode the men in her family hard, insisting they pitch in and help, demanding courteous behavior. And she was just a little thing. A little thing who could haul forty pounds of camera equipment everywhere she went. Ravon was already taller than her, but that hadn't made her meek at all. She could bring all three men in her house to their knees with one killer stare.

Lauren showed up looking sleek and rich in her workout clothes, her thick chestnut hair pulled back in a ponytail. Lauren didn't ever seem to sweat, either. She sat at Beth's breakfast bar with a bottle of water while Beth dried the last of the serving platters. "How was your party?" Lauren asked.

"Loud," Beth said. "Bunch of cops and their spouses and kids. All the usual suspects. They stayed too late and disturbed the neighbors. It was great, in other words."

"We went to a cocktail party for a retiring doctor. I overheard Brad tell a couple of men he had to take the management of the finances away from me before I ran us into the poorhouse. Now he lets me keep track of my little paycheck while he manages the rest." She sighed. "I don't recall ever being in charge of the finances."

"I was just about to ask when you were in charge of the money..." Beth wasn't surprised by this mean little dig from her brother-in-law. "If he poked at me like that, he'd pull back a bloody stump," Beth said.

"He doesn't realize this, but he doesn't have much longer as my jailer. I just don't want to stress Cassie. I've put up with him for twenty-four years, I can put up with him a few more weeks. Get Cassie out of college."

The sound from the den erupted in a roar—someone made a basket, goal, or hole in one and Beth's men yelled. "I wouldn't have been married to him long enough to get my babies out of nappies, much less college," Beth said.

"They can't hear us, can they?" Lauren asked.

"They couldn't hear us if we were talking right into their dense male faces," Beth said.

"I put a deposit on a rental property that will be available July 1. I'm going to talk to the girls and move out. I've scheduled my vacation for after Cassie graduates and the first week of July. I suppose it will be sweltering."

Beth's mouth hung open for a moment. "This isn't the first time you've said this," Beth said.

"It's the first time I've rented something," Lauren said. "I've been to the lawyer, planned this out carefully. Listen, I'm sorry you've had to put up with me and my rotten marriage, my vacillating, my lack of courage and my mean husband. I'm a load and I know it. And now I need a favor."

"You know you're welcome here," Beth said.

"That's not what I need. I'm going to pack up some boxes and suitcases. I also have to buy a few things—new linens, some new kitchenware, that sort of thing. I need a place to store it. Someplace no one will notice."

"The guest room," Beth said. "We'll close the door. Can I say one small thing? Can I say, please God, please really do it this time! There's still time for you to have a life."

"I'm going to do it," Lauren said.

Beth gave a heavy sigh. In spite of all the bad things, Brad and Lauren had also been generous. He'd loaned them twenty-five thousand dollars to try in-vitro fertilization; he'd loaned them another twenty-five grand to build onto their house to make room for the boys. He and Lauren stepped up when Beth and Chip needed an expensive tutor for Stefano because he had a learning disability. Of course, Beth had long suspected Brad liked giving people loans they would take a long time to repay because it gave him power over them.

"Honey would be ecstatic," Lauren said. And immediately her eyes filled with tears.

They'd lost their mother two years ago. She'd been killed in a car accident; a truck driver had a medical episode, lost control of his huge truck and struck three vehicles, killing three people. Honey had never known what hit her—her death was instant, thank God.

"I miss her so much," Beth said. "It's just the two of us. I'm there for you. You're there for me—let's remember that. You've been to this lawyer how many times?" Beth asked.

"Leaving a man like Brad takes very careful planning," Lauren said.

"Are you afraid of him?"

"Of course. Not afraid he'll physically hurt me. He never does that…"

"A pinch here, a squeeze there…" Beth said, inexplicably rewashing a perfectly clean serving tray.

"He calls it affection gone a bit rambunctious," Lauren said.

"Because he's a liar. An experienced gaslighter."

Lauren sucked in her breath.

"All right, all right," Beth said. "I'll try to say nothing and just hope for the best."

"Once Cassie has graduated, there's really nothing more to hold me back."

Beth looked into her sister's beautiful lavender eyes. Lauren looked like pure perfection. She was elegant, smart, nurturing, compassionate, talented in so many ways, yet somehow held captive by an arrogant asshole. But she wouldn't call him that. Putting Lauren on the defensive might prevent her from freeing herself. Why her brilliant, loving, educated sister had chosen Brad eluded her. Why she stayed with him had confused her even more.

She had been young. She'd had stars and Wolf appliances in her eyes.

"Okay, tell me what you rented," Beth said.

"It's small and quaint, a Victorian, on a street that almost looks like the Seven Sisters in San Francisco," she said, keeping her voice down. "Three bedrooms and a loft, a long porch and deep yard on a lovely old street in Alameda. The owner lived a long and happy life there, building a lovely garden. There are big, healthy trees. Her son is keeping the house as a rental so it's being remodeled—new flooring, patching, texturing and painting the walls, new kitchen and bathroom cabinets, new appliances. I'm signing a one-year lease with an option to have first right of refusal if he decides to sell. He let me have some input on the materials… Or, let's say, I told him I did videos for Merriweather and he assumed I was a great homemaker..."

"You are," Beth confirmed.

As Lauren described the house, she became animated and Beth had hope for the first time in a long time. Only her rich sister would call a Victorian on the island of Alameda "quaint." It was probably a million-dollar property.

They talked about the house, the fact that Lauren could get back and forth to work more easily, that she'd have a say in how the yard looked, that it would be homey and all hers. She would have room for the girls when they visited. She hoped they would but it wouldn't surprise her to find they preferred their rooms at her current house. "The most important thing is that they know both their mother and father love them," Lauren said. And then she shuddered.

"It's not going to be easy," Beth said.

"I know," Lauren said in a shaky breath. "I plan to have a big celebration for Cassie's graduation. Once we've all come down from that, I'm going to help Cassie move to Boston. Then I'll talk to the girls. One at a time. Then I'm going to tell Brad. I would tell Brad first but once I do, I have to leave. If things don't fall into place like I plan—if one of the girls tells him before I can, or something—I might have to impose on you. I can't really stay there after I make my intentions clear. Because..."

"Because he will be horrible," Beth said, finishing for her.

They had done this before. But, in the end, Lauren had always stayed. Beth knew about everything—the suspected affairs, the STD, the separate bedrooms. No matter how bad things got, Lauren always tried to make the best of it for the sake of her daughters.

"I'll help you in any way you ask," Beth said. "What makes you think you'll really go through with it this time?"

"If I don't, I might as well resign myself to living out

my life with a mean, cantankerous old man who thinks he's smarter than God."

"Pretty soon, that will be the only option," Beth said.

Lauren ignored her or at least pretended to. "So, we'll celebrate Cassie's graduation and when my rental is available I'll tell them. Cassie will be in Boston for the next three years at least. Lacey has her apartment in Menlo Park. Once I've dealt with them, I'll face Brad."

"Maybe you shouldn't do that alone…"

"I've worked this out with the lawyer," Lauren said. "She has an investigator who is willing to stand by." Then Lauren shuddered again.

Beth hoped her sister would finally do it. Beth was terrified her sister would finally do it. This could get ugly.

Another loud cheer erupted from the den.

Beth and Lauren talked for a while longer. Every once in a while Beth would glance through the glass patio doors to the chaos outside—wet towels on the ground, various men's shoes, the greasy grill, plastic glasses, trash cans that were used for refuse, not all of which hit the mark. Lauren's surroundings would never be in such disarray. Brad would have a fit.

Beth's marriage wasn't perfect. There is stress in the lives of a cop's family; there is challenge in all relationships. She and Chip had money issues, kid problems—both of her sons were multiracial and hitting that puberty stage. Sometimes it seemed like a constant struggle. But they were happy.

But Lauren was married to an impossible jerk. Sad to say, but that trumped everything. How do you resolve yourself to life with a guy like that? No, he didn't beat her but he did twist an arm here, squeeze too hard there. No, he didn't get drunk every week. He'd had at least a couple of flings, but he was so repentant he even bought jewelry and took the whole family on trips so amazing the girls hoped he'd have another one. He treated people badly, told lies, believed he deserved slightly more consideration and a slightly bigger cut than anyone else, bullied his wife, put her down. And...he thought he was always right, no matter what. How do you explain that to your children?

When Lauren left Beth wandered into the den. Oh God, she should never have allowed them to put furniture in here. Chip was stretched out on the couch, Ravon's legs were hanging off the end of the loveseat. Stefano was lying on the floor with his feet up on the coffee table. It looked like a frat house. Morty, their old chocolate Lab, had his head resting on Stefano's belly. She was going to have to spray the room down with Febreze.

Something happened on the TV and all of a sudden everyone moved and cheered.

"Hey," she said. "Why does this den smell like the inside of a tennis shoe?"

"This is not a den," Chip said indignantly. "This is a man cave!"

"I beg your pardon," Beth said. "It's pretty gamey in here. Isn't it a little early in the year for the Open? Isn't that a June event?"

"This is an old one," Chip said. "Ten years old. It's a replay."

She was completely stunned for a second. "You have *got* to be kidding me! My backyard looks like a war zone and you're in here smelling up the place and watching a ten-year-old sporting event? Come on—get out there and clean up from last night before the sun starts to go down! I mean it!"

The boys dragged themselves to their feet, moaning and groaning, their lazy Sunday afternoon ruined. Chip got up, stretched and dropped an arm around her shoulders. "Thanks, babe. I needed a little nap."

"Hmph," she said.

"I heard Lauren's voice."

"Yeah, she was here."

"She having problems?" he asked. "With Brad?"

"Why would you ask that?" Beth asked.

"Because you're all prickly."

"Do we have a perfect marriage?" she asked, looking up at him. Beth was five foot three and Chip was a towering six foot three.

He grinned. "I doubt it. But close. Because your wish is my command."

"Yeah, right. After four hours in front of a ten-year-old golf tournament."

"But see how much nicer I am now?" he asked. He kissed her forehead. "You can't do anything about Lauren and Brad."

"Promise not to say a word. She's focused on Cassie's graduation for right now."

"Beth, she's never going to do anything, you know that."

But Beth was thinking, this time she might. And although it made her feel sad and guilty, she desperately hoped her sister would really leave Brad.

CHAPTER THREE

Beau carried a forty-pound bag of fertilizer on each shoulder as he walked along the trail of patio stones that led to the vegetable garden. There he found Tim working on building a nice large pile of weeds. "I thought I might find you here," Beau said. "I brought you a present." He dropped one bag on the ground and lowered the other. "What are you up to?"

"Just hoeing around," the priest said.

"You're hilarious."

"I know. I haven't seen you in a couple of weeks," Tim said. Then he stepped over his plants and gave Beau a firm handshake that brought them shoulder to shoulder. "How's life?"

"Manageable, but busy," Beau said, returning the man hug. Tim and Beau had known each other since they were about ten. To say they took different paths in life would be an understatement.

"But is life any good?" Tim pushed.

"Lots of it is," Beau said. "Work is excellent. I'm almost too busy. Things are quiet at home. I watch sports all night."

"I guess the divorce is proceeding," Tim said.

He shrugged. "It's a little stalled. Pamela wanted to try counseling. I thought it was a waste of time that also cost money. But then Michael asked me why I wouldn't give it a shot." He looked down, shaking his head. "I don't know why Michael gets himself into this—he's twenty, a sophomore, has a steady relationship..."

"He's trying to put his life together—the life he wants to have. He doesn't want the one you and Pamela have. He wants to know how that works." Tim sank to one knee and stabbed the bag of fertilizer, ripping it open, releasing the rank smell.

"You almost sound like you know anything at all about marriage, *Father*," Beau said.

"I'm well trained," Tim shot back.

"Michael just needs to pay attention to the women he lets into his life, make sure there aren't any red flags. Maybe he should be in counseling. Just for his future."

"Not a bad idea," the priest agreed. "Have you told him the truth, Beau? That you stayed for them?"

"I might've suggested that," Beau said, sticking a shovel in the fertilizer and scooping out a big load, sprinkling it down the rows. "I told the counselor I'm there in body only. I don't want to fix it. I want to end it. Our mission in counseling should be to help Pamela let go. So she sobbed for an hour, babbling excuses and trying to explain her change of heart. And there was begging. My head hurt for two days. It's torture."

"Stop going," Tim said. He sat back on his heels. "Seriously, stop going. You are the worst victim sometimes. You can't do this for her. It was her choice, you gave her many last chances. She needs counseling but not marriage counseling."

"Well damn," Beau said. "What about the sanctity of marriage and all that?"

"Everything has an expiration date, my brother," Tim replied. "Really, I'm in the wrong order. I should be with the Jesuits. I'm living in this century. I can't tell perfectly miserable people trapped in abusive and unholy relationships to stick it out just because the church prefers it that way and we promised to turn the other cheek and all that. I wouldn't have lasted a year with Pamela."

Beau grinned. "If the diocese ever finds out about you, you're history."

"Eh," he grunted. He stood and started spreading the fertilizer with his hoe. "How about Drew?"

"Drew's good. Graduating in a couple of weeks. I'm having a party for him—mostly his friends and my family. Will you come?"

"Of course, as long as no one dies or gets married."

"Pamela is trying to get involved, combining families, throw in an ex who may or may not show up. I'm expecting Drew will get a card with some money in it from his dad—anywhere from twenty to a hundred, depending on his guilt. It's so awkward, my family and I'm sure her family know the circumstances but we have to make nice, act like we're at least getting along, look as if we're not getting divorced. I talked to Drew about all the subterfuge and he said, 'No biggie. Let her do it. Then we're done until I get married, which I promise you will be many years from now. Between now and then, I'm probably not going to make her unhappy.' You gotta love that kid. Everything rolls off his back."

"Or it seems to," Tim said. "Keep an eye on that. Still waters…"

"We spend a lot of time together," Beau said. "Just me and Drew these days. I think Drew has forgotten we have Michael's graduation in a year…"

"Things will be better by then. What did you tell the counselor?"

"I told her we've been separated four times, Pamela has had other relationships during the separations and when we're together she's almost always unhappy and we argue too much. She pokes at me until I poke back, so sometimes I leave the house or go in the garage or detail the truck. I told her I don't want to do that anymore. And of course she asked if we fixed our relationship so it wasn't like that, was I in? And I said, I'm sorry, not anymore." He dug out a shovelful of fertilizer. "I'd like to move on so my friends and family aren't constantly forced to ask me where we are now."

Tim stopped moving his hoe. "I'm sorry, Beau," he said.

"Aw, not you, Tim. I don't see enough of you for you to get on my nerves. That's a problem, by the way. I'd like to see enough of you for you to get on my nerves."

Tim grinned. "Basketball game Thursday night."

"Can I bring a ringer?"

"Absolutely. I haven't seen Drew in months."

"I'm in pretty good shape," Beau said. "You should pray."

"I'll think about it, Beauregard," he said.

When Beau was a kid, a relatively poor kid, Tim's well-off family moved into town. Tim's dad was a lawyer. Beau never went to school hungry but there were lots of times he wanted more to eat than there was and he was impressed by the bounty of Tim's table. Beau had two sisters and a brother, Tim had two brothers and a sister. Tim lived in a five-bedroom house on a big lot with a brick circular driveway. Tim's mom played a lot of tennis at their club and had a cleaning lady. But, despite the differences, the boys became friends and stayed friends all the way through school.

Beau's parents were amazed and impressed that he got himself through college in five years with no help from them. Tim, on the other hand, went to Notre Dame. He'd never admitted it to anyone but he'd always aspired to the priest-hood. He was spiritual and wanted to help people. Notre Dame honed that aspiration into reality.

Tim's parents were appalled. Tim, being so damn smart, would have made a good lawyer in his father's firm, but that didn't interest him. He studied theology and counseling. And his mother lamented that he wouldn't be a father. "But yes, I will," he answered with a smile.

As it was, Beau became a landscape architect, marrying his love of design with his love of growing things. And Tim, after being away for many years, had finally come home to a parish in California not so far from where he grew up. And he was reunited with his closest friends.

When Tim came back it was to find his best friend strug-gling with a failing marriage. And while Beau was so happy to have Tim close by, he found the good father at odds with his assignment in his new parish. Tim wanted to help the needy, the hungry, the disenfranchised of the world and here in Mill Valley he was tending the wounds of people with plenty of money and access to everything they might ever need by way of health care, private education and luxuries. True, the well-to-do were not without problems, but Beau knew Tim longed for grittier work. He felt he wasn't as use-ful as he could be.

They talked for a while about the vegetable garden and fruit trees, laughed a little bit about how Tim's boss, the bishop, just wanted him to get people back into church. "He wants the confessional bubbling 24/7 and while there are plenty of Catholics in the parish, they're more like you," Tim said. "Not too worried about having a priest guide them and in-tercede with Christ for them. And most gave up on church doctrine a long time ago."

"Your ego must be bruised," Beau said with a laugh.

"I'm bored," Tim admitted. "There isn't enough challenge."

"It's a rich parish. Surely you can find something to do with the money!"

"This isn't my dream job, Beau. In fact, sometimes I question my calling. Or better to say, sometimes I ask myself if I've done all I can do in this—"

Someone was walking through the garden and the men turned to see a lovely woman standing not far from them.

"I'll be damned," Beau said. "Lauren!" And he smiled, thrilled to see her.

Lauren left work a little early. It was a beautiful spring day and she wanted to stop at Divine Redeemer and see how far along the gardens had come. It wasn't Tuesday, she told herself. There was no harm in it. But inside she knew she wanted to see him. Just to hear him talk about the gardens. Or his boys. She wondered how his life was going. Maybe he would talk a little about his divorce. If she felt comfortable and even a little secure, she'd ask him how they broke it to the kids. Cassie's graduation was a mere week away. After that event and the celebration, when things had calmed, Lauren was going to stir it all up by telling her daughters her plans.

She was terrified.

The garden was looking so beautiful. In this part of the world, the humid spring brought everything to life in such a rainbow of colors. She sighed deeply. It made her feel calmer just looking at it.

Then she heard the laughter of men. She rounded the corner and there stood Beau and another man. Dear God, they were both hunks. Tall, broad-shouldered, lean. Beau had thick brown hair and the other man, straw-colored. Both had strong, tan arms; both held gardening tools—a hoe and a shovel. She just filled her eyes with them. Must be Beau's assistant or one of the church maintenance men.

"Lauren!" Beau said, and there was no mistaking the delight in his voice. Her heart soared and she smiled back.

"I never expected to run into you here," she said. "I wanted to check out the garden. I haven't been back here in weeks."

"Lauren, this is my friend, Father Tim. Tim, this is Lauren. We met here one afternoon. I was replacing a few plants and she was enjoying the garden. Then we ran into each other again at a fund-raiser."

"Nice to meet you," the priest said. Oh, he was much too handsome to be a priest. She immediately decided a bunch of women probably sought his counsel. Regularly.

"Nice to meet you, too. It's all looking beautiful. You must have dozens if not hundreds of people spending time here."

He shrugged. "When there are daytime functions at the church. Sundays, lots of people wander through. A few people come just to see the gardens. Surprisingly few, considering how beautiful it is." He gazed around thoughtfully, leaning on his hoe. "We need a fountain. Maybe I'll suggest it to the board. That'll give them something to discuss for a year and a half." He chuckled.

"I guess you like to get personally involved," she said.

"On a day like today, when I have no appointments, it's a good excuse. You must live around here."

"Mill Valley. I work in Oakland so this is on my way home. I discovered this garden a long time ago. My grandmother was a master gardener. She's gone now and so is the garden, I'm afraid."

"How have you been?" Beau asked.

"Well. And you?"

"Great. I have a kid about to graduate high school. My youngest."

She loved the way he talked about his stepsons as if they were his very own. "And I have one graduating college in two weeks. My baby."

"You must have been seven," Father Tim said with a laugh.

"Very nearly," she said. "I was quite young when I married and had children. And here they are—grown. My nest has been empty for a while now but with Cassie's graduation coming up I don't see them coming home except for visits." She took a breath. "It's bittersweet."

"I'm finding it only bitter," Beau said with a laugh. "Drew has no interest in leaving me anytime soon. He's going to UC Berkeley and it's close. Close enough to commute."

"He'll change his mind in short order," Tim said. "Once he sees all the good times on the campus, he'll get interested in leaving home."

Beau thought about this for a moment. "I'm not sure I take comfort in that idea. Trading one set of problems for another."

"You wanted to be alone, remember." Tim laughed.

"Show me what you've got going on here," Lauren asked of the men.

They gave her a nice little tour, introducing her to the lettuces, cabbages, root vegetables, tomatoes and potatoes. Melon and squash vines were growing, flowers appearing where there would be fruit. Cucumber, beans and zucchini vines were snaking all over. Beau had a pumpkin patch started and Tim showed her the ancient apple trees that surrounded the church.

"Impressive," she said. "The bounty. You guys do good work."

"I'm only part-time," Tim said.

"So am I. I didn't plant the vegetables," Beau said. "I tried to give them a design that would maximize their space."

"You have quite a kale farm going there," she said.

"You know what I heard about kale? That if you chop it and add coconut milk it's much easier to scrape into the trash."

She laughed but then she said, "I have some good recipes for kale. Kale and quinoa."

"Mm. Sounds delicious," Beau said, making a face.

The three of them talked about vegetables and flowers for about fifteen minutes while Tim and Beau spread fertilizer. Lauren, wearing a skirt and low pumps, couldn't get into the dirt, though she wished she could join them. She did bend over and pull a weed here and there.

She looked at her watch. "I'd better head home. I was going to stop at the store and I always get sidetracked..."

"I'll walk you to your car," Beau said.

"It was nice meeting you, Father," she said.

"I hope to see you again, Lauren."

Beau kicked the dirt off his shoes before starting down the walk. At first he had his hands in his pockets but within only a few steps, his right hand rested at the small of her back. It felt so protective somehow, as though keeping a light hand on her to be ready if she stumbled or tripped or was suddenly in the path of a speeding train. Brad always gripped her elbow. A bit too tightly. Not escorting her but steering her.

"I'm glad I happened to be here when you stopped by, though I know it was probably the last thing you expected," he said.

"It was, but I'm glad, too. I know it's meaningless but just knowing you're going through something similar... Really, I planned to wait for a time when I felt secure and comfortable to ask you..."

He stopped walking and looked into her eyes. His were dark, smoky blue and heavily lashed. She smiled. She had extra lashes applied so she wouldn't need too much mascara but this guy who liked to dig in the dirt had all the lashes in the world.

"I hope I don't make you feel insecure or uncomfortable. What are you going through that's similar? You can ask me anything. I'm pretty much an open book."

She took a deep breath. "How did you tell your boys you were getting a divorce?"

He put a comforting hand on her upper arm. "Our situations are probably different. Pamela told them she was moving out. She needed a breather, she said. She might be filing for divorce, she said, but she hoped a little separation would help. Then I had to tell them I wasn't willing to try again. But I also told them I wasn't going anywhere, that they were my boys and I loved them."

"And that was enough?"

"I thought so at the time. We'll see."

"I have to tell my daughters," Lauren said. "They love their father. They tiptoe around him, but I know they care about him."

"Good that they care," he said. "That's a good thing. I'm sure he's a great father."

"No... I don't know," she said, shaking her head. "But that's all too complicated. I just want to know how to tell them."

"Lauren, they probably already know. They live with you. Once you know how you feel and what you want, you have to be clear and honest. Don't expect them to be supportive. Aw hell, what do I know? I'm no expert. Our attempts at marriage counseling have been pretty dismal."

"Ours, too!" she said. "Brad walks in the door with a mission to win over the counselor! Within ten minutes she's thinking...it's almost always a woman...she's thinking the poor man has a nagging, half-crazy gold digger trying to bleed him dry of all his hard-earned money!"

All Beau could say was, "Gold digger?"

"Brad's older than I am," she explained. "He was a surgeon when we married. He's very successful. His family was rich. As I mentioned, mine was not."

"But you're a chemist. A working chemist," he said. "You're obviously not laying on the daybed watching your soaps and having your nails done."

She hid her hands. He smiled and pulled them out. They

were lovely, manicured nails, soft hands, but not because she was self-indulgent. She took care of herself. "I do my own most of the time. I get an occasional manicure but I just can't sit still for it."

"It's not a crime to be able to afford something like this. Pamela gets completely redone every six weeks. Maybe we have more in common than I thought," he said. "Is your husband a little overpowering?"

She nodded.

He chuckled. "If you knew Pamela…"

"Overpowering?"

"She makes the rules," he said. "Every couple of years she gets restless. Has he left you?"

"Never," she said. "Not physically. He's a very difficult, high-strung man. He knows everything. He has a bit of a temper."

Beau's face darkened with a low crimson brewing under his tan. "He hits you?"

She shook her head, shame preventing her from talking about what he did. What he did was so subtle. He hurt her in small ways that no one would ever notice. He had to have control. He was in total control all the time and if anyone got in his way or argued with him, he would fight back until he exhausted his opponent and they gave up or gave in. He belittled her. He loved reminding her she came from nothing. "I really should go," she said a little nervously. She wasn't afraid of being caught talking to a gardener in broad daylight at a church. She was nervous about exposing herself too much. If people knew how much she'd put up with, how could they respect her? She no longer respected herself.

"Wait," he said. "Lauren, who do you have to talk to?"

"I have family. My sister. I have friends. They're not all close but there are a couple I can confide in," she said. "There's Ruby. She was my supervisor at work but she's fifteen years older than I am and she's retired now and yet we've been close for a long time. It's just that..." Ruby's husband had been ill.

"I know marriage counseling hasn't worked out. Mine hasn't, either. Maybe she's like your husband, put the two of us in a room and Pamela has to win. She'll do anything to win. But maybe you should think about your own counselor. Just for you. Someone to help you get through the rough patches."

She had done that once, on the sly, a secret counselor. Maybe she should revisit that idea. "Do you have your own counselor?" she asked.

"I don't," he said. "It's been suggested and I might go that way yet. Right now, things are manageable. Not fun but manageable."

"I'll keep that in mind," she said.

"Listen..." He paused and glanced away. "I'd like to see you again. Is that possible?"

"Probably not. A complication right now..."

"I'm not suggesting anything illicit, but if you want someone to talk to... I know I wouldn't mind having someone to talk to."

"I can't depend on a man right now, not even for talking."

"I wouldn't want that, either," he said. He pulled out a card. "That's my cell number. If you want a cup of coffee. Or if you're sitting on a park bench worrying about things..."

"Thank you," she said. "It's doubtful I'll call."

"I understand," he said. "It's an offer."

"But you're a busy guy and I'm a virtual stranger."

"Doesn't really feel that way," he said. "Here we are, two people going through divorces with grown kids to deal with and... You know. It just happened that way. Neither one of us ran an ad or signed up for online dating."

"I appreciate the offer," she said, smiling.

"We'll run into each other again," he said. "Meanwhile, hang in there."

★ ★ ★

Father Tim was leaning on his hoe, waiting for Beau in a stance that looked like the old farmer stance, except that Tim was anything but an old farmer. Plus he was grinning mischievously, ready to give Beau the business. "Your friend Lauren is very attractive."

"Stop looking. You're supposed to be a priest," Beau said, lifting his shovel.

"A priest, not a corpse," he said with a laugh. "Did you notice her eyes are violet?"

"Must be contacts," Beau said. "No one actually comes with eyes that color."

"If they're born from a god and a high priestess."

"Spread the manure on the ground, Father."

He had noticed everything about her. He loved the sound of her voice, her easy laughter, her rich and soft brown hair that fell to her shoulders. It was the color of mahogany. He loved her sass when he ran into her at the fund-raiser and noticed that when the subject turned to her husband, her marriage, it sucked the confidence right out of her. She had that lean and strong look, like a thoroughbred. She was tall and she had kind of big feet, but tall women had to have a sturdy base or they'd blow over in the wind. And that thought made him smile secretly.

"You're seeing her?"

"No. She's going through a divorce. Or will be soon. No, I haven't been seeing her. It's like she said, we met accidentally a couple of times, that's all."

"How do you know about the divorce?"

Beau leaned on his shovel. "I told her I was separated. The next time we met she said she'd be in the same spot before long. So here we are, strangers with grown kids, getting divorced..."

"What are her issues?" Tim asked.

"I have no idea, Tim. We're not close friends."

"But you want to be," Tim said, then wisely shut his mouth and turned back to spreading fertilizer.

It was true. He wanted to be. "That was the last thing I was looking for," Beau said. "Pamela kind of cures you of women. She doesn't look like the kind of woman who'd make you want to jump off a very tall building, does she? But she's—"

"Pamela needs help, Beau. She'll never get it, but she's so temperamental and narcissistic, she's not going to function well in a relationship. Medication and counseling could help her but she's probably not open to that idea."

"I don't know if it's even been suggested," Beau said. "The mood swings almost killed me. And trying to make herself happy with things—outrageously expensive shoes or purses. And a better man. She always says she'd left the relationship before the man but I don't think so... Then when the grass isn't really greener, she comes home."

Of course Beau had told Tim all this before. Tim had been back four years now, came home to find his closest friend mired in a mess of a marriage with a selfish and manipulative woman.

"But I'll be forever grateful to Pamela for giving me a chance with those boys," Beau said. "They're good boys. When it's the three of us, when we go camping or fishing or hiking, we have a good time. One who thinks too much and one who lets everything go."

"Don't get yourself in a complicated situation with a beautiful woman who's trying to leave her husband," Tim said.

"Don't sin?" Beau asked.

"That's probably asking a bit much," Tim said with a laugh. "It's just that there's an intensity about Lauren..."

"Well, what would you expect? She's obviously pretty worried about what's coming. She asked me how I told the boys. She has to tell her daughters."

"I know you want to help her," Tim said. "I'd just like you to remember, Pamela needed support when you met her. She'd just come out of a bad relationship and found you to help her pick up the pieces."

"Hey, I don't know this woman, okay? But she doesn't seem like a Pamela! Manure on the plants, Father."

"All right. Don't get testy."

"I'm not," Beau said, digging a shovelful of fertilizer out of the split bag.

But he was. He was annoyed because Tim could be absolutely right. When he met beautiful, sexy Pamela, he didn't see a selfish, impatient, hard-to-please woman with a short attention span. Oh no—he saw a vulnerable and sweet young woman saddled with two hard-to-manage little boys, a woman so grateful to have a good, steady man in her life, a man interested in the parent-teacher conferences. It was a couple of years before he met the other Pamela. Oh, he'd seen hints of her here and there, but they were so fleeting he convinced himself that everyone has their bad days.

Lauren, at first glance, seemed like a good woman with a strong moral compass. She couldn't meet him even just to have someone to talk to if it could become a distraction, a complication. She wanted to be sure her daughters were informed in the best way of what was coming. She didn't trash the husband she was leaving, yet it was clear in her eyes and what little she said, she was in a bad situation. When he asked if he hit her, she rubbed her upper arms and said, "No." She was beautiful. Sweet and sensitive.

And in two years they could be at each other's throats. She could be railing at him about how dull he was, how uninteresting, how inattentive. He didn't dance. He had quiet friends. He didn't want to party. She could be explaining how her life had become unfulfilling, how her needs were not being met...

...how her sex life needed to be recharged.

"There were red flags with Pamela," Tim said. "You told me all about them, how obvious they were, how you convinced yourself you were overreacting because most of the time things were good. And besides, no one's perfect. You admit you have failings. In fact, you're a little too eager to admit your—"

Beau stopped shoveling and stared at his friend. "Stop reading my mind."

"Sorry," Tim said. "I wasn't sure I was."

"You do it all the time and it pisses me off."

"I said I was sorry. So, we can count on you for basketball Thursday night?"

"Yeah. Sure."

"Father?" a female voice said from the walk. "I'm sorry to interrupt you. I was just wondering…"

"Angela! How wonderful to see you! What brings you to my neighborhood?"

"A fool's errand, I think. It's still so early in the spring, but my shelves are bare of the fresh stuff and my clientele could use some greens. It was just a gamble, that you might have some lettuce that came in early."

"Beau, meet my friend Angela," Tim said. "She operates a food bank in Oakland. It's where a lot of our fresh stuff from the garden ends up."

"It's a pleasure," Beau said. He couldn't help but notice how Tim's eyes lit up. He also noticed how beautiful the Latina woman was, black hair in a single braid down her back. Beau guessed she was about thirty. Her eyes danced as she was focused more on Tim than Beau. She wore tight jeans with rips in the knees, hoodie tied around her waist. She was lovely. And Tim's entire mood changed.

"We don't have anything yet but I'm friendly with the produce manager at the big Safeway. One of my parishioners. Let's go see if he's clearing out produce. I bet we'll get something, no matter what his stock looks like. Let's go in your car, then you can drop me back here."

"I knew you'd help if you could," she said, smiling so beautifully.

"Let's go then," he said. He took her elbow to guide her, walked her away from the garden. He leaned down to talk with her and they laughed together.

Tim never looked back at Beau.

"Interesting," Beau said. Then he proceeded to spread fertilizer.

CHAPTER FOUR

The Delaney family home was in a posh, gated neighborhood in Mill Valley. Guests had to be cleared by the guard at the gate to enter. It was much more house than Lauren wanted or needed, especially with the girls being gone, but Brad found it and contracted the purchase without her involvement six years ago. It was an eight-thousand-square-foot showplace. She had been stunned but helpless. What was she to say? We don't need all this since I'm not planning to be married to you that much longer? She had two choices—she could sign the purchase agreement and at least be a co-owner of the massive property. Or she could refuse and he'd just buy it himself.

"Be sure to put your things away," he instructed before their guests arrived. "I don't want people thinking we have separate bedrooms."

"Even though we do," she muttered.

"You sometimes sleep in the guest room down the hall because of your hot flashes," he said, creating her lie for her.

"No one is going to be wandering around the bedrooms," she said. "And I don't have hot flashes."

He touched her cheek. He laughed. "Any second now, Lauren. You're not as young as you used to be."

Feeling a little ancient and emotional with her baby a college graduate on her way to law school, she lashed out. "What do you suppose they'd all think if they knew the truth?"

"Just what I think," he said easily. "You're a half lunatic who imagines ridiculous things all the time."

She gritted her teeth and remained silent, picturing that quaint Victorian in Alameda, how quiet and sweet it was. The girls had gone out to pick up a few last-minute items for the party and would be walking in the house any second. Guests would start to arrive in an hour. The caterers were busy; their van was parked in the garage so they had a clear path from the van to the party site, the kitchen, butler's pantry, dining room and patio. They were expecting about 100 people. Obviously she couldn't get into an argument with him now. Actually she couldn't get into an argument with him ever. Disagreeing with Brad was disastrous.

The last straw should have been when he had given her chlamydia. He denied it, insisted it wasn't him and his argument was so unflinching and convincing even she began to wonder where she might've gotten it. She hadn't had a lover, not ever. She began to worry about a contaminated tampon or used underwear someone had returned to a store with their germs on them. She knew better, yet her doubts, as ridiculous as they were for a woman who had studied chemistry, persisted. Finally, her gynecologist calmly and firmly said, "You could only get it from a person you had sex with. You can't even get it from a blood transfusion. Period."

Of course it had been Brad. He'd been unfaithful before,

hadn't he? Of course it was him. That's when she stopped having sex with her husband. Three years later she'd been emptying his pockets for the dry cleaner and there it was—a condom. Of course. Because he didn't want to get chlamydia again.

She'd left the condom on the pillow in his room. He told her she was an idiot—he'd picked up the condom in the nurse's supply station, they sometimes used them for external catheters and he thought he might need it for a patient but didn't and hadn't put it back. Why would he leave a condom in his pants pocket if he was screwing around? But she knew it was a lie and she stayed in the guest room. She told the girls she liked to stay up late reading and their father needed his sleep to be alert for early morning surgeries. They neither noticed nor cared—they were both in college and only home for visits. In fact, the girls liked it. On their visits overnight, the girls often gathered in her room, sitting on her bed, gossiping and laughing with her and at those times she was doubly glad she wasn't in his room.

She thought maybe they could get through this, weather his anger, but it could be rough and all she wanted was for her daughters to have a positive college experience.

Yes, they were spoiled and she had been complicit. She hoped it wouldn't lead to their ruin. Above all, she wanted them to be good people.

So what would he come up with to threaten her this time? What threat to keep her? Why the hell did he even want her?

She shook her head and forced her thoughts back to the daughter for whom this over-the-top celebration was planned. Cassidy had made good. She was going to Harvard Law. Tears came to her eyes. Not sentimental tears because of her pride, but sad tears because Cassie's gramma, her mother, Honey, would not be here. And she missed her so. The last time they were together, they had dinner—just Honey, Lauren and Beth. Lauren and Beth talked about their marriages. Beth's was usually crazy and dysfunctional in adorable ways and Lauren's was growing more awful every year. As they embraced to say good-night Honey had touched Lauren's cheek and said, "You don't have to give him your entire life, sweetheart. You don't have to sacrifice your entire life for your daughters, either, for that matter. Maybe you've gone as far as you should. And it's all right." Three days later Honey was dead and aside from missing her every day, she prayed Honey had not lost all respect for her as she grappled with a bad marriage and indulged two daughters who had already been indulged enough.

But now, Cassie would study law. Lauren was happy for her, even though Boston was so far away. Lauren would go with her to Boston to look around for a place to live. Cassie was going to get ahead of her class, hopefully get a job, get to know the campus and the area, settle in, try not to die of loneliness. She was leaving behind a boyfriend of over a year, her family and many friends.

Eighty-five-year-old Adele, Brad's mother, arrived in her town car, leased for the day complete with driver. She looked…rich. Rich and pinched and miserable. Beth, Chip and the boys arrived and it was all Beth could do to keep them from falling on the hors d'oeuvres like locusts. Ruby arrived and Lauren fell into her arms. "How are you holding up, girl?" Ruby asked.

"I'm fine," she said. "How's Ted?"

"The same," Ruby said. "I'm not going to stay long, I'm sure you and Cassie understand."

"Absolutely. Let me know if there's any way I can help."

"Thank you, but we're getting by just fine."

Ruby's husband had had a stroke and he was coming along fairly well, home from rehab now. But there was no getting around the facts—he'd taken a life-threatening blow and at seventy-five, progress came slowly and Ruby felt the need to stay close.

She could not visit her troubles or plans on Ruby.

This was Ruby's third marriage. The first took up nine years and brought her two sons. The second was very brief and painful, *Like a woman who had learned nothing on her first terrible match*, she had said. A few years later she married Ted, with whom she shared a warm and compatible relationship. It was Ruby who had said to her, *Do what you can to try to make your marriage work. If you don't try, you'll have regrets. But listen to me—don't wait too long or you'll find yourself a trapped old woman with no options and a beastly old man who has perfected abuse. Someday one of you will be sick, dependent on the other. That's hard enough when there's love.*

She hoped she hadn't waited too long.

"I'll stop by and see Ted soon," Lauren said.

"He'd like that," she said. "Everything looks so beautiful, as usual. You really know how to throw a party."

"There sure have been enough of them, haven't there?"

"A good many," Ruby said.

The Delaneys were known for their wonderful parties— with delicious food and good company—if you liked a lot of medical people and a few others. There was always an extraordinary atmosphere. There were plastic water lilies holding votive candle holders floating around in the pool, classical music, a complete uniformed wait staff circulating with champagne and hors d'oeuvres. The great room doors were open to the patio and the party flowed through the house. A plentiful buffet was set up in the dining room complete with a waiter slicing prime rib. The caterer had set up a series of round tables and chairs on the massive patio.

Over the years Brad and Lauren had hosted brunches, dinners, cocktail parties, summer pool parties, retirement parties, even a couple of wedding receptions.

For a moment she felt a touch of melancholy. She'd done a good job under difficult circumstances. Only once had she invited the people she worked with to a party exclusively for them and Brad had charmed them. Afterward, when they'd all left, he complained for at least a day. He didn't like a one of them.

Their entertaining was mostly Brad's suggestion. "I think we should have a Christmas party this year—we'll invite the office staff, a few friends, family. Let's say sixty people. Can you get it done?"

She never said no. She'd hire a piano player for the grand piano that occupied the foyer, sit down with the caterer, have Brad's secretary work up some nice invitations, put together a guest list for him to review. He'd look it over and invariably add names or say, "Adults only, all right," upon seeing her nephews on the list.

"But it's Christmas!"

"They can come to Christmas but children don't come to fancy cocktail parties and pour punch on the carpet!"

Just then she saw Sylvie Emerson walking toward her, Andy trailing behind her. Brad always invited the Emersons.

"Sylvie! How thoughtful of you to come!"

"How could I miss a chance to congratulate our future lawyer," she said, pulling a card from her large purse. "And to say this—I realize you've been very busy with all this going on, but when things settle a bit, I'll be waiting for the phone call about lunch."

"Absolutely," Lauren said. "I'm going to help Cassie get settled back east, then I would love to get together."

"Perfect. Take me to the graduate," Sylvie said. "We're not staying long. We have somewhere to be a bit later."

"Of course. And I'd like you to meet my sister and brother-in-law. He's an Oakland police officer and the daughter of his late friend was a recipient of one of your scholarships."

"Oh yes, please! It's funny that Brad never mentioned that connection," she said.

And Lauren wondered if Brad even knew.

The second Brad noticed Sylvie and Andy, he rushed to them and usurped Lauren's place as escort. She let them go, confident that Sylvie would insist on meeting Beth and Chip and congratulating Cassie. She knew she'd have a chance to thank Sylvie again before she left.

Lauren had become a master entertainer. And she'd be more than happy to give it up. She looked forward to things that Brad would mock. Maybe a book club that met one evening a month, sometimes at her less auspicious home. Or hosting a baby shower for a young co-worker, somewhere a little less intimidating than the Delaney manse. She just wanted to be calm and comfortable; she wanted a grandbaby to take care of sometimes. Would her daughters invite her into the delivery room?

That was years away, she thought. But then when the party was ending, when all the toasts had been made to Cassie, when the brandy and cigars had been indulged by Brad and a few of his cronies, Cassie asked to speak to her alone. She was holding her boyfriend Jeremy's hand. *Oh no!* Lauren thought. *What's this?*

"Mom, I have some wonderful news," Cassidy said. "Jeremy has decided to come to Boston."

"Huh?" she said oh so eloquently.

Cassie laughed. "He's decided to transfer to Boston University for his master's program."

"What? But haven't you started already? At Berkeley?"

"Yes, ma'am," he said. "I won't get in until after the first of the year but that's good. I'll work and get a leg up on my research. We'll settle in before we're both deep in our programs."

"Settle...in...?" she echoed.

Cassie laughed. "We're going to live together. I can't tell you how happy this makes me." She grabbed Jeremy's hand. "I honestly didn't know how I was going to stand the distance—each of us on a different coast."

"Are you...? No, you're not getting married."

"Not yet, no," Cassie said. "The subject has come up and we're talking about marriage. But we agree that law school and his master's is the first thing to consider. But at least we'll be together."

Lauren suddenly choked on a sob and covered her mouth. She loved Jeremy. He was a sensitive, wonderful young man. He was researching autism and he was by far the most decent and committed boy either of her girls had brought home. Cassie had been seeing him for over a year and Lauren knew they were serious.

"Mom..." Cassie said.

But Jeremy pulled her into a hug. "We'll be okay," he said. "We're not rushing. As it turns out, Boston will be better for my research in some areas. And you'd think I was stupid if I let Cassie get away."

"I would," she said. "But, oh God, it's another one of those big transitions."

Cassie laughed at her. "But you're happy for us, right?"

"Does this mean you don't need me to help you get settled?"

"Oh Mama, I really want to do this with you! You're so good at this sort of thing."

She wiped her cheeks. "True," she said. "I am the best." This was silly. She knew they were intimate. They were hardly children. She'd married at twenty-three. She laughed a little nervously.

Cassie asked Jeremy to go get them a couple of glasses of wine. When he was out of earshot, Cassie said, "Will you tell Daddy?"

Lauren frowned. "Shouldn't you?" she asked.

Cassie shook her head. "I shouldn't. He never likes my choices. Lacey could announce she's moving in with Charles Manson and Daddy would applaud her good taste, but I never please him. And he doesn't like Jeremy."

"Oh, I'm sure he likes Jeremy. They just don't have that much in common," Lauren said. And then she asked herself why she lied for him? Brad didn't like Jeremy because Jeremy was a sensitive intellectual who would never be rich. Jeremy was gentle and kind. Brad was not drawn to people like that.

"Will you please?" Cassie asked.

Lauren smiled at her youngest. She admired the choices Cassie was making. She admired that she'd chosen a good man who made her happy, a man who wanted her to be happy. "Is Jeremy coming with us to Boston to look at housing options?"

"No. He said that's entirely up to me. And he insists he'll get a job and pay half the rent."

That made her smile again. "Will he be coming right away?"

"A few weeks after me," she said. "He has stuff to wrap up and an apartment to clean out."

"Then maybe I'll wait a little while to tell your dad your plans."

"I know it's not going to be smooth with him," she said. "That's why I asked you..."

"And what makes you think I have any influence?" Lauren said. "He argues with me constantly!"

"But somehow you always get through it!"

"No, somehow I always survive it," she said. "I figured out how to live with him."

Damn, it was true! She managed her husband. He didn't love her, she didn't love him and they'd done this dance for years! She had no idea what Brad's stake was in the relationship—was it all to have a good housekeeper and hostess?

Because they weren't lovers. They weren't confidants. They weren't friends.

"You know, Cassidy, no matter what your father's opinion is, who you live with or marry is up to you," Lauren said.

"But he can make things pretty difficult when his opinion doesn't match mine," Cassie said.

"I know," Lauren said, giving Cassie's light brown hair a fond stroke. "I'm not looking forward to you moving so far away but I am looking forward to our time together."

"Me, too," Cassie said.

And I hope you choose more wisely than I did, she wanted to add.

But was every day a tragedy? Of course not. They'd had some good times together without being lovers, friends or confidants. They went to Italy last year and met some lovely couples they still kept in touch with. They went to St. Tropez every winter, sometimes taking the girls, and ran into the same people there, socializing like normal couples. Daily life was tolerable because they really didn't see too much of each other unless the girls were around. Brad was very social and when he made plans, she went along and was very agreeable.

Then once or twice a week it went south and crushed her spirit. He'd remind her she came from nothing. He'd tell her she was delusional or that she fabricated stories to make herself look like a victim of his cruelty. He'd shout at her, demean her.

Pinch her.

Those pinches were possibly the most demeaning thing he did. Weighing everything about their relationship, she wanted to leave him just because of that. He'd zap out a hand and find a tender piece of flesh, her forearm or the back of her upper arm, grab with his long, strong fingers and twist. Sometimes she'd bruise.

The worst part was feeling she had to build a case. She suspected men could leave because they'd lost that loving feeling, but women? Women had to be abused, assaulted, held prisoner or otherwise severely victimized before it was all right for them to walk.

Lauren turned her thoughts back to Cassie. "Be patient, all right? If I sense a good time, I'll tell him, but there's no hurry. I can promise you he won't be in Boston for moving day."

Beau met Pamela in the waiting room of the marriage counselor's office. She stood and gave him an affectionate little hug. He pulled away before she could embrace him, hold on to him.

"Well, I guess I got the message," she said.

He just smiled at her. She was beautiful and looked sophisticated in her work suit. Only Pamela could make a work suit look so sexy. It didn't exactly cross the line but it rushed right up to it—conservative jacket, low-cut silky blouse, straight skirt, slit up the thigh, heels that were at least three inches. The color was right for her and right for spring—pale coral. It set off her blond hair and blue eyes. The blond was not authentic and she wore colored contacts. That had never mattered to Beau. Women wanted to be pretty. He understood that. He didn't even mind that she liked being sexy and pretty for men. Depending on your self-confidence, that could make a husband feel a little puffed up and proud.

Sometimes Pam took it over the edge.

She barely resembled the young jeans-clad single mother, struggling with two rambunctious little boys, living in a one-bedroom apartment and keeping an old car running on meager support from their fathers and food stamps. Sometimes he missed that girl. She was holding it together somehow.

"We've talked about this, Pam," he said. "I will be happy to explain my feelings to the therapist. He seems like a nice enough guy."

She sniffed in a breath through her nose and stiffened. "I'm hoping he can help put us back together. Aren't you?"

Beau didn't answer. He gave a small, melancholy smile and stuck his hands in his pockets. Then he looked at his watch. "You have to be somewhere?" she asked tartly.

"I have appointments this afternoon, but I have some time now," Beau said.

"Why are you so distant?" she asked. "We had such a successful weekend, Drew's party, the whole family together for once… I really felt we were making great progress!"

"It was a nice weekend, wasn't it? Drew really appreciated it. He's also glad it's over so he can get on with his life. He's ready for the next chapter."

"I can feel you pulling away…"

Only Pamela. How many times did she have to call a time-out before it was truly over? She moved into a sublet flat in the city, took a ten-day vacation to Maui, did a little traveling for work, plastered pictures of her fun times all over her Facebook page, but now she was done and wanted a smooth return to her base. There seemed to be one man's face in many of the photos, including what looked like a partial profile of him in Maui. He must have left.

"Maybe you're right," he said. And then thankfully the door opened.

"Come on in folks," George said. "I hope everyone had a good week."

"A very good week," Beau said.

"Before we get started, anything I should know?" George asked.

"Yes," Beau said. "I'm afraid I'm not going to continue with this counseling," he said.

"He has someone," Pamela said.

"I don't," Beau said. "I wouldn't mind, though. I thought it would be decent of me to give this a chance, but I just can't work up the enthusiasm. This is the fourth separation and you're our seventh counselor. Just by the numbers, we're probably done. No criticism of you, George. I'm sure you're one of the best."

Pam put her hands over her face and began to cry.

"Pam, you should stay," Beau said. "Really. I think you want to end this phase in your life, this marriage, and find some new direction. But I'm not it. If we got back together now it would be nice for a few months and then tense, then difficult for a long time until you decided it was too difficult, then we'd have another time-out. It's your pattern and I'm done."

She broke into loud wails.

"Aw, Jesus," Beau said.

"What brought this on right now, if you don't mind me asking," George said.

"I don't mind at all," Beau said. "I have a good friend who is also a counselor. I was talking with him about going to counseling for a marriage I don't want anymore and he suggested I be more honest about my feelings. Look, no offense intended, but Pamela doesn't want to be married. At least not to me. It's usually more about another man…"

"It is not!" she spat.

"Yeah, it usually is," Beau said. "And I don't even care. Just let us end it."

"Then you'll have to move out of my house!" she said emphatically.

"Folks, these are not the kind of things negotiated in therapy, but if you want to dissolve the marriage, I can help with the emotional part," George said.

"Then help Pam with the emotional part," Beau said, standing up. "I'd say Pam has some doubt about us staying married—we've done this too many times. I'm going to call it."

"The counselor he talked to is a *priest*!" she shouted.

Beau just shrugged. "He didn't quote me scriptures," Beau said. "He's just a friend. But he does a lot of counseling. Look, I should stop wasting your time and Pam's. I'm not going to have a fifth separation. The boys are adults now. They still need parents. They'll always need parents—"

"You're not their father!" she said.

"I'm not their biological father," he said. "I've supported them for a dozen years and we're very close. I'll be their parent as long as they'll let me."

"I can't believe you're giving up on us so soon!"

"Beau," George said. "Why don't you sit down and let's just talk about this issue."

He thought about it for a second. He even began to take a seat; he'd always been so accommodating. Being cooperative and helpful had worked for him. He firmly believed it had made him successful. Then he remembered that Peacekeepers were also bombs and he stood again. "Sorry, George, this is the end of the line for me. Thanks for trying to help. Look, see if you can convince Pamela to get a little personal counseling. She's angry and unhappy."

"How *dare* you say that about me!"

"I'll tell the boys I just didn't have one more try in me."

He turned and left the small office. He was surprised by how terrible he felt. He had expected to feel free and nothing could be further from what he felt. He felt disappointment and heartache and sheer dread. And there was guilt because he had plotted out this day carefully and while Pamela shouldn't have been surprised, clearly she was broadsided. She had expected him to go on like this forever.

He had two appointments. First the lawyer and then the locksmith. Sonja Lawrence, the attorney, was a woman in her sixties who had been doing this for a long time. They had met for the first time two months ago and after a brief interview, she gave him a list of things to do and to decide. She pulled the list right out of her top drawer—so clinical. It was like the list the dentist gave you after he'd pulled a tooth. He tried to explain to Ms. Lawrence about the separations, the other men who Pamela referred to as a little casual dating during a separation, the counseling, the toxic environment—

"Really, Mr. Magellan, it's irrelevant. This is a no-fault state. No one has to be right or wrong. The lawyers have to work on negotiating the division of property."

"She's going to take half my business, isn't she?"

"I imagine she will try," Ms. Lawrence said.

He gave a huff of forlorn laughter.

"I know it's not funny," she said.

"No, it wasn't that. It's just that… I like you, I really do. I don't want anyone else. I didn't set out to find the meanest lawyer in the Bay Area. But you remind me of my grandmother… When I was younger, of course. But will you be able to get me a fair deal out of this?"

She smiled patiently. "Don't let looks deceive you, Mr. Magellan. Most of the time they never even see me coming."

CHAPTER FIVE

Lauren and Cassie flew to Boston, rented a car and proceeded to a real estate office that specialized in rental properties convenient to the Harvard area. Even though they came from California where the cost of living was high, the sticker shock almost buried their otherwise high spirits. They spent every night in their hotel room looking at the listings and discussing what Cassie needed. Cassie had brought her tape measure and recorded room sizes in a small notebook. Most of her belongings had been container-shipped, ready to be delivered when they found adequate space.

By coming early in the summer they had so many more options in the search to find a flat or apartment. Graduates had just left, new students hadn't started to arrive and the availability was high even with waiting lists on some flats. But the prices were ridiculous.

"I don't know how we can justify the cost of this," Cassie said, doing some figuring.

"Harvard," Lauren said in one word. "There's going to be some debt here but you'll pay it off faster than you think and I'll help you all I can. You'll just have to be one helluva great lawyer."

"That's what I'm worried about," she said. "Making as much money as I can isn't exactly my goal. I'd like to make as much right as I can."

That made Lauren smile because Cassie had such a good heart. It was peculiar—Cassie looked more like Brad with her light hair, short stature and blue eyes. Lacey's temperament was more like her father but she resembled Lauren right down to those unique eyes.

Lauren got a little teary. "I'm so proud of you. You have no idea how much I'm going to miss you."

At the end of their third straight day of looking, they were shown a small, one-bedroom flat on the third floor. A walkup, of course. It was tiny and old; the building was quite ancient but had been remodeled a few times. The floors were wood and scarred, the bathroom tiny. "You would definitely have to take a number," Lauren said of the bathroom. But unlike many of the student flats, at least they wouldn't have to share a bathroom with another tenant. The kitchen was just one notch above a galley kitchen but the stove and refrigerator weren't more than ten years old. Lauren remembered the appliances from her college days when they were either avocado green or a fleshy pink. These were white. There was room for a small table and two chairs. And the bedroom would barely hold enough furniture to accommodate a couple.

But the living room was spacious for the size of this flat. It was bright and airy, the ceiling high, with a large window that faced the park across the street and the city in the distance, rising above the trees. There was plenty of room for a sofa, a couple of chairs, a coffee table, bookcase and maybe a small desk if they arranged things cleverly.

"Oh Mama, I love it," Cassie said, standing in front of the living room window.

"I hope you're sure of Jeremy," Lauren said. "If you get on each other's nerves, there's no escape in this little space."

"It's on the bus line," Cassie said. "The street is lined with shops and eateries. I imagine we'll be spending a lot of time at school, the library, study groups, maybe work, if we're lucky. But really, isn't it darling?"

Lauren tried to remember how love made the worst dump look like a honeymoon cottage. Then she recalled she'd never had that experience. "Well, IKEA here we come," she said cheerily. "And the Home Store, etc."

They got right on it. Lauren was determined to try to see her daughter set up before leaving her. She had planned on two weekends and her five-day workweek of vacation but in the end she called the company and took two extra days. Eleven days to find a flat, furnish it, have everything delivered and set up, and that didn't even allow the days it took the landlord to complete a credit check. She was pretty astonished at how much thought Cassie had given this whole transition, right down to plastic storage tubs for her sweaters and boots that could slide under the bed. She bought a couple extra for Jeremy, though she said he didn't have so much in the way of wardrobe. A few plates, four tumblers, four wineglasses, four bowls, flatware and three pots. Lauren got some extra items, place mats, serving dishes, candles, kitchen linens. "No dishwasher," Lauren observed.

"I'm a college graduate," Cassie said. "I'm going to be able to figure out washing dishes."

They bought serviceable furniture. Not cheap but certainly not what Cassie was used to. The furniture store also sold area rugs and they bought an impractical fluffy one for the living room. "It'll help this winter," Lauren said. They put together a desk and bookcase, added two wooden folding chairs for the compact table with two chairs for the kitchen. The table had a leaf and they could host a meal for four if they wanted to.

Lauren spent the last two nights of her leave with Cassie in her new/old flat. They shared a bottle of wine, a pan of chicken stir-fry with rice and ice cream for dessert. Lauren looked around. "It's not much, but it's cute."

"Aren't these supposed to be the struggling years that we look back on with sentimental bliss and humor?" Cassie asked.

"It wasn't like this for me," Lauren said. "Your father was a surgeon. He came from a rich family, or so they've always told me. We never lived in an apartment. He bought a house. It was a perfectly nice house but he never talked to me about it. He just bought it. That should have been a red flag…"

"You've always made the excuse that he's not an easy man," Cassie said. "I was terrified all through college when people said girls marry their fathers. I love him, I can't help it, but I definitely didn't want someone as high-maintenance as him to share a life with."

Lauren took a breath. "I want to give you some advice and then I want to tell you something. I haven't told your dad that you plan to live with Jeremy. I think you should have any roommate of your choosing. You don't need permission."

"I'm right, aren't I? He hates Jeremy!"

"Hate? I hope not. Jeremy isn't tough and ambitious enough for your father. Jeremy is gentle and kind and brilliant. There's absolutely no reason a man with those attributes can't be hugely successful."

"Oh, you only know the Jeremy he lets you see," Cassie said. "Yes, he's very kind, very fair, but he has integrity and can really dig in when he sees injustice. He's not timid and Daddy doesn't scare him at all. There's more power in that integrity than in a blustering, arrogant fool who thinks he's king. Oh! I didn't mean Daddy. Or maybe I did, but not intentionally."

"It's all right, sweetheart. Everyone knows. Apparently he's a gifted surgeon, though some nurses have said he has the personality of Attila the Hun. The ones that aren't in love with him, at least. Listen, this is very hard for me but I can't leave you here without telling you. I'm planning to ask him for a divorce. No, that's not accurate. I'm going to go home and tell him I'm filing for divorce. Then I'm leaving right away. I've already rented a small house for myself."

Cassie's mouth hung open; stunned silence hung heavy in the air. And then she began leaking tears.

"Oh honey, listen, I've given this a lot of thought and it's not an easy choice…"

"After all this time?" Cassie said, grabbing her mother's hands. "I wondered if you ever would!"

"What do you mean?"

"Mama, do you think I'm completely dense? As if I don't know about him? I've known since Disneyland!"

"Disney…? What?"

"Don't you remember? Or did it just blend in with all the other times? Remember your argument over where to have lunch? Remember what he did?"

Lauren frowned, trying to remember.

"He wanted sushi. You said we girls wouldn't eat sushi. I was seven. I wanted a hamburger or hot dog. You said you were going to take us to McDonald's. He told you we could eat rice, but we didn't want rice. He argued and argued and we started to act up because we were hungry and he started to pick on you and said that we were spoiled brats and it was your fault. Pretty soon you just turned to walk away and he—"

"Oh God," Lauren said, covering her eyes with her hand. He had tripped her. She went down hard, fell flat on her face, bloodied her nose. And he rushed to her side saying honey,

honey, you all right? And a man nearby also rushed to her and said, *What were you doing, man? You tripped her!* And Brad said, *Don't be ridiculous, this is my wife!* And the man insisted, he'd seen Brad stick out a foot, hook it around her ankle…

"He tripped me," Lauren said.

"That sort of thing happened a lot," Cassie said.

"No, that was very rare," Lauren said.

Cassie bit her lip and held silent for a long moment. "Even once isn't right," she finally said in a quiet voice. "You have to do this, Mama. Please."

"Thanks for coming over, Mike," Beau said. Drew, of course, already lived at the house. "I have new keys for both you guys. I've changed the locks. It's official, we're getting divorced. I'm going to do everything I can to keep this from turning into world war three."

"You're *what?*" Michael said. "I thought you were in counseling!"

"Yes, we went a few times. It wasn't working, I'm sorry."

"Did you *try?*" he demanded. "Really try?"

There was so much Beau wanted to explain. He wished he could make them understand how demoralizing it is to have your wife, your partner, completely unable to commit, unable to take responsibility. The sense of failure at never being enough for her. She was happy once… "I've tried several times. I was the one to say it—I think it's time we let it end. I don't want to do this anymore."

"So that's it? And you changed the locks? What's she supposed to do?"

"She's hardly homeless—she has a pretty swank flat in the city. Her half of the closet is empty. Here's what's supposed to happen. Our lawyers are supposed to talk about how we divide our property. In California it's called No Fault. That means—"

"I know what it means!" Michael said. "And you locked her out of the house. It's her house, too!"

"Hey, Mike, back off," Drew said. "This isn't Beau's fault, you know that!"

"She's not locked out," Beau said. "She's welcome any time, as long as someone's here. She can have anything she wants, but it has to be documented for the lawyers so that at the end of the day, it's fair. When a couple goes through as many separations as we have, it doesn't exactly look like the marriage is working. Come on, it's obvious to you guys it's not going to work. It was probably obvious two separations ago. I did my best."

"You don't seem all torn up about it," Mike said.

"Hey, what's up your butt?" Drew asked. "It's not like Beau hasn't jumped through all her hoops!"

"She's our mother!" Mike said. "She's brokenhearted!"

"Aw shit, she called you," Beau said.

"Last night," Mike said. "Crying!"

"Listen to me, don't let anyone put this on you!" Beau said. "It was her decision to leave, her decision to move out. This is a marriage, not a revolving door!" He took a breath. "She's only brokenhearted because she didn't get her way. She calls it off, she wants to turn it back on, then off again, then—"

"You know she's never happy," Drew said to Michael. "Come on. It's not like you didn't expect this."

"Neither did your mom," Beau said. "I guess she thought we'd do this for life, back and forth. But I don't want to spend my life like that. I'm sorry if it hurts, I'm sorry if you're angry, but I'm done. I think a divorce will give your mom a chance to start fresh without looking back all the time. I think it's time we all found some peace. That's all I'm looking for. Peace."

"So you locked her out of her own house," Michael said, angry.

"She's not locked out, she just can't live here now. I bought the house. I lived in it before I met you guys and your mom. And *she* left. I didn't ask her to leave. I asked her to stay and try to work it out. But she needed space and some freedom. Now she has it. And we'll resolve this fairly. Whatever settlement the lawyers can come up with that works for everyone involved, that's what we'll do. I'm not punishing anyone. I just want to get on with my life. For that matter, I want you guys to be able to get on with yours." He looked at them imploringly. "Haven't you been through this enough?"

"You just don't love her anymore?" Mike asked.

Beau pulled out a dining room chair and sat at the table. "Michael, in a way I'll always love your mother. For starters, she's your mother—she gave me you guys. Watching you grow up has been the best part of my life so far. I care about Pam. But I can't fix what's wrong."

"So now I guess you'll just go?" Michael said.

Beau was stunned. Drew made a sound of disgust, as if he couldn't believe his brother just said that. "Why would I go anywhere? Worst case, I have to move out and let your mom have the house. So if that happens, I'll find something else. There will always be room for you two. And your families, when they come."

Michael got a little teary. "Sure," he said. He swiped an arm under his nose like a seven-year-old.

"Mike, I know I'm not your biological father but I've always thought of you as a son. You have to know that."

"Then why can't you make it work?" he asked.

"Don't be dumb," Drew shot out. "It's not Beau's fault and you know it. Mom can be a pain in the ass."

But Beau knew that wasn't the problem Mike was having. "I'm not going anywhere, Mike. The only way you'll get rid of me is if you don't want me in your life and I hope to God that never happens. You're an adult—you choose your friends and family. I want to be your chosen family. But that's up to you. Not to your girlfriend, your grandparents, your teachers or the cops—just you. And incidentally, if your mom puts pressure on you to break off your relationship with me, telling her no is an option. I want to be there for you, like always. If you'll let me."

"It's just that she wants us to be all together so much," he said, sounding pitifully like a child.

"Tell her, Michael. Tell your mother there's nothing you can do about her marriage. Ask her to please not fuck up your head over this. It's not fair."

"Don't say anything to her, okay?" he said.

"I'm not getting between you and your mom," Beau said. "But please don't let her do this to you. You don't have to get in the middle of this to prove you love her."

"I can't stand to see her hurt," he said.

Pam had been doing that for years, putting her boys in the position of parent and protector. Drew was more resistant to that pressure. Or maybe he was just more oblivious. Good-old easygoing Drew. He seemed to have known since he was about seven there was nothing he could do about his mother or his father. When Pam went on a rant, he just withdrew until the storm passed.

"I know. It's hard to see someone you love hurting. But remember. This was her choice. Now she's going to have to be the grown-up and get through it. I'll take care of her the way I always have—she has a great job and is far from broke. Michael, divorce is unpleasant as hell, but it's not fatal. At least half your friends have been through it. All I want is that your future marriage doesn't suffer. Learn from this."

Michael just hung his head. He hadn't wanted to blame Beau, Beau knew that. The poor kid couldn't help it. His father practically abandoned him. His mother was unstable half the time.

"Hey, I was going to suggest we go out to dinner but if there's a chance it could get emotional, let's order in, get a pizza or something. I want you to be able to talk about this if you have questions or something. I'll call and—"

"Nah, I gotta pass," Michael said.

"Drew?" Beau asked.

"I'll go out with Mike for a while," he said, though he didn't look too happy about it. "I won't be late."

"Just drive carefully," Beau said. "I think I'll go out for a beer or something. Just an hour or two. Then I'll be here the rest of the night. Come here, Michael," he said, opening his arms. "I love you, man. We're still a family. This will settle down."

"Yeah," he said with a sniff. "Sure."

When the boys had gone, Beau called Tim. "You got any cold beer?"

"I might have a couple," he said.

"Good. Because I feel like shit. I'll be there in twenty."

Lauren had taken some pictures on her cell phone of Cassie's new flat and said it was really adorable. "Looks like an adorable dump to me," Brad said. She didn't waste any more of his time. She did her laundry from her trip, folded it and put it away. She had prepared for this moment, organizing her things into bureau drawers so that she could quickly and effortlessly lift them out and into suitcases and duffels. She had listed exactly what household items she would need; she'd already taken two boxes of such items to Beth's garage. Her lawyer had warned her that it might be a while before she got back into her house.

The time had come. Finally.

She had not told Lacey yet but after Cassie's reaction, she was optimistic—obviously her daughters had witnessed some of the vulgar things that had passed between them. She would call Lacey as soon as she could.

On the lawyer's advice, Brad would be served with not only divorce papers but a legal document instructing him that there would be penalties if he emptied out their accounts or ran up charge accounts in her name. She'd contacted her own credit card companies—the ones he routinely paid—and canceled them. She opened new ones and had a debit card from her personal bank account. She took no money from their joint accounts. She had put aside some money over the past several years, money he didn't know about that allowed her to make the deposit on a rental and would get her through the first few weeks of separation. And then there was the money from the sale of Honey's house. It was in a trust, safe from Brad's hands. Beth guarded it carefully. And Lauren fully intended to give it all to Beth if she eventually received a settlement from the divorce.

With the proceeds from the sale of the house, her little stash and her job, she'd be all right even if Brad found a way to freeze her out.

She dropped her things off at Beth's, then went to work. She told her boss first. Bea said, "Oh Lauren, what a shock! I'm so sorry." Of course everyone at work thought she lived a charmed life—that's what she'd intended them to think. First of all, she felt she was liked at work yet had no close friends there. She was rarely included in their away-from-work so-cializing, probably because they all thought they had nothing in common. She never let on that life in that big house was cold and heartless. She never complained about Brad.

Then she told some of the people who worked for her, warning them that she might run into scheduling problems if she had legal emergencies. Again, they said they were sorry, but she detected in their voices that they didn't really feel sorry for her at all.

Brad texted her three times. Pick up my cleaning. Make an appointment for my car to be detailed while I'm at the hospital, Tuesday is best. What's for dinner?

She answered: Okay. Okay. Maybe takeout.

Then she went home and waited for him. She sat at the kitchen counter, still dressed in work clothes, and tried to stem the trembling. He was not later than usual but it felt like she had waited for hours. She didn't have a glass of wine but when this was behind her, she was having a big one. Very big.

He walked in through the garage door, briefcase in hand, and seemed surprised to see her sitting there. He didn't smile or say hello. He pretty much ignored her. "Your cleaning is in the closet and you have an appointment for the detailers at noon on Tuesday. Meet them at the car. I told them it would be in the doctor's lot. And I'm leaving."

"Going somewhere?" he asked, leafing through the mail.

"I'm filing for divorce, Brad. I've arranged to have you served at the office tomorrow—you can either tell your office staff or just say you're expecting some legal documents. If you're not there, there's always the hospital. But I thought you'd appreciate telling those people yourself."

He put down the mail. "What brought this on?"

"Twenty-four years of abuse," she said. "I've canceled my charge cards and had my mail forwarded."

"Going with the clothes on your back?" he asked. Then he smiled mockingly.

"I've packed some clothes but I'll wait for our settlement before taking anything else from the house."

"And where the hell are you going?"

"My cell phone will be turned on if you need to talk to me. If you harass me, I'll block your calls."

"You're such an idiot," he said. "You'll regret this."

"I believe it will be difficult but I don't think I'll regret it."

He continued to smile. "Oh, I'll make sure you regret it."

"Why bother? Really. Our marriage died years ago. What am I besides a housekeeper and arm piece for your social obligations?"

"A very well-paid housekeeper," he said. "And not that much of an arm-piece anymore. You came from nothing, Lauren. Is that what you want to go back to? Nothing?"

"I came from a loving if modest home and I can support myself."

"If you walk out that door, you won't get another dime from me. I'll make you suffer, wait and see."

"I'm sure you will try," she said. "When you get the papers, you'll have my attorney's contact information."

"I won't pay another dime of support for your daughters, not for education or living expenses," he said.

"That would be so sad, Brad. They're your daughters, too. Do you want them to resent you? Hate you for cutting them off?"

"I was very clear—if you divorce me, I'm done supporting any of you. You're doing it to them, not me. You know the price you'll pay for this is high. I've warned you."

"Why?" she said imploringly. "We haven't even shared a bedroom in years! We're not friends! What the hell does it matter to you? I don't delude myself that you love me! By now you've made it abundantly clear I mean nothing to you! On some level, you actually hate me."

"I will if you do this. You don't make the rules."

"Then tell them you ended it!" she said. "Your secret is safe with me. Tell people I'm a hopeless drunk or a shoplifter or drug addict and you threw me out! Who cares? For the sake of our daughters, let's end this amicably. Someday we'll stare over the same baby's head at a christening and—"

"I doubt that very much, Lauren," he said icily. Then he went back to leafing through his mail. As though she didn't exist.

And she left.

She had never prepared herself for the idea that he might be ready for this. Cassie wouldn't have told him. But would she have leaked something to Lacey? Or perhaps Brad had been expecting this for a long time. He should. She'd been as compliant as was possible but when he'd pushed her into a corner, she fought back as much as she dared. He might've said a lot of mean things, but she hadn't exactly been silent.

Sex came to mind. She'd always had a hard time with orgasms and it displeased him, as if she was doing it on purpose. More than once he said, "You could try a little harder, Lauren." And more than once she'd said, "Are you sure you're trying?" But that made him angry and when he wasn't getting his way, he pouted or became abusive or looked for ways to punish her.

She had to see Lacey now. She hadn't planned to see her tonight, but now she would have to. Brad would probably call his daughters. He was very good at building alliances when he needed to. So, instead of setting up some time with her oldest daughter for tomorrow evening, she called and asked if she had a little time tonight. To talk.

"We'd better talk," Lacey said. "I hear you've lost your mind."

She took a breath. "Not at all, honey. Do you have some time now? I can drive over. Or we can meet somewhere."

"There's no one here at the moment," Lacey said. "Come right now and we can get this misunderstanding handled."

CHAPTER SIX

All the way to Lacey's apartment, Lauren's stomach was in a knot. It was a familiar feeling. She'd spent most of the last twenty-four years with a tight stomach thanks to Brad. She was kind of amazed she hadn't worked it into an ulcer, swallowing her feelings like she did.

Lacey lived with a roommate in a quaint little apartment in the Menlo Park area, close to Stanford. It was ridiculously expensive, very upscale, which had always been important to Lacey. But, like Cassie's, it was solid and safe and comfortable. She wondered how Lacey would manage when she was finally on her own. She'd never really worked. She'd had token jobs that didn't interfere with her life too much but she'd never had to struggle.

When Lauren arrived, Lacey had candles lit, though the summer sun was still up. She was sitting at her small kitchen table, drinking a glass of wine.

"Hi, honey," she said, kissing Lacey's cheek.

"Midlife crisis?" Lacey asked acerbically.

Lauren sat down across from her daughter. "No, Lacey. This is something that has to be done and I'm sorry to say, it's long overdue."

"There's wine chilled. Help yourself if you like while we sort this out."

"No, thanks. I don't think there's much to sort out. I've moved out. I rented a small house in Alameda."

Lacey looked shocked beyond belief. "You didn't go to Aunt Beth's?"

She hesitated. How much to tell her daughters was the big question. She didn't have any intention of persecuting Brad but neither did she want to carry the whole load. She settled on trying to get by with telling Lacey what she already knew. Or should have known if she'd been paying attention. "I didn't want to do that again. I'm able to take care of myself. And sometimes too many opinions only makes things worse."

"You've been planning this?"

Lauren sighed. "Remember when I took you and Cassie to Aunt Beth's? You were so young then. It was very spur-of-the-moment. I hadn't planned it or thought it through but there was something that just put me over the edge. It was psychological abuse, emotional abuse. Your father was on a tear and I couldn't take it—"

"But we know he gets like that," Lacey said. "The life-and-death pressure he's under..."

"There's no excuse for abuse, Lacey. But when I thought I could break away, he threatened me and blackmailed me. I tried to fight back but it was pretty well established I was no match for him and so we went back. You begged to go back. Aunt Beth's was small, crowded and chaotic."

"What do you mean he threatened you?" Lacey said derisively. "Aren't you a big enough girl to weather his little tantrums?"

Oh, how Lauren wanted to show her daughter the bruises on her upper arms from being pinched! They went away but there were still discolored spots here and there. Brad always blamed her, her behavior, when he lost his temper or treated her badly. "I always took the brunt of it to spare you girls. And I always hoped he'd mellow over time. But he threatened to do everything in his power to take you from me. Later, he refused to pay tuition for you. He said he could be forced to pay child support until a child was eighteen but not after. I talked to a lawyer who told me there would be a settlement and it was highly possible arrangements for tuition could be part of the settlement. At least half of the tuition. Your father does not fight fair, Lacey. He fights to win. I took you back. I weathered his little tantrums, as you call them. I didn't want him to punish you girls."

"And now?"

"I'm done," she said. "I've done all I can do."

Lacey got tears in her eyes. "What did you expect? You moved out of your bedroom! Don't pretend this isn't your fault!"

"He cheated on me!" she blurted.

"No," Lacey said. "No, he didn't."

Lauren rubbed the bridge of her nose. One of many things she hadn't wanted to dump on her daughters. But, she was sure they'd known. She and Brad had fought so much about it. "He did," she said. "More than once, and he denies it."

"You're just being dramatic!" Lacey said. "You've always been like that."

Lauren heard Brad's voice saying those words and lost her composure. "He gave me an STD! There's only one way to get it and I've only had one partner in my life."

Lacey clearly didn't know what to say. "Well, is he sorry?" she asked, at a loss.

"No! He won't admit it. Come on, you know how stubborn he can be. And he's always right, no matter what. You lived in our home. You know how often he belittled me, humiliated me, shouted at me! He accuses me of pushing his buttons, forcing him to behave badly. Do I really need to tell you that's not true? And even if it were, that's no excuse. Lacey, I'm almost fifty. I can't take it anymore! I know that makes you unhappy, but—"

"You have to try harder," Lacey said.

"I'm sorry, but no. I've given him all I have to give."

"But what about the things we've planned?" she asked. "What about my wedding?"

Lauren was momentarily gobsmacked. "Are you and Sean getting serious?"

"Not really, but I will get married someday. What's my wedding going to be like with you and Daddy hating each other? No family times with all of us together? What about when I have my first baby? Do I have to take turns between you and Daddy? And decide who gets to hold him first?"

"You're kidding me, right?" Lauren said.

"Of course I'm not kidding!" she said, tears running down her cheeks. "You just can't do this to me. We have a family. For better or worse, right?"

Lauren leaned closer so she could look into her daughter's eyes. "You would have me stay in a place where I'm painfully unhappy so you can pretend to have a perfect wedding?"

"Well, you married him, not me!" She turned and grabbed a tissue and began crying in earnest. "You can't just change everything because you're not getting your way!"

"Not getting my way?" she asked. "Oh Lacey, can you really be that heartless?"

"Me? I'm not the one walking out on the man I promised to love and honor!"

"Lacey, he made those promises, too. And he never kept them. At first I thought I could fix it, our marriage. Then I thought I could live with it until you girls were a little older. Then I thought I could take it until you were through with high school. Then college. Would you really ask me to sacrifice the rest of my life so you can have a fairy-tale wedding to some completely unknown groom?"

"It's more than that and you know it!"

"Is it? Oh right, who gets to hold the baby first..."

"If you leave Daddy and ruin my family, I will never forgive you!"

Lauren felt the tears rise in her eyes. "That would be such a shame." She got up and walked around the small table, bending to kiss the top of her daughter's head. "I know this is hard for you and you need some time to absorb this. But it's time I stand up for myself and do what's right for me. I love you," she said to Lacey as she walked out the door.

Lauren thought about going to Beth's house for the night. Most of her things were still in Beth's spare room, but in the next two days the furniture she'd ordered would be delivered and she'd move in completely. Right now there was only a couch in her new home but it would be comfortable enough for one night. She wanted company but did not want Beth and Chip to see her anguish. If she even saw her sister, she would tell about her conversation with Lacey and Beth would condemn her, pronounce her a spoiled brat.

She knew this would be hard. She had been terrified. She even feared Lacey wouldn't be sympathetic or supportive. But she hadn't predicted the cruelty of her words—the echo of Brad's voice.

Surely she would come around in time...

She went to a little grocery market in Alameda, her new home. She wasn't exactly hungry but she put a couple of wedges of cheese, a box of crackers and some fruit in her basket. Then she went to the wine case and picked out a nice bottle. There was a part of her that thought she might down the whole thing, but she knew she wouldn't. The more sensible part of her thought too much wine would only make her cry, and was that such a good idea? She threw a corkscrew and one single knife in her basket.

"Kind of a long way from home, aren't you?"

She turned abruptly, nearly dropping the basket, which Beau caught very deftly while hanging on to his own. "Did I startle you?" he asked.

"I was surprised at the sound of your voice," she said. "You're the last person I expected to run into here."

"And the last person you expected to run into in a church garden or at a fund-raiser," he said with a smile. "I live in the neighborhood. If I only need a couple of things, I like this market. If I need a lot, I hit a bigger, cheaper and more crowded store. But this is all fresh. All good."

"You live around here?" she asked.

"Just a few blocks away," he said. "Is this on your way home?"

"In a way. I'm renting a house nearby. Also in the neighborhood."

"Seriously?" he asked, shocked.

She nodded. "This is my first night. Nothing in it but a couch. And soon there will be cheese, fruit and wine. Badly needed wine."

"Oh boy."

"Yep, this was the day. A very trying, painful day."

He reached out and touched her upper arm, giving her a supportive squeeze. "Want to get a cup of coffee? There are lots of nice little spots around here."

"I...ah... I really need to get out of these shoes. It's been so stressful."

"I understand completely. I had a go-around with one of the boys the other night. He was upset about the pending divorce, like it hasn't been coming for years."

"Really?"

"His mother got to him, wanting him to pressure me to try again. It was awful."

"I think that's what happened in my family. One daughter seems to understand completely and the other thinks I'm a monster. I'm trying so hard not to explode and list the terrible reasons this is the only option for me."

"You don't want to blame him to the kids," Beau said, knowingly. "Eventually you're going to, you know. It happens. Hang in there."

"I don't feel like going to a café or bar, but if you'd like a glass of wine and some..." She looked in her basket. "Some cheese and grapes?"

"I don't want to complicate your life at such a touchy time. But I sure wouldn't mind a glass of wine. The only person I've had to talk to about all of this is a priest." He grinned. "We should do this. We have war stories to share."

"That sounds miserable."

"It's going to be perfectly nice. You'll see you're not the only one and you won't tell me anything you're not ready to talk about. Lauren, it would be nice if it was simple and amicable. I've heard that happens sometimes. But if you ask me, it's damn rare. I thought I could just be strong, be a big guy and weather it, but I'm having a rough ride like most people do. You know what's good, though?"

"I can't imagine."

"It won't last forever. In my case, Pamela will find someone to take her mind off me. She usually does."

She thought about this for a second, the idea of having him

over. She wished she had her mom to talk to, but Honey had been bitter in some ways, having been abandoned herself. Not only had her young husband walked out on her and left her with two babies to support alone, but Brad had never fooled her. She knew he was a bastard from day one. At least there was Beth, who could be sympathetic and supportive, but Beth had a storybook marriage. Very human and earthy, married to a cop and with money always tight, but at the end of the day, she was secure in her marriage. There was only Ruby. And Ruby's husband was recovering from a stroke.

"I need to get some plastic cups and plates," she said.

"Great. Then I'll follow you." He lifted his basket. It contained only milk, bread and eggs. "Can I borrow your refrigerator?"

"Sure."

For the first time since deciding to leave Brad she did not feel utterly alone. It would be good to have a friend who understood what it was like to end a marriage.

Beau followed Lauren to a neighborhood he knew and to a house that was easily as nice as his, but he'd bought his as a fixer-upper before he even met Pamela. Lauren unlocked the door for them and went straight to the kitchen, turning on the overhead lights. She set out the wine and cheese and some plastic plates and cups on the counter. "I don't even have a coffee table," she said. The house was vacant but for a single couch.

"I'm a guy," he said. "I can put my drink on the floor and the plate on my knees. And I won't spill."

"Would you do me a favor?"

"Sure."

"Would you open the wine while I bring in some bags from the car?"

He held out his hand for her key fob. "I'll open the wine and bring in the bags. Where are they?"

"Trunk. And thanks. I feel like I've just finished a marathon."

"I know the feeling."

He opened the wine then made fast work of bringing in the bags. She sat on the sofa—the kind of fancy, curved sofa in a light beige he wouldn't have dared buy for his living room with two boys growing up. "You have more furniture coming?" he asked politely.

"Yes," she said with a laugh. "A full complement, most of it in the next two to three days. Tables, chairs, television, bedroom furniture, guest room furniture. I'm taking some time off. I did that to meet deliveries but now I'm so glad I have the days off. I'm emotionally drained."

"How'd your husband take it?" Beau asked.

"As though he'd been expecting it for years but didn't think I'd ever have the guts to really do it. And then he warned me—he'd make me regret it. He didn't say he loved me and couldn't live without me, which wouldn't have worked in any case. He said I was humiliating him."

Beau winced. He recovered and said, "Look, I'm sorry to pry, but is there any chance he'd become violent?"

"Physically?" she asked. "And hurt his hands?"

"Is he the kind of man who could cause you physical harm? Disable your car? Set your house on fire? Anything?"

She stiffened, instantly at alert. "He's so good at abusing me without lifting a finger, those things never occurred to me. He's more likely to try to keep me from getting anything from the marriage or turn the girls against me. He loves to tell me I can't get by without him when actually, I think the opposite is true. He texts me all day, giving me chores to do for him, lists of things to buy for him, settle for him. It is said most doctors can't make it without a good nurse and a good wife. Brad has a great sense of entitlement. I don't know for sure but I suspect he was born with it. He was the only child of wealthy parents."

He just shook his head.

"He's mean and spiteful. I need to remember that."

"I'll come over tomorrow and install some good locks for you," he said. "I'll get one of those camera doorbells that you can access with your cell phone."

"You don't have to do that..."

"But it will help," he said.

"So you've had a bad week?" she asked, only to take the focus off her for a moment.

"Predictable, but not fun. I didn't expect Michael, my twenty-year-old, to come to me in tears practically begging me to let his mom come home. I hated looking like such a beast. I changed the locks on the house. I told them their mother isn't forbidden to enter by any means but to please be sure someone is there. When she's done acting hurt and begging for another chance, she's going to get angry. And when she gets angry, she can be malicious."

"What are you afraid of?" Lauren asked.

"I'm not sure what to be afraid of. She could take lots of stuff she doesn't need. She's living in a furnished flat in the city and all she needed was her clothes and she took almost all of them, leaving very little behind. She thought she was never coming back, that's my guess. I suspect another man. A man that didn't last. That's been our pattern. She leaves because the marriage is troubled, she says, but I think she gets bored. A few months later she regrets it and wants to come home. Quite suddenly, every time. All I'm lacking are the facts."

"And you were expecting that?"

"I was. I told her the last time she left I wasn't going to be welcoming her home after her vacation. I told her if she left, it would be the last time. Apparently she thought she could turn that decision around. At Michael's insistence, we tried marriage counseling. And not for the first time."

Lauren actually laughed. "We've had marriage counseling at least six times."

"I guess it didn't work for you, either."

"It will never work," Lauren said. "Brad sees himself as smarter than the counselor. He manages to control the session. He educates the therapist, diagnosing me as a chronic liar who is frequently delusional, imagining him having affairs, exaggerating things he said, picking fights over nothing."

"All untrue?" he asked.

"My sister calls it gaslighting. He says, 'You're imagining that,' or 'That's just another gross exaggeration,' or 'You're dreaming again, Lauren.' And, 'Sometimes I genuinely fear for your sanity.' And my favorite, 'My wife is suffering from depression and anxiety and she's in denial and won't get help.' He's called me bipolar, manic depressive, a borderline personality and malicious."

"Did you imagine him having affairs?"

"No," she said. "Not affairs, I don't think. I think I might've guessed if he was really invested in another woman. Flings, I think. And no it wasn't my imagination. He had me almost convinced I was paranoid. Then there was proof."

"That'll do it," Beau said. "Ever ask yourself, how did I get to this place?"

"I'm pretty sure I know how and it doesn't reflect well on me," she said. "You?"

He nodded. "I know exactly how. I loved Pam and her kids."

"Well, I was very young and hopeful. And Lacey came along right away. The kids were still very little when I realized it was hopeless. I didn't think my heart could break any more. Until my daughter said she'd never forgive me if I divorced her father, even though she knows how difficult he is to live with. Then I knew real heartache."

"And your other daughter?"

That was almost as painful to think about. "Very support-ive…because she remembers his abusive nature and mean-ness way better than I want her to. It tears me up to think she grew up with that knowledge."

He leaned toward her. "There are some things you're going to have to understand, Lauren. Even though you did your best and no more could be expected of you, you'll feel guilty. You're going to be judged. You're going to be worried about what he can do to you. He might want to do battle. Your daughters might love you a lot and still not be supportive—to them it's not ideal for you to walk away now. Would they have you spend the rest of your life unhappy just so it won't inconvenience them? I'm afraid so. You're going to have to do what you think is best in spite of what other people, in-cluding your kids, think. And depending on how tenacious your husband is, this could go on for a long time. Are you sure you're up to it?"

"We haven't even shared a bedroom in years. I'm not spend-ing the rest of my life like this. I may crumble sometimes, but I'll pick myself up. I regret that I didn't do this years ago. I thought I was doing right by the girls by staying, but I was wrong. Obviously I didn't do anyone any favors. Including Brad."

He looked at her for a long moment, sympathy in his eyes. "Buckle your seat belt."

Lauren had made two phone calls before arriving at her new rented house with Beau following. She called Beth and said, "I'm not coming over. I'm going to my house. I bought a bottle of wine and some cheese and crackers and right now

I really need a little time to think. Can I call you in the morning?"

"Was it terrible?" Beth asked.

"Kind of, yeah. But highly survivable."

"Call me," her sister said.

Then she called Cassie. "I left the house and came to my rental. It was terrible and I need a little time to process. Is it okay for me to call you later?"

"Yes, but Lacey already called. Oh Mama, I'm sorry she was so selfish!"

"Well, she was shocked, I suppose. Let me take off my shoes and relax, get a grip on my feelings and call you later."

"I'll be up and if not, call anyway."

"Should I wait and call tomorrow? I'm having the day off."

"Call tonight to say good-night. I'll be up till midnight. Then we can talk tomorrow, too."

"Thank you for being so understanding, Cassie. I'm sorry to put you through this."

"He put us all through it. It was harder listening to the way Daddy put you down all the time. I know you were putting us first. If it hadn't been for me and Lacey, you would have left him years ago."

She prayed there was a way Cassie and Lacey could remain close through this, but that seemed impossible, given the differences in the way they both felt.

Then Lauren had unlocked her front door and carried in her meager groceries, followed by the flower man. And a whole new world seemed to open up to her. At first they drank a glass of wine and dumped their bad marriage tales on each other, but after an hour, almost by mutual decision, they moved on to other topics. He told her about his house in Alameda, a Victorian he renovated and remodeled almost entirely on his own. He had a job that never required dressing up and all summer he worked in shorts. He had an office and an associate, three assistants and several landscapers he'd worked with for years.

"I built the business from the ground up, at first I was designing and planting with a small crew to help. I only worked for someone else for a couple of years after college, then I bet it all and struck out on my own."

"I don't mean this in a nosy way, but is your company successful?" she asked.

"It is," he said. "But more importantly, I still love it. Both the boys have worked for my landscapers. Drew still does. It will get him through college and make him strong. It's hard work. Tell me about your job."

"It's not very interesting," she said. "It's just product development. We're the people that help marketing introduce new products and investigate ways to use them. We work closely with the dieticians and chefs. We call them chefs but they're not official chefs—more like cooks. In fact some of our best cooks are men and women who are semi-professional but have great success in the kitchen. They take something as simple as freeze-dried or frozen chicken strips and create a packaged chicken Alfredo that's inexpensive, nutritious, easy and fast."

"And full of preservatives," he said.

"Don't you ever eat prepared meals? Like frozen pizza?"

"Of course," he said. "I'm giving you a hard time."

"Because I haven't had a hard enough time today?" she countered, lifting one brow.

"How do you make your eyes that color?"

"Believe it or not, it's real—violet. It's rare. Elizabeth Taylor had violet eyes. It's a mutation, I'm told. It can also be done with contacts, which explains why we're seeing more of it."

He was looking into her eyes, not talking. Then he took a sip of his wine and seemed to gather himself up. He swallowed. "Men must have fallen in love with you all the time," he said.

She looked away from his intense gaze. "Not that I noticed," she said. Not since Brad. Brad had said, *I just want to
look into those eyes for the rest of my life.* She'd fallen for it and it
turned out not to be true.

"Well, maybe you'll notice once you're not going through
the upheaval of divorce. You're a beautiful woman, Lauren.
I think your life is going to take a nice turn after the storm."

"And is yours?" she asked.

"It was pretty slow and easy until Pamela decided she
wanted to save our marriage, then it started to get rough
again. It'll pass. After she's gotten everything she can get."

"Oh God, I can't even think about all that," Lauren said.

"I hope you got yourself a good lawyer," he said.

"I had to. I've always known my husband would be terrible. He's been kind enough to warn me. Do you? Have a
good lawyer?"

He nodded. "She has an amazing track record and a great
reputation, but she looks like my grandmother. She says it's
her secret weapon."

In spite of herself, Lauren laughed. "And my lawyer has a
reputation as a barracuda, but she's always been very nice to
me. Where it all breaks down is when it's time to do something ruthless. And I can't. I'm not that person. I never have
been."

"Me, either. Oh brother," he said. "We're screwed, aren't
we?"

"Kind of sounds like it."

He looked at his watch. "I'm going to get out of your hair.
Do you need anything before I go?"

"I think I'll get by just fine. I'm glad you stopped by. Maybe
everyone needs a divorce buddy."

"That's very cute, Lauren," he said, standing. "You have
my cell number. If anything comes up, if you have a problem
or if you're worried about something…"

"I'm fine. Really. I need to make a couple of phone calls."

At the door he paused. Hesitated. Then he gave her a brief hug. "Hang in there."

"You, too."

Lauren called Cassie first, told her she was fine and they'd talk the next day. Beth had been chomping at the bit to know how she was. "He must know I'm serious because he isn't showing his hand," Lauren told her sister. "He likes to think he's smarter than everyone and capable of a sneak attack. Even after all these years, it's impossible for me to anticipate Brad."

After that, she pulled a blanket out of a box, put her pajamas on and reclined on the sofa with her last glass of wine and her laptop. She checked her mail, listened to some local news and before she knew it, her eyelids were drooping. Using one of the sofa throw pillows for her head, she curled up on her new couch and went to sleep.

She slept like a baby. When she woke, birds were chirping and the sun was streaming into the living room windows.

How is this possible? she asked herself. After the stress of the day, how could she sleep like that? She thought she'd be awake all night, worrying about her daughters, dreading Brad's anger, hearing odd noises... But she was strangely at peace. She couldn't remember her dreams this morning but she thought there was a familiar presence there. She thought it was Beau, smiling that reassuring smile. What a surprising gift he was—a friend who understood what she was going through just when she needed that most. A divorce buddy was not a bad notion. When she got to know him better, she might be able to talk him off the ledge just the way he had for her.

She checked and saw there were no missed calls on her phone. The world was at peace. She showered, dressed in jeans and sneakers and roared into her day, starting with the nearest Starbucks. She treated herself to a sausage biscuit and called Cassie from the store patio. She listened to her daughter's concerns, then told her firmly, "Don't let your father or anyone make this your problem—this isn't about you. This is our marriage that's ending and we're the only people responsible. And don't let Lacey try to get you involved. I know in the end it will be difficult and painful for you girls, but I'll do my best to reassure you, then we just have to move on." She took a deep breath. "I'm sorry for the inconvenience."

Hah. What tripe! she thought.

Then she called Lacey, who was every bit as unpleasant as she had been the evening before. "Have you come to your senses yet?" Lacey said.

"I'm afraid you're going to have to get used to the idea that I'm not going to be married to your father any longer. It will take a while to sort out, but this doesn't have to be about you, Lacey. This is about your father and me."

"Oh really? And who's going to take care of him in his old age?"

A rush of protests were on her lips, the most obvious being, *You can't treat a person like an irrelevant servant for years and then expect them to be your faithful caretaker in old age!* Instead she said, "And who's going to take care of me in my old age, Lacey? You? Because we both know it wouldn't be your father."

She heard her daughter suck in her breath, but nothing more.

"Never mind," Lauren said. "I'll pick out my extended care facility before I need it. I've given your father twenty-four years and I've given you most of that, too. Since no one seems particularly concerned that I be happy or cared for, I'll do it for myself. Call me when you're done blaming me."

"How can you? How can you destroy our family like this?"

"Me?" Lauren asked. "Stop it, Lacey! There are no more excuses! Your father has been, at the very least, horrible to me. Cruel! Mean! I'm done. That. Is. All." And she hung up.

She had a million things on her to-do list, but she chucked the cardboard cup and took a brisk walk down the main street. She needed to uncoil that tight knot in her gut. She'd awakened so fresh and rested, but Lacey could tax anyone's patience.

She was familiar with the area, of course, but she saw it this morning through fresh eyes. The grocer was putting out his fresh fruits and vegetables and wished her a good morning. The café across the street had people lining up for breakfast. The bookstore was just opening its doors, as was the real estate office and bank. The bank was now her new bank and one of the tellers who was walking in gave her a wave.

Lauren walked for about a mile, then walked back to Starbucks to fetch her car. By the time she got home she was feeling better. Lacey was another reality she was going to have to accept. Despite the fact that Lacey knew only too well how hard Brad was to please, to get along with, she had managed to wrap him around her little finger. Cassie was right, Lacey was his favorite. He bought her spur-of-the-moment gifts he didn't get Cassie. Not small gifts—a four-hundred-dollar purse, designer shoes they saw in a window and he said, "What the hell, huh?" Anything Lacey wanted, Brad would give her. It was entirely possible that the future belonged to Lacey and Brad as a family. Lauren excluded. Cassie excluded.

It stung. But it was a reality she'd been aware of for a long time.

Cassie, on the other hand, probably wouldn't trade anything to keep a relationship with her father. She had already been clear, she wouldn't throw her mother under the bus. Cassie's eyes had been wide open since she was about seven.

So, this was where she'd failed. She shouldn't have stayed with Brad so long. The first time the backs of her upper arms were shocked with small bruises from his nasty little pinches, she should have left him. In her naive attempts to fix her marriage or keep the meanness invisible for her daughters, she'd failed and in the end may have lost one of them. In fact she'd let one of them become spoiled and self-absorbed, while the other was all too aware of the abuse in their family. She worried that she'd failed all around. She hoped it wasn't too late for them to heal.

She hurried to Beth's to load up the things she had left at their house. Despite the darkness of her troubles, she felt a burden lifted. She was finally starting over. Beth wanted her to sit down for coffee and breakfast but Lauren had already eaten and just couldn't be still—she had so much to do. She declined with a smile.

"Boy, you must be feeling kind of confident," Beth said. "Didn't he unleash any of his dominance on you?"

"I didn't listen," she said. "He's going to make me suffer as much as he can. So what else is new? I defied him. He's pissed. How surprised am I?" And she actually laughed. "Stop by when you have time. You know the way."

Her phone was buzzing before she got home. The bedroom furniture would arrive within the hour. Another buzz announced the two large area rugs for the living room and master bedroom were ready to be delivered. The dining room and bar stools were en route. And she was suddenly very busy. She was sorting through new purchases from pillows to kitchen towels. The bedroom furniture arrived ahead of the area rugs—she'd figure that out later. Maybe Chip would help her move furniture.

An electrician came by to check some of the outlets that weren't working properly. The landlord stopped in to see how she liked some of the painting they'd done. It was nonstop.

There were three angry texts from Brad. They served me at the office! said one. Who's going to pick up my paperwork from the transcription service? And, her favorite, Let's have dinner and talk this over! She responded calmly to each. I told you, I don't know and No, in that order.

Then midafternoon when she was up to her eyeballs in boxes, recently delivered furniture and other items, and starting to wilt from the work of getting settled, Beau walked in the door that had been left standing open. He was carrying a toolbox.

"Hey," he said, looking around. "Looks like you have a lot to do."

She was never so happy to see anyone in her life. He'd come to install the safety locks and cameras. She wanted to hug him.

CHAPTER SEVEN

Beau helped Lauren rearrange her bedroom furniture to accommodate the area rug. He reinforced her locks, made sure the windows had locks and installed the doorbell camera, which had an app on her phone to show who was at the door. He even helped her put her linens on her bed and all the while, they talked. It was exactly what she needed. While Beth and Chip were as supportive as they could be, they were always treading so carefully, clearly fearful that she'd cave in and go back as she had before. There was something about Beau's empathy that was better—he didn't tread carefully. *You will be judged and you will feel guilty.* Boom.

She spent the rest of the week and through the weekend getting settled. It wasn't too complicated—she didn't have that much. She spent some money on odds and ends like baskets, candles, pictures, stacking tables—the personal touches that would make the house hers. And Beau dropped by several times. By the end of the week he said, "I'd call or text but I don't have your phone number." She decided it was probably safe to give it to him since she never hesitated to open her door to him.

She learned that he supported the family and paid all the monthly bills; Pamela paid her charge accounts and only occasionally picked up family expenses or paid for clothes or athletic supplies for her sons, but since they filed a joint tax return, he was well aware of how nice her paycheck was and that she had her own savings account.

"That doesn't seem fair," Lauren said.

"I caught on within a few years," he said. "That's how she was able to take breaks from the marriage, rent nice space and travel. So I started an equity account in the business for savings and started college funds for the boys. I'm not trying to hide anything, but I'd like to level the playing field because she's going to want half the house and half my business."

"Your business?" Lauren asked, aghast.

"Divorce is a rough game, Lauren. And I made quite a few mistakes along the way. For one thing, I should've filed the last time she left. I should've done it right away, before she was tired of her vacation. If my guess is right, she wouldn't have flinched. She was occupied and wanted to be free of me."

"And I should have divorced Brad when the girls were small."

"But you didn't," he said.

"He said he'd take them away from me. He said, 'Lauren, you'll never make it. I have money and you don't. I can fight you every step of the way until I starve you out and get the girls.'" She shrugged. "I believed him. I was young. I was married to a man who got everything he wanted. And then there's that other little thing…"

He furrowed his eyebrows in question.

"I didn't want the girls to grow up the way Beth and I

did." She blushed in embarrassment. "We weren't unhappy, I don't know what I was thinking. Our mother and grandparents loved us, did their best by us. It was hard, though. Barely seeing Honey because she worked at least two jobs, not having enough money to join clubs or teams. I thought, Brad couldn't provide love and kindness, but he could provide." She sighed. "I was a fool and I made a deal with the devil."

These were the kind of truths they shared. Lauren wondered what kind of deeply personal things Beau was keeping to himself because she was barely scratching the surface when sharing with him. She was telling her new friend only those things she was comfortable making public.

Lauren was seeing that divorce was an emotional mine field. Brad was calling and texting her several times a day, alternating between harassing her, sweetly cajoling her to stop this madness or demanding she take care of his errands. She stopped responding but his messages and texts were well preserved on her phone.

She went back to work the following week and told her supervisor and most of her colleagues how the move had gone and that she was living not too far from the plant. She was surprised by the kind reception. She hadn't expected them to be sympathetic. Bea, the division director and her immediate supervisor, asked her if she had a good lawyer and said, "If there's anything I can do to support you, let me know."

She thought it would be a good idea to contact Sylvie Emerson. They planned for a Sunday brunch, just the two of them, at Sylvie's beautiful home on Nob Hill. "Andy will be playing golf, so he won't bother us!"

Lauren hoped he wasn't playing with Brad.

She took a leafy red geranium in a pretty pot and she settled with Sylvie at a table on the patio, surrounded by plants, shrubs and flowers. It wasn't a large yard, it being a city home, but it was beautifully landscaped with lots of outdoor furniture and a brick fireplace. Lauren assumed they did quite a bit of entertaining here.

After a cup of coffee and a little fruit cup, Lauren broke it to her. "I have something to tell you," she said. "It's official now. Brad and I will be divorcing."

Startled, Sylvie gasped. "Oh my God," she said. "Are you all right?"

"I'm fine," Lauren said. "Sylvie, I was the one to file for divorce. I have to be honest with you—this is not premature. But I understand that Andy and Brad are good friends and if that means you wouldn't be comfortable as my friend, I completely understand. I would never put you in the middle of it. It's messy."

"Not be my friend because of a messy divorce? Bullshit. I've known Brad for fifteen years and I consider him more of a business associate of Andy's than a close friend. He's been helpful with medical matters. Brad would move mountains to get any of our family or friends a speedy appointment or referral and we appreciate that. Of course, we're grateful for anything he'll do for the foundation. But Lauren, we're not friends. Brad does favors for Andy, Andy takes Brad to his club or includes him with a group of friends when they take the boat out. It's a business relationship. Not like our relationship, which is not business. This is personal. If you need anything at all, *anything*, I hope you'll come to me at once! And I didn't get where I am today being afraid of a mess here and there."

"You are incredible," Lauren told her.

"You and I are going to get together more often," Sylvie said. Then she smiled. "I imagine it will drive Brad out of his mind."

"Brad is very fond of Andy. And you," Lauren said with a touch of nervousness.

Sylvie lifted the silver top off a serving platter. There was a beautiful, cheesy omelet, just a few slices of bacon and toast points on the side. She reached for Lauren's plate and began to serve the food. "Darling, I know a lot of men like Brad. He's pretty obvious..."

"Oh?" Lauren asked.

"I think Brad likes attaching himself to people he thinks are important. He practically drools when he is introduced to someone he thinks might be important. Or maybe that's too judgmental of me. Maybe he likes being associated with men like Andy because Andy does so much for the community. But there is no hiding the fact—Brad is not an easy man."

"How would you know that?" she asked, genuinely curious.

Sylvie handed her the plate and began to serve her own. "I'll be honest with you, if I can trust you to keep it to yourself."

"Oh, believe me—I'm not talking to Brad! And I'd never say anything that might betray you."

"Well then. It's very easy. I've known him for fifteen years and I knew immediately. He's not gracious to anyone he perceives as beneath him. He's impatient with servers, valets, groundskeepers, bartenders, laborers. Andy put himself through college working at the docks. He started his first company on government grants. I don't think Brad would have paid him much notice then. Do you?"

"Brad's family was wealthy," Lauren said. "He had a lot of advantages..."

"Neither of us came from money. I worked as a waitress, then eventually a teacher. We worked hard. Our kids had jobs in high school. It's true, we've been very fortunate lately, but it's still fresh to us. Which explains Andy's interest in the less fortunate."

Lately? Lauren thought. She couldn't remember a time the Emersons weren't extremely influential in San Francisco society. But then, they were now in their seventies. They had a son nearly as old as Lauren.

"Always remember this, darling—people will be judged by how they treat the most important person in the room and the *least* important. That will tell you everything you need to know about a person."

For a while as they ate, Sylvie talked about the early years of her marriage, when the children were small, and times were lean and sometimes terrifying. One of the kids would get sick and they worried about medical costs, not to mention the difficulty of working out childcare so they could both work. It was a struggle to even find family time. But eventually, when the kids were in their twenties, Andy's company was doing well and they took it public in a big stock offering that shocked their wildest dreams. After that, Andy sold and started a new company, also a success. But the years of struggle were not only remembered clearly by Sylvie and Andy, but also by their children.

Lauren talked a little about her young years and how amazing she thought it that a successful young surgeon would want to marry her. But those early years of marriage with two babies were not easy; Brad was always busy, always on call, leaving early, coming home late. He was high-maintenance from the first day, but she hadn't expected life with a doctor to be a paid vacation.

Their brunch lasted over two hours. Then Lauren said she'd better get out of Sylvie's hair.

"I want us to schedule another brunch or a lunch right now," Sylvie said. "Do you have your calendar?"

"I do," she said, pulling out her phone.

"Two weeks? Three? And are Sundays good for you? They are for me. If the family's coming over, they don't pester me in the morning."

"I would love it, but Sylvie...how are you so sure you can believe me? Trust me?"

"I've known Brad for a long time," she said. "And I've also

known you. I think I'm right about you. And when all your friends run and hide, you've got me. So—two weeks?"

"Perfect," she said, smiling.

In the third week of separation, she had a couple of decorator shelves she wanted mounted onto a wall and she confidently leaned them against that wall in anticipation of Beau stopping by. He texted on Thursday afternoon and asked if he could either stop by or meet her down the street for a glass of wine. She countered by asking if he would hang her shelves, and for that she would happily treat him to the wine.

She'd met him in March. She hadn't told anyone, not even Beth, that there was a new friend in her life and he was male. She could admit to herself that she was afraid of how it might look, as if she relished the end of her marriage so she could find a better man. People might assume that, especially if they met Beau.

It was almost August and so far the split hadn't been too traumatic. It seemed as though she was thoroughly prepared for everything Brad would do. He was dragging his feet on providing support payments while they were separated. He had steadfastly refused to help Cassie with law school and she had bravely said, "Don't worry, Mama. I'll get loans while we figure things out. Most law students are up to their eyebrows in loans anyway." Lacey was still angry with her and while it made Lauren sad, she was doing pretty well at letting that be Lacey's prerogative.

She did not cry late at night. Instead she sometimes shuddered to think what her life would be had she stayed any longer.

After he hung the shelves, she and Beau decided to walk down to a local restaurant for drinks and sliders, which would be a great dinner for both of them. They talked about their work weeks, their kids, their divorces. Michael was slowly coming around, Beau said. Pamela was spending a little more time with her sons these days. "I'm so jaded, I think it's all about stopping this divorce because she doesn't have anything better going on. I wish I wasn't that way. I want to believe it's genuine love for the boys..."

"And Lacey said she might move home—she's thinking about it. Probably to comfort her poor father from the evil witch who left him and will rob him blind. You're not the only jaded one."

It seemed they couldn't avoid the topic of divorce for long but that wasn't the only thing that came up. They talked about their childhoods, high school and college. They both grew up without luxuries, but they had friends and good times.

"Except, I grew up without a father. My grandparents were alive then, so I did have family," Lauren said.

"I don't know what I would have done without my dad," Beau said. "Four kids. Two boys and two girls and we lived in two and a half bedrooms. My dad worked all the time, job after job. When we weren't in school, my brother and I went with him. My mother cleaned houses and my sisters helped her when they could, but you know what? My parents were always good-natured, always. They have always had this deep sense of gratitude for what they did have. They were grateful for health, for family, for the energy to work. God, did they work."

"That explains you," she said.

"How do you figure?"

"The way you've managed to keep your boys out of the conflict, keep your home and family together even when your wife left you. And left you and left you..."

"What about you? Where do you get your stamina? What drives you?"

"Well, undeniably my daughters. I'm sure I follow in my mother's footsteps, if a little awkwardly."

"Now why would you say that?"

"My mom was abandoned by her husband. She never heard from him again, didn't know if he was dead or alive and didn't care. Holding body and soul together was a constant challenge for her. But even as hard as it was for her to be a single mother, she never would have put up with Brad's meanness and she was very vocal about that. My mother was pretty and poised and strong and smart. She was killed in a car accident two years ago—she was seventy-one and vivacious. Compared to my mother and sister, I'm a wimp. I'm not proud of the fact that I let myself be bullied for so many years."

"Listen, we do our best," Beau said. "I'm strong and like to think I'm smart, but I was bullied, too, by Pam. I didn't fight back and used the excuse that we don't fight girls."

They talked about what their favorite college courses had been, what they planned to do with their new lives. "Breathe," Lauren said. "Walk down the street for breakfast, sometimes for dinner. Have a book club again. I belonged to a book club years ago and I loved it, loved the women in it, but it became too much for my schedule and I had to give it up."

Beau told her about his real history with Tim, going back to grade school, and some of the trouble they got into when they were on the loose. They both went to Catholic school, of course, but Beau was on a scholarship. They put a frog in Sister Theresa's desk only to find out she could handle frogs like a pro. "Be glad I don't make you dissect this little guy for science class," she'd said. Tim got caught shoplifting once and was forced to go apologize to the shop owner. He also cut class a lot when they were in high school.

"He's much too handsome to be a priest," she said.

"If you'd seen him with the girls in high school, you'd be shocked they let him in the priesthood. No one knew his secret, that he intended to end up a priest all along. That didn't stop him from finding out what he'd be giving up."

"Oh yeah?" she asked, grinning.

"Oh yeah. He found out before I did," Beau said.

By the time Beau was walking her home, they were laughing and enjoying the summer evening. It was still light when she said good-night and let herself into her house and he drove away.

She leaned back against the front door and sighed. "I hope this is what I'll be doing with my new life," she said aloud. She made a decision right then—she wasn't going to breathe a word about Beau to anyone until all this divorce business was behind her, behind both of them. She hoped it wouldn't take too long. She pushed herself off the door and headed to the kitchen, putting her purse on the counter and getting a glass of cold water from the refrigerator.

The chime on her phone alerted her of motion on her front step. Had he come back? So soon?

She started for the door but then thinking better of it, she stopped and took her phone out of her purse. It had two chimes—one for motion and the other for when the doorbell rang. The doorbell rang. She hadn't locked the door yet. The sun was just going down and it wasn't dark. It must be Beau, she thought. Perhaps he forgot something. She looked at her phone.

She saw it was Brad. He had found her. He was fidgeting impatiently. She put her phone down and crept closer to the door. "What do you want, Brad?" she asked.

He pounded on the door. "Open the damn door, Lauren."

"This isn't a good time," she yelled.

As she reached for the lock he opened the door and stormed in. "So that's how it is," he said, scowling. "It's not about our marriage. It's about a man."

"What are you talking about?" she asked.

"I saw you," he said. "You were with a man!"

Poor Brad. He was so completely self-absorbed he didn't

even recognize Beau, whom he had met. She frowned and backed away. "He's a neighbor, Brad. He hung some shelves for me and I bought him a beer and sliders at the pub down the street."

"It looked pretty cozy to be just a neighbor," he said, approaching her rapidly.

"You're crazy. It wasn't cozy at all. It was—"

Lightning fast, he reached out and pinched her upper arm.

"Ouch! Don't do that!" she exclaimed. But he pinched the other arm. "Stop it!" she shouted and she tried pushing his hands away.

He grabbed her wrists. "The most stupid thing you can do right now is lie to me!"

"Get out," she said. "Get out right now or I'll call the police!"

He laughed at her. "And what hand are you going to use to do that, Lauren? Huh? You know no one ever believes you because you're a liar and a lunatic and sometimes you're delusional."

"You're hurting me! Let go of me!"

With just the powerful grip of his hands around her wrists, he shook her. "You'll be sorry," he growled. "I'll make sure you're sorry." He let go of one wrist to slap her, first the left cheek and then the right. And then to her shock, he curled up his fist and cold-cocked her, right in the cheek and eye. She hit her head on the breakfast bar on the way down. When she was down he said, "You're just a stupid whore." And he kicked her in the face. She managed to draw her hands over her face to protect herself somewhat but she felt it in her teeth. Then she felt herself fade out.

She was only out for a moment, she thought. She opened one eye and saw that the front door was standing open. She looked at her hands; they'd been trying to cover her face and now were covered with blood. She could hear birds, unless that was ringing in her ears. She could see the slant of the setting sun. She pulled herself to her feet. Everything hurt. Her head felt like it weighed a hundred pounds and she could taste blood in her mouth.

She grabbed her phone and the hand towel from the counter and slowly moved to the couch. The new couch. She mustn't get blood on the new couch, but she had to sit down. He'd never done that before. He had pinched her, embarrassed her, shoved her, tripped her, verbally abused her, but he'd never slugged her or kicked her. But then, as Cassie made her see, she'd been in denial about what physical abuse really was. *How much of that is too much?*

She dialed 911.

"Emergency," the operator said.

"Help," she said, spitting blood. "I've been assaulted." She gave the address three times because her words were garbled.

"Do you need an ambulance?"

"I don't know. I need the police. Maybe medical assistance…"

"Is the assailant still in the house?"

"I don't think so," she said. "I might've lost consciousness. He kicked me in the face. In the mouth. I can feel it in my teeth…"

"Help is on the way, ma'am. Stay on the line with me until they get there…"

"Do you think he was going to kill me? He was going to kill me, I think…"

"Stay with me…"

"I'm passing out, I think…"

"Hang in there. You'll hear sirens in a moment. Tell me when you hear sirens…"

The police and medical arrived at almost the same time. She tried to imagine all the flashing lights on her quiet little street. While paramedics assisted her, did a cursory medical exam and provided an ice pack, one of two police officers asked her if she knew who the assailant was.

"My husband," she slurred. "Dr. Brad Delaney. We're separated. He lives in Mill Valley. He's angry."

"No kidding," the paramedic muttered. "We're going to start an IV, just to keep a vein open in case you need drugs. We're going to transport."

"Is that really necessary?" she asked. "I'm starting to feel better..."

"No reason to take chances with a head injury. And I think we should check for facial bone damage."

"My teeth feel loose. Do I have all of them? Are they whole?"

"I think they'll make it, but you have to go to the ER."

"Ma'am," the officer said. "Did anyone besides you and your husband witness this assault?"

She held out her phone. He recognized what she was showing him—the doorbell camera and speaker. While the door stood open, the sounds of Brad growling at her, threatening her and Lauren begging him to stop hurting her were loud and clear. The sound of him hitting and kicking her were clear. The image and audio recording would last for up to seven days, but she could save it now.

Typical Brad. They had closed circuit security at their Mill Valley home but he must not have considered that Lauren might have it at this old Victorian. He thought no one would ever know...

"I think we're going to have to have this phone," he said.

"No, you don't," she said. "You can dump everything on this phone if you want to but I need it. It's the only way I can reach people who will help me now, and there is no house phone here. I can email you this image and recording right now."

"That would help, if I'm going to pick him up."

"What are you going to do with him?" she asked.

"He's going to jail, ma'am. There are two offenses for which at least twelve hours in jail is mandatory—DUI and battery domestic. One, so the offender can sober up and is no longer a menace on the road and the other, so the victim can ensure his or her safety."

"So he'll be in jail all night?"

"I can assure you," the young officer said.

"Even if he's a very rich surgeon with a bunch of lawyers?" she asked.

"Even if," the cop said.

"Here," she said. "Email this to yourself."

"You're not going to beg me to leave him alone?" the officer asked.

"No," she said. "Take him to jail."

"What's going on?" Beau shouted from the door. "What the hell? Where's Lauren? Lauren!"

She was already on the gurney, sitting upright, holding the ice pack on her face. Beau was pushing his way through the paramedics and the two police officers instinctively grabbed his arms, holding him back.

"Let me go!" he said. "Let me see her! What happened to her?"

Lauren lowered the ice pack.

"Jesus," he said, looking at her weakly.

"Let him go," she garbled. "He's a friend and neighbor."

He rushed to her. "What happened? Who did this?" he kept his voice soft.

"I think you know," she said, her speech slurred.

Beau followed the ambulance to the hospital and paced in the waiting room while Lauren was with doctors and nurses.

Lauren was in the ER for three hours, holding an ice pack

to her mouth and cheek. She had stitches inside her mouth where her teeth had cut her lip and she felt swollen from her neck up. Her CT scan was negative—no fractures of the skull or facial bones. At almost midnight one of the officers who had come to her house returned to the ER. He spoke quietly with the doctor before approaching her bed. She was sitting up, getting ready to make her escape as soon as the paperwork and insurance nonsense was complete.

"So, it's going to be okay, I'm told," the officer said. "You'll heal and maybe get better locks?"

"I have good locks," she said, but she sounded more like *I hab goo wocks.*

"Your husband has been cited, arrested and taken to booking, but is there somewhere you can stay or someone who can stay with you?"

"I'm going home," she blubbered. "He's obviously not coming back. I'm a mess."

"That guy is still in the waiting room," the officer said. "Is he someone you can trust?"

"He's a neighbor. I've known him a few months and he's been helpful and kind. He's still here, huh?"

"Waiting to see you, I guess. Hopefully take you home..."

"That's nice. I can get a cab if he wants to get home."

"I wish you weren't going to be alone. Your husband is a piece of work. He tried to convince us you did this to yourself. The problem with that story was that when we found him, he was icing his hand."

A huff escaped her. "His precious hands. Insured for millions..."

"Then there's the recording. So he tried saying it was your boyfriend..."

"I don't have a boyfriend," she said. "The man out there is a new friend. Not that new." She groaned and said, "I met him at church."

"Your husband's voice on the recording is recognizable," the officer said. "Is there someone who can stay with you? You should contact a family member. This is a traumatic injury. You might get home and realize you wish you weren't alone and the doctor says you can't drive. Not for at least twenty-four hours. As a precaution."

"I agree," the doctor said, pulling back the curtain to enter the little cubicle. He held a chart. "I'd admit you for the night but it isn't absolutely necessary and hospitals aren't the coziest places. They're noisy, for one thing."

"I want my own bed."

"Then call someone," the officer said. "Someone who can make sure you're home and inside and helped to your bed. There must be someone..."

"The neighbor says he's going to get her home, stay with her until she's settled. And he lives a few blocks away so if she needs assistance, she can call him. That work for you, Mrs. Delaney?" the doctor asked.

She nodded. "I don't want to call my sister or daughter this late. I must look a wreck. I haven't even seen your handiwork."

The doctor opened a drawer and pulled out a round mirror, handing it to her. She lifted it to her face. Her lip was three times its usual size on one side, her face was distorted, one cheekbone swollen, her eye was puffy and black and blue and her blouse was covered in blood and drool.

She almost passed out and both the doctor and officer caught her before she fell back on the bed. They helped her sit back upright.

"Oh my God," she said. "This would terrify my sister. And her husband is a cop. He could lose his mind."

"Cop? Where?"

"Chip Shaughnessy. Oakland."

"I know him. Good guy. Want to call him?"

"Want to really test his control?" she asked.

The doctor handed her a clean washcloth because every few words brought a new drizzle of pink spit. She didn't want either Beth or Chip to see her like this. Beth was angry enough with Brad. She didn't mind that she hated him. In fact, she liked that. However, when she was trying to stay focused, stable and smart, she didn't need haranguing. Her lawyer had prepped her well to listen only to her advice and not that of relatives and friends. And her brother-in-law, sweet, laid-back Chip, why tempt fate? This could be the thing that tipped him over the edge and he might just go beat the hell out of Brad. Truthfully, that could feel quite satisfactory, but why should Chip land in jail?

"Beau can take me home," she said. "He's trustworthy. And very kind. My phone?" she asked.

"In your purse," the officer said, handing her the purse that had come with her to the hospital.

She scrolled through her text messages and found the last one from Beau.

Are you still here?

I'm here. How are you?

I'm ready to go home. Can you give me a lift?

Ready when you are. I'll move the truck to the loading zone and come for you.

"He'll take me home," she told the officer. "He's moving his truck. Would you bring him back here?"

When Beau got back to the cramped ER space, his eyes narrowed and he ground his teeth. "Where does it hurt right now?" he asked.

"Where you can see," she said. "I almost think he wanted it to show."

"We have to get you to a safe place," Beau said.

"Home. Please. Leave me with my door locked and my ice pack. He's not coming back. At least not tonight."

"How can you be sure?" he asked.

"I called the police," she said. "He's in jail for the night. I'll be talking to my lawyer tomorrow. I think we're beyond negotiating agreeably. Don't you?"

"I'll take you home," Beau said. "Can we get you a sleeping pill? I'll stay on the couch, just as a precaution."

"No sleeping pills on top of a possible concussion," she said. "But I want my bed. I'm not afraid. Not right now." She dabbed at her lips. "I should have locked the door right away, but it was still light and I saw him on the monitor. I told him it wasn't a good time. If the door had been locked…"

The doctor stretched his hand toward Beau. "I'm Dr. Kraemer. You're the escort home, I presume?"

"Yes, sir," he said, though it was possible the doctor was younger than Beau. "I'll stay with her tonight. Anything I should watch for?"

"Yes. Keep an eye out for disorientation, nausea and vomiting, unconsciousness… Her CT was negative, but let's be observant. If she's asleep, don't wake her. If she passes out and won't rouse—call for medical assistance." He looked at Lauren. "How's the head?"

"It feels like I've been kicked by a mule."

The young doctor smiled wanly. "You have. Here are a few business cards—shelter, social services for victims of battery domestic, Lt. Sanders of that unit at the police department. Please make an appointment with your family physician…"

She let go a pathetic laugh. "My husband is a physician. Surgeon."

"If there's no one for you to call, just come back to the

ER and I'll handle taking out the stitches for you in a week. Here's my card. I know how that goes—doctor in the family, you either let him handle your issues or it's one of his friends. Don't do that, Lauren. He's obviously dangerous."

"He's locally very well known," she said.

"I know. I never liked him. Take care now. Call if you need us."

"Let's go," Beau said, taking her purse and her hand. "I'm parked in the loading zone. We'll be home in ten minutes."

"I really appreciate this," she muttered, towel still hovering at her chin. "How did you happen to see the commotion around my house?"

"I went to the market for milk and bread. When I came out there were police and fire department vehicles in front of your house. Took about ten years off my life."

"Mine, too," she said, hanging on his arm as they walked through the waiting area and outside.

"Let me lift you up into the truck. Hand me the towel and ice pack."

"You don't want to touch this…"

"Gimme," he said. "Grab the handle, we'll go slow."

He drove cautiously on the way to her house. What he'd done by following her to the hospital, he'd involved himself. He was in now. He knew instead of making it easier for them to bond it would make it more complicated. Both of them would wonder if it was vulnerability rather than pure attraction. He didn't care and there was the danger. That's what happened with Pamela—she was needy. She was a single mother on a limited income with limited potential and two sweet, rambunctious little boys. She needed a man, needed him. It wasn't genuine, it was artificial and he knew it. Even so, even having that history, he wanted Lauren to find a hero in him. But this was new territory. Pamela had never been physically beaten. She'd been fooled and abandoned by first one man and then another, but no one had ever punched her in the face.

"Here we are," he said. "You okay?"

"Hm. Sure."

"I'll come around and help you down—sit tight. Is there a key in your purse?" he asked.

"I'll get it," she said. She found it and opened her own door. "I'm going to be fine now. You can go home and sleep."

"Let's get you settled. What are the chances you have frozen peas on hand?"

"As a matter of fact, I do."

"Then how about if you change into something clean—pajamas or sweats or something. Do you need help?"

"I'll manage. I'm not really ready for you to see me in my underwear."

"I could do that without assuming you're flirting," he said.

"I've got this," she said, wandering into the bedroom and closing the door behind her.

He called Drew.

"I woke you, I'm sorry."

"Everything okay?"

"Yes and no. My friend had an accident and needed a ride home from the emergency room. She's all bruised and has some stitches. I just wanted you to know I'm staying here to make sure she's all right tonight. She lives alone. There's no one to look out for her so I'll hang out on her couch."

"Are *you* okay?" Drew asked.

"Yeah, but after the ER doc told me to watch for things that meant she should get back to the ER, I don't feel like I should leave her. You're all right alone, aren't you?"

"I've done it before, Dad. I work in the morning. Call me and let me know everything is okay."

"Sure. Get some sleep. My phone is on if you need me. I'm

not far away." Then he found the frozen peas and a dishtowel from a kitchen drawer.

A few minutes later, the bedroom door opened and Lauren stood in a set of un-sexy pajamas with long sleeves and long pants. At first glance it looked like they were covered in a print of ice cream cones. On closer look he saw they were flowers.

"Come on," he said, turning her around to send her back into the bedroom. "Let's get you comfortable and I'll give you a shoulder rub. It's guaranteed to make you relax..."

"You really don't have to," she said.

"I know. But I'm here and I'm not leaving. Once you're snoring, I'll grab a little sleep on the couch. Just give this a chance. You won't regret it."

He helped her position herself on her side, her head elevated because of the swelling, the peas balanced over her swollen lip and bruised cheek. He kicked off his shoes and climbed up on the bed behind her. Then he started to gently knead her shoulders and neck. "You won't be able to go to work for a few days. You definitely won't be filming any cooking videos. The good news is, the swelling will go down in a couple of days and you might be able to disguise the bruising with makeup. Or you can just say you were in a car accident... Or tripped and fell... Or you can be honest. I know this stuff happens. I'm not naive. But anyone who hits his wife, even the wife he's not getting along with, is an animal. A dangerous animal."

"He has a lot of people fooled," she whispered.

"Not the ER doc," Beau said. "Could he ruin his reputation?"

"Nah. Privacy laws."

"Too bad," Beau said. "Well, he's screwed. If he thought there was any hope of restoring his sad marriage, it's impossible."

"I think he knows that now. I think he finally realized it was the end of the line and he left me with a reminder of how cruel he can be."

"Was it twenty-four years of that, Lauren?"

She sighed. "Like many troubled marriages, maybe like yours, there were times it wasn't awful. But when you live with someone whose mission it is to control everything, even the good times were just a place holder."

"That's going to change," he said. He massaged her neck, her shoulders. Softly. "For now, just let go and see if sleep comes. If you have to think at all, just think that you've turned a corner and from now on you'll accept only the most perfect treatment. Because you're a good person and you deserve it. You're a good, beautiful person and no one gets to treat you like you're not. I'm not just talking about the man you're finally leaving for good, I'm talking about all people. You're not without options anymore."

"Turned a corner," she repeated.

"Headed for a better life," he said.

She gave a huff of laughter. "I don't think it's going to be that simple."

"Maybe not, but in the end it's going to be better. You can't have a person like that stalking you. We'll work out some details tomorrow..."

She sighed softly, relaxing into his hands. The same hands that dug in the ground, drew designs of beautiful gardens, remodeled his fixer-upper house, raised his stepsons—those hands, gently caressing her shoulders and neck. She began to doze off, then jerked in her sleep.

"Shhh," he said. "You're okay."

"You don't have to stay," she said. "I'll lock the door. I'm safe."

He eased down behind her, spooning her, one arm sliding lightly over her waist. "I'm not leaving you, Lauren. I'm right here if you need someone, if you're afraid, or if your head hurts, if you need a fresh ice pack."

"I shouldn't let you stay…"

"It's okay if you want me to," he whispered. "And I want to. Don't worry. No lines will be crossed."

"With my lip like this, I'll probably snore…"

"It should be a regular symphony with my snoring."

"Some people would call this an affair…"

He laughed sharply. "And what would they call what happened to your face? A love tap gone too far? Just relax and feel safe. If that's an affair, you should have had more of them."

"Yeah," she said. "I should have. I never did."

CHAPTER EIGHT

Beau had his assistant, Cheryl, move his morning appointment. There was only one and it was to review a plan. He pled a personal matter that wasn't too complicated, just had to be taken care of today. He was not the secretive sort so when he offered no further explanation, Cheryl didn't ask any questions.

He heard Lauren call her supervisor, heard her say she'd fallen and had a black eye and split lip and needed a couple of days for the swelling to go down. She explained she was released from the hospital after getting some stitches but was still in pain. He fixed a soft breakfast for her and they had to make do with some frozen corn while he refroze the peas.

She was feeling a little bit better but looked worse. Her lip was still grossly swollen and the bruising around her cheek and eye were intensified, which was what happened with bruises.

They started out bad and only got worse for a couple of days. It was horrific. He insisted she take a picture of her face.

"The police already did," she said.

"Have one of your own," he said. "You might need it. Email it to your lawyer. You should think about an order of protection."

"And what? Wave a paper at him while he's coming at me?"

"No, I've got a better idea," he said. "I'll be right back." He went to his truck and came back with a baseball bat. "Be glad I don't clean out the truck bed too often. This has been in the storage box since last spring. If he comes here and somehow gets past the locked door, call the police first and start swinging second."

"I hope the police have their A-game on," she said. "I can barely lift the bat."

"Well, if all that transpires, tell him goodbye because it will be hard not to kill him. And really, I'd hate to kill even a bad man. I'm not a fighter. I'll be back after I get some groceries for you—soup, eggs, yogurt, ice cream, that sort of thing. I checked your fridge—you need some soft foods."

"You're really going above and beyond..."

"I'm glad I happened along," he said. "You have to talk to your family right away. Both daughters. Show them what happened to you when you defied your husband. If you have to explain, which you shouldn't have to, this is not normal behavior. And they should beware of him. If he'll hurt you..."

"I know. I know. Listen... I can order groceries. The market delivers."

"If you don't want me around, just say so. But wouldn't you rather not show the delivery boy your face today?"

She looked down.

He lifted her chin with a finger. "Lauren, it's not your fault. But you need ice packs and privacy, not a lot of panic and questions."

"Of course you're right," she said.

"Those cards the doctor gave you, you might want to check in with some of those people. I'm afraid you might be downplaying this. You've gotten so good at keeping the peace, it could leave you unprepared for the kind of violence he's capable of."

"I will call someone, but I'm not unprepared. You might want to run for your life. It was seeing me walking home with you last night that set him off."

"You didn't mention that," he said.

"I wasn't going to but this is crazy. If we're not honest with each other, we'll just be starting the same cycle all over again."

"Tell me," he said. "Tell me about your life before today."

They talked for another hour, then he got her resettled into the bed with a bag of frozen Italian cut beans, nice and soft.

Before going to the grocery store, he drove toward Mill Valley, to Divine Redeemer. He hadn't called ahead. Part of him hoped Tim was busy, then he'd just check in at his office and maybe return some phone calls.

Tim was in the sanctuary. It being summer, school was out and he was meeting with some altar boys, having a quiet discussion about their duties. They seemed awfully young. He sat in a pew nearby and waited until Tim noticed him.

Tim raised a hand and excused himself from the kids. He leaned on the pew. "This is a surprise," the priest said.

"I can see you're busy," Beau said.

"I'm done."

"I'm looking for someone to talk to," Beau said.

Tim raised a tawny eyebrow. "Office or parsonage?"

"How many people at the house?" he asked.

"Just Mrs. Johnson, cleaning. She's pretty much deaf. Father Damien is away today."

"Aren't you afraid you'll get arrested for making little old ladies work like that? Elder abuse."

Tim just smiled tolerantly. "I can make us some coffee."

"Got anything stronger?" he asked.

"Of course, but isn't it a little early?"

Beau stood. "I want to invoke the Seal of the Confessional without getting in that damn little box."

"Come on," Tim said, leading the way out the back door to the parsonage kitchen. Once there, he set about making a fresh pot of coffee while Beau took a seat at the table. "When have you ever had to ask me to keep a secret?"

"I don't know how you do it," Beau said. "I bet your ears are burning with juicy stuff."

"Spit it out before Mrs. Johnson smells the coffee."

"Remember Lauren? From the garden? I spent the night with her last night."

Tim was silent for a long moment. "What do you want from me? To say you sinned and give you ten Hail Marys?"

"It wasn't for sex. We had dinner together and ten minutes after I left, her house was surrounded by police and emergency vehicles. I'd stopped at the market for bread and in the space of a few minutes, she'd been assaulted. She was battered."

"Dear Mary," Tim said.

"Her face," Beau said, a catch in his voice. His eyes filled with tears. "It's indescribable. It's horrible. Her husband did it." Beau wiped impatiently at his eyes, not sure if it was the pain of grief or rage that brought the tears.

"Listen, Beau, you don't have to tell me, but are you involved with a married woman? A married woman with a violent husband?"

"Not exactly," Beau said, sniffing loudly and wiping the tears from his eyes. "One of the first things we learned about each other was that we're both going through divorces, both separated. She's living in her own house now, one she rented. Coincidentally not too far from my house. A complete and unplanned surprise."

"On the island?" Tim asked.

Beau nodded. "I ran into her at the market. We shared a bottle of wine. I stopped by a few times. She always saved a chore she needed help with—changing locks, hanging shelves, that kind of thing. Nothing serious. No dating, no texting or calling. Well, just texting to see if she wanted to walk down to Park for a drink or sandwich. She's been out of her house about a month. Pam's been out of mine over six months. We've both served papers, so I thought it was possible we might date. Down the road."

Tim pulled out a chair across from Beau. He folded his hands on the table. He moved a box of tissues closer to Beau. "Beau, you might want to put that on the back burner for a while. Let the dust settle..."

"And leave her defenseless against a man who kicks her in the face? *Kicked* her in the face, Tim! She took some stitches in her lip and it's about as big as my thumb."

"This can get way more complicated. She's a battered wife..."

"She won't quite admit that because this is the first time he slugged her and kicked her, but we talked about the abuse. He talks down to her, tells her she's a liar and a loser and has this ugly little habit of pinching her, hard, leaving her arms speckled with small bruises. But this..." He sniffed again. "This demonstrates what he's really capable of doing."

"And trust me, he wouldn't mind doing it to you."

Beau's face took on a mean twist. "Bring it," he said darkly.

"You should step away. Find her some good resources and step away," Tim said. "Help her get safe, and walk."

"Too late," Beau said. "I can't do that now. I won't do that now. I know what you're saying but tough shit. I dare that bastard to—"

Tim whistled. Long and loud and high. "This is starting to sound eerily familiar..."

"Pamela was never battered," Beau said.

"Not physically, which kind of amazes me," Tim said. "She's the most aggravating and dysfunctional woman I know, and I know some beauts. Even I wanted to belt her sometimes."

"Now you're going to hell," Beau predicted. "There are many differences between Pamela and Lauren. Many."

"Oh hell, you're not objective! You're a rescuer! You always have been. When we were kids you tried to help the dorks wear their socks right so they wouldn't get picked on. You stood up for the little guys and took a few shots for it. You took the ugliest girl in school to the prom!"

"She wasn't ugly," he said. "And that group of bitches set her up to get dumped right before prom and how could I let that happen, knowing? Besides, she was really nice. And smart. That's probably why they hated her." He blew his nose. "Lauren is really smart."

"This isn't going to end well," Tim said.

"I think we kind of need each other right now," Beau said.

"Oh Christ," Tim swore. "Listen, you can tell her, you know. You can be honest. Tell her you really like her but things like this usually backfire, so you're going to help her find the right protection, counseling, security system, whatever it is. And then you're going to step away until these matters of divorce get settled. Including yours. And then you can revisit the idea of spending more time together."

"Yeah, that would be really smart," Beau said.

"Hallelujah!"

"That's just not going to do it for me," Beau said. "I want to be the one to help keep her safe. Be with her. Know her better."

"Oh God," Tim said. "I'm almost drowning in the testosterone here, could you ease back on that? I'm a priest. I try to keep the male hormone under control… Are you perfectly hopeless?"

"I hope not," he said. "I'm not as pathetic as you think."

"What if I told you it might be better for *her* if you backed way off?"

"She wanted me to help. She had other people to call, even a brother-in-law cop, but she was glad I was there." He shrugged. "She likes her brother-in-law and didn't want him to commit murder."

"Well, I knew the second I met her, she's a very giving and kind woman…"

"I gave her a baseball bat, just in case…"

Tim couldn't help it. He let go a little huff. Then he burst out laughing. "You haven't changed one bit in all these years." He shook his head. "I'm going to be on my knees a lot over you, you know that, don't you? Why don't I pay her a visit? I'll wear the collar. I'll carry a bible. But I'm still pretty tough if anything comes up. I could be her protector until things—"

"Maybe when she feels better," Beau said. "Give her a little time, then by all means, lend your very fine clerical support."

Tim just shook his head. "They didn't write enough prayers for you."

"I know." He stood up. "I'm really glad we had this little talk."

"I made coffee," Tim said.

"I have to go to the store, get Lauren some soft things to eat, some more frozen peas to put on her face. And I should talk to Drew…"

Lauren hadn't spoken to her daughters, though she called both of them. She left them messages to call her back. She called her lawyer and emailed the video and was forced to take a selfie because Erica Slade demanded it. "I'll come over there and take one myself," she threatened. She was still on the phone with Erica as she received the selfie and listened to the tape. Erica gasped. "Don't leave the house!" she said. "Keep the doors locked! I'm going to get the arrest report and find a judge. You'll have a restraining order by noon. I'm going to pin this bastard's ears back!"

"You're kind of terrifying," Lauren said.

"Terrifying is what you need right now, since you've been pounded into mush. Don't go anywhere. I'll be in touch."

Lauren made one other call, hoping it had not been a mistake to involve another person in her drama. She called Divine Redeemer and asked to speak to Father Tim. He was very surprised to hear from her and she sensed a little hesitation in his voice, but he offered to help in any way he could. "There is something I could use help with, if you have the time. I need to talk with you about Beau."

"Of course," he said. "I'll make time."

Lacey knocked on her door at ten in the morning. Her beautiful Lacey, wearing white summer jeans, torn in all the most fashionable places, a fitted tee that showed her midriff, tall, lean and tan all over.

"I can't believe you," Lacey said before she said hello. "You sent him to *jail*?"

Well, that explained one thing. Brad had called his favorite daughter.

"I called for medical assistance and the police came. They took him to jail. But thanks for your concern."

"He said your new boyfriend did this!"

Lauren made a sound that was almost a distorted laugh. "Please, it hurts to laugh." She pulled her phone out and clicked on the ring icon. She turned the volume up so Lacey could hear her father snarling at her and then slapping her, hitting her, calling her a whore. Lauren winced at the sound of her own begging, whimpering.

The look on Lacey's face illuminated her shock. Her pretty

mouth hung open. Her eyes welled with tears. "This is fake," she said. "This must be fake. He wouldn't lie to me."

"He has always lied. He'll say anything."

"Tell me the truth, Mama—did you fake this?"

"Oh for God's sake! Of course not! The police arrived within five minutes of when I called them. This is a closed circuit security camera. I showed the officer and paramedic. The officer emailed himself the video and they arrested your father for battery domestic violence."

"You could have told them he's not like that."

"He *is* like that! And they didn't take him to jail because I told them to—that's the law!"

"I lived in that house! He didn't beat you!"

"Honestly, Lacey! Do you think I'm getting a divorce because he adored me and treated me with love and respect?"

"You have a boyfriend?"

"Oh my God, of course not!" She split her lip open and a little trickle of liquid ran down her chin. She wiped at it thinking it was drool, but it was bright red. She went for a towel in the kitchen. Holding the towel against her chin, tears rolled down her cheeks. "The man is a neighbor, a man I met months ago in the Divine Redeemer gardens and again at the Andy's kids fund-raiser. Your father met him, too. I ran into him at the market and we discovered we both live in the neighborhood. He hung some shelves for me and I bought him a beer and sliders to thank him. He's a friend. He's kind and honest and helpful. But I'm sure this face and the presence of a violent husband will end the friendship." She went to the freezer for an ice cube. She pressed it to her lip. "He wouldn't hurt a fly."

Lacey was sitting on the sofa, weeping quietly. "I don't know why you couldn't just manage the way you always have."

Lauren's eyes filled with tears that rolled down her cheeks.

She just shook her head. She had longed for a husband who would tenderly hold her, comfort her, especially after her babies were born. She had craved kindness and love, praise for everything she did to keep him happy. Appreciation. She'd learned how not to admit how lonely it was in that house sometimes. Lauren and a couple of babies, her husband either away or finally home but angry.

"You can think about that awhile and maybe you'll come up with an answer," Lauren said.

"I know you'd get impatient with him, but—"

"Impatient? Oh Lacey… If he didn't have his way all the time, he was intolerable. Just avoiding his abuse was a full-time job!"

"He didn't abuse you!"

"He called me a liar! He kept telling me I was poor and uneducated, that I was weak and stupid! He inflicted pain! He could be a monster!"

"But he was also good to you!" Lacey argued.

"By allowing me to live in a big house? Wear good clothes? Take vacations?" Lauren went to the sofa and sat beside her daughter.

"Lacey, I love you. I have always loved you so much. I did everything I could to make your life good. But there are some things you understand, whether you'll admit them or not. You know there have been endless arguments, temper tantrums from your father that made us all want to run and hide. You know that as often as he was nice, he was mean. He was demanding, he was bitter and angry. He's been sued by employees twice! You know I haven't slept in the same room with him for years. And now you know—he *kicked* me in the face! If you think I'm going to cower and give him another chance, you have lost your mind. And if you're going to find a way to excuse him, that's going to be your problem."

"If he's so terrible, why didn't you divorce him a long time ago?"

"Twenty reasons but mostly to protect my daughters, to ensure your safety and private education. He's a mean man. But you're an adult now. You can take an objective look. You can look back at our family life and decide for yourself. If you want to blame me for *this*," she said, pointing at her face, "you'll have to live with that. It would make me sad, but I am done explaining myself. That any woman would have to explain something like this…" She shook her head. "I am done."

"I just wonder if you really tried," she said.

"No matter what your father says, you do not do this to a person you care about," Lauren said.

"I don't know what to do," Lacey said. "I don't know what to think…"

"Maybe it'll come to you," Lauren said. "I thought, after our many long talks, after the discussions we had, you would know exactly what is okay and what is not okay. But take your time, Lacey."

The doorbell chimed and Lauren noticed that Lacey still held the cell phone in her grip. Lauren reached for it and clicked on the icon that would show her who was at the door. "Oh dear God," she said, heading for the door. "Father Tim! Um… Please, come in."

"I had some time and happened to be in this part of town," he said. He had a package. "Is ice cream the medicine of the day?"

Lacey was standing. "Is this the boyfriend?" she asked icily.

"Not hardly. I'm a Catholic priest. We're not allowed to have girlfriends," Tim said. And he smiled. "If you're busy…"

"It's all right. Lacey was getting ready to leave. Lacey, meet Father Tim from Divine Redeemer. I called him. He's a counselor as well as a priest."

"You don't go to that church, do you?" Lacey asked.

"I've been known to stop in," Lauren said. "I asked the Father to call me when he had time for a chat."

"I had a couple of appointments cancel and although you were willing to come to Divine Redeemer, I didn't think you'd feel like going out yet. But I can come back another time. I'm a little impulsive. I should have called to say I was coming."

"I'll just leave you two," Lacey said. "Mom, I'll talk to you later."

"Yes, please," Lauren said. She reached for her daughter and they hugged very carefully. Lauren patted her daughter's pretty brown hair. "I love you."

When Lacey had gone, Lauren turned away from the door and looked at the priest standing in her living room.

"I'm so sorry," Tim said. "That was awkward."

"A bit, but when you said you could see me at my house, that came as such a relief. I don't want to wander around the church office looking like a prize fighter. The loser, at that," she added. "Can I take that?" she asked, reaching for the grocery bag in his hands.

"Sure, yes. Put it in the freezer. It'll come in handy as something to eat or press on your lip." She took it to the kitchen and turning back, she invited him to have a seat. "After you," Father Tim said.

She sat in the corner of her sofa and he took the chair diagonally from her. "You didn't even wince," Lauren said.

"I actually did get training," he said. "I'm a licensed counselor. But listen, if you're not feeling up to a chat today, I'm very flexible. And I can find things to do and come back at a better time."

"I'd like you to stay," she said. "It might not really qualify as a session. I'm still a little rattled. And my daughter… She rattles me more."

"We'll just get to know each other a little bit," he said. "You could start by telling me why you called me."

"I was raised Catholic, but we weren't exactly devout. And

when my husband's mother wanted us married in the Lutheran church, I didn't argue. Maybe there's something from my childhood... But as I recall, my mother didn't put much stock in... Oh hell, I don't know. You seemed nice. Beau's nice and you're friends."

"Not a terrible recommendation," he said with a smile. "How are you feeling?"

"Do you promise not to scowl at me?"

"I can manage that," he said.

"I feel vindicated," she said. "My husband can be the cruelest man but I always felt that no one believed me. And it was the funniest thing, the ER doc said he'd never liked him and that was so wonderful to hear. And a woman I know who I always assumed thought he was wonderful...it turns out she's been onto him for years. I've spent twenty-four years thinking everyone loved him but my mother and sister."

"They didn't?" Tim asked.

"You can't fool the people you spend holidays with. They saw him, heard him. He was always so superior, with his cutting remarks, his insults. But he's never done anything like this before."

"Is this worse than the emotional and psychological abuse?" he asked.

"Not at all, but it's more convincing." She looked down. "He accused me of having an affair. I never had an affair."

"Did you go to counseling with your husband?"

"Several times—it never helped. But I also went by myself, on the sly. He didn't want me to go alone. He said if I needed to talk about the marriage, he was entitled to be with me. Listen, I have a concern. Are you going to tell Beau about this? I know he's your close friend, and in fact that's one of the reasons I thought talking to you—"

He was shaking his head. "Beau won't know unless you tell him."

"But I'm not a parishioner," she said.

"Lauren, I'm doing my job and it's all confidential."

"What if he drops by and finds you here?"

"I spoke to you and took the liberty of bringing you ice cream. Beau is very smart but he won't question my word. By the way, why did my friendship with Beau prompt you to call me?"

"I have an important question that I think only you can answer. I believe you'll tell me the truth. Am I right to trust Beau?"

He looked surprised for a brief moment. He took a second to consider his answer. "I think Beau is one of the finest men I know and I trust him completely, but I'm a bit biased. He has been a good friend for a long time."

"I thought so."

"That doesn't mean I would recommend you get involved," he said. "You have some more immediate concerns, I would think."

She got up and went to her purse, pulling out cards. "I have these," she said, passing them to him. "All given to me by the best ER doc I've ever seen. He was kind and gentle and concerned. Cards for victims' support groups, shelters for victims, counseling for victims, housing assistance, the domestic violence police unit to help me get a restraining order, although my lawyer is taking care of that. I even have the doctor's card—he's willing to meet me in the ER for the removal of stitches so I don't have to see any doctor associated with Brad. But...but I don't know these people. I'm sure they're great, but I don't know them and have no point of reference. I met you. You've known Beau since you were about ten. And I haven't known Beau that long, but I think he's a good man. There's no question about it. He couldn't have a thirty-five-year friendship with you if he wasn't good."

"Sometimes he's a pain in the ass," Tim said.

She was momentarily shocked, but she smiled crookedly. "Are priests allowed to talk like that?"

"I'll say ten Hail Marys. Actually, it's a trick. If I use a little harmless profanity, you'll let your guard down somewhat and feel less like you'll be judged for what you say. And by the way, you can't trust a person just by the collar."

"I don't, and I know that. I trust Beau. If he's fooling me, he's way better at it than Brad was."

"For what it's worth, Beau is good down to his bones. He should probably be the priest and I should be a farmer."

"He's more than a farmer..."

"Still... I have a question for you. Did you have a good rapport with that counselor you saw on the sly?"

"Excellent, really. Why?"

"You should probably see her again. I'd be happy to talk to you anytime, I'd be honored to be your friend, I'd be pleased to be your priest, but I have a conflict. You have a conflict. We have Beau in common and now he has us in common. I just want you to have the most objective counselor you can find."

She smiled her pitiful lopsided smile. "I plan to. Being afraid my instincts are rusty or just plain off, I wanted your endorsement of Beau. Because liking him and trusting him during this chaos is risky for me. Yet, I can't help it."

He transferred himself to the sofa beside her and touched her hand. "Beau would never intentionally hurt you," he said. "And I suspect you wouldn't knowingly hurt him. Just the same, do be careful. You are both on shaky ground, I think."

Beau was pressing hamburger into patties when Drew came home from his job. Since it was summer landscaping, the guys started at sunup and quit in early afternoon. Beau knew he'd be starving, though it was early for dinner.

"Hey," Drew said. "You work at home today?"

"For a couple of hours this afternoon. I ran some errands and stopped by the office to check appointments and get messages."

Drew eyed the salad and hamburger. "We having company?"

"Just me and you." Beau made a face. "You wanna get a shower before you touch my food?"

"Sure. Is something wrong?"

"No, but I want to talk to you. Over burgers. When you don't smell like sod, manure and other outdoorsy things."

"Stay tuned," Drew said with a big smile. He ran up the stairs to his bedroom and bathroom. Beau started the grill and within ten minutes, Drew was back, looking damp but clean. He was such a handsome kid. Always happy. Beau hoped he wasn't about to disappoint him.

"What's up?" Drew asked.

"I just wanted to tell you about my friend who was injured. She's a woman named Lauren. I met her several months ago. In a garden," he said.

"Of course," Drew said with a laugh.

"We're not dating or anything. Remember that fund-raiser for the scholarships? She was also there. I ran into her three or four times over the past few months, then I bumped into her at Stohl's Market and learned she lives in the neighborhood. She was buying wine, cheese and fruit and she invited me for a glass of wine. She lives a few blocks from here. Nice lady."

"And you're getting ready for dating now?" Drew asked.

"No. Well, I hadn't been. Running into her was a surprise. Then I drove by her house and saw it was surrounded by emergency vehicles."

"Right," Drew said. "Accident?"

"Actually, no. She was assaulted. Beat up. By her husband."

Drew whistled. "She's married?"

"About as married as I am," Beau said. "She's separated,

pending divorce. I didn't know her husband was violent. He's a doctor, for God's sake. And apparently she never expected an attack like that. I followed the ambulance to the ER and then drove her home. I stayed in case she needed something. Later, after we eat, I'm going to text her and see how she's doing. I'm going to offer to sleep on her couch just in case she's scared. I guess he could come back."

"Yeah? You could let her come here."

"I thought of that, but I'm sure she'd turn down the offer. She might be embarrassed. She's got a big black eye and a fat lip."

Drew looked shocked and disgusted. "Who would do that?"

"We should have a talk."

"You gonna tell me not to hit women?" Drew asked sarcastically.

"I believe we've had that talk already," Beau said. "Here's what I want to explain. Things are probably going to change for me. I'm not going back to the way things were, Drew. I'm not going to patch things up with your mom. As soon as this divorce is settled, I'm going to be a single father with two grown sons. Even though you don't need me like you did when you were younger, you can always count on me. But things are bound to change. Our property, for one thing. I might be forced to give up the house in the divorce, but don't worry—I'll find another house. Anywhere I live will have room for you and your brother."

"Oh, that should go over well..."

"There are always options. If you don't want to have to choose who you're going to live with, you can always opt for your own place closer to the campus and if you do, I'll be able to help with the expenses. I know you're not made of money. But having that option should take some pressure off because I know you don't want to get your mother riled up. Anything can be worked out, Drew. I just want it to be clear—there is going to be a divorce."

Drew shrugged.

"You might have to interpret that gesture for me," Beau said.

"I figured," he said. "You said so before."

"Drew, I'm moving on. My marriage to your mom is ending. We don't love each other."

"Just so you know, she says she still loves you."

"I know she says that, just like she has before. I don't believe it. A woman who loves her husband doesn't leave him repeatedly. And I don't have one more try in me. So let's do this— let's make sure we're communicating. If you have any stress or worries about this situation, talk to me. No matter what's been going on with me and your mom, we're the same, me and you. We're not breaking up. At least, I don't want that."

"So...we're going to be a couple of bachelors?"

"Looks that way," Beau said.

"And you'll be dating, I guess?"

He sighed. "A couple of months ago I would have said, no way. After a failed marriage, another relationship seems pretty risky."

"Then you met her..."

"I like her," Beau said. "That doesn't mean anything. She's got some pretty big issues of her own. I'm telling you the truth—we've only seen each other a few times and had a few conversations. I have no way of knowing if we'll ever be better friends. But meeting a nice woman made me realize that maybe I don't have to be a lonely old bachelor for the rest of my life. For right now, let's just say I'm open to the idea. But I'm in no hurry."

"You going to ask me not to tell Mom?"

"When have I ever asked you to censor anything you say to your mom?"

"I wasn't going to tell her anything," he said with his infectious grin. "Just wanted to know what you'd say. And I won't be throwing any parties here while you're out running wild, either."

Beau just shook his head. "Much appreciated," he said.

The door chime rang through Lauren's phone and she gasped as her heart began to pound. It wasn't yet five, Beau had already dropped off a few soft grocery items for her, Father Tim had come and gone... Was this horrible fear going to happen every time someone came to the door? She had always dreaded Brad's dark moods and abusive nature but she hadn't had fear before. She was terrified of being beaten again. Once might have left her feeling vindicated but twice could break her.

She looked at the camera image on her phone.

Cassie!

She flew to the door and opened it. Cassie stared at her with wide, horrified eyes that quickly filled with tears. "Oh Mama!"

CHAPTER NINE

"My God, what are you doing here?" Lauren asked her daughter. Lauren enfolded her in loving arms and let Cassie weep against her shoulder. "Come inside, darling. We're making a scene on this nice quiet street." She laughed in spite of herself. "I'm sure my neighbors expect nothing less, after this week."

Cassie pulled herself out of her mother's arms and reached behind her for her bag, pulling it inside. "Oh Mama, Daddy did this to you?"

"I wish it weren't so," Lauren said.

"How badly are you hurt?" she said, reaching out trembling fingers to touch Lauren's tender cheek.

"Possibly a mild concussion," she said. "But no brain damage. My teeth feel loose. Lots of anger on my part. But why are you here? I left you a message this morning, but didn't hear from you!"

"I didn't get your message because I was flying. But I heard from Lacey. Good thing I don't trust her a bit. She told me you and Dad got into a physical altercation and you had a black eye but there was some doubt about whether it was really Dad. She said you have a boyfriend?"

"No, there is no boyfriend," she said, shaking her head. "I have a neighbor who has become a friend since I moved in. He's helped me—done a few handyman things for me. Your father made some assumptions about him when he saw us on the sidewalk together. In broad daylight, not touching. And this was his response."

"What is the matter with him?" Cassie said, crying again. "And what is the matter with *Lacey*?"

"If Lacey didn't tell you how bad it was, why did you come?" Lauren asked.

"Lacey said Dad went to jail over this."

Lauren nodded. "Yes. Because I called for help..."

"I'm so glad you did," she said, grabbing Lauren's hand. "I got a call from Lacey early this morning. I wanted to talk to you, but didn't want to call in case you were trying to rest. I knew you'd try to downplay everything, say you were fine... And Jeremy told me to just go. I have this week before orientation and classes. I caught the first flight out that had room for me this morning. That would have been 6:00 a.m. your time. I would have called you sooner but I had to change planes."

"But how did you afford it? I haven't been able to send you anything!"

She smiled a bit tremulously. "I have a credit card. I guess we're going to become very good friends, me and Ms. VISA. Tell me, Mama. Everything."

"Oh Cassie... I didn't want this to be your divorce. I hoped that in spite of everything, we could one day be civil, be co-grandparents."

Cassidy reached into her small purse and pulled out a compact, flipping it open. She held the mirror up to Lauren's face. "I think it's too late for you to protect me from the ugly side of this. We have plenty of time. I'm all grown up and I want to know the truth."

Lauren made them tea and while the water boiled, she responded to Beau's text offering to stay with her and explained that Cassie had shown up for a surprise visit, so she would have company for the night and the next few days. Then she and Cassie began what would be a long conversation.

Of course Beau had been completely right—the girls lived in the house with them and were aware of the friction, sometimes terrible friction. In Cassie's view it seemed Brad had a major meltdown about every six months, maybe a little more often, but the rest of the time he was a rigid, difficult man who liked to win every argument and have his way. He was controlling; his daughters frequently pointed that out to him and he responded by asking them what they expected from a man who had to make life-and-death decisions every day, sometimes every hour.

"I think it's too late for any hope of an amicable split that will allow the two of you to be together, even for family events," Cassie finally said. "He won't change in this lifetime. He will never be remorseful and he will never compromise. Just give up on him, Mama. I have."

"Oh Cassie, I didn't want a hand in you hating your father."

"You didn't. You always tried so hard to buffer his meanness. I'm telling you, it's no longer necessary. I figured him out long before you did, I think."

"But not Lacey?" Lauren asked.

"Lacey likes her wardrobe allowance and car," Cassie said. "She's willing to trade a lot for that.

"What does Aunt Beth say about this? I've seen the way she looks at him sometimes, like she'd like to smack him!"

Lauren bit her lip. "I haven't told her or Chip. I'm afraid she'll explode."

"Oh Mama, you have to tell her right away."

Lauren reluctantly called Beth and asked her to stop by after work. "I think you should know, I had a serious fight with Brad and he hit me. I'm fine now. I went to the emergency room and except for some ugly bruises and a fat lip, I'm okay." Beth wanted to drop everything and rush over but Lauren stopped her. "Cassie is here with me—she surprised me with a visit and her timing is perfect. If you could come by after work, that would be great. I'd like to spend the rest of the afternoon with Cassidy."

Lauren and Cassie had only had one cup of tea and less than an hour to talk when there was a knock at the door again. The motion sensor made a chime on her cell phone and Lauren checked it. Lacey was back, this time with a bouquet of flowers. "Your sister is back," Lauren said. "Will you let her in?"

Lacey was speechless to find Cassie in California.

"And you didn't even call me?" Lacey said.

Cassie stiffened her spine, standing tall even though she was a few inches shorter than her sister. "Frankly, I don't know if I'm ready to talk to you yet. You said you weren't sure Mama was telling the absolute truth, yet you saw the security video and you saw her poor face."

"I hadn't seen the video yet, I just heard about it. And I didn't want to take sides," Lacey said.

"There is only one side," Cassie said. "You can't make this go away. And you can't ignore it."

"I know, but I can't help wishing this wasn't happening..."

"I want you to ask yourself something, Lacey. If some man pummeled your face, do you think Mama would make excuses for him?"

"Don't be so hard on me!" Lacey shouted. "I'm just trying to understand what went wrong!"

"You knew things were bad with them! We talked about it! We worried about it! Our parents fought a lot and Mama always lost!"

Lauren watched and listened. *This will be the moment that estranges them*, she thought.

"Sometimes!" Lacey shot back. "But I didn't think it was any worse than anyone else's parents!"

"Like who?" Cassie asked.

"Like most of my friends and probably most of yours! At least half of their parents are already divorced and the rest of them fight all the time!"

Cassie was quiet for a moment. "Wow," she said in a near whisper. "Lacey, you seriously need new friends."

My God, she's just like me! Lauren thought suddenly. All these years she'd wanted to blame Lacey's entitled nature on Brad. Had she just not wanted to acknowledge that it was in her shallow nature that Lacey took after her? Lauren hated to think of herself as selfish, but there was no question that years ago she had been like Lacey. Maybe not as obvious, but still, the similarities were there.

Her mind took her back to her engagement to Brad, how bossy he was, how hard to please, how willing he was to spend money to make things perfect. If he'd bullied Lauren or her mother or sister, he was quick with the gifts and excuses. Well, she'd grown up poor! She loved what she misinterpreted as his efforts to make amends for his thoughtfulness. She loved the status that he was a surgeon. He was difficult but rich and offered the kind of security she'd never known. Her mother and sister were even drawn into that state of mind. Brad represented safety. They wanted Brad as much as she did.

For a while.

Then Beth and Honey figured him out. They heard him say dismissive and unkind things to her. Saw that he was moody and angered easily. Pointed out how he made amends with money or that which money could buy. And he had an ego the size of Montana. *They're talking about me all over San Francisco. Some people are saying I'm the best young surgeon in the Bay Area.* They warned her, saying, "Lauren, this does not bring happiness, it brings struggles. Rethink this. At least live with him first."

"I love him," she said. But it was a lie. She wanted to be a part of his world. She had seen the house he bought and helped pick out the furniture. She didn't want to live in a rented room in some old lady's house or jammed into an apartment with four roommates, just getting by until she could save enough money for something decent. Honey had never quite gotten there, though they scrimped their entire lives. Lauren had been trying to find a good job after college, one that had real career potential, but with Brad, she didn't even have to work! She knew he had his rough edges but she believed she had the ability to provide him with the comfort and kindness that would smooth out their relationship. Soon, he would have no reason to be cross!

She had wanted life to be easy. She had ignored her mother's warning, *If you marry for money, you'll earn every cent.*

And that's what Lacey was doing right now, defending a man who would beat a woman. Defending him because she thought that man held her perfect future in his checkbook. She was denying his character was dangerous because she had plans! Her plans included her dream life as the daughter of a semi-famous surgeon and it was wrong of her parents to mess it up with their bickering.

Lauren knew that she had been nearly the same way when she was younger. And she'd been managing to do exactly what Lacey was doing by laying low, keeping peace by being quiet, flying under the radar.

"Oh, this has to stop!" she said, drawing the attention of both of her daughters.

"We're not fighting," Cassie said. "We're not going to fight, I promise. But I'm not accepting this attitude that Daddy is difficult and that's okay. He passed *difficult* when I was two."

"Not you two," Lauren said. "*Me*. This will stop with me. I am done pretending. And I'm not going to be controlled or manipulated anymore. I'm finished with protecting him. And I won't be controlled and manipulated by you two, either..."

"Protecting him? You called the police and put him in jail!" Lacey accused.

"I didn't," Lauren said calmly. "I called for help and the police put him in jail. I wasn't even asked to press charges and won't be asked to testify against him. I was warned it will probably be a misdemeanor first offense or dismissed, but it's not my case to pursue. He did it to himself. There are consequences when you assault people, when you hurt people. I stayed with him for all the wrong reasons and look what it got me."

"She did it for us, you dumb-ass," Cassie said.

"You two fight it out or work it out, I really don't care. My sister is coming over in about an hour and I'm going to get a shower."

"What about these flowers?" Lacey asked. "They're from Dad."

Lauren looked as though she'd been hit by a truck. *Lacey checked on her dad.*

"You can have them," Lauren said. "Or throw them in the trash."

With that, she left them and closed her bedroom door.

Lauren stood under the spray of the shower for a long time, thinking. The blow-dryer and the circular brush hurt when she touched certain places, but she got the job done. Her

THE VIEW FROM ALAMEDA ISLAND

lip was disfigured and she was bruised, but she tried a little makeup. Not for Beth. For herself.

She didn't hear the girls fighting. Maybe they were talking. Maybe Lacey had left and it was just Cassidy. Yes, they were like Lauren and Beth had been. Lauren and Beth had fought like tigers when they were young.

But Lauren and Beth had forged a truce after Lauren was married and they learned to tiptoe around the subject of her pathetically dismal decision to marry an egomaniac. Beth was Lauren's biggest champion now. Maybe, down the road, if Lacey matured a little, Cassie and Lacey would become close. Time would tell.

Lauren didn't think of her childhood as bad but she was well aware of the difficult parts. Her mother always worked. Always. Lauren and Beth spent a lot of time with their grandparents, sometimes with friends and neighbors, and when they were finally old enough, alone. They were fed and clothed, but there wasn't money for extras and they learned to help with all the household chores when they were very young. Grandma and Grandpa lived a few houses away so there was always someone they could rely on but poor Honey was constantly on the run to her first job, second job or somewhat later, night classes. It was not surprising that their mother was seldom cheerful.

There were things Lauren was able to do with her children that Honey couldn't—like playing games, helping with homework and reading together. In adolescence, when kids were sometimes cruel and always competitive, Lauren and Beth relied on their own part-time jobs to buy clothes or go out with friends. They didn't have the use of a car. Once in a blue moon they could talk Grandpa out of his. And while both of them achieved partial scholarships, college was brutally hard—they worked their way through and of course they had to live at home.

By the time Lauren graduated from college, Honey Verona had achieved her own degree, but hers came through years and years of part-time school. Honey had worked job after job, leaving one job for the next if the pay was higher. She worked in a library, nursing home, self-serve gas station, convenience store, as a secretary on a military base and even in a police department motor pool, washing and cleaning cars. When Lauren was twenty-two, Honey had a degree with a teaching certificate and taught freshman English. But she also started working at an upscale cosmetic counter at a department store—two nights a week and weekends.

That job was perfect for her. She looked amazingly young and fit until the day she died. When she retired from teaching just two years before the accident, she kept her job in cosmetics. She had a discount at the department store, wore her own makeup like a pro, dressed beautifully in casual chic clothes, even taught her granddaughters how to apply their makeup so they wouldn't look cheap or inexperienced. Beth had never cared that much but Lauren had always made good use of her makeup lessons, as did Lacey.

Lauren remembered having rich fantasies about how her life would be different from Honey's when she was grown up. She would have an easier life and there would be luxuries now and then. And travel. And good clothes and a cleaning lady and a nice car.

She laughed softly. "And didn't I just manage to get all that. And how exactly was it better?"

Dressed in jeans and a comfy chambray shirt, she opened the bedroom door. There sat Cassidy alone on the couch, texting or writing emails on her phone.

"I thought it was pretty quiet," Lauren said. "My other daughter and her flowers are gone?"

Cassie put her phone aside. "Yes, but she didn't go quietly. I made her cry."

"Oh Cassie, why?"

"Because she's selfish and spoiled and never thinks of anyone but herself."

Lauren sighed. "That's pretty normal in a young woman her age. She'll grow out of it. Hopefully."

"I don't care whether she does or not," Cassie said. "I decided a long time ago that I was just too unforgiving and everyone else in my family had more tolerance for Daddy than I did, but now what I realize is we all let this happen, let him build up momentum until he went too far. I'm done with him."

Lauren was saddened by the fact that that made her feel good. She hadn't planned to throw him under the bus to his daughters, even if he deserved it. "So, you're not feeling forgiving?"

"Oh, maybe I'll forgive him eventually, *if* he asks. But that doesn't mean I'll be spending time with him. Wouldn't you say he's crossed the line now? He's a selfish and dangerous bastard. Don't you *dare* go near him. I'm just terrified to leave you here alone."

"I'll be okay now. I outed him. I have friends and family here."

"I'm terrified you'll cave-in and go back to him!"

"Oh no, Cassie, no. I have my lawyer working on a restraining order. In fact, she said I'd have it today."

"That's a relief. For a nickel I'd kidnap you and take you back to Boston where I can watch over you and be sure Daddy hasn't somehow manipulated you into thinking you can't leave him!"

Lauren attempted a smile, but she was sure it was hideous. "And here I was worried that you were too timid to practice law."

"I'm not timid, I'm quiet. You should watch the quiet ones," she said.

"Yeah, so I've heard," she said, thinking of Beau. "And how are things in Boston? Now that you're sharing your flat."

"You know one of the main reasons I love Jeremy?" Cassie asked earnestly. "He's nothing like Daddy. He's a good man who would never disrespect me. He would never lay a hand on another human being except to defend himself. He doesn't even verbally spar with me. He's honest, brilliant, tender and strong. I will have children with him, Mama. And he will be the best father in the world."

Lauren nearly grabbed that cut lip in her teeth as she finished Cassie's description in her head. *They won't have to listen to their father belittle and yell at their mother. Our children won't see their father trip their mother, then lie about it.* "Cassie, I'm so sorry," she said softly. "I know there were times..."

"Stop," she said, placing a hand on Lauren's arm. "Lacey was right. Don't tell her I said that, okay? But she's right, a lot of our friends are from divorced homes and some of them have really shitty family situations. I managed to weed through and find some stable people to hang with, Jeremy being one. I knew you were putting up with more than you should. But honestly? I thought you'd put up with that forever." She got tears in her eyes. "I wish he'd gotten better. I so wish he'd gotten better."

But Lauren asked herself, *Could I have loved him if he'd gotten better? I could have stayed, but could I have ever loved him again?* Because abuse kills love. And the real tragedy was—that wasn't always the case. Some women, bruised and bloody and fearing for their children's lives, will say, *But I love him.* Just as Lauren had oh so many years ago.

It was not yet six when Beth arrived. She took one look at Lauren and said, "Oh baby Jesus!" Then she pulled Lauren into her arms. "If Honey were alive, she'd kill him!"

"It looks worse than it is," Lauren said.

"I doubt it," Beth said. Then she hugged Cassie. "You came to your mother. You're a good daughter."

Beth examined Lauren's face more closely. "That's it," she said. "*I'm* going to have to kill him and leave my sons motherless while I rot in prison!" She sighed and said, "I brought wine. Not enough, that's for sure."

"Actually, I happen to have wine, too," Lauren said. "But you're driving."

"There are ways around that," Beth said. "I'll call Chip. Or Uber my way home." Then she smiled. "Are you taking any drugs?" she asked Lauren.

"No, I'm fine. I'm pretty tired now, if you want the truth. It's been quite a day. Lots of surprise visits. First Lacey. Then a priest I know. Then the guy who drove me home from the ER brought me a bagful of soft food. Then Cassie. Then Lacey again, with flowers from her father. As you can imagine, it's emotionally exhausting…"

Beth and Cassie were frozen in place, speechless. Quiet enveloped them for a good minute, which seemed like forever. Lauren could read their minds. Priest? Guy? Flowers?

Beth cleared her throat. "You have that wine open yet?"

It was the best evening in forever. That made no sense at all and yet absolute sense. It was rare for Lauren to have this kind of evening with her sister and daughter and absolutely unheard of that her barriers were down and she was completely frank about her husband. She kept thinking, *this is not Brad's house.* She could say whatever she wanted to say. As soon as the shock and horror passed, they seemed to relax. They all felt it. *This is it; this nightmare will finally be over.*

Having her sister and her daughter together in *her* house with not a single thought toward needing to get home or expecting her husband to come home and disrupt the gathering, this was perfect. They had a glass of wine and talked honestly about what had happened. Then Cassie called for Chinese takeout—egg drop soup and mild lo mein for Lauren, spicy shrimp and garlic pork and egg rolls for those without stitches in their lips.

Beau leaned back on his sofa, feet on the coffee table. After their hamburgers, Drew had gone out to meet some of his friends at a driving range, sharpening his skills to eventually whip Beau and Tim on the golf course. Drew had to be up by four for work but he was eighteen—he didn't need much sleep. There was still plenty of daylight. Beau vaguely remembered having that edge of youth. He flipped through the channels, looking for something to watch with a ball in it. Anything would do.

He heard the sound of a key in the lock at the front door. Drew was back already? He'd only been gone about two hours. He sat up. But the door didn't open. Then there came a pounding and he felt a sick feeling grow in his gut.

"Let me in!" Pamela shouted from the other side of the door.

He took a deep breath. He sighed. He lumbered up off the couch. He slowly opened the door. "It would be better if you called ahead," he said. "Is there something you need?"

There was a grim set to her mouth but, oh, Pamela was so beautiful. She was constructed to be, of course. She wore her streaked, honey-colored hair long. She bought a chin years ago, for starters. Then boobs. Lipo. Tummy tuck. Botox. Her lips were a little puffier—collagen injections, he had learned. Her nails were a classy length and she had an awful lot of eyelashes. She was tanned and buff. Pamela worked very hard on that face and body.

Beau thought she did so because she had a troubled soul. He thought she'd been much prettier before adding and subtracting so much.

"I need my house back," she said.

"Well, unfortunately, it's not your house."

"You always said it was *our* house and I lived in it for thirteen years, so move over, darling."

He blocked the way. "It will be part of the community property, I understand that, even though it was my house for six years before we met and it's still in my name. And I'm sorry, but since our divorce is pending, since you've been served divorce papers, we can't live together. It just wouldn't work. And on advice of counsel, I'm not leaving."

She looked shocked. "You never put the house in my name, too?"

"At first I just didn't because it made no difference—neither of us would have singular properties. It's a 50/50 state and that's the way it is because there's no prenup. But I brought this house to the marriage and you left," Beau said.

"Well, I'm coming home," she said.

He leaned slightly, spotting the suitcases behind her. Two large and one carry-on size. "I'm sorry, Pam. No. You left. You had a flat in the city. And I told you several times, I'm done with this arrangement."

"And where am I supposed to go?"

"Back to your city flat, I suppose."

"I let it go," she said.

"Before making arrangements for your next residence?"

"I don't have to make arrangements to come home to my house!"

"Not your house, Pamela. It's where I live, it will be community property." He glanced over her shoulder to the newish BMW in the drive. "Just as your car will be community property. And your other assets."

"My car will not be community property!" she said, sneering. She tried to push her way in and he blocked her. "God

165

damn you, let me in. You can go to a hotel. Or your mother's. Or go to the goddamn rectory for all I care."

"Mom," Drew said from behind her. "Stop it."

Beau hadn't seen him arrive. Since Pamela was parked in the drive, he'd parked in front of the house next door and had silently approached. "Drew!" she said. "Sweetheart, tell Beau this is my house and I'm coming home!"

"Pam, don't put Drew in the middle of this," Beau said. "It's not the boys' problem, it's ours. Let him be."

"But I want to come home and live with my son," she said.

"I'll take you down to the restaurant and we can have a cup of coffee or ice cream or something, talk things over, then you have to leave," Drew said. "This is Beau's house and he's been really fair."

"I don't want an *ice cream*," she snarled. "I want this house! How can you take his side? What's he to you? He's not your father. I had to beg him to take me on with two little boys but he was never your father. He can't—"

Drew took a step toward her. "He wanted to adopt us, me and Michael, but our dads wouldn't give permission. My 'dad' didn't even come to my graduation." He shook his head. "Mom, Beau is right. You left. I asked you not to leave—I had a feeling it was going to be the last time. You can't just keep changing your mind."

"Drew, you don't have to—" Beau was going to say, *Fight my battles*, but he was cut off.

"Don't get sucked into pity for poor Beau," she said. "You have no idea how difficult and complicated marriage can be!"

Drew chuckled, but without humor. "Don't I? I've been watching you and Beau since I was just a little kid and, Mom, I think everything in your life is complicated and difficult. I'm sorry it is. But this isn't your house anymore and I'm not going to be quiet while you beat up on Beau. Beau's been a good dad. And you don't want to live with me. If you wanted to live with me, you wouldn't have left."

"Seriously? You're taking his side? Over your own mother? This...this...stepfather who doesn't care about his own wife?"

"Pam, don't..."

"Yeah, I am," Drew said. "Do you need me to help you get those bags back in the car?"

"Where do you expect me to go, since I'm denied my home?"

Drew stiffened and put his hands in his pockets. "I know you have somewhere to go. You probably have a lot of places you can go. But you gotta stop being so mean and so unfair. Beau was always good to us, good to all of us. I love you, Mom, but sometimes I really don't like you."

"Drew!" she gasped. "How can you say that? To me?"

"Michael might let you sleep on his couch," Drew said.

"You are so ungrateful, Drew," she said, turning on him now. "After all I've done for you, you side with the man who's throwing me out in the street? He was a lousy husband, a useless stepfather, an unfaithful—"

"Come on, Mom," Drew said, taking her arm. "Let me help you get these bags back in your car. You can scream at me for a while if it makes you feel better. Enough of this drama out on the street."

Beau watched as Drew pulled Pamela to her car, watched as she shook him off and stomped her foot. But he didn't watch long because he knew what was next. She would strike him and then cry and while he felt an overwhelming desire to protect Drew, Drew was a man now. Drew knew his mother and if Beau was exiting this marriage, he couldn't be the buffer between Drew and his mother anymore.

He stood just inside the door for a moment, listening. He could not make out the words but clearly Pam was arguing with him. Loudly.

Beau sat on the sofa and hoped Drew would not have to endure too much of that but it was ten minutes before the door opened. How could anyone put their child in the middle of a disintegrating marriage? Even an eighteen-year-old child? It was unconscionable.

"Drew, I'm really sorry that happened. The last thing I want is for this to be hard on you."

"I know. It's okay."

"I think the craziness will die down before too long. I'm really proud of you, the way you handled yourself. You were calm and respectful and I know it must have been hard. Come on, we can—"

"I gotta be alone right now, if that's okay. I don't feel so good."

"I understand," Beau said. He sat back down on the couch.

But after a few minutes, he stood up again. Drew had acted so much the way Beau would, exactly the way Beau had taught him. Face your mother's anger with calm, don't lose your cool, it's her temper not yours, the storm will pass. And now he was acting as Beau did.

Beau knocked on Drew's door. The voice inviting him in was small and hurt. Drew sat cross-legged on the bed and his eyes were a little red.

Beau smiled at him. "You couldn't be my son any more if we shared DNA," he said to Drew. "You got through the whole ugly business with your dignity and now you're sealed off, inside yourself, suffering. Just like I always have. But let's not do that, Drew. Let's talk it out. It'll pass faster that way."

"I'm not sure how," Drew said miserably.

"Your mom has troubles," Beau said. "I'm not sure what kind of troubles and if I could help her with it, I would. I'm sure you would, if you could. But you can't. She's mercurial and sometimes selfish. She's probably going to be a handful forever. She attacks when what she really wants is to surrender and just be loved. Understanding that won't help her, unfortunately. She's got to help herself. And she never will until we stop picking up the pieces and giving in."

"I hate when she's mad," Drew said. "Life would be so much better if she could just be happy. But she just can't be happy. At least not for long."

"Not for lack of trying," Beau said. He sat down on the bed. "The hardest part, but the most important part, we have to remember we didn't do anything to cause her pain or unhappiness. We have to try to let it be her problem."

"Easier said than done," Drew said.

"Tell me about it," Beau agreed.

CHAPTER TEN

The rest of the week while Cassie visited Lauren was like a gift. Lauren thought it might be the last time her daughter came home like this, all by herself. She and Jeremy were now a couple. They might wait to get married but they would probably take their vacations and visit their friends and family as a pair from now on.

By the time Cassie had been in town for a couple of days, Lauren's lip was less swollen and she was mostly able to conceal her bruises with makeup and dark glasses. Still, when they walked down the main street to grab lunch and do a little shopping, the waitress in the pub noticed and said, "Oh my word, sweetheart." She leaned close and squinted.

Lauren just smiled and whispered, "Minor cosmetic surgery."

"Well, darling, you didn't need it!"

"That's very nice, thank you," she said. Then she smiled, a slightly lopsided smile.

Lacey joined them for lunch one day and they managed not to discuss the divorce, nor did the girls air their differences. But it wasn't warm and loving. It was merely cordial.

Lauren and Cassie enjoyed the business district of Alameda together in the afternoons, checking out the shops, stopping at Stohl's grocery for a few items for dinner, getting an ice cream cone for their walk home, then sitting out on the porch with glasses of wine in the late afternoon sun. They sat on wooden folding chairs that Lauren bought to accompany her kitchen dinette set.

"You need better chairs," Cassie said. "Like maybe rocking chairs."

"I'll keep that in mind," Lauren said.

They waved at strangers who passed by; everyone in Alameda got out and about on sunny days. Neighbors jogged, pushed strollers, pulled kiddie wagons behind their bikes or just walked. The parking spaces along the main street in front of the shops and restaurants were always full, but Lauren couldn't imagine ever taking her car four or five blocks for a glass of wine or burger, unless it was a driving rain.

"I have loved having you here for a visit," she told Cassie. "The reason you came so suddenly and expensively, not so much. But just having you here? It's wonderful. I'm sorry about your sister."

"She'll probably come around," Cassie said. "When she figures out all this little mood is going to get her is Dad, she'll probably rethink the whole thing."

"She has a sweet side," Lauren argued.

"As long as it suits her purposes," Cassie said. "I wish we were close, but I'm not compromising with her anymore. She stepped over the line."

"It worries me to think she might not know the difference

between squabbling and abuse," Lauren said. "Beth never approved of my marriage but she stuck by me. Your sister will need you someday. And there's something you should know—I was more like Lacey than like you. I had a feeling I might be getting in over my head with your father, but I pushed it aside. He was so powerful, capable and rich. He's helped Beth a lot. He offered to help my mother but she refused him." She laughed at the memory. "Honey said, 'How very sweet, Brad. No thank you.' When he blustered she added, 'Just give it to a charity.' He was furious. But you know your father can be generous and charming when he wants to be."

"I loved those times he was happy," Cassie said. "Christmas parties, birthday parties, summer barbecues. I didn't trust them, but I liked them. It's just that all the stress leading up to the party was awful and after all the company left, he so often took a turn for the worse."

"When something didn't go the way he expected," Lauren said.

"I really don't want to leave you," Cassie said.

"Well, you're going to," she said with a laugh. "I have to go to work on Monday and you have to go home. I can't have you hanging around watching over me. It's time for both of us to get on with our lives."

"It didn't seem like the East Coast was so far away before…"

"I'm going to be fine and you have Jeremy and law school to think about. Just promise me one thing, Cassie. Promise me that if things don't feel right with Jeremy, you won't spend your entire life trying to change them. Take the shades off, Cassie," she said. "See *honestly*. Don't lie to yourself. And please—don't be afraid. I was too afraid of what he might do to us."

"I'm not the one with that problem," she said. "I'm thinking about putting off law school for a year," Cassie said. "I'd like to come back here, work, reapply, live closer. I talked to

Jeremy. He understands. He wouldn't mind getting back to the West Coast, though he's starting to think of Boston as an adventure, but—"

"No!" Lauren said. "No, no, no! We're going to move forward, you and me! I'm going to work and get divorced and this winter I'll fix up this house. After the divorce is settled, I might buy it. Next spring I'll plant a garden. And you're going to get the first year of law school under your belt. We'll Skype. We'll get this big transition handled—my first year on my own, your first year with Jeremy and with law school. Maybe we'll live closer down the road but for now? We're going to move ahead with our plans."

"Who will help you, Mama? If things get bad again? If he tries to hurt you? Who will help you?"

"I have assembled a good team," Lauren said. "A good lawyer, my sister, my brother-in-law, a few friends… There's a record and a restraining order. The sale of Honey's house—that money is tucked away and keeping me afloat. I hope that after it's over, I can help you with your expenses. We're going to be fine, you and me. We're going to—"

A truck was driving by and it slowed, catching Lauren's attention. The driver backed up and stopped in front of the house. He got out and looked over the hood. He grinned. "Lauren! How's it going?"

She stood from her chair. "Beau," she called, waving. "Come and meet my daughter."

He smiled and reached into his truck to stop the engine. He came up the walk to the porch and stuck out a hand. "How do you do," he said. "I'm Beau Magellan. We're neighbors."

"Cassie Delaney," she said.

"Beau, will you have a glass of wine with us?" Lauren asked.

"Aw, sorry, I don't have that much time. I have groceries in the truck and a kid at home I promised to feed." He looked at Cassie. "You live around here or just visiting, Cassie?"

"I'm just visiting. I live in Massachusetts now—going to school. I'm from around here, though."

"I guess I can't really take a rain check, then," Beau said. "Unless you're staying a long time."

"Just a couple more days," she said. "But I love the pace of this town—walk downtown, sit on the porch, take it easy. This is such a nice little town."

"It's full of movers and shakers. Lots of people want to raise their children here but take the ferry or BART into the city to work. I've been here quite a while," he said. "I bought an old fixer-upper on a street that seemed to be dominated by them. Now we have one of the best-looking streets in town."

"Did you fix it yourself?" Cassie asked.

"I did, with a little help from family and friends. It took years. I'm a landscape architect by trade." He grinned handsomely. "The yard is beautiful." He glanced at his watch. "I'd love to stay. I'm sure you'll visit again sometime, Cassie. Lauren, if you need anything, just call or text—I'm just around the corner." He stuck out his hand. "Really nice meeting you, Cassie."

"You, too," she said.

They didn't speak as Beau jogged to his truck, jumped in and gave a brief wave as he drove off. Then Cassie looked at Lauren and said, "Wow."

"Huh?" Lauren asked.

"He's very handsome," Cassie said. "How well do you know him?"

"I haven't known him that long," she said. "I'm still getting to know him. I bought him dinner at the pub where we had lunch as thanks for putting up shelves. And we spent the whole time talking about our pending divorces. He's been separated since months before we met. He was working in the gardens at Divine Redeemer—that's where I met him. I thought he was a groundskeeper—those gardens are so beautiful. The priest there is his childhood friend." She paused. "And he's the neighbor who followed me to the hospital and brought me home the night your father…"

"He's the one! You must see that he likes you," Cassie said.

"I hope so," she said. "I like him. But if you think I'm going to rush into another dysfunctional relationship, you are completely mistaken. I'm thinking about freedom and some independence, Cassie. Not another man."

"Well, good for you," she said. "But he's cute. Thirty seconds and I would have fallen for him."

"Tsk, tsk, what would Jeremy say?" Lauren teased.

"I'm just saying—"

"It's nice to know a guy other than your uncle Chip, who can help if I run into trouble or need a little carpentry, but I am absolutely not in the market. Period. I am looking forward to getting to know him a little better, though. On the surface of things, he seems so utterly perfect." She sighed. "I assume that means he's probably a psychopath."

"I think the sad truth is, my dad is the psychopath. Not your garden-variety *Criminal Minds* psychopath. More of a CEO or billionaire type of psychopath."

"Oh Cassie, I didn't want that for you."

"I think it's time we stopped glossing over the facts, Mama. That's Lacey's job. You really want me to ignore what he did?"

"No," Lauren said. "I just didn't want you to be hurt."

"You might want to rethink that," Cassie said. "Pretending is lying. Lying hurts."

Early Monday morning, Lauren and Cassie said goodbye and Lauren went to work. She still had to try to camouflage her purple bruises, but at least the swelling was down. The first people she ran into at the lab said things like, "Welcome back! I heard you had a fall! Are you okay?" She said she was fine but was pretty ugly there for a few days. Then invariably they would say, "What in the world happened?"

"One of those klutzy slips while unpacking the kitchen. You know, up on the step stool, down on the floor, whacking the countertop on the way down and biting my lip."

And if she wasn't mistaken, she got a few quizzical looks wondering if that was really the whole story. Her decision had already been made, but if it hadn't been, those few looks would have been convincing. But she was going to tell her boss first. She asked her supervisor, Bea, for a few moments of her time.

Bea frowned. "Yes," she said tightly. "How about right now?"

Lauren tensed up. Bea always treated her fairly but there was something about the response Lauren felt that made her wonder if her supervisor disliked her. It hardly mattered—they worked together successfully, respected each other's boundaries, played by all the right rules. Lauren always thought the distance between them was because they had little in common. Left to their own devices, Lauren and Bea wouldn't meet for lunch or drinks, but they both joined in when the office staff went out together. Bea was the single mother of four grown children and now had several grandchildren. She had a great position as director of the product development lab and owned her home, but it was not in posh Alameda and she had never had a surgeon husband to go home to. Lauren tried not to speculate, but thought it was possible Bea was just a little jealous. If only Bea had known the truth...

"Sit down, Lauren," Bea said. "You obviously took quite a header."

"I wonder if we can have a confidential conversation," Lauren asked. "Because I didn't exactly fall. I really don't need the details all over the lab."

"I don't talk about my employees," she said.

"My husband did this to me," Lauren said. Her eyes briefly

filled with tears, not because her heart was breaking but because she was embarrassed.

"Dr. Delaney?" Bea asked in shock, half rising from the chair behind her desk.

Lauren nodded.

"How long has this been going on?" Bea asked, her face grim. Lauren thought she detected a blush in that beautiful ebony complexion.

"Nothing like this has happened before, and I say that honestly. I'd like to think I'd have filed for divorce long ago if it had, but I'm no longer sure. I managed to lie to myself so many times, in so many ways. Yes, he was always abusive. Yes, I left a couple of times. Really, this is all such dirty laundry..."

"Don't worry about it," she said. "It'll go no further. But you're kidding yourself if you think people don't pick up the signals."

"Oh God, has there been talk?"

"That he's been beating you? No, not at all. That he's a mean and superior son of a bitch? I've heard a whisper or two. Do you have some good help to get you through this?"

"Help?"

"Legal help? Psychological help? Emotional help?"

"Oh, of course. Yes. Listen, it's not that I'm ashamed, but—"

"Lauren, anyone who has been through what you have has felt ashamed," Bea said. "Believe me, I know. My husband was abusive. We divorced thirty years ago. I was so young. There were all those children. It was the hardest time of my life. And I never learn. I frequently make the mistake of thinking there are some people who are immune, who live charmed lives, just because they appear to have it easy. But you never really know what is going on in another person's life. Don't worry, I won't be talking about your issues with anyone else.

I respect your privacy and I completely understand. And if there's any way I can be of help…"

Lauren was deeply touched. "Bea, would you like to go to lunch sometime?"

Cassie went to her father's office on her way to the airport. She left her suitcase with security at the front entrance and went upstairs. The receptionist in his office actually recognized her immediately and grinned a big hello, until she saw the firm line of her lips.

"Will you please tell my father I'd like to see him at the earliest free moment he has? It's urgent."

"Of course!" she said. "Are you all right?"

"I'm fine, but he'll want to speak to me before I leave town."

"Yes," she said nervously. "Yes, of course. I'll tell him."

Just a moment later a nurse came to the reception area and called for her. Cassie couldn't remember the woman's name but she was very sweet and asked her how she was liking Harvard. It was so like her father to brag about her accomplishments as if he had anything to do with them, yet refuse to help her with tuition to punish her mother.

"Classes haven't actually started yet," she said. "I came home for a family emergency."

"Oh no!" she said. "The doctor didn't mention anything. Is everyone all right?"

"I think she will be," Cassie said. She walked straight to her father's office.

Of course it was furnished with the best of everything, as was the rest of the office. The examining rooms held the latest equipment and were smart and efficient. Brad Delaney sat behind a large mahogany desk, surrounded by bookshelves and a couple of TV screens even though most of the medical files were now accessible via computer.

He rose. "Cassie?" he said, as if shocked.

"Stop it," she said. "You know I've been in town. Lacey is reporting every tidbit to you. I came running the second I heard Mom had been so badly hurt. *You* never contacted me."

He took on the expression of a slapped toddler. "I was under the impression you didn't want to see me."

"But I *do* want to see you," she said. "I'm leaving today. I came here to tell you something. I think you know, you're in trouble. You have a problem."

"I certainly do," he said. "My wife of twenty-four years is leaving me for a younger man."

"I don't know about that," Cassie said. "She has filed for divorce because of your abuse. You could get help, you know. It won't save your marriage. It's really too late for that, but it could save your life. And if you got help and changed, you might be a part of your grandchildren's lives. As it stands, you won't. You're not safe. You're a dangerous megalomaniac who hurts people."

"She's lying," he said. "She did that to herself and blamed me! She wants a big divorce settlement!" he spat out.

"There is proof, you know. You, the great saver of lives, have inflicted so much pain. On the people who loved you most."

"Do you think it's smart to accuse me this way when you're hoping to have your tuition to law school paid?"

"First of all, you already threatened to pull your support, just like you do every other month. Lacey seems willing to be held hostage but I'm not. I'll find a way. For that matter, it would feel dirty now, knowing how cruel you can be. Since I assume you won't try to change, won't get help, I suppose this is goodbye."

He glowered, not speaking, his eyes narrow slits. If this office was like all others on the face of the earth, someone would have an ear to the door and the word would travel. She decided to make the most of it.

"My mother's face has healed enough for her to go back to work. I'd like you to know one thing. If you ever lay a hand on her again, you will be sorry. I would ride into hell to make sure you're sorry. Leave her alone."

"Get out, Cassidy," he said, keeping his voice carefully quiet.

She turned and left but she was acutely aware that one of his staff looked at her hard. She wasn't sure if the expression was one of disdain or pity. Perhaps he had already briefed his staff that he was being railroaded by a greedy soon-to-be ex-wife.

She had an Uber pick her up to go to the airport. She'd lived in the Bay Area her entire life and she loved it, earthquake rumbles and all. This was her part of the world. Leaving her mother here during what could be one of the most stressful, frightening times of her life didn't feel good at all, but she would be back. Leaving her mother terrified her, but she was right—they had lives to live right now. There were important transitions. They were headed for new lives and it wouldn't be too long until they'd be together again.

Lauren would be safe, she reminded herself. She had a baseball bat, she had Beth and Chip. Too bad they no longer had Honey. Honey had been looking for an excuse to pound the crap out of some man for almost fifty years.

But then there was the guy. Beau.

She was pleased to hear her mother was being overly cautious. After her father? Beau would not be around one second after he *pinched*.

Lauren heard from Cassie that she'd been approved for a low-interest student loan, just enough to get her class schedule started. Lacey was knee-deep in her master's of English education and when Lauren saw her, they avoided talking about the divorce. And Brad was silent.

Lauren's lawyer was not silent. She'd had no difficulty securing a restraining order but she was having a hard time getting an accurate accounting of the Delaneys' net worth, since Brad handled all their finances and investments. She had copies of the couple's tax returns so she knew what the family income was, but the value of property, medical equipment from his private practice and his total investments was a little murky.

"I suspect we need a forensic accounting," Erica Slade said. "He's offered you a settlement, which usually means he'd like to get off cheap."

"A settlement?" Lauren asked. "Seriously?"

"Four million. The house plus two million. I suggest you reject it. It almost certainly means your estate is worth far more than eight."

She was dumbstruck. "He's worth more than eight million?" she asked in a whisper. "Really?"

"Lauren," Erica said. "You contributed mightily to that. Your income and blood, sweat and tears. Quite literally."

She thought for a moment. "The house is probably worth closer to six, but there is a big mortgage. The practice must be very valuable, though I never thought of it as *ours*. The investments—I can't imagine. He controlled the money. This is terrible. I feel so pathetic and incompetent. Why don't I know what we have?"

"Because your husband didn't want you to know," Erica said. "He was obviously never secure. He may have been concerned that you might file for divorce throughout your marriage. When we get a believable accounting, we'll talk about a settlement. In the meantime, I'll get his lawyer to agree to a stipend during your separation."

"Is there something I should be doing?" Lauren asked.

"Yes," Erica said. "Begin to rebuild your life."

She was more than anxious to do that. She began by making an appointment with the last counselor she had seen and felt comfortable with, Jan Straight. In the first session, they renewed their acquaintance and then Lauren filled her in on what had been happening in the last six months, including Brad's violence.

"I didn't realize I'd been in denial," Lauren said. "The more I confront the truth, the more comes to the surface. Stuff I just didn't want to believe, so I ignored it or tamped it down…"

"Give me an example," Jan said.

"Well, he was sued by an employee. She alleged he kicked her in the operating room. When she did something he didn't want her to do or failed to do something he expected, he kicked her. Not hard, but still… Of course he said she was crazy—it never happened. Eventually, he settled with her and she quit her job. I never learned the details. He said he had deep pockets and was a target as a result and it was to be expected people would go after him from time to time. And I accepted that.

"Then, a couple of years later I went to the dentist, a new dentist. Oh my gosh, he was a handsome young man with the most beautiful smile. His assistant was a young woman who'd worked for the previous dentist who'd retired. She was a single mother, was gentle and kind with a good sense of humor.

"During the procedure, he corrected her twice, harshly. Then he kicked her leg underneath the back of my reclined chair. I said, 'Stop! Did you just kick her?' And he said, 'Of course not! Please relax, Mrs. Delaney.' I couldn't relax. I was on high alert. Then he did it again. And she winced. And I knew in that moment—Brad was guilty of doing that to one of his nurses. I tore off the bib, pushed away his tray and with my mouth stuffed full of cotton, I sat up and spit it out. I told Ashley she should sue him and if she needed a witness, she could call me. I walked out. And cried all the way home."

"You're sure that's what happened?"

"I have a mental closet full of those things," she said. "Sometimes I buried them so deeply, I couldn't even remember them. Like the time he deliberately tripped me at Disneyland—my daughter Cassie never forgot it, but I did. Or at least I refused to think about it. Because if I thought about it, I'd have to do something about it. And that took way too much courage."

"But you found the courage now?" Jan asked.

"My daughters are grown," she said. "They've moved away from home, though their bedrooms are still preserved for them. I can't live there anymore. Especially now."

"Let's set up some appointments," Jan said. "I want to help you through this."

September brought Lauren's very favorite time of the year and she began to relax as the air became crisp and cool. The harvest from the farmlands of the central valley brought out the most delicious displays of fresh fruits and vegetables in bins outside the grocery and at roadside stands. The last of the tomatoes were displayed among ears of corn and ripe apples. Next would come the squash and pumpkins. She brought home artichokes by the bagful, so cheap they were practically free. The fall colors gave her a sense of renewal, a hopefulness.

Lauren's do-over began. She pushed herself to become friendlier with her coworkers, beginning with Bea. They had lunch together soon after their meeting and while they spent a little time discussing their war stories, they soon moved on to their very similar childhoods, both of them being raised by single mothers. Then she pushed her way into the small cliques that met to lunch together. She asked if she could join them. She was welcomed and quickly realized that *she* had been aloof and kept herself separate from the social side of work.

"Of course you were," Bea told her. "I imagine you didn't

really want too many people to understand how imperfect and secretive your life really was. Time to get some counseling and support, Lauren."

"I'm way ahead of you," she said. "I started counseling already."

She shared some of the beautiful vegetables she bought at out-of-the-way roadside stands. She made cookies and brought them to the office. And she kept her appointments with Jan Straight. For the first time she felt she might actually realize her hopes and dreams for a new kind of life.

She grew comfortable in her new friendships. She went out for drinks with the girls from work one evening and they all giggled like children. They were women she'd known for a long time and yet hardly knew at all. Carly, in her early fifties, was single and her widowed mother moved in with her as she grew older and had medical issues. Merline was just thirty-five, married to a contractor and the mother of three young children who drove her crazy most of the time. Shauna was forty, divorced and the mother of two teenage girls. Anne was sixty with her seventy-eight-year-old husband now in memory care. Her children were grown and didn't live near enough to help out.

Lauren was pleasantly surprised to fit right in. They were all dealing with personal challenges of some sort. Some of them seemed rather alone, some had large families they were close with. But none of them had worked at Merriweather for as long and remained as remote as Lauren. They all supported each other and were willing to support Lauren, too.

"Sorry about the divorce, Lauren," Carly said. "But I'm glad you decided to come out and play."

"Me, too," she said, and meant it.

"Congratulations on taking your life back," Jan said after their first few sessions.

The changes that started with a new house and fresh vegetables proceeded to lunching with coworkers, seeing Lacey without arguing about the changes in their family dynamics, talking for at least a little while with Cassie almost every day and meeting Beau for an occasional glass of wine at the pub a few blocks away. She and Beau easily graduated to laughing over ordinary things like one of his fussier clients or some of her failed recipe experiments. On one lovely fall evening she made them gourmet artichokes, the leaves stuffed with blue cheese and bacon, doused in garlic butter. They ate on the front porch, drank wine and watched the sun set.

"Do you hear from him?" Beau asked her.

"Through my lawyer, and that's all. Do you hear from her?" she asked.

"Constantly. But it's all the same old stuff. Nothing new. She can't turn the boys against me—they're men now. Sadly for her, they're men who know how mercurial she is. So she's threatening to wipe me out, leave me completely broke."

Lauren gasped. "What if she does?"

He smiled, a smile she had come to depend on. "I don't care. I can start over. She can't get more than half. Right?"

"Why do I feel guilty, asking for half?" she asked. "I'm not the surgeon. I didn't endure a decade of medical school and residency. I didn't build the practice...okay, on his father's money, but still. It wasn't mine."

"Maybe you don't need half," Beau said, surprising her. "Maybe what you need is what's fair and reasonable. But before you settle on a number, you should know what there is. And you should see if you can count the pinches. The bruises. And I don't know that much about your marriage but... Could he have done any of it without you?"

"Yes," she said quietly. "With a maid, nanny, assistant, secretary, household manager...and whipping post."

CHAPTER ELEVEN

At the end of September, when the leaves were turning colors and people were putting fall wreaths on their doors, Beau called her one Friday afternoon. "How's your poker game?" he asked.

"Poker?" she repeated.

"You know, cards. Your poker game."

"I'm not sure I even remember how to play," she said. "I might've played a couple of times in college, but we mostly played hearts."

"Great! I'm getting a table together for tonight. Tim, my son, Drew, his current girlfriend, Darla, me and you. I'll have food. Poker food. Seven. Will you come?"

"Oh… I don't know…"

"I'll tell everyone to go easy on you," he promised. "Come on, it will be fun."

Lauren took the address from Beau and opted to drive

herself to his house, though she was tremendously nervous. Would Father Tim frown in a paternal way? Though Tim didn't seem that fatherly, except in the clerical sense, and surely he would not be wearing a collar or robes... Would Beau's son show his disapproval of her presence out of loyalty to his mother? And the girlfriend—would she be snooty and proprietary? Why ever would she think or worry about those things? Lauren didn't know. Perhaps because she worried about many things.

"Hi," Beau said when he opened the door. "Come in! We're all here!"

She presented her offerings, though she wasn't asked to bring anything.

"What's this?" he asked, taking a couple of large, sealed containers from her.

"Stuffed mushrooms and a cheese ball." She lifted a bag. "And crackers."

"That was nice of you," he said. "I didn't mean for you to go to any trouble..."

"Well, I wanted to," she said. "You'll love it."

"Will you have a glass of wine?"

"I... I... Yes, sure," she stammered.

He grinned at her. "Aw," he said softly. "You're nervous."

She glanced around. The house was so nice. It wasn't in any way fussy, but the walls, woodwork, cabinetry, window coverings and furniture were classy and well cared for. There was, of course, a big-screen TV mounted on the wall in the family room and a U-shaped sectional facing it. It was, in a way, masculine, so she wondered about his wife and wanted to see the kitchen. Clearly the dining room would be the poker table, since that's where the cards and chips were.

"Lauren!" Father Tim called, coming to her at once to greet her with a hug. He wore jeans and a sweater. An emerald-green sweater that brought out that green in his eyes.

"I'm so glad to see you! Beau mentioned that it's been a while since you played poker so I took the liberty of writing out a little cheat sheet for you." He pulled a slip of paper out of his pocket.

"Ah, wait a sec," the young man who must be Drew said. "You'd better let me check that…"

"You suggest I would mislead her? An innocent like Lauren?"

"I wouldn't put it past you. Hi," he said, sticking out his hand. "I'm Drew. And this is Darla. I'm really glad you could make it. My dad's mentioned you now and then for months, obviously trying to pretend he's not dating anyone…"

"Actually, I don't think he's dating me. We've just met at the pub down the street a couple of times. Back in the day, that wasn't quite a date," she said.

"It qualifies," Drew said. "Let me check that cheat sheet." He grinned at her and pulled it from her hand. "Hm. Looks correct, but don't take his advice, okay? He'll do anything to win. He doesn't exactly cheat, but he wrangles."

"I'm offended," Tim said. "First of all, it's *poker.* Second, I'm not on the clock right now. I play by the same rules you reprobates play by." He turned his attention to Lauren. "You're looking wonderful. I haven't seen you in a while, but it looks like you've been well and happy."

Her whole demeanor softened. There was nothing like a handsome priest and an attentive suitor to put her in the best possible mood. "I've been very well, thank you, Father."

He leaned toward her and whispered. "Tim is fine, if you're comfortable with that."

"Yes, thanks. Tim."

"Good. I want you to be at ease while I clean your clock at poker."

"Is this some kind of grudge match?" she asked.

"It's *poker,*" three male voices said at once.

"Oh boy," she said. "I'm going to have to pay attention."

They had their drinks and loaded up their plates with what Beau had referred to as poker food—nachos, a veggie platter with dip, lettuce wraps stuffed with chicken salad, vinegar chips. Lauren's stuffed mushrooms and cheese ball fit right in. They sat at the table, visiting and eating, for about twenty minutes and then Beau explained the game to Lauren. "We play for chips," he said. "The white are a penny, the blue are a nickel, red are twenty-five cents, purple are fifty cents, black are a dollar. We'll front you for your first time and if you don't want to bet..."

"Like if you have a gambling problem or something," Drew said.

"No, I want in like everyone else," she said. "Though I hope you'll be patient with me. I've never been good at card games."

"We'll be very patient," Beau said.

"Then can I just have a bunch of penny chips?"

"Okay, Lauren, to stay in the game you're going to have to bet along with the rest of us. You'll have to 'see,' which means to match a bet to stay in, or 'call' which forces them to show their hand. Every move costs chips. And they'll do the same to you."

"Okay," she said uncertainly. "So, what should I do? Twenty dollars?"

"That's good," Beau said. "And you only have to play as long as you're comfortable. If you want to get out of the game and just eat, drink and watch, that's okay. And if you need help, just ask me."

"No way, pardner," Drew said. "She asks me."

Lauren dug in her purse. "Can't believe he's so scared of a girl who hasn't played poker in at least twenty-five years..."

"You just take your time," Beau said.

He counted out her chips while everyone put their money

in the pot and took the appropriate chips. Then Beau dealt the cards and asked her if she wanted to open.

"Sure," she said. "How much? A few pennies?"

Everyone groaned.

"Well jeez..."

"Look at your cards, see what you have, you can discard up to three and pick up new ones. I'll open. I'm in for fifty and I'll take two cards."

Around the table they went, then went again. Lauren stayed in. When they were going around the third time and it was just Tim, Drew and Lauren, she very politely raised her hand. "I have a question," she said.

"You don't have to raise your hand," Beau said. "What's your question?"

"What's a full house again?" she asked, showing her cards.

There were more groans as everyone folded their hands.

And so it went. It was not long before they refused to let her ask questions and told her to check her cheat sheet and follow her instincts. Before long, Darla gave her chips to Drew and retired to the sofa to read, a plate of snacks balanced on her flat belly. That left Lauren as the only woman at the table as she played each hand in an ultra-polite manner, asking permission, saying please and thank you, laughing softly as the men groaned while she scraped her chips toward her. After about two hours she was the big winner of the night. Tim threw the party, Drew was hurting from his losses and Beau was amused in spite of himself. .

"That's it, I'm out," Tim said. "I've emptied the collection plate."

"Me, too," Beau said. "I'm out."

"I should quit and take Darla home," Drew said.

"Awww... Don't you want a chance to catch up?" Lauren asked.

"No!" they said in unison.

"Jeez," she muttered, stacking her chips. Then she grinned and said, "Nice doing business with you."

"It better not turn out you're faking," Tim said.

"Faking what?" she asked, grinning slyly. "Being a prodigy at poker?"

"Yeah, yeah, yeah…"

"How about some coffee before you make that long four-block drive home?" Beau asked. "There's cake. Not homemade, but it is cake."

"Does it have *preservatives?*" Lauren teased.

It was down to Beau, Lauren and Tim sitting around with coffee and pound cake. Tim slowly got over his pique about being the big loser, though Beau had a hard time letting it rest. He seemed to enjoy it more than Lauren did.

Soon it was time for Lauren to say good-night. Beau walked her to her car and Tim rather conspicuously hung back. "The holidays are just around the corner," Beau said. "Have you made plans?"

"I've barely thought about it," she lied. "There's my sister, I guess. Every other year, we went to Beth's. On alternate years, Adele, Brad's mother, hosted. It was catered, of course. This would be Adele's year. Beth could be planning to go to her mother-in-law's house, but I'm sure they'd all be happy to drag me along or adjust for me. The girls…haven't said anything…"

"How homey," he said, smiling. "I took a proactive stand— I'm cooking. I invited my whole family. Of my two sisters and one brother and their families, I don't know who's interested yet. They all have in-law obligations, too. And the boys are free agents."

"How do you do that? Just tell them it's up to them?"

"Exactly," he said with raised eyebrows. "The only caveat being, I'm not cooking for their mother. The first set of holidays will be hard on the people that don't want the divorce to be happening. That's one person—Michael. The divorce makes Drew uncomfortable, but he gets it. I have a feeling he wouldn't be married to his mother, either."

"Why do you say that?"

"He's got some really firm boundaries with her. But Michael? I'm pretty sure he wishes I would have applied myself and fixed her. But the point is, once you figure out your holiday calendar, I'm having Thanksgiving here probably for a bunch of people. I'd love for you to join us, if you feel like it. Your girls, too, if they want to."

"That's so nice of you," she said.

"Just an option to think about," he said. "You might want something different this year, just to change things up." He put a hand on her shoulder and squeezed softly. "I'm really glad you came to poker night. Even if you did wipe us out."

"You men aren't exactly good losers."

He chuckled. "You raised your hand to speak, just like a schoolgirl."

"You won't underestimate me next time," she said.

He leaned toward her. "I sure won't."

She instinctively backed up slightly when what she really wanted to do was lean into him. Obviously sensitive to her movement, he pressed a brief kiss on her cheek. "If you'd like me to follow you home, make sure you get in safely, I'd be happy to do that."

"I'll be fine. I'll be alert, the street is well lit, the locks are good. Thank you for a fun night. Talk to you soon." And she withdrew into her car.

He leaned on her car and she lowered the window. "If anything seems odd or weird, don't get out of the car," he said.

"Beau, I've been getting myself home from evenings out for weeks now," she said. "I won't take any chances."

"When you're home and safely behind locked doors, will you text me?"

She grinned at him. "You're an old woman in a man suit."

"I guess," he said. He gave her car door a couple of pats and stepped away.

Tim was lounging on the sofa with his feet up on the ottoman, coffee balanced on his belly. He appeared to be in no great hurry to go anywhere. "That took a while," he said to Beau.

"I was asking about Lauren's holiday plans," Beau said.

"You mean, you weren't getting kissed?"

"I wasn't, as if it's any of your business," he said.

"You've been chasing her for months! You used to have game," Tim said.

"Lauren is understandably cautious," Beau said. "And I am foolishly not."

"Ah," Tim said, sitting upright, feet on the floor. "So, you admit, this is moving too fast..."

"Not at all. Moving too slowly if you ask me. My marriage was over years ago. Pam and I have been separated almost a year now and if she'd just put away the damn calculator and wrap it up, it would be officially over. As for Lauren..." He ran a hand over his head. "It's only been a few months for her. You're right, I should slow down."

"I didn't say a word," Tim said, feigning innocence.

"You learn that in priest class, don't you? Getting information without exactly asking."

Tim laughed. "With you, no lessons were required. You've always worn your heart on your sleeve."

"Yeah, you're right. No game." He sat down on the couch. "What about you? What's going on with you? You haven't complained about your boss in quite a while now."

"I have no issue with my Boss," Tim said. "It's the earthly managers who wear me out. Maybe the problem is mine. I don't feel useful."

"Still that, eh? We should pull together a pumpkin give-away—we have some good stock this year..."

"Is the phrase, 'live with the smell of the sheep,' familiar to you?" Tim asked.

Beau looked stunned. "Ah, no. But it doesn't sound real appetizing..."

"It comes from the pope. He deftly pointed out that when priests and bishops aren't out with the people, working with the people, directly helping the people—and I think he meant tilling their gardens and helping them fix their plumbing as well as providing spiritual guidance—they become managers. Let me put that more succinctly—they become bureaucrats. The bishop gave me a good book for some leisure reading. *Three Easy Steps to Becoming a Bishop.*" He laughed. "He's such a political animal that when he heard the pope calling for priests who lived with the smell of the sheep, he immediately came looking for a lowly priest with political potential and that's how he found me in that poor little parish in the central valley and got me transferred up here. So he could look me over. I guess I cleaned up pretty well. Now he wants me to apprentice under him in the See. He wants a bishop to come from his archdiocese."

"I didn't know there was such a thing," Beau said. "A bishop apprentice."

"It's a glorified secretary. A valet."

"You're on the path to become a bishop," Beau said. "Congratulations. We'll throw you a party or something."

"Except, that doesn't really interest me," Tim said.

Beau was stunned. "Wait a minute. I thought you wanted to be the pope!"

"No. I wanted to be Bing Crosby," he said. "Maybe when I was a kid, I thought being the bishop was such an achievement, but what really propelled me was the idea of a nice little Brooklyn neighborhood parish filled with hardworking men and women in need of more than prayer, in need of sustenance and opportunity and a good singing voice. Children who could be encouraged and filled with hope. I never wanted anyone to be sick or hungry, you know? But there were going to be people in need. I wouldn't be able to right all the ills of the world, I knew that. But..." He became quiet. "I wanted to help, to give comfort."

"Did you want to be a hero?" Beau asked.

"I wanted to be another pair of hands," Tim said, his voice soft and earnest. "I wanted to work, not write canon law that controlled people and kept them from being human. I wanted to be needed. No, that's candy-ass—I wanted to make a difference in ordinary lives. They need another bishop like they need a rash."

"Oh boy. They're about to grace you with this high honor and you're...you're..."

"Losing the fire," Tim said.

Beau was quiet. He watched his friend closely. It was unusual for Tim to be this serious, this grave. "Why have you never said anything?" Beau finally asked.

"The real question should be, why am I saying something now? Because, my brother, I feel there could be changes coming. I know you need me right now. I hope you understand if I'm unavailable for some reason."

"Of course," he said. "Listen, take care of yourself, Tim. I'm good. I want you to be happy. You didn't sound happy just then..."

"God didn't put me here to be happy," Tim said. "He put me here to be useful. That's happiness right there. So you see, in the end it's entirely selfish. It makes me happy to dig my heels in and work alongside the poor and disenfranchised."

"You should have skipped the seminary and the vows and just hired out as a missionary. I can think of a hundred nonprofits who would kill to have someone like you, someone willing to break his back for a bowl of soup."

"Tempting," Tim said, causing Beau to look at him with amused surprise.

Beau shook his head. "You're one of a kind, you know that."

Lauren had tried not to think too much about the upcoming holidays, but the truth was it popped into her mind often and it worried her. She would bring it up to Cassie first. She was the most loyal and reasonable. Then she would talk to her sister; she would offer all the cooking and hosting she was able to. Maybe Beth would have no interest in having a holiday meal at Lauren's new house, which was perfectly all right. She would go anywhere that seemed agreeable. She even had passing thoughts of going to Boston, though she was sure Jeremy's family would invite them home and Lauren suspected they would include her.

But who would rear an ugly head this holiday season? Would it be Lacey, angry that the family she had known was splitting apart? Would it be Brad, furious that the holiday he had designed was not to be? Would the holiday spirit throw him into a rage?

Brad loved the Christmas season particularly. He liked attending parties; he liked throwing parties. Though he played host and had specific ideas about what should be done, he didn't do any of the work. He liked showing off at all of the parties, but he wouldn't like it while going through a divorce. Adele had never joined them at Beth's house. Instead, whether Thanksgiving or Christmas, he would make a run by his mother's house and have dessert with her, dragging Lauren along. But while he paid homage to Adele by having a holiday meal with her now and then, he didn't much enjoy it. He didn't stay long and his mood was usually dark when it was over. What he liked was hosting a lavish celebration at his house, whether it was for his friends or even Lauren's family. That's where he was comfortable—the king and his subjects. Whether Thanksgiving or Christmas Eve or Christmas Day, he liked it when people gathered at his house.

That would never happen again. The only way he could do it without Lauren was to have it catered the way Adele did, without his queen to oversee the details and do the work.

But perhaps he was working on his next wife, she thought cheerfully. That would eliminate a number of problems, if she could just pass him off to the next woman. That she pitied her successor went without saying, but she couldn't help the mysterious her.

But would he snap? That was her real worry. When the holidays didn't go the way he'd like them to go, would anger overwhelm him? Would that restraining order keep her safe from him?

Erica called her. It was the second week of October. The leaves were turning. It was still warm in most of the Bay Area while the coast was still cool and damp. The harvest was almost over. "Dr. Delaney would like to have a face-to-face conference with you. He termed it a renegotiation," Erica said.

"A what?"

"I have no idea what he means by that," she said. "Given your history with the man, I suggest we just say you're not interested in a meeting."

"What does he want?" Lauren asked. "Sorry, I'm thinking aloud. You just said you have no idea what that's about."

"Think about your experience with him," Erica said. "What does he do?"

"He lies and manipulates and here's the hook—I get sucked in because I wonder what he's going to say. I wonder so passionately that I can't wait to hear what he wants now. But you're right. Please tell his lawyer that I don't want to meet with him. He can talk to you."

Erica sighed deeply. "I'll listen to any offer, present it to you, and we'll go from there."

"And here I was just thinking how well things are going—he hasn't bothered me, nagged or intruded on me, and I'm getting a stipend to help with finances. It was too good to be true, wasn't it?"

"We don't know yet," she said. "His attorney says his request is very sincere. Of course, that's exactly what I would say. I'll be in touch."

Three days later Erica called again, this time asking Lauren to stop by the office. Erica Slade kept offices in a chic Victorian building that housed several lawyers, paralegals and clerical staff. She was located on a fashionable San Francisco street that also had residences—very upscale, as were Erica Slade's fees.

"I gave him a couple of hours of my time, which he will pay for, just as he will pay for the time I'm presently giving you. I wanted to see your face when I tell you this. I have accustomed myself to surprises but I've never grown to like them."

"Oh dear," she said weakly.

"He is willing to make a substantial cash payment to you with a few stipulations. He would give you five million in cash, transferable bonds and stocks if you will give the marriage another go. He would agree to a post-nuptial agreement that would keep the settlement from being a part of your future community property if your attempt at reconciliation fails. He wants you to agree to six months effort for the transfer of funds. And—"

Lauren shook her head. "You really don't have to go any further. There is no possibility for reconciliation."

"You don't want to hear the rest?"

"Is it even interesting?" Lauren asked.

"Well, yes. At least informative. If you move home for what he considers to be a substantial reward, he will be responsible for your daughters' post-graduate studies. Harvard Law is pricey, to say the least. If you won't try again, he will refuse to help them with their educational costs. We can make it part of our negotiation, but…"

Lauren pinched her eyes closed and a little moisture gathered on the lashes.

"What did that trigger?" Erica asked.

"They're *his* daughters, too," she said in a whisper. "How can he be so uncaring? So selfish? Is everything a negotiation with him?"

"You know him better than I do," Erica said rather coldly. "One more thing. If you find these terms unacceptable, he'd like to take this matter of property settlement to mediation."

That brought a bitter laugh out of Lauren. "I wouldn't dare," she said. "If you could see the way he brought marriage counselors to their knees… I should go to court and have a jury!"

"You won't get a jury. You could draw a family court judge and bear the same risk as with a mediator. However, I can exercise some small bit of control with a mediator. I've worked with quite a few, as has my opposing counsel. We can strike a deal for joint approval of the mediator. I cannot choose a judge, however."

"He really knows how to turn on the charm—he knows how to get what he wants."

"Lauren—you're not going to exit this marriage broke, I can guarantee that. But listen to me—those of us who have been working in the divorce business for a number of years are understandably jaded. Cynical. We have a hard time believing anything we can't see, touch, hear, smell or count. I don't trust anyone. And most of my colleagues are the same way, mediators included."

"Me?" Lauren asked. "You don't trust me?"

"You're a nice lady. I think you've been treated badly. I think your decision to divorce is sensible and I like you. But there are always two sides. I think you'd be okay with a mediator and it might speed things up. In any case, we should bring a motion before the family court to issue a deadline for this proceeding. And I'm still waiting for that forensic audit. That's one of my holdouts—we don't do anything without that audit. We have to know his net worth. His *real* net worth."

"Can I think about it?" she asked.

"Think about going back to him?" Erica asked.

"Oh God, no! About a mediator versus a judge versus a settlement for less than is fair. I just want to think it through."

"By all means."

Lauren's resources with people who had been down this path were limited. She had only Beau. She asked him if she could buy him dinner at the pub in exchange for a little advice, for a sounding board. He agreed immediately. Once he had a cold beer, she had her glass of wine and their food was on order, she told him about the offer.

"I'm reluctant to weigh in on this," he said. "I have a vested interest. I want you to be single."

"I want to be single, too," she said. "I don't think for the same reason. I just want my life back. It's been so long, I'm not sure I'll recognize myself. I just want to be friends, Beau. I'm not ready to think about another—"

"Oh God, I know," he said. "I hear you loud and clear. I'm in the same boat, Lauren. But while there are these crazy spouses stirring things up at every turn, we can't even look at our friendship without it being confused. Here's all I know— I have a cousin who was married to a jerk and she needed a divorce. She said all she wanted was to get out so she didn't get a lawyer, didn't fight for what was fair. He got away with no alimony or child support, he left her with a little furniture and the clothes on her back. She got her divorce, two little kids, no car, and the struggle was long and hard. The second she was on her feet she said she wished she'd been smarter. A little tougher and more patient. But at the time she was so worn down. So all I have to say is—don't make any decisions from a position of weakness. Take your lawyer's advice. I know you're not greedy and the most important thing is getting your life back, but don't let him trick you."

"Is that what you're doing? Trying to fight back and be patient?"

He laughed uncomfortably. "Lauren, my ex-wife wants everything. My house, my business, my boys, my soul. She's made similar offers—if I just let her come home, she'll promise to leave the business alone. But I know she doesn't keep promises. And let's be honest, that ship has sailed. No way I'm going to live with her again."

"I completely understand that," she said.

"There's only one problem in my life at the moment," he said. "I get lonely." He reached across the small table and took her hand. "I never thought that would be a problem. Then I met you."

CHAPTER TWELVE

Tim left an unpleasant meeting with the archbishop of the diocese; His Excellence was understandably disappointed. He had plans for Father Tim, but Father Tim had plans of his own. He had already begun transitioning out of the priesthood. He felt a rush of fear and grief at the prospect, but there was no question in his mind it was the right thing to do. It was not a question of faith; his faith was deep and strong and he would find a way to do the Lord's work as a civilian. But his political disagreements with doctrine were too strong.

The archbishop might be disappointed in his decision but he found a great deal of support within the diocese from other priests and a great deal of compassion and understanding from one of the bishops. His Grace, Bishop Michael Hayden had been ordained forty years ago and Tim would have expected him to think of Tim as just another flaky young priest with doubts and worries and selfish whims to break through the barriers that bound him, but instead they talked it over and the bishop was kind and sympathetic. He reflected that when he'd only been a priest for a dozen years, he'd spent a lot of time praying over his own commitment. "We're not a vague lot," the bishop said. "We wouldn't be here without tremendous passion and a powerful urge to be of service. That alone comes with a price. But what will you do?"

"I'm not concerned about finding a place to be useful," Tim said. "We're surrounded by need. More than I can ever remember. I've been a priest for twenty years."

"Of course I'll pray for you," he said. "You've been a good priest. The Lord will light the way."

His kindness softened the unhappy words of the archbishop. It was not a good priest who screwed with the political plans of an archbishop. His Excellence had wanted Tim to serve as his assistant while he was en route to the hierarchy of Rome. And Tim was not on board with that whole scene. He never had been.

To lighten his mood, to feel more human, he headed for Angela's Pantry in Oakland. His trunk was full of the last of the produce from the vegetable garden at the church. His volunteer board selected the pantry for the third year in a row. It was a charity outpost of free food, open only twice a week in a crummy old warehouse on the north side of the airport. There were a lot of homeless people in the area and further inland there were a lot of run-down neighborhoods. There were also a great many rich and well-tended neighborhoods, not to mention aristocratic homes speckled around the Bay Area. Angela Velasquez had started the food pantry five years before out of a rented storage unit about the size of a two-car garage. She was burglarized several times while she applied herself to writing grant applications and searching for a larger, more secure facility. It wasn't long before her pantry was absorbed by a larger nonprofit that operated a number of facilities from soup kitchens to food pantries in Bay Area neighborhoods. That allowed Angela to move to a safer warehouse, draw a modest salary and retain a number of dependable volunteers.

Angela was young and so beautiful. She must be thirty, but to Tim she looked like a mere girl of twenty. She had been raised mostly in the central valley, the daughter of a migrant farm worker, but had somehow managed an education and citizenship. Her family was large and all were in the States now, most of them married, all of them pursuing education and careers.

He'd seen her frequently over the summer, bringing her fruits and vegetables as frequently as he could. He'd been doing so for years now. Honestly, she stirred something in him. He had not stopped being a man when he took his vows. But it was more than that. She made him buzz with happiness. It was probably no secret—he had a crush on her. But if she knew, she never let on.

"Well, Father, I didn't expect to see you again this year," she said, flashing him that beautiful smile. "That has to be the last of your garden."

"I might have one more visit in me, if the garden holds up," he said. "Most of it is picked clean and I should save the pumpkins for the kids, but there are still a few things hanging on. Some squash, some melons, even some tired-looking peppers and intrepid artichokes. We are one freezing night away from ending the days of the lettuces, but I have a nice laundry basket full for you."

"Great! My friends need the greens in their diets. You didn't by any chance grow any disposable diapers or formula?"

"I scraped together some donations and bought them," he said. "I know how badly they're needed."

"Oh, bless you, Father! There are never enough. I tell the families not to ration them, not to let the little ones get a rash or infection. I have a list of places they can get those items. Let me help you get these things shelved. Let's clear the way. I have a couple of trucks coming in today and we're open for business first thing in the morning."

"I was hoping you had a minute for a conversation," he said.

"Always," she replied, grabbing a box of vegetables from the church van. "Shoot."

"For this, I want your full attention," he said. "I can wait until you're free."

She put the box on the ground. "Let's not wait if you have something on your mind." She focused on his eyes. "It's okay. It will all get done."

It made him smile with true joy. Angela was accustomed to helping people in trouble; people who were needy and hungry and frightened. She was focused. Half the time just having someone being attentive and listening was as much help as people really needed. "I would like to speak in confidence."

She raised her eyebrows in surprise. "Isn't it usually the other way around? A person asking the priest for confidentiality? But of course, Father. I owe you more than that."

"You owe me nothing," he said. "Your work is a godsend and I think you are an angel."

"My father named me for the angels, but I'm sure I've fallen short. What's on your mind?"

"I haven't talked to many people about this. My parishioners don't know yet. I'll be leaving the priesthood after Christmas. Christmas can be a stressful time for people. I won't add to that by leaving them without their priest. Father Damien will assume my position. More and more of my duties are falling to Father Damien and the lay pastors, but there are still those who rely on me. And I know you're incredibly busy this time of year, but I was hoping… I don't know how to put this. You've been in service to the community your entire adult life." He laughed lamely. "I don't even know how old you are, Angela."

"Thirty-four, Father. I never told you, I considered the convent at one time, but that would have been a bad idea. It was a brief consideration. Besides, I was a child. Why, Father? Why leave the priesthood now?"

"It's nothing concrete. It's not a crisis of faith or dissatisfaction with my work or unhappiness about celibacy or loneliness. But as the places I can go become more bureaucratic, I become less so. I have found myself in a selection pool I didn't apply for."

Shock registered on her pretty face. "Well, that's a first," she said. "You're quitting because they're threatening to promote you?"

"The bishop considers it an elevation of status. And I'm not interested. I guess that sounds ridiculous," he admitted.

"Yeah, because I've never met a priest who didn't want to be a cardinal," she said.

"I bet you have, but never mind that," he said. "You've been feeding people for years and I'd like to know how it happened. I'm going to be looking for options pretty soon. There are lots of things I can do to keep the rain off my head. They'll probably let me sweep out the rectory and polish pews until I find a proper job, but I'm interested in meeting some more basic needs. Like you do. If you're willing to talk about it..."

She stepped closer to him, her pretty brow wrinkled, her eyes narrowed. "Talk about what?"

"How you found your calling? How you began your food bank? What other work you've done? What bureaucracy you battle—"

"God isn't going to be mad at you for leaving the priesthood, Father. Are you looking for a way to make it right with God?"

"No. As far as I know, we're good, me and the Boss. It's what makes my heart beat."

"Then I will ask you this, Father. Have you ever been really hungry? So hungry that hunger no longer has a feeling? Have you ever fled your own home in the dark of night? Been chased by police? Run out of your house and slept on the cold ground for days? Had no one to help? Begged for food or clothing? Been afraid you would not live another day? *Dios!* Ach." She stopped and rubbed the back of her neck. "My apology, Padre, I didn't mean to unload on you." Then she continued. "That is how I found my calling—in my anger. I am angry that in a world as plentiful as ours there are hungry children. Isn't it bad enough that there is disease we can't conquer? Isn't it bad enough that no matter how hard we work, there is still poverty?"

He was respectfully silent while she calmed herself. Finally he said, "I'm sorry, Angela. For what you must have endured."

She jolted in surprise. "Oh no, Father—I wasn't talking about me! We did all right. We were immigrants and field workers but we had family. It's the people I've come to know. A large number of them are veterans, alone or some with families. If they have issues and can't hold a job, they get evicted, live in shelters or on the streets or in their cars, if they have a car. And yes, I see quite a few families from south of the border—if they're undocumented, they can't get any government help, like food stamps. For some of them the pantry is essential to their survival.

"When the shelves in this warehouse are full, I sleep so well, even though we can't cure the problem. But there are days I'm so sad. Like the day I sent a woman, a young mother, away with one dented can of cream-style corn. I don't do this because it's good. I do it because I'm driven, not always in a good way."

"I was going to ask you to coffee after the holidays, when

our rush is over, but I think we should meet for a drink instead."

"I would like that. I think we have stories to share. But I'm not going to be here long after the holidays. Mrs. Bennett is going to take over the pantry when I leave. She's run food banks before and she knows this one."

"Where are you going?" he asked, instantly sad.

"I've been accepted by an international rescue charity. I'll be in training for months before I find out where I'm going. I offered to go to Syria but they'll send me to a refugee camp in Greece until I get my sea legs. They can't afford to have an inexperienced volunteer in a dangerous place."

"Let's get one of your volunteers in the warehouse to help us unload and watch for your trucks. Then, let's take an hour. I have to hear about this! Please!"

"Oh Father, what is that strange light in your eyes?"

Without thinking, he reached for her hand and held it briefly. "I'm not sure where I'm going to land but every day I spend in an office is one day too long."

"There's a special job for everyone, Father. In every neighborhood. I know you're needed there…"

"Of course," he said. "I'm proud of the work we've done at Divine Redeemer. People who aren't starving are sometimes hungry in other places. We all have needs. But there are a lot of priests standing in line to get that job. I've been praying for years for an opportunity to go somewhere very few people are willing to go."

She looked at him in shock, her mouth hanging open. "I think you already had that drink…"

He laughed. "How dare you make fun of me! Look what you're planning to do!"

"Yeah, my mother has blisters from working the rosary beads over me. If I'm not in a terrible neighborhood, I'm on a waiting list to go to a war zone…"

"Let's get these boxes inside and see if we can find someone to cover for you for a while. If I don't corner you now, I might miss my opportunity! I'll make it up to you—I'll get the Boy Scouts rounding up nonperishables for your holiday rush!"

"You'd better," she said. "I'm holding you to that promise!"

Lauren handed out Halloween candy for the first time in years. She had decorated her porch. She hung a ghost in the tree out front, carved a large pumpkin and sat a scarecrow in her porch chair. She dressed up like a witch, a friendly witch with a pointed hat, no warts, all of her teeth. She didn't want to scare anyone, especially not the little ones, but she wanted to get into the spirit of things. She lit a few tall orange candles inside and made a big fuss over every costume from spaceman to princess. It was a good time to say hello to the neighbors as they brought the children around.

She tried to remember the last time she handed out candy or the last time her girls went trick-or-treating. Cassie was probably only ten. Brad had shamed her out of it. It's for little children, he would say. And it's a stupid, dangerous undertaking. It made him furious when people brought kids from other neighborhoods to theirs, but Lauren stubbornly bought piles of candy and handed it out generously. Brad was either at the hospital or kept to his home office, refusing to answer the door. By the time the girls were in junior high, he insisted they keep the front of the house darkened, front light off. They never had many children come to the door anyway, tucked away as they were in their wealthy gated neighborhood. Even before there was a guard at the gate, there had been a gate.

But on this night in her new neighborhood, she had a wonderful time, trading stories with young mothers, asking small children about their costumes, handing out fistfuls of candy. She visited with her neighbors and to her satisfaction, no one seemed to look at her strangely or ask her about the night of the police cars and paramedics. It was so social and entertaining, she hated to see it end. But the little ones were scuttled off home where their parents would check their candy and run them around a little bit to burn off the sugar.

After eight there were only a few older kids, but she left her light on. She was going to ride it out to the end. She wasn't sure how she could have done things any differently, but it made her wonder what her life would have been like had she left Brad years ago. There would have been friends, spontaneous and happy times rather than only the perfectly orchestrated events. She would have had such a different life.

The doorbell rang and she plopped the witch hat on her head and opened the door. There stood Beau, grinning, holding onto a bottle of wine by its neck.

"I ran out of candy," he said. "So I came over here. To see what everyone was talking about. I heard the sexiest witch in Alameda was here."

"Clever," she said, but she loved it. "Did you have a lot of kids?"

"Dozens. Darla was at our house and Drew looked thrilled when I said I was going out for a while. Should I open this?"

"Absolutely! There are only a few stragglers left."

"I thought about the pub but I passed it and they're having way too much fun. It's loud."

"It's not loud in here. Nice and quiet." She went to the kitchen for the corkscrew and a couple of glasses. "Did you have fun tonight?"

"Sure." He opened the wine. "I'm not as into Halloween as some people but the boys always have been. I could hardly convince them it was time to stop when they were in high school. Drew answered the door as a pirate tonight. I remember when they went through a stage of the bloodier the better." He handed her a glass. "You do make a spectacular witch. Cheers."

She smiled fondly. "Cheers, my friend," she said, clinking his glass. "Tell me about your week."

"Nothing much of interest. A few new clients that I'm drawing up plans for but we're not going to execute during winter. I'm planning a couple of rooftop gardens and some yards for new construction, but planting will be minimal until March. Then we'll blast through months of being swamped. That's my favorite time of year."

He talked about the catching up he would do, designs he would create, bids he would prepare over the winter. Taxes, there were always taxes to take care of, though he had a trusted accountant. Running a business meant the accumulation of plenty of paperwork.

The doorbell blessedly did not ring. They talked about his work slowing down when the planting season grew less hectic. Her business, on the other hand, grew more hectic as the holidays approached. "Food is a very big business right up to January. I look forward to things slowing down a little bit. But I'm enjoying work so much more than ever before."

"What was the big change?" he asked.

"The change was me, and it was a complete accident. I always felt like I didn't really belong. I felt apart, as though I wasn't like the other women in the food lab. As though I didn't have the same kind of struggles. You know—because I had a cleaning lady and a successful husband. It was an embarrassment of riches. Then I did the most unexpected thing. I stopped protecting myself and told them the truth. That my husband was abusive, that I was separated and filing for divorce. And they swarmed around me with comfort and support that had been there all along. I was the one who held myself apart. We started socializing—lunch now and then, going out for happy hour after work sometimes. I am friends now with people I've known for years.

"In the spring, I'm going to have a garden," she went on. "I'm going to plant flowers and vegetables. Maybe you can give me a few pointers. I've never had anything to say about the yard. I've never had a garden of my own."

"I can help with that."

"At your busiest time?"

"There will always be time for you," he said. He put his wineglass on the coffee table. Then he slid his arm along the back of the sofa and rested it gently on her shoulder, giving her a squeeze. "Come a little closer, Lauren."

She didn't hesitate. She slid toward him just as he leaned toward her. He touched his lips softly to hers.

"We've managed to go very slowly but we're both feeling it. I'm definitely feeling it," he said. "And I think you are, too."

"I thought it would be safer and less complicated if—"

"If all the legal crap was behind us? If that's what you want, I can do that, but there's a good chance our exes are going to drag this out as long as possible. And there is absolutely no possibility I'm ever going to live under the same roof with Pamela again. I'm pretty sure you're finished with the doctor, too. If you're not, all you have to do is tell me..."

"Oh, I'm finished. But I wouldn't want anyone to think..."

"That we had an affair?" He took her glass from her hand and put it beside his on the table. "There's almost nothing we can do to control what people think no matter what we do. But the truth is, I fell for you the minute I saw you. Way back in the church garden, before we knew anything about each other. If you hadn't been so vulnerable, I might've been a little more aggressive. That's not because that's in my nature. It's not. But I wanted to get to know you better right away. I wanted to spend time with you. Then he hurt you and I had to keep a safe distance from you, to protect you. I knew you couldn't deal with your issues plus a rambunctious guy. But no matter what we do or how long we keep a polite distance, people will think what they want to think. Just like your husband did."

"This really wasn't in my plan," she whispered. "I wasn't looking for a man."

"I know. And I was planning to be a lonely old bachelor. And anyone with a brain or anyone who has read an advice column will tell you, don't move very fast because the rebound lover usually doesn't work out. But that hasn't changed how I feel. I want to take you up into the hills to see the fall foliage before it all freezes off and there isn't much time left. And in the spring, I want to take you to see some special gardens. I want to go places and do things…and I also want to walk down to the pub for sliders. On those rainy San Francisco nights, I want to build a fire and stay in."

"What special gardens?" she asked, her lips still close to his.

He rubbed a thumb along her jaw. "There are so many. But we should go to Victoria, British Columbia. The Butchart Gardens for one. The whole town is beautiful and there's always something in bloom. They have a perfect climate."

"Victoria?" she whispered. She would love to go to Victoria with him. "I wasn't hoping to find a man," she said again. "What if this is just infatuation because of what we've both been through…"

"Then I guess we deal with it," he said. "But what if it's *not*? What if it's real? And good? And *right*?"

"I've made so many mistakes," she said, letting her eyelids fall closed.

"Welcome to the club," he said.

Then he covered her lips in a searing kiss. Her arms reached around his neck and his went to her waist, pulling her closer. She moaned softly because she had wanted this for a lot longer than she cared to admit. She returned his kiss, opened her lips for him, held him so close she felt like they'd be bonded together forever. She loved the sound of his sigh as his lips slid to her neck, his hands running up and down her back. Then they shared a deep and open kiss, tongues playing. It lasted for a minute, at least. Then two. She loved his scent and the taste of him. She could detect a manly cologne and something like freshly turned, rich soil...or perhaps she imagined that because he was so comfortable in a garden.

She held him close, letting her fingers wander into the short hair at the base of his neck, kissing him deeply for minutes. And minutes. Their breathing became labored. She broke from his lips and rested her head on his shoulder, holding him tightly, as if he might slip away.

He held her and stroked her hair. "You have no idea how much I wanted to do that," he said.

"Have you been practicing?" she asked in a whisper. "Because you're very good at that."

"You're pretty good yourself. If it matters, I haven't kissed a woman in well over a year. But I sure wanted to kiss you. I want to do it some more, too. But maybe I should go. I don't want you to feel pressured."

"You don't have to go," she said, snuggling closer.

They stayed that way for a little while, silent and comfortable. Finally he kissed her again, almost desperately. God, it felt so good to her to be wanted with this kind of passion. Tender but strong. She yielded completely, finally unafraid of where this might be going.

He broke the kiss. He looked into her eyes. "I should go," he said. "I probably shouldn't get any more worked up. This... us...we could move a little too fast and go off the rails."

"Okay," she said.

"You did say you thought it would be best if we got our legal shit handled before we—"

She nodded. She still thought that would be the smart thing, except she wanted to be less smart right now.

They stood. They hugged. He held her face in his hands and kissed her again. Then he went to the door and she followed. He stopped before opening the door. He paused. Then he turned and grabbed her around the waist, turning her so that her back was pressed against the door. He kissed her again. "I don't want to leave," he whispered against her lips.

"Good," she said. "I don't want you to."

"Even if it's not smart?" he asked.

"It's the smartest thing I can think of at the moment," she said.

"I want to make love to you," he said. "For three days straight."

She laughed softly. "I think we're going to have to start off slower than that. I have to work tomorrow."

"But now?"

"Now is good," she said.

He leaned his head against her shoulder. "I promise. I'll take good care of you," he said, his lips against her neck.

"I know," she said.

He lifted her up into his arms. "Time to undress the witch," he said. And he carried her to her bedroom.

Standing at the side of the bed, they shed their clothes quickly, leaving everything in a heap on the floor. "Condoms," he announced, putting a couple on her bedside table. She didn't stare at him, though she wanted to. What she could see without looking down was his beautiful chest and strong shoulders. He was so fit and strong. She was feeling shy suddenly. It had been a long time since she'd seen a naked man. It had been a long time since she'd been hopeful about sex. Fortunately, he pulled her into his arms so quickly, she didn't have to struggle with her awkwardness. His lips on hers gave her confidence.

He stared at her, however. "Oh God, you're perfect," he said, running his hands down her sides, brushing over her breasts and down her rib cage and over her hips. "This has been so crazy, this friendship," he said. "I've told myself to be careful, to not come on too strong, but every time we said goodbye, I missed you. I thought about you all the time we've been apart." He fell on her gently, holding his weight off her. He kissed her deeply and she could feel the strength of him pushing at the apex of her thighs. "And soft. And so *long*," he added, running his hand as far as he could down her legs.

All her height was in her legs, she knew that. But Beau had quite a huge erection there. The way he was pressing at her and kissing her, she was quickly filled with urgency, but she slowed herself down, taking the time to touch him. She ran her hands down his arms, his back, his hips. She wound her legs around his; she could match him for length. His skin was soft and smooth, his hands a little rough. His hands felt so good on her breasts, on her hips. But his mouth was amazing, kissing her in a way that seemed like they'd been kissing for years.

"You feel so good," she whispered.

"I feel good because I have you in my arms," he said. "I've been dreaming about this for so long..."

"You have just exactly the right weight to your touch," she said. She stroked his face. "You know, you're handsome and sweet. You could have any woman..."

"There's only one I want," he said. "And I want you so damn bad."

"How can this feel so familiar?" she wondered aloud.

"Because it's right," he said.

His hands and lips were on the move. Everywhere he touched filled her with tingling desire and when his fingers inched low to her soft center, she moaned deeply. "Can you reach that condom?" he whispered. "I don't want to lose my place."

"Oh, so you're a lovemaking comedian?" she asked with a soft chuckle.

"Hurry, Lauren," he whispered. "I seriously need it."

He sat back on his heels for a moment, then once ready, he was hovering over her again. He was in the right place, just barely moving into her. "I think we have a nice fit, sweetheart." He lifted her knees, then was kissing her deeply as he entered her.

She held her breath for just a moment, then let her eyes close, holding him tightly. She rocked with him, the fullness of him inside her bringing her both comfort and excitement. Soon she was pushing against him and spontaneously slid one leg over him, pressing him into her.

He muttered softly against her lips as he moved harder and faster. The passion of it took her away and she could hear herself crying out even as she clutched him tighter. And then her world lit up as she enjoyed a completely magnificent orgasm that left her panting. She heard something of a growl come from Beau as he held her tight and enjoyed the spasms. He pushed into her as hard as possible and she gasped.

"God," he whispered.

Then it took him only a few deep thrusts to join her. It showed on his face—his clenched lips and eyes—his pleasure was as complete as hers. They both lay trembling and weak with satisfaction. Neither spoke, but they held each other. Shivering, Beau reached down and pulled the sheet and blanket over them, but he didn't let go of her. He rolled with her to their sides.

He kissed her again and again. "That was incredible," he finally said. "Wasn't that incredible? You're wonderful. Perfect."

She started to laugh. She actually started with a snort and she didn't just chuckle girlishly, she laughed hilariously.

"How is this funny?" he asked, propping himself up on an elbow.

"Oh no… No, I can't bring ghosts of past experiences to our completely new and wonderful…" She laughed more. Then she cleared her throat. "I've been told…" Laughter caught her again. She coughed, cleared her throat and tried again. "I've always been told I should try harder. That I was a disappointment."

Beau was clearly not amused. He didn't join in the laughter. "Sounds like someone else should have been trying harder. You're amazing."

"That was pretty perfect, wasn't it?" she asked. "It felt that way to me. I suspect it was you, though. I was just responding because I couldn't not." She smiled. "And that's perfect, isn't it?"

"Completely. But with a little practice, we'll become slightly better than perfect. And I look forward to that."

"It just kind of happened," she said, snuggling close to him. "I've been thinking about it a lot."

"I've been thinking about it for *months*…"

"I wondered if I would be afraid, if I would be nervous and self-conscious, if it was too reckless. I'm never reckless, you know."

"Was it any of those things?" he asked.

She shook her head. "I felt very natural. Very good. Very right."

"Lauren, don't panic. Just let me show you how important you are to me," he said. "We've only nibbled around the edges of this subject but I know you don't feel free to move on in your love life. I've tried to keep that in mind. God knows, I don't want to scare you off. Coming off a painful marriage, the thought of diving into a new relationship must be terrifying…"

"Is it terrifying for you?" she asked.

He shook his head. "It didn't just occur to me that I could fall in love with you. It's been growing in me. The more we've gotten to know each other, the stronger my feelings are. I've never felt like this before—there is zero doubt in me. We're going to be happy together."

"I have to ask you something," she said, her hand on his cheek. "Was there doubt the last time? With her?"

"There was," he said. "I made excuses for her—she'd been through a lot. She'd been abandoned by the fathers of her sons. She'd been left to struggle. Why should she trust me? I cared about her. I had sympathy for her situation. I worried about the boys—they needed a constant and stable role model. I thought in time when she could see I could be trusted, we'd be all right. I don't regret it, Lauren. I'm not sorry I took them on."

"I know," she said.

"And you? Did you ever have doubts?"

She laughed as if embarrassed. "Yes, I had doubts from the first and almost didn't go through with it. Mrs. Delaney ordered everyone out of our room and then she dressed me down. She was so terrifying. I wanted to run for my life. Instead, I did exactly as she said. I dried my tears, put on fresh eye makeup and married her son. I spent over twenty years being ashamed of my lack of courage."

"You had to be strong to get through those years as well as you did," he said.

"Not the right kind of strong. My boss and new friend, Bea, she threw out an abusive man and raised four children alone, working and going to school with no one to help her—she's the kind of strong I'd rather be."

"I agree, that's admirable."

She smiled tenderly. "Oh Beau, I thought we'd be friends and wondered how I would manage to make you more. You're so damn chivalrous."

He laughed. "Am I?"

"Buying a coffee, waiting in the garden, staying with me after Brad attacked me, coming by the house with soft food… you are the most perfect gentleman. And I love it."

"I just want to be with you," he said. "That's all. I can be patient, I can be discreet, but I'm ready."

She grinned. "I think I'd like to have a boyfriend."

"What will your daughters say?" he asked.

"I'm not sure," she said. "But I will remind them that they've brought a very entertaining variety of boyfriends to my house, some of them truly awful, and I've always been welcoming and courteous."

"You were?" he asked.

"Damn straight," she said. "If I wasn't, they'd have married them before midnight! I might not be good at marriage, but I know how mothering works."

He stroked her back. "I think you know how everything works…"

"I had a lot of doubts with Brad," she said. "With you, I have none."

CHAPTER THIRTEEN

Beau's life changed instantly. In a day. Maybe in an hour. When he told Lauren how deeply he cared for her she responded and the bond was sealed. In her body, he found ecstasy.

Over the next few days, he couldn't be away from her much. He tried to move slowly but it was agonizing. They'd spent months carefully discovering each other and after making love, they found there were more discoveries awaiting them, the kind that forged a new and intimate relationship. One that felt immediately secure and deeply fulfilling. "I was content with my life," he whispered to her. "I wasn't aching for something more, something or someone to make me happier. But you've filled up an empty place inside me that I didn't even know was there. You're everything to me."

"Oh, I definitely wasn't looking for anyone," Lauren said. "I didn't trust myself. I was afraid I wouldn't know the real thing if it knocked me over. But this feels right. Please be careful with my heart, Beau. It's so fragile."

"Your heart is safe with me," he promised. "All of you is safe with me."

They began seeing each other almost daily. Whether it was for lunch or dinner or a drive up the freeway to the foothills where the last of the leaves were turning color, they spent quality time together. Beau cooked for her and Drew, but she wouldn't stay late. Then there would be a knock at her door and he'd wrap his arms around her.

"Oh Beau, what about Drew?"

"It's all right," Beau said. "He's not thinking about what we're doing because he's busy doing it himself."

"That's different," she said. "We're not eighteen."

"Yeah, you know how you can tell? At eighteen they're doing it all the time."

"It kind of feels like we're doing it all the time," she said.

"I haven't hit the saturation point yet," he said. "Have you?"

An emotional hiccup escaped her. "You have to understand, I didn't think I'd ever have this in my life."

Lauren had a long talk with Cassie about Beau. "The very one you thought was so handsome," she said. "He's a lovely man. You'll love him. He's the single father of grown sons, we live in the same neighborhood and I've started seeing him. Given what we've been going through with our spouses, we're taking it slow. But I wanted you to know we're dating. I think this weekend we're driving up to Napa to have a nice lunch and get some wine."

"Oh Mama, that makes me so happy. But promise me you'll be careful. I don't want you to go through another bad relationship experience."

Lauren laughed. "When did you become the mother?"

Two weeks before Thanksgiving, she spoke with Lacey.

"I don't know how you want to spend Thanksgiving. Cassie will come home for Christmas, but not Thanksgiving. It turns out I have a lot of invitations. My boss, Bea, invited me to join her family. Sylvie Emerson wanted to include me in her holiday meal with her family. Beth is having most of the Shaughnessy tribe and of course invited us."

"And Daddy?" she asked.

"I have no idea how he's spending the holiday," she said.

"Aren't the Emersons including him?" Lacey asked.

"No, Lacey. Sylvie is my friend, knows this divorce has been contentious and wouldn't set me up like that. I think the best thing for me is to go to Beth's house. Would you like to come?"

"I want to make sure Daddy's not alone," she said. "I'll let you know."

Poor Daddy, Lauren thought. It probably never occurred to him there might be consequences for kicking his wife in the face.

"Are you ever going to forgive him?" she asked.

"Lacey, he hasn't asked for forgiveness." She took a deep breath. "Just let me know if you want to join me." She decided not to tell Lacey about Beau. The timing just didn't feel right. Lacey was still so bitter about the divorce, still expecting Lauren to endure anything to put it all back together for her.

Another invitation was to Beau's house. If it worked into her schedule for that day, she would stop by his house for dessert. There were people to meet.

Beau's brother lived near Alameda, one of his sisters lived in Redding and the other in San Diego. Their mother had recently moved in with their Redding sister and they rarely got together as a whole group.

Lauren did tell Beth all about Beau. Beth, like Cassie, was delighted and nervous.

"They're afraid I'll get sucked into some terrible relationship, like the last one," she explained to Beau. "It won't do any good to tell them how different this is. Instead, I'm just going to throw you out there and let them have a look. Beth wants to make a big Sunday meal at her house. It's strategic— you can escape if you get uncomfortable, the boys can run off to Xbox if they get restless and you can help with dishes to keep your nervous hands busy."

"I won't be nervous," he said. "From what you've told me about them, I'll like them a lot. And your brother-in-law has a big screen in his man cave. I'll be fine."

"Is this a little quick for us to be meeting the families?" she asked.

He shook his head. "We're not meeting the families to get their approval so we can get married. We're meeting so they know who we're spending our time with. No one has proposed to me. Has someone proposed to you?" he asked, his mouth quirking into a smile.

"We're going to be dating a long time—it's not serious."

But of course it was. Serious. She couldn't imagine another man ever putting his hands on her. And she knew that in Beau's mind it had been serious almost from the beginning.

"How do you define serious?" he asked her.

"Engagement or plans for marriage, which will not even be discussed anytime soon," she answered. "Years, probably."

"Okay, we have different definitions of serious. My definition of serious is that I miss you every second we're apart, can't keep my hands off you, you are my one and only, other women don't even register in my vision and I plan to be with you and only you for a long, long time. As long as you'll have me."

"By your definition, I guess we're serious," she said.

"What about Lacey?" he asked. "When are you going to spring me on Lacey?"

"I've already told Cassidy about you and she's anxious to

meet you again. Given the strained relationship she currently has with her sister, I doubt she'll share the news. As for Lacey, if she pops over unexpectedly while you're at my house or if we run into her while we're out, I'll make an introduction. Otherwise, I plan to wait until the holidays have passed or the divorce is final, whichever comes first. My divorce would be final by now if Brad wasn't trying to make sure I don't get anything. What he doesn't understand is I don't really want anything. I just want to make sure my daughters have some legacy from that marriage. For their education. And for therapy if they need it. I can take care of myself."

He chuckled and said, "I think at the end of the day, we'll take care of each other, babe. We know how."

Lauren saw Beau nearly every day and when they couldn't spend an evening together, they talked on the phone. She felt thirteen. Every time she said, "I missed you all day," her cheeks flamed. Was this absurd? To feel that kind of infatuation so soon? Was it soon? She didn't know the rules. He claimed to have fallen for her instantly and the truth was, she'd fallen for him just as fast. When she showed up in that garden to find the book they had talked about and a couple of coffees, she was doomed. Yes, he was handsome, incredibly sexy, smart and wise, but what registered the most on her poor battered heart was his kindness. His thoughtfulness. He wasn't only kind toward her but everyone. He held doors, asked after people's families, carried heavy parcels to cars for older people, made babies laugh, scratched dogs behind the ears. Polite. Sweet. He had not once walked away from a person and muttered a rude or hateful comment. He was completely considerate.

She loved his goodness.

Her eyes were held wide open by her own memories. Beau could not hide an evil or hateful nature for this long. Thinking back, Brad had not hidden his true nature for even a week.

There had been red flags all over the place, but she had made excuses. Why had she made so many excuses for him?

"Because you were twenty-two," Beau said. "Instead of being mad at yourself for missing the obvious, be proud of yourself for trying so hard to keep your family intact. You really gave it all you had."

"And you did, too," she said.

"I tried," he admitted. "I wasn't hopeful, but I tried. I gave myself a real steep goal—when I had to let go I wanted to be sure I'd done my best."

"We're so alike," she said. "Is that enough for us?"

"I think there's a lot more to us than that, but I have great instincts. I doubt everything but my gut."

"There was Pamela," she reminded him.

"It didn't feel like this," he said. "And there was Brad..."

She gave a short laugh. "*Nothing* like this."

The second week in November, Beth hosted a dinner so they could meet Beau. She chose a Sunday because there would be no photography jobs and she guarded the date. She cleaned like a wild woman and rode Chip and the boys hard. She was going to make her best dish, which happened to be a pretty ordinary slow-cooker lasagna that tasted wonderful. Along with that, fresh spinach salad with red onion, mushrooms and hard-boiled eggs. She'd make jalapeño poppers to start—guys loved those. And Lauren promised to bring a cake for dessert.

It wasn't a complicated meal, but it took Beth two days to get ready. She wasn't sure exactly why. It wasn't so much to impress this new guy Lauren said was wonderful. It was more the anxiety of hoping this wasn't another mistake for her sister. If this was a good guy, she wanted it to work. True, Lauren had only been on her own a few months, but she'd left her marriage and been alone for years. Only Beth knew how truly lonely her sister had been, especially when both her daughters were living away from home.

"No, you're not wearing that," she said when she saw Chip dressed in sweatpants and an oversize Giants T-shirt with grease stains on it.

"You said it would be casual," Chip argued.

"That's not casual," she said. "That's the vagrant look. I put your clothes on the bed."

"Seriously?"

"When your friends and family come to dinner, you can dress yourself," she informed him.

She had also put out clothes for the boys. For once in their lives they didn't grumble or argue because they could tell she was on a tear and life wasn't going to get any easier until this "introduction dinner" was behind them. Beth put a little extra time into her own prep. Although she kept her hair short and easy, for this party she used the blow-dryer and applied makeup. Even eye makeup, which she never wore because looking into the camera made it smear and glop. She put on a sleek black pantsuit, one she reserved for their nights out. On her way to the kitchen she stopped off at the man cave, straightened up, sprayed air freshener all around.

When she went into the kitchen she saw Chip leaning against the counter, drinking a beer. He tilted his head toward the great room. Stefano and Ravon sat side by side, hair combed, faces scrubbed, wearing the clothes she had put out for them. Ravon held on to Morty's collar so he wouldn't run around like a dog. Which he was.

"Look at you," Chip said to Beth. He grinned lasciviously. "Maybe they'll go home early."

"I'm counting on your manners."

"What happens if we just act normal?" Ravon asked.

"I'll make your life hell," she said.

The doorbell rang.

227

"Showtime," Chip said. And Beth whacked him in the arm.

Lauren, Beau and Drew came in. Lauren was carrying her cake. She looked like she always looked, slacks pressed with a crease, boots with a heel, cashmere sweater. "Wow," she said. "Look at the Shaughnessy family. We going to church tonight?"

"Funny," Beth said. "Hi," she said, sticking out her hand to Beau.

"Beau and Drew, meet my sister, Beth, brother-in-law, Chip, nephews Ravon and Stefano. And Morty," she added. Morty was straining at the hold Ravon had on his collar. He desperately wanted to jump on the company.

There was hand shaking, smiling, welcoming.

"Nice place," Beau said.

"Great yard," Drew said, stretching his neck to look through the patio door. "Is that a basketball hoop out there?"

The boys nodded. "We're not allowed to have fun tonight," Stefano said. "Or she'll make us pay."

Drew loved it. "Not if I talk you into it. Show me the back. Come on. And let go of the dog before he passes out."

Chip put a hand on Beau's shoulder. "Let's get you a drink."

"I'll take one of those," he said with a nod toward Chip's beer.

"Thank God you got here before she made us paint and reupholster," Chip said.

The table was set, the lasagna was ready and staying warm, the poppers were ready to go in the oven. Chip took Beau outside with the boys and lit the fire pit. The men were going to bond.

"Beth, you went to a lot of trouble," Lauren said.

"I did," she admitted. "If we don't love each other after tonight it won't be my fault. Want wine?"

"Absolutely," Lauren said. "And relax—everyone loves Beau and Beau loves everyone. As far as I can tell, Drew is just like him. Michael declined. He's still struggling with the divorce. I haven't even met him yet."

"Does that worry you?" Beth asked.

"No. I have a pissy one of my own. We decided we don't much care. It'll all fall into place eventually."

"Pissy kids could make it harder," Beth said.

"What can you do?" Lauren asked. "Stay in a bad situation till they finally give you permission to have a life?"

"God," Beth said, handing her a glass of wine. "You're so calm."

"Amazing how you feel when you're spending time with a calm, rational person. Cheers," she said, lifting a glass to her sister. "And thank you for this. It's all beautiful."

"My pleasure. As soon as we get to know each other a little, we're going back to our slovenly ways."

The dinner at Beth's house was a roaring success. Chip, Beau, Drew and the boys bonded, laughed, clearly liked each other. Drew threw baskets with them, putted with them on the backyard putting green, laughed like idiots when Morty got in the pool and then shook, leaving everyone's pants speckled with water. They joked and talked through dinner. "We sure never had this much fun with the last guy," Stefano said.

"Stefano!" Beth shouted, going completely pale.

"It's okay, Beth," Beau said. "We all know there was a last guy."

A week later, Beau talked Michael into meeting them for dinner at the pub. He wanted him to meet Lauren. Michael was a little quiet and standoffish at first, but Lauren plied him with questions about school and future plans, and before long Michael was almost as personable as Drew. She thought *al-*

most because it was hard to top Drew for personality. That kid was just magic.

At least Michael did not seem angry or resentful and that was all she hoped for.

The weekend before Thanksgiving, there was another poker night and this time Michael and his girlfriend, Raisa, joined them, along with Darla and Drew and Father Tim.

"Your favorite third wheel is here," Father Tim said.

"We don't think of you that way," Lauren said. "You're our favorite, however."

They had fun, Lauren got along wonderfully with Raisa, Michael opened up even more and it looked as though the holidays might not be as stressful as she feared.

Cassie had confirmed she would not be back in California for Thanksgiving but would be home for ten days at Christmas. Lacey agreed to spend the early part of Thanksgiving with Lauren and Beth, the later part with her father. Brad would be having Thanksgiving dinner at a restaurant with his mother.

Lauren, Beth and Beau did a little working behind the scenes to arrange a workable schedule. Beth would host the Shaughnessy clan for an early dinner served at about four o'clock, a dinner that would go on and on and on, ending with at least two desserts and one session of leftover grazing. "The Shaughnessys are like locusts," Beth said. "They eat forever."

Beau would serve a later dinner at around six. That way Lauren could drop by on her way home from Beth's and have dessert with them, a dessert she would supply. She could meet his brother, sisters, their spouses, his nieces and nephews, his sainted mother. In fact, she was supplying three pies, which she would bring over in the morning.

Beau's boys reported that Pamela was taking a holiday, spending Thanksgiving in Cabo with some friends. "If I'm reading them right, Drew and Michael are relieved," Beau said. "Pamela has little family, they're not close and they tend to get into squabbles. Holiday dinners with some of them is a game of Russian roulette. But I pointed out to the boys that from now on, if they have a woman or wife in their lives, they'll be working out and sharing a holiday schedule so no one feels left out. It won't be about their parents so much as their partners. I could see on their faces they liked that idea better than trying to work things out between their divorced parents."

"No doubt," Lauren said. "Poor Lacey is going to a restaurant with her stuffy father and stuffier grandmother."

"It'll probably be delicious," he said.

"And lonely." Because Lacey was the one who didn't want anything to change even if what had been was pretty bad.

It all went off as if perfectly choreographed. Lacey joined the Shaughnessys and visited a little with Beth's in-laws. She had a glass of wine and some hors d'oeuvres before going off to the city to meet her father and grandmother. No one in the Shaughnessy household had breathed a word about Lauren's plans for after dinner and when Lacey left Beth nearly collapsed in relief.

"Were you worried?" Lauren asked. "It was fine."

"I threatened to cut their tongues out if Stefano or Ravon spilled the beans. I hope you're going to tell Lacey pretty soon, let her have her tantrum and we can all move on!"

"I'm sorry, Beth. I don't mean to make it so hard for you."

"Hard? This is the most promising holiday we've had in a very long time! It's nerve-racking, trying to keep things from exploding, but I'm so relieved you're finally doing this. It was so painful to think of my big sister as a victim of that asshole."

"I wasn't a victim, honey," she said. "I'm starting to realize I was an accomplice. I should have done this so long ago. It's time for Act II—Beau's house for dessert and coffee and meeting the family."

"They will love you."

There were a lot of cars parked along the street, a lot of lights showing from inside the houses as though big families were gathered in almost every one, leaving only a few houses dark. She had to park a block away, which she didn't mind—it gave her time to settle her nerves.

Beau answered the door, his smile big, drawing her into a hug. "How was Beth's?" he asked.

"Lovely. Lacey escaped before anyone dropped it that I have a boyfriend, but I'm not going to make it past Christmas. I thought I was the only one afraid of her temper. It turns out everyone is!"

"Well, come in here where everyone is dying to meet you. My mother and sister are cutting your pies."

"I hope they're good," she said.

"Don't be nervous," he said, squeezing her hand. "The boys have been telling everyone how sweet you are."

She stopped walking. "Even Michael?" she asked.

"Even Michael," he assured her. "Come on."

Once inside she found the place swarming with people. She was introduced first to Beau's mother, Christine, a sturdy white-haired lady with a bright smile who grabbed both of her hands and exclaimed it was so nice to meet her. Beau's brother Jeff introduced his wife and one of his two grown sons and a daughter-in-law, Beau's sister Jeanette, her husband, two kids and one of them had brought a friend. Beau's sister from San Diego couldn't make the dinner. Beau's boys both said hello, then Drew, apparently after thinking about it, gave her a hug. Michael had brought his girlfriend, Raisa, but Drew said he was headed to Darla's house a little later. There was a lot of chatter as they asked her about her daughters, oohed and ahhed over their impressive pursuits and asked Lauren all about her job.

"I work in product development for Merriweather Foods. Sometimes I make cooking videos."

"I think I could do that," Beau's mother said.

The women talked jobs and kids and Lauren wanted to know all about Christine's garden when the kids were growing up. The men wandered off but Beau was never too far away. They joked about growing up in a too-small house and told stories about Beau that had everyone laughing. And before Lauren knew it, over two hours had passed. The words *divorce* or *ex-spouses* never came up. And she was exhausted. The stressful anticipation of wondering how she would be accepted, wondering if anyone would challenge her as the other woman, of worrying that Lacey would suspect something while they were at Beth's house, a full day of people and food, left her tired and anxious to pull the shade on this day. Then she noticed Beau's mother stifling a yawn and knew it was time.

"Are you sure?" he asked. "Another piece of pie? Coffee? Wine?"

"You've got to be kidding me." She laughed. "I've eaten so much today, I'll be lucky if I can roll over in bed!"

It took as long to say her goodbyes as it had to make the introductions and it was after nine by the time she was walking out the door. Beau insisted on walking her to her car. They were barely ten feet down the drive when he pulled her to a stop, put his hands on her cheeks and kissed her in a way that made her wish they could be alone for a few hours. "Thank you for being so wonderful to my family," he said.

"They're wonderful people, Beau. They were very nice to me. They didn't ask a single embarrassing question."

"They're good that way," he said. Then he kissed her again. "After everyone has left and Drew has gone to Darla's, I'm coming over."

"You don't have to do that..."

He laughed wickedly. "Tell me you don't want me to come..."

She laughed right back at him. "I want you to come and never leave..."

"Soon, baby," he said, kissing her again.

"So, this is how it is," a woman said. Beau jumped.

He turned. "Pam, what are you doing here?"

"I changed my plans, so I thought I'd swing by and say hello to the family." She shook her head. "So this is why you won't give us another try. You were cheating. I knew it all along."

Lauren couldn't help but notice how beautiful she was. She also couldn't help but notice that large tears had formed in the dark, lacquered eyes.

"I never cheated on you, but all that's irrelevant now. You have to leave. I don't want you to upset my mother. Or anyone else."

"I love you so much," Pam said, the tears flowing. "I told you I'd do anything to make it right! But you just had to get yourself a side piece!"

"Stop that! Don't be vulgar! We're not going to have it out on Thanksgiving in the driveway with the boys and my family inside!"

"I did everything I could," she whimpered.

"Beau, I have to leave," Lauren said. "This isn't for me to see..."

"Beau, please, send her away. Please talk to me," Pam said.

"Jesus Christ, Pam, no more drama! There's nothing more to talk about! I'm done!"

"Send her away and talk to me, please..."

"Beau, talk to her," Lauren said. "I'm getting out of here."

Lauren took off at a brisk semi-jog, heading down the block to her car.

"Shit," she heard him say behind her. "Pamela, don't you

dare go near that front door. Stay right here!" He ran up behind Lauren. "Lauren, you go home and I'll call before I—"

The door to the house slammed. "Oh God! Just shoot me
now!" He turned and jogged back to the house.

Lauren sped home. She put her car in the drive, let herself
in the house, locked the door and cried. For about a hundred reasons.

Is that what his wife thought? That they hooked up before he was free. Did he tell her the truth? About the many
separations, that she'd left him six months before they met?
Was she there to get his sons and family to put pressure on
him to save his marriage? Is this how it would be, ex-spouses
constantly drumming up trouble? Would people think they'd
strayed on their spouses and that's what caused their divorces?
Would she turn the boys against her?

The day had been so perfect, so positive. And was coming
to a close with a very nasty twist.

Pamela was already in the living room, putting on a real
show, by the time Beau got back in the house. It was like the-
ater in the round—the boys, his family, his mother, all sitting
around or standing, speechless while Pamela sobbed that she
would do anything to save her marriage, that she didn't know
Beau was cheating on her, she never suspected, that even her
sons had betrayed and turned against her, that she wanted to
come home, live in her house again, be the wife and mother...

Beau looked around the room. His mother was twisting her
hands and had a pained expression on her face, Michael's eyes
were pinched and he also looked as if he might be in pain. But
everyone else looked disgusted and bored. Of course. They'd
seen her in action before. Many times. They'd been to Beau's
house during those times Pamela was on sabbatical and witnessed for themselves that the closets were stripped bare of
her things. His mother had no idea what was happening on

Facebook but the boys and his siblings did. They all saw pictures of her dancing, sunning herself on sandy beaches, doing shots, grinning over the tops of martini glasses, relaxing and enjoying life. The party girl.

"Pamela, you have to leave now," Beau said. "Boys, would one of you see that your mother gets safely to her car?"

"All I want is a little of your time! We've been together for so long! Are you going to throw it all away for your cheap side chick?"

"Mom!" Michael said, rising to his feet. He threw a forlorn look at Beau's mother, his step-grandma. Oh God, they had to be as embarrassed by her volatile behavior as he was.

"Come on, Mike," Drew said. "Let's get her to her car."

One of them on each side, her sons escorted her out the front door.

Beau was left to look at most of his family. He faced a room of such oppressive silence, his ears rang. He met each pair of eyes. His mother was shaken, his brother's pregnant daughter-in-law looked horrified, his sister Jeanette looked like she was contemplating murder.

"Well," his mother said. "Lauren seems very nice. Shall we be sure this time?" she asked.

The room was filled with laughter.

CHAPTER FOURTEEN

Father Tim spent Thanksgiving evening serving dinner at the mission in downtown Oakland. He usually presided over mass on this holiday. Instead he was with Angela and her friends. They had nearly finished cleaning up the kitchen, saving some meals in the warmer for latecomers, but the rush was over.

He'd been talking to Angela a great deal since he'd brought her his last crop before Thanksgiving. He wanted to tell her what he was doing, that he was re-entering the secular life. That led to other discussions, including how he felt about her. And to his thrilled surprise, she returned his feelings. She admitted to being fond of him. He had spent every spare minute with her since.

"How was it to miss mass?" she asked him, wiping her hands on a towel.

"I'm sure Father Damien did fine."

"Are you going to call him and check?" she asked.

He shook his head. "He'll call me if there's anything to report."

"So, you're still determined, are you?"

He nodded. "I've been sure for at least a year. I'll be explaining my departure to the board right after Christmas. They won't be surprised that I'm leaving—just the reason why. They've been expecting me to move to the diocese to work for the bishop. But I'll be around until I find my next job. There will be parishioners with questions. Maybe concerns."

"What will you tell them?" she asked.

"The same thing I told you. I'm not leaving God's work or the faith or the church. I'm resigning from the priesthood, that's all. And I was wondering if you had a date for New Year's Eve?"

"Father!"

"Stop calling me that," he said, laughing. "Am I too old for you?"

She blushed.

"To see you blush is quite a beautiful sight," he said. He reached for her hand. "I don't mean to put you on the spot."

"It's not that. It's just that... You haven't dated anyone in over twenty years. I don't think I want to be your experiment. You'll end up breaking my heart. You know how much I like you."

He looked around, then he kissed her forehead. "I bet if there's any heartbreaking going on, you'll be doing it."

"You're not quite free..."

"Yes, I am," he said. "I stopped celebrating mass, communion or hearing confession a while ago. I can still assist Father Damien if he needs me but he doesn't need me." He chuckled. "It's all he can do to keep from grinning like a fool. His secret is he's happy to have me out of his way."

"Aren't you close?" she asked.

"I like him," Tim said. "He's a good man. We're driven by different things." He held her coat for her to slip into. "It's cold and wet. Let's go find a quiet bar with a fireplace. I want to tell you about my applications."

Her face lit up. "You did it? You applied for the international rescue mission?"

"Yes, I'm going to follow you around the globe. And I heard about some other groups I think we should look into. I'd love to talk about it. I'll buy you a cup of coffee or glass of wine."

"On Thanksgiving? Where?"

"I know a place close by, on the island. Just a little pub."

"Listen, don't take this the wrong way. I don't think I want to be seen dating a priest…"

He laughed. "I'll only hold your hand under the table."

"I should never have told you I was attracted to you! You started it. Coming clean with me about your silly crush on me. Now look what we've got! I'm not exactly a virgin."

"Me neither," he said.

She gasped. "Father!"

He rolled his eyes. "Could you call me Tim, please? You inspire guilt where there is none. There were quite a few years before I took the vows, Angela. I admit, I examined my secular options."

She laughed in spite of herself. "This is going to be a disaster," she said.

"Just follow me to the bar. It's very nice and I'll protect you from all the sad people who have no place else to go. We can talk about this disaster in peace."

She agreed and twenty minutes later they were tucked into a corner booth near a brick fireplace. Angela sipped red wine while Tim enjoyed a beer.

"What makes you think we have anything in common?" she asked him.

"We have everything in common. We're drawn to the same kind of work, we share a need to rescue the disenfranchised, we're the same faith, we're looking for the same things and you turn me on."

"Oh God," she said, resting her head in her hand. "It is so hard to hear that from someone I have known as a priest."

"Get this—you turned me on while I was a priest. I just wouldn't act on that feeling. I had an oath. Now I don't."

"You hung up the collar for sex, didn't you?"

"No," he said with a laugh. "But that is likely to be a benefit."

"Well, it's not going to be me! Not until I know you a lot better!"

He touched her hand. "I'm not going to pressure you, Angela. I like you. I can't wait to spend more time with you. If it works, I think that would make me very happy. But if it doesn't, I'm still grateful you're my friend. And grateful you showed me some options for my civilian life. There are Catholic charities all over the globe!"

"You're really jazzed about this, aren't you?"

"It's what I've always wanted. To be a working priest. With the smell of the sheep."

"Why?" she asked.

"Same reason you do what you do. It's necessary. It's vitally important. It's not for everyone, which makes it more important that those who can, do. It feels right."

"This is insane," she said. "I've known you for years. We've never even flirted! And believe me, I've known women who flirt with priests."

He laughed. "So have I. Listen, it wasn't always easy. At least some of my vows weren't easy, but that's what made them important and worthwhile. But having certain oaths didn't mean I didn't have feelings."

"You were always friendly, happy, but not flirty."

"Of course not," he said. "That would put you in a terrible position. It's different now. But Angela, I don't want you to struggle with your conscience over me. I want you to be at peace."

She just gazed at him, shaking her head slightly, smiling. "It's going to be very hard not to fall for you."

He was quiet a moment. "Praise be," he said.

Beau texted Lauren that he was on his way over. When she opened her door, she had a tissue in her hand and her eyes were pink and wet.

"Oh honey," he said, pulling her into his embrace. "Have you been crying for the last two hours?" he asked.

She nodded against his chest, sniffing.

He pulled her into the room and sat with her on her sofa. "I'm so, so sorry."

"What happened after I left?" she asked, a hiccup in her voice. "I saw she went inside."

"Hardly anything," he said. "Most of my family has seen her drama before. I felt sorry for the boys, though. They are the ones who've seen the most. I asked them to escort her out, get her in her car safely. It took just five minutes and they were back inside. I don't know if they were brokenhearted or embarrassed. Probably both. But they had places to go where they'll get comfort without the shame of it all. Darla spent the day with her family so Drew went over there. Michael and Raisa went to her married sister's house. Both of them will be among friends. After just a little while and a lot of goodbyes, everyone dispersed. My sister, brother-in-law, kids and my mother were all staying over at my brother's house. They'll head back to Redding first thing in the morning. Of course I welcomed them to stay at my house but Jeff's is larger. And frankly, I think Pamela might be the reason they didn't want to stay at my house."

"Were they all upset?" she asked.

He lifted her chin so he could look into those beautiful lavender eyes. "Listen, last Thanksgiving Pamela was gone. She'd been gone. Gone for the holidays. While other people with troubled marriages are trying to hold it together through the holidays, my wife packed up and headed for Maui. She didn't call Drew and I assume she didn't call Michael. We went to San Diego. Yes, I made sure Pamela knew where we'd be so she could call her sons, but she didn't." He took a breath. "My family has been shaking their heads for years... For the most part everyone in my family has had decent marriages. Happy marriages. I'm the only one who never figured it out."

"My sister and Chip are happy," she said with a sniff. "But my poor mom... My dad just disappeared, leaving her to handle it all..."

"My parents were always happy as far as I remember. Lauren, I can't tell you the recipe. But I didn't give up early."

"She was so heartbroken," Lauren said. "I would never do that to anyone. I would never get in another woman's territory."

"You didn't," he said. He touched her cheek. "What's really wrong?" he asked.

"What if I'm wrong?" she said. "What if we're both wrong?"

"Wrong?" he asked, frowning. "Are you afraid I'm lying to you?"

"My husband lied about everything," she said. "And your wife was so *shattered*!"

"Lauren, you knew he was lying," Beau said. "You'll know if I'm lying. You have time, Lauren. You have time to learn me, I have time to learn you. No one's going to get backed into a corner."

"I would never want to hurt anyone," she said.

"Of course you wouldn't," he said. "And you didn't hurt

Pamela. She's been making bad choices for so long. Trying to come back to our marriage would just be one more."

"She won't ever let you go," she said.

"The doctor might not let you go, either. We might be stuck with them for a long time. So, let's do this. I've already let Pamela go. You do what you have to do."

"Oh God," she said, leaning against him. "She's so beautiful."

Beau held her. "She was actually prettier when I met her," he said. "She's changed a lot in her appearance. She's enhanced some body parts, reduced others. She's very pretty, but the girl I knew was less perfect and much more real. Pam has always had an issue with wanting more. She's never been happy with what she has."

"You said you had no regrets," she reminded him.

"None," he said. "It wasn't always easy but it was worth it. I can honestly say the boys grew up in the best home I could provide. Not a flawless home. But we did all right." He looked into her eyes. "I never left them."

"I got a little worked up," she said. "I'd just met your family and this poor, shattered woman..."

"It's okay. It's better than okay. You have questions and you should have them. You'd be crazy to get yourself in another abusive situation. So would I. But it's going to be all right because we have lots of time to figure each other out. We're not in a hurry because our clocks are ticking, are we?"

"Funny," she said with a huff of laughter.

He wrapped his arms around her. "I figured this holiday period could be a little sketchy. Unpredictable. And we haven't even heard from the doctor yet. He could weigh in at any time. You still have that bat handy, right?"

She shuddered.

"I'm willing to just soldier on, take it one day at a time, get to the other side of all this bullshit. I don't want a lot, Lauren. I just want to enjoy life with someone who cares about me while I enjoy caring about her. Nothing fancy or complicated. Some balance and a little compromise." He kissed her cheek. "Everything is going to be okay. I hope."

She sighed. "I'm kind of glad in a perverse way that your ex-wife showed up and went a little crazy. Brad must be hopping mad by now. Thanksgiving dinner in a restaurant with his mean old mother. I'm surprised he didn't burn my house down."

Beau was quiet for a moment. "You don't smell smoke, do you?"

"All the years I contemplated this—divorcing him and getting on with my life—I never pictured it would be like this. I never thought he'd hurt me so badly. I never thought I'd fall for a man running from a crazy wife. Can we last through all this?"

"I know I'm doing the right thing and I believe in you," he said. "I'm not going to lie to you about anything. If you lie to yourself, I can't help you with that. If it doesn't feel right, you have to make the move."

"And will you? If it's not perfect for you, will you tell me?" she asked.

"Absolutely. I'm not going to trick you. There would be nothing in that for me."

"No one's waiting up for you?" she asked.

"No. They all ran for the hills after Pamela. They were probably afraid she'd come back."

"Will you come to bed and hold me?" she asked.

"Just waiting for the invitation," he said.

In the small hours of the morning, she snuggled against him. She felt secure. Secure and satisfied and peaceful. She lifted her head from his shoulder and kissed his chin. "I love you," she whispered. "I love you and I want to be with you forever."

He tenderly kissed her mouth. "Me, too. Me, too."

The week following Thanksgiving everything seemed a bit calmer to Lauren. She took Lacey out for a nice dinner and some shopping and heard all about Thanksgiving, secretly a little gleeful that Lacey had had a perfectly miserable time with Adele and Brad. Unsurprisingly, he was in a foul mood, stuck with his mother, spoiled daughter, with no whipping post on hand.

It never occurred to her last June that six months after moving out, she still wouldn't be divorced, wouldn't have any property from her old house. Therefore, there were no Christmas decorations. But Lauren knew how to make centerpieces and wreaths and bought herself a few flameless LED candles that lit and went off on a timer. Red and white candles. She stopped by the craft store to get florist supplies and ribbon. She knew where to get greenery scraps at a great price by driving north to the warehouses that supplied flower shops. She offered to make a wreath or centerpiece for Beau if he'd come along.

It was just the perfect distraction for Beau, loving gardens and flowers as he did.

They filled the back of his truck with varieties of fir, pine, juniper, eucalyptus, cedar, holly and other holiday greens and pinecones. Lauren put a sheet over her dining table, got out the florist's clippers she'd bought and got busy creating wreaths and centerpieces.

Beau brought in all her cuttings and hung around to watch. He was so intrigued by her creations that she showed him how she was doing it. "Can I try?" he asked.

He was irresistible. "Sure. Let me show you. The centerpiece is easier, we'll start with that."

By five they had made ten centerpieces and several wreaths. Their fingers were sappy and sticky. Beau looked at his watch.

"Got an appointment?" she asked.

"I'm hungry," he said. "How's your beer and wine supply?"

"All set, but that's not food."

He went to the sink and started washing his hands. "I'll go get us something, unless you feel like going out."

"I want to use up all these greens while they're fresh," she said. "I'd eat anything you feel like eating."

There was a tapping at the door and when she opened it, there stood her boss, Bea.

"I'm sorry. I should have called. This was impetuous. It's about work..."

"Come in," Lauren said. "We were just making Christmas decorations. Bea, this is my friend Beau and Beau, Bea is my supervisor at Merriweather."

Beau put out a hand and nodded. "Pleased to meet you, Bea," he said.

"I think I'm interrupting..."

"Not at all. Beau is ready to quit for dinner. Let me wash my hands and let's have a glass of wine," Lauren said. "You've never been to my house. Well, my rental. But I'm kind of proud of it—my first house of my own."

"I don't want to take up too much of your time and I can see..."

"I'm on my way out to get us something for dinner," Beau said. "Will you join us?"

"No, but thank you. I just need a few minutes."

Lauren was washing her hands vigorously. "This must be something important. This is the first time you've ever called on me on a weekend to discuss company business. I've been there over a dozen years..."

Bea was looking at the greenery lined up on the countertops—centerpieces of all sizes, a few wreaths leaning against the cupboards. "These are beautiful. You're such a talent."

Beau dried his hands and came to Lauren's side, kissing her on the cheek. "I'll bring you something you like. I'll take my time."

"Thank you," she said. As Beau left, Lauren continued chatting with Bea. "Since I still don't have access to anything in my house, I have no Christmas decorations. So I set about creating some from scraps. My daughter and her boyfriend are coming for the holidays and I'd like it to be—"

"Lauren, I'd like you to know I'm going against direct instructions and against policy in coming to your home, but this is important. And it's not good news."

"What's wrong? What in the world…"

"I've been informed that you will be terminated next Friday."

Lauren let a short, confused huff of laughter escape. "The Friday before the holidays? Why?"

"Human Resources will handle that and I can't wait to hear what they come up with since every ounce of documentation from me shows exemplary performance. Here's what little I know—the decision came from very high in the company and they've decided to eliminate your position for budget reasons. Someone, somewhere has decided it won't take a director to run your department but they are not offering you a chance to stay on as a supervisor. And they don't have another director's position open for you." She shook her head. "It's insane. Can you think of anything? Any reason? Any connection?"

Lauren was stunned and shook her head. She had to lean on the counter in the kitchen and take a few deep breaths. Then she went to the living room couch and sat down. "Why?" she asked.

Bea just shrugged. "I smell a rat," she said.

"Does someone at the company have a grudge?" Lauren asked. "Do I have an enemy somewhere I don't know about?"

"Not in our department," Bea said. "I may not be the most powerful senior director on record but I raised four children. I have a sharp eye and good instincts. Lauren, could your husband have anything to do with this?"

"I don't see how," she said. "He's not even friendly with my coworkers. No one in our department is important enough to do him any good."

"But is this something he would do if he could? Cost you your job?"

"I don't know. I don't see how." She blinked a few times. "What should I do?"

"Well, I'll do what I can, but I don't have much influence. Right now, before it actually comes to pass, I have zero power and could lose my job just for defying direct instructions not to tell you. So for now, we're both going to have to be clandestine as all hell and keep a good poker face. I don't know who knows. I got my instructions from the VP of marketing. He doesn't know any particulars. I argued this was insane, that of everyone in product development you were probably the least likely to be terminated. You're going to have to be so stoic this week."

"Maybe I should call in sick..."

"Take a couple of short days if you want to—no one would notice. Everyone is sneaking out to see their kids' holiday activities from classroom parties to Christmas concerts. You should contact a lawyer and think, Lauren. Think if you can connect the dots. Somebody has a personal vendetta. I might be crazy but I don't know anyone in our division with that kind of influence. When it happens, you should be ready to fight it."

"Just what I need," she said. "Another lawyer."

"When I think of someone losing her job right before Christmas, I think this is personal and vengeful. Don't you?"

"If I worked in the medical field, he could probably easily sabotage my employment. But the food industry? It's not like he socializes with— Okay, this is crazy. Didn't Sylvie Emerson sit on our board of directors about five or six years ago?"

Bea was shaking her head. "Lauren, I haven't kept track of board members. I'm not high enough in the food chain to pay attention. What would that have to do with anything?"

"Brad thinks of himself as a friend to Andy Emerson. But I honestly can't imagine either Andy or Sylvie..." She shook her head. "That just doesn't come together in my head. They're good people. When I told Sylvie about the divorce, she was very frank. Brad never fooled her. She isn't fond of him. She wouldn't do him a favor. Especially a favor like this."

"Maybe you should talk to her," Bea said. "Just keep your source out of it for now."

"I can do that. Now that I'm separated, Sylvie and I see each other regularly." She stood. "I think we'd better have that wine."

"I don't know," Bea said. "I should get out of here before that young man brings you dinner."

"Don't leave on account of Beau," Lauren said. "I've known him quite a while but we started seeing each other recently. He's nothing like Brad. Let's have a glass of wine and see if the grape brings any ideas to the surface."

"Just a small one," Bea said. "I've been racking my brain..."

"I'm not going to let Merriweather toss me on the trash heap," Lauren said. "I've never had a bad report or been disciplined in over a dozen years. I've been a loyal and trustworthy employee."

"I vouch for that," Bea said, sitting up on one of the stools at the breakfast bar. "I'm sorry this is happening, Lauren. Divorce can get so ugly."

"I'm learning that."

When Bea was leaving about forty minutes later, Lauren handed her a centerpiece. "Merry Christmas," she said. "I had intended to bring you one this week."

"Thank you," she said. "I'll treasure it. I'm devastated. After all these years of knowing each other, our friendship came so recently. I can't bear this."

"No matter what happens this week, we will stay friends. And now you know how to find my house."

Going to work every day was a terrible strain, but Lauren managed to keep from letting on that she knew. If she had not had Beau to talk to, to sleep with, it would have been so much harder. On Thursday afternoon she left early and went by a local flower shop and bought their greenery scraps for a pittance. She made a long thin centerpiece that would fit on Sylvie's dining table. She texted her, not knowing what Sylvie's holiday schedule might be, and said that she thought she might have Friday afternoon free and wondered if she could stop by.

Sylvie Emerson returned the text and asked Lauren to please stop by.

And right on schedule, as promised, the head of Human Resources came to her office with a couple of assistants and explained that for budget considerations, Lauren's position was being terminated. When Lauren asked, she was told no severance package was being offered, but she was entitled to unemployment insurance.

"You're terminating me, without cause, and offering no severance or benefit package?" she asked.

"I'm very sorry," the HR director said. "I'm just following instructions. If you plan to appeal, here are the steps you should consider taking." And with an obvious nervous tremor, she handed Lauren a sheet of paper.

Lauren looked at the page with a list of suggestions, then looked at the director. Termination, no severance, no exit package, no benefits. This was somehow related to her divorce, it had to be.

"I'll certainly take this into consideration. Thank you. Can you get me a cart to help me get my belongings to the car?"

"Absolutely," the director said, relieved. "And my assistants will help you."

Lauren sat in the parking lot of Merriweather Foods and called Beau. "It happened," she said. "It really happened. No severance, no nothing. I was expecting it and yet I'm still stunned."

"We'll figure it out," he said. "I've been researching and looking for good attorneys. Are you going home now?"

"No. I'm going to Sylvie's house to give her a centerpiece. I was planning to do this anyway and now I'm going to ask her advice. She must know Merriweather, she once sat on their board of directors. Will I see you later?"

"Of course. Would you like to go out? Stay in?"

"I don't know," she said. "I'd like to cry but for some reason I can't. Let me call you after talking to my friend."

When Sylvie answered the door the first thing she said was, "Oh, how perfectly amazing!" referring to the greenery. When she heard what had happened to Lauren she said, "That's just impossible! That was not how Merriweather treated employees! If it was, I would never have served on their board!" And finally she said, "Something is very wrong and I'm going to help you get to the bottom of this."

CHAPTER FIFTEEN

Christmas would be a negotiation from now on and Lauren accepted this. That's how it is after divorce and with grown children who have coupled up.

Cassie and Jeremy flew in from Boston on Saturday; Christmas Eve was Monday. They came directly to Lauren's house, moved their bags into the guest room and had a snack before going to Menlo Park where Jeremy's family lived. "Do you have plans for tonight?" Cassie asked.

"I'm at your disposal," Lauren said. "At some point we should talk about Christmas Eve and Christmas Day and where you'd like to spend them. We have a flood of invitations but I know you guys have to make plans with Jeremy's family. But can I just tell you how thrilled I am that you'll stay here? Thank you. I know that in the future I'll share you with Jeremy's family."

"That's probably true," Cassie said. "But right now, when

you haven't been on your own for long and have gone through so much drama, we want to be here to support you."

They indeed had piles of invitations. Beth wanted them all to come to her house on Christmas Day. Beau was hosting dinner on Christmas Eve and he'd told Lauren to please invite her daughters and Beth's family. His boys, maybe their girlfriends and Tim would join them for ham and scalloped potatoes. Then Tim was going to attend midnight mass and anyone who wanted to go along was welcome. Although Lauren hadn't asked yet, she wondered if Cassie and Lacey had invitations from their father; she didn't know if Beau's boys had invitations from their mother.

"Can we have dinner together tonight?" Cassie asked. "Can you invite your new friend, Beau?"

"He's already on standby and I've included his sons and their girlfriends. I've already made a very large chicken parm and am ready to throw a spinach salad and baguette at that. I haven't figured out dessert."

"What about Lacey?" Cassie asked. "Will you invite her?"

"I'm going to leave that with you," Lauren said. "I haven't talked to her about Beau and she hasn't met him yet. If you decide you want to include Lacey tonight, please tell her she'll be meeting my... Oh dear God, what should he be called? A gentleman friend?"

Cassie laughed. "You should relax. He's the man you've been seeing the last couple of months. Am I right about that—couple of months?"

Lauren just nodded. "I don't feel like a scene. It's Christmas. Tell her to please come over if she'd like to meet my friend. If she's pissy, I'm not in the mood."

After a lovely dinner of chicken parmesan, Lauren reminded herself that every situation would be touch and go for a while. Everyone had come. Lacey looked like she'd been invited to the gallows. She was stiff and uncomfortable and somewhat grim. But Beau expressed how happy he was to meet her, Cassie and Jeremy welcomed her with hugs and Beau's sons made her laugh. Then there was a fair amount of teasing from Drew and Michael about the new couple, Lauren and Beau.

Lacey seemed a little rigid in the beginning, trying not to like them, but in spite of herself she fell for them all. Beau and his sons were funny, charming and sweet. Not to mention attractive.

From that point on, the days were magical. Lauren spent every bit of time with Beau while Cassie split her time with Jeremy's family and Lacey split her time with her father. Cassie did not receive an invitation from Brad and didn't care. In fact she was relieved; she hadn't heard from her father since August when she confronted him in his office. Nor had he offered her any help with law school.

On Christmas Eve everyone except Lacey went to midnight mass in Mill Valley where Father Tim assisted Father Damien for the last time. By now the word had gotten out and he was seen hugging parishioners, and telling them that he'd be taking calls and visiting with anyone who wanted to see him for another two weeks. He encouraged anyone with questions to call his cell phone.

In the wee hours of Christmas morning, after midnight mass, Lauren and Beau were alone in Lauren's living room. Cassie and Jeremy had gone to bed. Michael was staying overnight at Beau's house and Beau had gamely told them not to wait up. In this little bit of time alone at Lauren's, they exchanged gifts. Beau had a wrapped gift for her and she opened it to find a most beautiful diamond pendant on a platinum chain. "I can't put a ring on your finger but I can show you how I feel with this."

"Beau... It's so beautiful!"

"Let me," he said, pulling it out of the box to fasten it

around her neck. He looked at it for a moment, then treated her to one of his best kisses. "I wish you could wear this to bed," he whispered against her lips. "This and nothing else."

She laughed softly. "We might have to wait until company is gone…"

"I don't know if I can last that long," he said.

"I don't know if I could have made it through this holiday without you," she said. "You and the boys—they were terrific, softening up Lacey."

"Tim was good, too," he said. "I hope he's okay. I told him to call or text if he wanted to talk…"

"I have something for you," she said, distracting him from Tim. She got up and went to the Christmas tree. She reached into the boughs and pulled out a long, slim envelope.

He smiled as he took it. "We were going to go easy since we don't have any idea what kind of finances…"

She touched her pendant. "You forgot," she said, smiling.

He opened the envelope. There was a lovely card inside and some folded pages in the card. He unfolded them to find a printout of airline tickets and an itinerary—San Francisco to Victoria, British Columbia, leaving on Valentine's Day. He was speechless and just stared at her in wonder.

"The gardens, Beau. They're beautiful all winter and your busy season really kicks in in March. Someday, when things settle down, we'll also go in spring."

He pulled her close. "I guess you forgot you're unemployed at the moment."

"Oh, who could forget that," she said with a laugh. "But I saw the travel agent before I was fired, thank God. We'll figure it out. I don't know how, but we'll figure it out. Just hold me."

It was almost two in the morning by the time Tim exited the rectory and went to the truck parked in the small lot behind the house. He tossed a small duffel into the truck bed, jumped into the passenger side and looked at the pretty woman in the driver's seat. "Would you like me to drive?" he asked.

"I can manage."

"It's a long drive..."

"I'm fine. How do you feel?"

"I don't know," he said. "If I tell you I feel a little lost, will you think I'm not sure of myself?"

"Are you sure of yourself?"

He leaned toward her. "Come here, Angela," he said. When she leaned toward him, he slipped a hand around to the back of her neck and pulled her closer, covering her lips with his. He kissed her deeply, lovingly. "I'm sure of this," he said against her lips.

"Woo," she said, almost a sigh. "Merry Christmas."

"There could be phone calls," he said. "I think a few of my people are worried about losing touch, worried about where I'll go and what I'll do."

"But are you worried?" she asked.

"No, it's in God's hands. I've known Him a long time and it's been my experience that when you offer to be of service, your cup runneth over."

She laughed at him and put the truck in gear. "You have no idea," she said. "It's never quite enough. I have ended every day for the last eight or ten years wondering how I could do more."

"The woman with one can of cream-style corn," he reminded her. He reached across the console and patted her thigh.

They were on their way to Lake Tahoe. He had reserved a nice room. They were going to drink some champagne, toast the future together and sleep in one bed. Their room would be ready early, when they arrived during the predawn hours.

They'd planned a leisurely Christmas Day and night, then they would drive back to Oakland to the Velasquez house the day after Christmas. Tim would ask Senor Velasquez for his daughter's hand in marriage. The Velasquez family were not his parishioners but he would explain that he had recently transitioned out of the priesthood and while he'd known Angela since he returned to Mill Valley—a few years now—they had not had a romance. Not until recently, when he was officially transitioning into the secular community.

"Are you sure it's all right for you to do this?" she asked.

"Angela, I began the out-processing five months ago. If you're talking about the archdiocese, they've known for months. I'm leaving them in good hands. Father Damien is young, energetic, driven and alive with the spirit."

"My mother is going to faint," she said.

"And your father?" he asked a bit nervously.

"I think he will not only grant permission, he might try to get you to the church long before you're ready."

"I wouldn't worry too much about that," he said. "I'm ready."

Their plans had changed, but only slightly. They were still hoping to assist with the refugee program, but that might come later. For now they would be assisting Catholic charities as volunteers in Puerto Rico where there was still so much hunger and destruction after the terrible hurricane. And based on a wonderful recommendation from the Monsignor, they'd been accepted through the New York chapter and would be helped with lodging. That probably meant a room in someone's house. One step at a time, one day at a time. *At least we're going forward together,* Tim thought.

"Did you say something?" she asked.

"I didn't think I said it out loud— Together."

Sometime in the future, hopefully the not too distant future, they would blend their special skills to form the right kind of team. They weren't sure which resource they would attach to—it could be one of any of the many wonderful organizations committed to easing hunger and disenfranchisement and pain. But they would find the right mission as a team.

"God, I'm so grateful for you," he said.

"*Dios,* I'm about to spend the night with a priest," she said.

He laughed. "Not exactly. *Ex*-priest." And then he thought, *it was a very good run.* In twenty years he'd done some good. He'd had some rewarding experiences. And when Beau heard about this new adventure he was going to mess his pants, for sure. "Wait till I tell my best friend."

"I thought you had!"

"No, I told him I was moving in a new direction. He's going through a nasty divorce and I apologized and told him he might need me and my head could be elsewhere. I spent the evening before mass with him and his family. He has a very nice woman in his life and his sons seem to be supportive and in a stable place. I haven't told him about you yet, but I don't think it will surprise him. When I finally catch up with him and tell him everything that's going on, he's going to flip. I should be sure you're with me. It's fun watching Beau freak out."

It was early in the morning but still dark when they got to Lake Tahoe. Tim asked for a champagne breakfast to be sent to the room. Then they sat in their hotel robes with their room service breakfast, curtains open to catch the rising sun in a couple of hours. They clinked glasses, fed each other small bites of omelet and crepes between kisses.

And finally they tumbled onto the large bed and clumsily touched, caressed, kissed and eventually made love. When both of them were exhausted and satisfied, Angela gasped and said, "I think you're lying about your chastity. That was excellent!"

"That's the thing about love, sweetheart," he said, brushing her thick dark hair away from her brow. "No practice required. It's pretty natural."

★ ★ ★

Angela slept in his arms, her head on his shoulder, one leg thrown over his hip. For the first time in a long time he felt at home, at peace. He had never strayed from his vows, though he'd felt the occasional temptation, as any man would. He had exercised a lot of denial and struggled with control— hormones, that's all it was. It was when he saw Angela for the first time after telling His Excellency that he'd be leaving the priesthood, that's when he felt something more. This wasn't just hormones; it wasn't just a man struggling with his God-given urge to mate. This was perfection.

He didn't expect this to happen. He thought maybe some-day he'd meet someone. He knew he was open to the idea when he was no longer a priest.

He toyed with her dark hair and she stirred against him. The right woman, a woman who shared his passion for being of service, a woman who shared his faith and his drive and his love for humanity. Angela had been doing God's work for years and in her, he would find his way. Hopefully in him she would find her completeness.

He pulled her closer and his lips touched her brow. She lifted her head and looked into his eyes. "I hope I can make you as happy as you've made me," she said.

"We're a work in progress as a couple," he said. "Every day will be a new canvas. If you just hold my hand, we'll do the right things. Can we get married right away?"

"You in some hurry, Tim?" she asked.

"It's my nature, I think. Once I decide, I take an oath. Don't let me rush you if you need time to think it over."

"Tim, I wouldn't be here now, like this, if I were unsure. But I'd like to be married by a priest. It might be old-fash-ioned, but it's how I roll." She grinned and ran her fingers through the hair that fell over his ear. "Will we have a hon-eymoon, do you think?"

"Probably not a typical one. I still have things to clear out of the rectory and I'll have to spend a little time there, but I'm not going to stay nights there anymore. Everyone has my cell phone number. If any of my old parishioners need reassurance, I can keep appointments at the church until January first. Then we move on."

"Do you need my help with that?"

"No, there isn't much. What I can't pack I can donate or leave with my parents. I'm going to get us a hotel room in the city for a couple of weeks. We have people to see and a marriage license to get. When we're not busy doing that, I want to spoil you a little. I have a feeling it's going to be a long time before we can indulge in good restaurants or things like whirlpool tubs and big showers."

"Good mattresses, fancy linens, hotel bathrobes…"

"If this ever becomes too much…"

"You're following me, remember? I never preached in a big rich church or lived in a cushy little mansion like that rectory. How many times have you slept in your car?"

"Not that many," he admitted, though there were a few times in the central valley when he'd given up his lodging to someone in need.

"It was the most wonderful Christmas morning of my life," she said.

"Me, too," he agreed. He tenderly touched her cheek. "Me, too."

Cassie and Jeremy were very busy the week between Christmas and New Year's Day. This was the part of the world where they'd completed their undergrad work and there were still many friends in the area. Not to mention Jeremy's parents, a married sister with a baby, an aunt and uncle. That gave Lauren plenty of free time, which she needed, but high on her list of priorities was getting her girls together for lunch. Just the girls, no boyfriends or extras.

Since she was fired the Friday before Christmas, she'd had a very interesting call from Sylvie Emerson. Sylvie had taken the liberty of talking about Lauren's situation to her personal attorney, no names of course. "Call your attorney and tell her you want to contest your termination because they claimed no cause. Don't take another job without talking to me—I have a couple of excellent ideas. But while you're unemployed, ask your lawyer to push hard for a settlement. If you agreed to mediation, get it scheduled. Your husband has dragged this out for over six months in a no-fault state when you're not contesting the laws. Push, Lauren. Then please talk to me."

Lauren said that of course she would; she would appreciate any suggestions.

When she called Erica Slade, she had to leave a message. And, Lauren being Lauren, it was apologetic. "Erica, I'm so sorry to bother you during a holiday week, but I've had a few things come up and hope to discuss with you when you're next available. I lost my job. They have no cause and it seems pretty suspicious, but I can't figure out if there's anyone to blame. And that's even more reason I have to try to get this divorce settled. I have expenses, of course, that I was hoping to cover with my paycheck. I'm sorry to have to bother you."

It wasn't even an hour later when her phone rang. "Lauren, I'm a divorce attorney. You think I'm not used to holiday crises? I'm afraid it comes with the territory. Everyone loses their marbles at Christmastime. Mother's Day, Father's Day and the Super Bowl are also bad. I'm going to take a vacation in February. Now, tell me what's happening."

Their conversation was brief. Erica agreed to file a complaint contesting her termination and to start petitioning for either a mediation or date in family court ASAP. She requested the results of the audit she had asked for. "If he stalls anymore, I'll petition the court. His lawyer knows he has to have a case to drag this out and he has no case. You've submitted all your statements and earnings records."

That had occupied her, but that was not the reason she wanted to meet her daughters for lunch. Cassie and Jeremy were going to be returning to Boston on January second. It would probably be a long time before the three of them were together again. Lauren chose the neighborhood pub she enjoyed so often with Beau and she walked down the street with Cassie, though the weather was damp and cold.

"You know, Mom, you don't have to send Beau home at night to protect me from your relationship. As long as I don't hear screaming and spanking..."

"Cassie!" she said with a laugh.

"I'm just saying, I'm sure when I'm not in town, you have a much more interesting private relationship. I like Beau. He has a nice family. And I'm glad you found someone like him."

"It's a complete surprise," Lauren said. "I wish I'd met him after the divorce was final, but at the rate we're going..."

"When exactly did you meet him?" Cassie asked.

"Back in March. On the very day I put down a deposit on the house and asked my lawyer to have your father served right before my July first move-in date. I was prepared to stay with Beth but the landlord gave me the keys a few days early."

"But he had nothing to do with—"

"Of course not," she said. "He never made any such overtures. I ran into him the first day I shopped at Stohl's and that's the first time he told me he lived in the neighborhood. I had no idea. I invited him over for a glass of wine and he came back the next day, without being asked, to install new locks and that camera doorbell." She was quiet a moment. "He helped me move some furniture, hang some shelves... and he kissed me four months later..."

"I wouldn't say you're rushing things," Cassie said. "I made out with Jeremy on our first date! Made out like a rock star!"

"I'm trying to be sensible and cautious," Lauren said. "And so is he. He's going through a divorce, too. The difference is, he's been separated over a year now. It should be over but..."

"But you both have spouses who won't let it go?" Cassie said.

"And why?" she asked. "I don't know what's going on with Beau's ex, but I do know she left him. And what's up with mine? What does he want from me? All evidence suggests he despises me. Why doesn't he want this over with?"

"He wants to win," Cassie said.

"What would he win? A beaten-down, unhappy woman?"

"I didn't say it was logical," Cassie said. The pub came into view as did Lacey's little BMW, parked out front. "Oh good, we're not going to have to wait for her today."

Lacey had herself a spacious booth and was already sipping a glass of white wine. She smiled when Lauren and Cassie came into view and that was such a relief. The girls had done well over the holidays—no squabbling, no taking sides. Of course they avoided the subject of the divorce, and for that Lauren was relieved.

"Are we late?" Lauren asked Lacey, giving her a peck on the cheek.

"Not a bit. I might be early. This is a great little hole in the wall. I love it. Walking distance for you, too."

"I love this neighborhood," Lauren said. "I've been known to walk down to do a little light shopping or grab a breakfast sandwich at Starbucks or a salad right here."

They chatted while Cassie and Lauren looked over the menu and ordered; Cassie invited Lacey to come to Boston for a visit, though all she could offer was the couch and a door that closed. They even managed to laugh at Lacey's complaints about Christmas with her father and grandmother. "I can't believe you have left me to deal with him!"

"Hold on, sister mine! You did that to yourself—you don't want to give up the allowance and for that luxury, you're going to have lots of family dinners."

"Lord, I hope not. Cassie, be a sport and make up with him! Then we'll at least have each other and you'll probably get back on the payroll!"

"What have I done to you two?" Lauren said, resting her head in her hand.

"I admit it, I'm a little spoiled," Lacey said.

"A little?" Lauren and Cassie said together.

Their lunches were delivered, they laughed through lunch and Lauren felt a glimmer of hope. She'd filed for divorce right about June 28th. Today was December 28th—six months had passed and they were making crude and somewhat evil jokes about their parents throwing them into poverty.

"Not me," Lauren said. "I just want to live a life free of control and meanness. And I'll help you all I can while you both finish your educations, but that's one of the reasons I wanted us to get together before we're separated again. I have another challenge ahead. I was fired from my job."

"What?" Cassie said. "You've been there forever! What was their reason?"

"They said that I hadn't done anything wrong, but they were taking product development in a new direction and my position was no longer needed. I've heard it said, very cautiously, that it's not really true and doesn't make sense."

"Oh Mama, what in the world!" Cassie said. "What will you do?"

"I'll look for another job," Lauren said. "And I've asked my lawyer to turn up the heat and get your father to sit down with a mediator over the property. We need to wrap this up for everyone's sake. So, what I'm telling you is it may take me a while before I can help you with expenses. I've still got my retirement funds, but I'm trying to save that for emergencies."

Cassie grabbed her hand. "Listen, I can do this on my own. I might run up a lot of debt but I sure won't be the first and I'll work my way out of debt like everyone else. Jeremy is going to earn some money teaching while he finishes his PhD. You can't believe how many law students I know whose family isn't able to help them at all. The only ones living like normal people come from those *fine old families* and—"

"Lacey?" Lauren asked.

Lacey was looking down at her plate. Her hands were folded in her lap and she was crying.

"Lacey, your father will probably pick up some of your expenses since you haven't deserted him, but if that doesn't work out, I'll do everything I can to at least help you. Just please be patient. I'm in a fix right now. An unexpected fix."

Lacey lifted her eyes and a big tear spilled over. "He did it," she said.

Cassie and Lauren just looked at her, confused and speechless.

"He did it. I didn't get it at the time. He and Grandma were laughing about how freaked you would be, how you wouldn't know where to turn, you wouldn't have any income, you'd be begging him for help..."

Lauren frowned in confusion. "But how?" she asked.

"I don't know, not really. After a minute of not understanding what the hell they were talking about, I tuned out. I remember he said it paid to know the right people in the right places and that golf was an excellent game for all kinds of favors. That meant nothing to me at the time."

"That is not how my company operated!" Lauren said, realizing after the fact, she was echoing Sylvie's words exactly.

"I don't know how, Mama," Lacey said. "This is probably my fault! I should have done exactly what Cassie did. I should have told him how much I hated what he did. But I didn't. I didn't because I hate this divorce!"

Lauren was quiet for a long moment. "Me, too. I waited too long. And now look how complicated and terrible it is for everyone."

"I couldn't figure out why he and Grandma were so happy and laughing. He wants you on your knees," Lacey whispered. "God," she said, a sob escaping. "This is the most horrible thing…"

"It's not your fault," Lauren said. "It's not your divorce. It's my divorce."

"Lacey, don't let him manipulate you anymore," Cassie said.

"But you don't understand. I don't have anyone. I don't have my sister—we've been on opposite sides of this. I don't have my mother—you must hate me for the way I took his side. He's using me, I don't have a guy, my girlfriends don't want to hear about it. I don't have anyone. And I'm not in law school with some big dream. Do you know what teachers make?"

Lauren just smiled. "It's not pretty," she said. "But you will always have a mother. Even when we're on opposite sides. I don't blame you for wanting to stay on civil terms with your father, just don't work against me. That would be hard to forgive."

"But he says you're trying to hurt him with this divorce," Lacey said, clearly misunderstanding the terms.

"Of course I'm not," Lauren said. "The law is clear. Our possessions and investments that were obtained during our marriage are divided equally with the exception of personal retirement funds. Everything accrued prior to our marriage is not part of the equation. I worked at least three jobs my entire marriage. I cleaned, cared for the children, took care of your father's needs—professional and personal—and then held down a full-time job. Your father never volunteered in

your school, never cleaned the house, never went to the grocery store, doesn't know where the dry cleaner is, gave me
lists of chores to do for him or things to buy for him, and my
paycheck went into the joint account. Lacey, I don't want to
hurt him, even though there's an argument that he deserves
to be hurt. All I want is my life back."

Lacey was quiet for a moment, then she said, "I don't think
he's going to make that easy."

"Sweetheart, I knew that before we'd been married a year."

CHAPTER SIXTEEN

On January eighth Beau took Lauren with him to a wedding in a small Catholic church on the outskirts of Oakland. Beau was going to stand as best man for Tim Bradbury. It was supposed to be a very small, private affair but by the time Tim and Angela included their families, small was impossible. Angela lost control of the wedding early on as her mother, aunts, grandparents, siblings and cousins took over. At the end of the day their intimate little wedding was over one hundred strong with every woman bringing covered dishes and the mariachis from a couple of towns over arrived. There was also a dance band. The flowers must have been ordered from afar, it being January, and they were plentiful. There were piñatas for the children, beer and wine aplenty and the most delicious Mexican food imaginable.

It came as no surprise to Beau that the Bradbury family, a well-to-do professional family, blended in beautifully and had the best time of all. Beau mentioned it to Michael and Drew and they wouldn't miss it, so they were there with girlfriends in tow. There was music, dancing, singing, laughing, toasting and toasting and toasting. Beau gave the bride and groom a roaring good speech.

"I don't think any couple I've ever met has been more married," Lauren said. "They really know how to do it right."

"Did you have a big wedding?" he asked her.

"Of course," she said. "It wasn't a fun wedding, however. It was prim, proper and stick-up-your-butt boring."

Beau erupted with laughter, then grabbed her in his arms and spun her around the dance floor—the church basement— one more time. It was after midnight when a limo ordered by Tim's father arrived at the little church and whisked Tim and Angela away, back to the city where they'd been staying.

And Beau took Lauren back to her house where they stumbled into her bedroom, peeling off clothes along the way, their lips locked together the whole time. Within seconds they were on the bed, naked, holding on to each other. The moment Beau touched her, she opened to him like a beautiful flower and he filled her with all his love and lust. Her skin, so soft and perfect to his touch, grew warm and supple and her hips moved beneath him.

This was what perfect love felt like, when there was trust and devotion and passion. Beau tried to count the number of satisfied emotions every time they made love. There was blinding pleasure, there was unparalleled contentment, comfort, excitement, a need quenched, a desire gratified. Body and soul came together for him and he knew complete fulfillment.

"I can't believe you're mine," she whispered.

"Oh, I'm yours," he said. "I'm yours like I've been waiting for you my whole life. This is how it's supposed to be." With his lips on hers, his hands all over her, filling her, moving with her, it wasn't long before she came to a thundering climax in his arms. It was so quick; it was always quick. Her body responded to his body and together their love was powerful yet easy. Then his favorite part, holding her as she came back to earth, as her body trembled and her breathing evened. He gave her a flood of small kisses to mark the way home and she held him to make sure they were together for the ride.

"That was so nice," he whispered. "Hard to believe you had trouble with orgasms before. They come to you very easily now."

"Hm, now. The second you touch me, I have to hold back so you can come with me."

"Loving you is the best part of my life," he said.

She touched his handsome face. "I never thought I'd have this," she whispered. "I was planning to be alone. Alone and quite content."

He chuckled. "So was I. But at least neither of us was planning to be a priest."

"Weren't they the most beautiful couple? The chemistry was rolling off them in waves. It was really hard for me to imagine Tim that way, lusty and sexual and..."

"And not a priest?" he finished for her.

"There was nothing priestly about him at the wedding," she said, snuggling closer. "Every time I saw him, he was kissing Angela. I think he's thoroughly in love." She kissed him. "I'm thoroughly in love, too. In case you're interested."

They made love again, the urgency sated. It was slower and sweeter but no less wondrous. Wrapped in each other's arms, they began to drift into sleep.

Then there was an explosion that shook the house.

Beau's truck in Lauren's drive was ablaze and he acted quickly. He didn't go outside and told Lauren to stay in the kitchen, far away from the windows. He called 911 and explained that his truck was on fire and there was no explanation for it, but there had been a loud explosion. He heard sirens before he completed the call and within a couple of minutes there were fire trucks, a paramedic rig and lots of police vehicles.

"Get dressed, Beau," she said, handing him his jeans.

He saw that she'd hurriedly pulled on jeans and a sweatshirt and some slip-on tennis shoes. While he was getting into his pants and T-shirt, there was pounding at the door.

Lauren opened the door to a firefighter. "Everyone in here all right, ma'am?"

"I think so," she said. "We woke to the explosion..."

"I'm going to need you to evacuate for now. You can sit in one of the police cars. The bomb squad and arson investigators are going to take over when the fire is out. Then I'm going to suggest they have a run through the house."

"The house?" she said, her hand going nervously to her throat.

"It looks like it was some kind of bomb. I have no idea how sophisticated it might be. Anyone looking to hurt you?"

Beau came to the door while tucking in his shirt. "It seems preposterous, but you never know. We're both going through divorces and the exes aren't happy. And before you ask, no, we're not the reason for the divorces."

"Right," he said. "You can explain all that to the cops."

"They're a pain in the ass, our exes, but... This could have hurt someone!"

"You need to get jackets," the firefighter said. "It's cold tonight."

They were relegated to the back of a squad car and all attention was focused on evacuating the neighbors on either side of Lauren. "My neighbors must hate me," she said.

"We'll talk to them together," Beau said. "We'll explain we don't have any idea what this is about and promise to give

271

them the details when we have more information from the police."

"They're going to hate me just the same. This was a quiet, well-kept little neighborhood until I came along."

"Have you had any contact from Brad?" Beau asked.

"Nothing," she said. "I told you what Lacey said, that she thinks Brad somehow managed to get me put out of a job, but she can't be sure. It could be the things he was saying meant he thought he'd finally outsmarted me and will get even in the settlement. I have no reason to suspect him of blowing up your truck. Oh God, what if that was meant to hurt us? Or kill us?"

"Let's not go there until we get more information," he said.

"But what if one of them, probably Brad, wants that level of revenge?" she asked.

"Come here," he said, pulling her into his arms. "We're going to figure this out. We're going to be okay."

They spent the rest of the early morning in the police department, answering questions. What was left of Beau's truck was towed to a special section of the impound lot for examination by detectives and the arson investigator, although the remnants of a pipe bomb were discovered. It appeared the pipe bomb could have been tossed in the bed of the truck, which actually brought Beau and Lauren a small bit of comfort. Had it been wired to explode while they were occupants in the cab, it would have been so eerily terrifying.

They were separated and answered many questions for about three hours before they were released and asked to remain available to police. The first order of business was a nap—at Beau's house. Then they visited the neighbors on either side of Lauren's house to explain as much as they could and Lauren packed a small bag.

There was a devastating black charred mark left on the driveway.

"This is so scary," Lauren said. "Is there any way to clean that away? Just looking at it is a horrible reminder."

"I'll find a solution to that," Beau said. "I think you have to stay with me now. Just to be safe."

Drew was shocked and agreed, Lauren should stay with them. No one was sure who the target was—Beau or Lauren or both of them or just the property—but no one was willing to take any chances. Beau had installed security cameras a few years earlier. He looked at the footage surrounding his house for the past month. There was only one suspicious figure—Christmas Day, a little after 3:00 a.m. It was a female in a disguising hoodie. He wasn't 100 percent sure, but the woman moved like Pamela.

Lauren was a bit surprised by how easily she slipped into living in Beau's home. From the very first morning after a full night's sleep, when she was sitting at the table in her robe, working her crossword puzzle and Drew came into the room. He said a pleasant good-morning as though this was a typical routine. He began rooting around for cereal and toast and Lauren said, "Let me make you a couple of eggs. It'll only take a minute."

"Um, you have time?"

"Right now I have nothing but time, but when I get back to work you'll be on your own again. I'd love to right now."

"Um, sure," he said.

She turned a couple of eggs in the pan, microwaved a few slices of bacon, made him some toast and presented a plate in five minutes or less. She filched a piece of bacon for herself and opened a yogurt.

Drew dug in. "You sleep okay?" he finally asked.

"I did, but I admit, I woke up a lot. Every little noise."

"Try not to worry," Drew said. "Dad's got this place wired. No one's getting in here without a lot of bells and whistles."

"I'm relieved by that," she said. "Are you off to school?"

"I don't have classes today so I'll run by my dad's office and see if there's anything for me to do around there. When I'm not working with landscapers, I do stuff around the office. Then I'll meet Darla after her classes. I don't know if I'll be around at all today. Do you need anything?"

She shook her head and smiled. "Thanks, Drew. I'm fine. I have a few errands."

"Be very careful," he said. She had to remind herself that Beau was not Drew's father—he looked so much like him, especially when he was solicitous.

"Believe me, I will," she said.

Beau was planning to try to buy a new truck but Lauren was going to see Sylvie Emerson. It was so coincidental that Sylvie had called yesterday and asked if she could manage lunch. Lauren didn't say anything about their adventure with the bomb and couldn't imagine Sylvie knew.

Lauren genuinely admired Sylvie. She would be like her if she could, giving so much to so many important causes and reigning over society with such grace and kindness, yet having that no-nonsense grasp of reality. Just the way she had admitted Brad had never fooled her—that wisdom and intuition—if Lauren aspired to anything, it was that.

Sylvie was a lot like Honey, Lauren realized.

Even given all that, Lauren didn't feel like a close friend, but rather a friendly acquaintance. That was all right; Lauren didn't run in Sylvie's circle, nor did she want to. All she really wanted was Sylvie's respect and she believed she had that.

The day was dark, foggy and wet. Lauren took the ferry to the city and a cab to Sylvie's large home. Sylvie answered the door herself, even though there was staff in this house.

"Lauren," she said, giving her a friendly hug. "So good of you to come out on a day like this!"

"While I have the time, this is my first choice of things to do. Thank you for inviting me."

"I've looked forward to this and I finally had some free time. We're set up in the library. Let me take your coat."

Before Sylvie could take the coat a casually attired woman Lauren recognized from her last visit took the coat and whisked it away. "Thank you, Mary," Sylvie said. "Come with me," she said to Lauren.

They walked down the hall past a sitting room, an office and a dining room to the front corner of the house. Lauren had been here a few times but had been unaware of the library. It was beautiful with floor-to-ceiling bookcases, a couple of ladders, a leather sofa and a blazing fireplace. A small table occupied the center of the room and was appointed with a linen tablecloth and delicate china. The chairs were leather captain's chairs, comfortable and deep. The room was dimly lit and without windows but there were a couple of flickering candles on the table.

Lauren was mesmerized. "Sylvie, this is beautiful!"

"I thought it was best for today, since the garden is out of the question." She flipped a switch and bookshelf lighting came on. "It's a dark room but I find it cozy, especially in winter."

"Do you use it much?"

"Not as much as I'd like," she said. "I carry whatever book I'm reading around with me. I read in the living room, the bedroom, wherever I happen to be. Now and then I'll come in here and just remind myself what books I've hoarded and kept." She pulled one off the shelf. A copy of *Treasure Island*, tattered and yellowed. "I read this to the kids. I could replace it but is there anything quite as lovely as a book that's been well read?"

"I read it to my kids, too," she said.

"Sit down, Lauren. Did you drive into the city?"

"No, I took the ferry and a cab. The roads were destined to be clogged with traffic on a rainy day and I like the ferry, even in weather like this."

"Well then, let's have a glass of wine, shall we?"

"Perfect," she said.

"And you can tell me the latest in your life," Sylvie said.

"By now you should be afraid to ask," she said.

"Oh no," Sylvie said, pouring them a glass of wine. "Has something happened?"

Lauren first toasted Sylvie and said, "It's so good to see you again." Then she explained that Beau's truck had exploded and that the police said it was a bomb of some kind.

"Oh dear God," Sylvie said. "Do you suspect Brad?"

"I have no idea what to think, but to be safe, I'm staying at Beau's house. I don't know if it was meant for one of us—the truck was parked in my drive—or if it was just malicious mischief. It's just that there's so little crime on the island and we both have hostile exes."

"And what of this man, Lauren?"

"Oh, you met him. It was almost a year ago at the fundraiser. I had barely met him myself at that time—the landscape architect who creates rooftop gardens."

"I remember him!" Sylvie said.

"After knowing him about six months and with my divorce dragging on and on, we started dating. He has two grown sons, I have two grown daughters and we have nothing and everything in common. He's a lovely man. I certainly hadn't intended to be living in his house, but circumstances being what they are..."

"Listen, if you ever feel vulnerable and without options, or even if this is merely the best option, you're welcome to stay here. This house is a fortress."

"That's so generous, Sylvie. I also have my sister and she's married to a police officer. She also has two messy, loud sons so her house is safe but crazy. But once I decided to take a chance on Beau, whose youngest son is still living at home, I realized this is an opportunity to really get to know him. The real Beau. Rest assured, one red flag and I'm gone. I am certainly not afraid to get out of a bad situation now. I so regret staying in a terrible marriage for so long."

"Is there any hope of this being resolved anytime soon?"

"My lawyer has a court order for him to produce his financial records by the end of the month so in one respect, yes the end is in sight. In another—he might be a problem for as long as I live. But it wouldn't be better living with him."

Mary brought a couple of salads and ice waters, then quietly left.

"I have something to tell you," Sylvie said. "I spent a little time at Merriweather with corporate officers I knew from my time on the board. I have no proof of this but I believe Brad convinced the VP of marketing to eliminate your position, a position he is now advertising to fill. There is no memo, no email chain, no witnesses that I know of. Just one very guilty and remorseful VP who has offered to get in touch with you and reinstate you to your former position."

Lauren's fork was on its way to her open mouth when it stopped. Her first bite of salad was hovering inches from her mouth. "Stu Lonigan? I can't believe it!"

"Believe it."

"I always considered Stu Lonigan to be a smart and fair boss. My boss also respected him. My daughter spent Christmas with her father and grandmother and she has no details, just that she believes Brad somehow convinced someone to fire me. She said something about a deal made on the golf course."

"It may be as simple as that or even more complicated, I don't know. But Stu Lonigan may find his job in some jeopardy. You were given an exit package, were you not?"

Lauren returned her fork to her salad plate. "No."

"I wouldn't blame you if you decided to go back to Merriweather. It's familiar, no doubt you have friends there, and despite all this I've always considered Merriweather a good company. Believe me, I checked them very thoroughly before agreeing to sit on their board. As a local philanthropist, I can't associate with a corporation that discriminates or abuses employees. This situation is unusual. And, I think, personal. If it's a corporate habit, they've hidden it well. I don't believe it is. Still, it's so disturbing."

"Is Stu in trouble now?"

"When someone terminates an employee without cause, without negotiating a healthy exit package, leaving the company open to lawsuit, you can bet the board has an issue with that. Your lawyer contested the termination so everyone knows. Mr. Lonigan is on very fragile ground. And, it's my opinion that your soon-to-be ex-husband has been risking his medical license. I know he settled two lawsuits. They were not for malpractice. They were for abuse and harassment."

"You know about that?" Lauren asked. "They never went to court. I only know what Brad told me."

Sylvie took a forkful of her salad. She tilted her head and chewed slowly. "Well, when you're in the habit of giving away a great deal of money, you soon learn not everyone is your friend. We have to research individuals, charities and foundations very carefully. It's routine, I'm afraid."

"And you researched Brad?" Lauren asked.

"In a way," she said. "I hope you won't be horribly offended. I had good reason. We researched you. I uncovered the extent of your injuries at his hand, the order of protection, the lawsuits. I knew Brad rubbed me the wrong way, but I admit I had no idea things were that bad. I'm horrified. Don't worry—it's all confidential. It's meant to protect our foundation. That money is meant for people in need."

In spite of herself, Lauren blushed. "Why would you research me?" Lauren asked. "Were you afraid I was lying about the divorce? About anything?"

Sylvie laughed. "Not at all. I asked my assistant to do the research. She's so good, so sensitive. I asked her to do that because I liked you. I thought you were smart and I guessed you had a personality I could mesh with. Then things tumbled a little bit, you had a lot of stuff happening at once. Your divorce, your job loss. I was thinking along these lines anyway. My assistant, Ruth Ann, is planning to move out of the Bay Area when her husband retires. We've been scouting around for her replacement. It's not easy. Ruth Ann has been with me for ten years. Several people have been suggested and they just aren't meeting my expectations. Perfectly nice, very professional, but... I'm looking for someone I admire, someone I like, someone with the kind of perseverance and heart I can respect, a devoted mother and loyal employee. And someone who can keep a confidence. It's a hard job sometimes. It can get very busy, it can involve travel. There are also easier weeks. It pays well. And there are excellent benefits and a retirement fund."

Lauren could not close her mouth. "You admire me?" she asked in a whisper.

Sylvie put down her fork and sat back in her chair. "Lauren, you were raised by a single mother. So was I. It's hard on a girl. You lost your mother just a couple of years ago. You protected your children and raised them well, though it had to have been difficult. You held a responsible position in a large company for many years. You were dependable, you didn't give up easily, you have a close relationship with your sister's family and your daughters. And you're smart. We get along so well. You're the kind of assistant I want." She touched her napkin to her lips. "I won't take it personally if you're not interested."

Lauren laughed. "Well, there's a lot more you have to tell

me about the job. I really loved Merriweather but I don't want to go back. In any case, I haven't heard a word from Stu or HR. And I can't think of anything I'd like better than having you for a boss. But good God, I'll have to be trained! I've never investigated anyone in my life!"

"Don't worry, that's the easy part. It doesn't come up that often. The hard part is getting to the bottom of the charities and foundations that want our money."

"Are they often crooks?"

"Hardly ever," Sylvie said. "But sometimes they're exclusive. We insist on inclusive giving. Oh, I think you're going to find this fun. This is the greatest fun in the world. Giving to people who not only need it, they will pay it forward. You'll be helping to make a better world, Lauren. That's all we care about now. We have more than we need, our kids have more than they need, so what should we do? Buy another boat or plane or feed and educate people who weren't as lucky as we've been?"

Lauren felt tears cloud her eyes. "Oh Sylvie, that you would trust me to help with this. I'm humbled. And wait till I tell you about Beau's best friend, formerly Father Tim Bradbury. We attended his wedding a couple of days ago. He's a study in charitable works."

"Tell me," Sylvie said. "Tell me all about him."

Lunch lasted three hours. Lauren enjoyed telling Sylvie about Tim and his new wife, both of them soon to be traveling to Puerto Rico to work on the restoration. She passed on what she'd heard about Angela and her food bank. Sylvie told Lauren about all the foundations they were involved in, all the special projects that took up most of Andy's time. They both talked about their families at great length. And then Sylvie explained what her assistant would be expected to do and Lauren was so excited, she wondered if Sylvie could see her wiggle. It presented an entirely new life for her, one that was both challenging and fulfilling.

When they were finishing second cups of coffee, Sylvie asked, "What's it like, Lauren? Being in love now, after ending a twenty-five-year marriage?"

She thought for a moment. "Startling," she finally said. "So unexpected. So shocking, really. Like my heart is full of sunshine. Like I just woke up and everything is all right. Finally."

Lauren eagerly accepted Sylvie's offer. She couldn't wait to tell Beau. When she got home she found him cleaning out the garage with Drew's help. It was a detached garage but they needed room for two vehicles and since Pamela had left, it seemed to have filled itself up.

When Lauren told him about the job offer, he hugged her and said, "That's wonderful, honey. When will you start?"

"I'm going to start going over there afternoons right away. Her current assistant will start showing me the ropes, introducing me to some of their projects. I'll be the liaison between Sylvie and some of their fund-raisers. They hire event planners for golf tournaments, auctions, dinners and other things. She's going to have us to dinner soon so we can all get better acquainted."

Beau chuckled. "Dr. Delaney is going to shit himself."

"I'm going to avoid talking to him about my new job," she said.

There were a couple of people she was anxious to tell, along with an explanation about where she was now living and why. Lacey immediately asked if Lauren suspected Brad of the bomb and Lauren said, very honestly, "I can't imagine it. Not the way your father values his hands. I've not only never known him to play around with explosives, he never even talks about things like that. And Beau is so well liked by everyone, no angry clients, nothing... I bet we find out it's random."

281

To her surprise, Lacey did not get her back up about Lauren staying with Beau and Cassie was relieved to hear it—she wanted her mother to be as safe as possible. Beth wanted Lauren to stay with them but understood why she'd rather stay at Beau's. "I come with a lot of baggage," Beth said. "But promise you'll come to dinner soon and bring that young man. Drew. The boys love him."

When Lauren went to the Emerson home the next day, there was a shiny stained oak table sitting in the middle of the library. A laptop was open on it along with a couple of new iPhones. "What do you think?" Sylvie asked. "Would this be a good office?"

"Oh God, it's delicious. Is this where Ruth Ann worked?"

"She moved around a lot—my office, the kitchen, sunroom. You might do that, too. But this is a good place to start. We cleaned out a cupboard for you," she said, opening a couple of cupboard doors, the shelves inside empty and waiting for her use. "We're almost entirely paperless now but you'll need the scanner and computer."

It was like a dream come true for Lauren.

There was one more poker night before Tim and Angela left town and it was a wonderful celebration filled with laughter, but at the end of the evening, during the goodbyes it was a little emotional. When Tim took Lauren into his arms and said, "I'm so happy Beau has a good woman in his life," she completely lost it.

"Please, please, please be safe," she said, sobbing onto his shoulder.

It took a lot of comforting to get her under control again but before all was said and done, lots of people were crying.

There was a lot going on. Brad failed to provide his financial records and was cited with contempt and fined by the judge who had made the order. Brad's response was to stop sending Lauren monthly support payments.

Beau was checking with the police about the progress of their investigation almost weekly. One of the first things he learned was that the detectives had interviewed Pamela and Brad, separately of course, and both had alibis for the night of the bomb and were not suspects, however they now both knew that Beau's truck had been destroyed.

Lauren was going into the city to work with Sylvie daily and at the urging of both Sylvie and Lauren's lawyer, she did not withdraw her suit against Merriweather. "Please do it," Sylvie said. "They shouldn't be allowed to do this to someone else in the future."

Lauren was offered her old job back, but she declined on the grounds she just couldn't trust them again. She had a long conversation with Sylvie and said if there was a financial settlement, she'd donate it to one of the Emerson foundations. "I'd rather you donate it to law school for someone who doesn't plan to make herself rich but plans on doing some good in this crooked world. Know anyone who fits that description?"

The first week in February everyone at the Magellan house rose to go to their jobs—Lauren to the city, Drew to school, but Beau was wearing a suit.

"Today I have mediation with Pamela," he told them.

"You didn't say anything!" Drew said.

"I wasn't being secretive," he said. "I knew it would cause some anxiety and I just want us all to stay calm. It might take more than one meeting. It might take more than two. I'm hoping for a peaceful outcome that's fair to everyone."

"I'm really surprised Mom hasn't called me, tried to get me to wrangle something on her behalf."

"I'm a little surprised by that, too," Beau said. "I hope it means things are calming down and we're getting to the end of hostilities."

And Lauren thought, wouldn't that be nice. But she had an ugly feeling the end was not yet in sight.

CHAPTER SEVENTEEN

Beau's day of mediation was surprising, to say the least. One surprise after another. He had worn his best suit and, for a landscape architect, that was saying something. He was typically seen in jeans, khakis or shorts. There was hardly ever a business meeting that required this much of a suit, however there was the occasional wedding or funeral.

He thought of this meeting as a funeral. He expected to be buried. He came to the marriage with so much and it never once occurred to him to create a prenup. Not so much because of his ferocious trust for Pam but because he wanted the boys, his boys, to be well cared for right into adulthood. Their fathers had pretty much bailed on them. Beau was going to hang with them till his last days.

The mediator had looked over the figures, done all his own figuring, calculated again and again and gotten his own value estimates on things like the business and the house. There were things that Pam was asking for that had a red line run through—like her legal fees—that adjusted the total by quite a bit. She wanted the house and half the value of the business. The mediator explained the law very patiently, it was assets accrued during the marriage.

Their lawyers argued about their research—the value of the house and business at the time of marriage versus current assessments. The mediator split the difference.

Beau had to concentrate to close his mouth. He really hadn't expected to get a break on this.

Alimony was out. She didn't need alimony—her income was substantial and she wasn't supporting her kids. Her income was nearly as good as his and not only were the boys still living on his income rather than hers, he was paying their tuition. She wanted half of his substantial retirement funds, but those were off the table. They had agreed early on to stick to the standard no-fault parameters. That put her retirement off the table also, but the difference was, Pam had socked away a little, paid cash for her fancy car and since she had a 401K retirement fund, she'd built a tidy little investment portfolio. She'd been taking vacations, partying, buying clothes, living it up. Beau had been investing in the boys and saving for the future. By the time Pam had left him twice, he increased his retirement fund and put away a substantial amount for college educations, money he had wisely put in the kids' names, keeping it safe.

Once Pam saw the totals on the college funds, she wanted half of that as well. She loudly protested her assets were being added to the mix; he was allowed half of that. By the look on his face, that soured the mediator. Pam lost ground when he realized she would take from the boys.

It took three hours to go through the financial reports, then they each met with their lawyers. Pam and her lawyer went out to lunch, Beau and his very astute and grandmotherly attorney ate in her boardroom while figuring.

"It's my opinion, you're coming out in good shape. Given the value of your home, possessions, business and investments, if you accept this settlement, she is due about 27 percent of your house value and 34 percent of your business value. We can negotiate that you'll pay her a fixed amount based on current appraised value, but not due until you sell the house or in ten years. But you're not going to be so lucky with the business. To keep it clean, you have to buy her out or she can put a lien on it. Trust me, you don't want that."

"Do we have a number?" he asked fearfully.

She turned around a page and ran a red circle around a figure. $1.3 million.

"My business is worth three times that?" he exclaimed.

"More. Much more. Your net worth is very respectable. Impressive. We're not negotiating based on your net worth but income accrued during the marriage. Thank God you lived with her for a while. We were able to depreciate a lot of your office equipment, office space, salaries and benefits, et cetera. You have a very successful operation, Beau."

He started to laugh. "Don't tell anyone but I could work from home if I had to. I'd be damn busy, doing all my own paperwork, but that's how I started."

"Believe me, I won't tell. But your business assets are all tied up," she said. "You'd better arrange to clear that debt right away."

"Yeah, but I can get that much," he said. "I have a house to live in. When I bought it, it was falling down. I spent a lot of money and did almost all the work myself. It's paid for. It was already fixed up when Pam moved in." He laughed. He ran a hand through his hair. "Damn."

"I have a question," Sonja said. "What kind of man has every receipt for every nail he ever bought?"

"A businessman," he replied, and laughed. "Plus, the bank

is there to help. They can get bank statements from years ago. I love computers. Don't you?"

She made a face. "Not particularly."

"All I want right now is for Pamela to let me go."

"I can't vouch for her leaving you alone but you'll be free of the marriage. You both agreed to final mediation and I think the mediator did a very good job. This settlement is fair. No one is suffering unduly. Your wife should get along just fine and the boys will be able to finish their educations."

"Ex-wife," he said. "Can she take me back to court?" he asked.

"Listen, anyone can sue anyone for anything. Winning is another story. And bringing a frivolous suit to court is risky business. It wears badly on an attorney."

"Where is Pamela now?" he asked.

Sonja gathered up papers and put them in a large envelope. "I imagine she's having her lips sutured shut by her attorney. I'll have this packet copied for you. Do you have a safe?"

He nodded.

"Keep track of this," Sonja said. "Something about Pamela strikes me as relentless."

"You don't know the half of it," he said.

It had taken all day and he was grateful it hadn't taken more than one day. The necessary paperwork had been signed by both parties and would be filed; the official dissolution would be forwarded through the attorneys in about ten days. Pamela's lawyer must have told her she wouldn't do better. Plus, she had never had that much admiration for a landscape architect. She thought of him as a landscaper who had fixed up an old house to live in. She was probably surprised by that settlement figure; likely she hadn't thought he was worth much.

He couldn't wait to get home. *Home.* He looked at his watch. With this new job of Lauren's, he couldn't keep track of her hours. He hadn't really tried, for that matter. He knew she would go early and stay late if that's what it took. But if she wasn't there now, she'd be there soon. The important thing was he was not only free, he had a home, a job, a good reputation, plenty of work and a good woman. No matter what happened with Lauren and the doctor, he wouldn't have any trouble supporting them. Himself, Lauren and the boys. He was left pretty much intact. He felt like he got off with a bargain.

He laughed out loud. A million-dollar bargain? The truth was as long as he had his house, his business and his boys, he could always rebuild. He texted Tim.

Divorce final. I paid and I'm a single man.

I'm glad, brother. It was a hard bargain.

Are you well?

Very well, Beau. Angela sends love.

If you ever need anything...

Thanks. Back atcha.

Love to Angela.

When he got home, Lauren's car was in the drive but he didn't see Drew's car. He unlocked his door and walked in—they kept the doors locked these days. She was at the dining table on her laptop and she stood expectantly.

"Where's Drew?" he asked.

She shook her head. "I got home a couple of hours ago and he hasn't been here."

He let out a breath. He went to her, pulled her into his arms and kissed her neck. "I'm done," he said softly. "It's over."

"Over?"

"It will have to be filed so it's just paperwork. It's not my paperwork."

"You don't have to do anything more?" she asked.

"I have to write a big check," he said, and he laughed. "That's easy. That's so much easier than the stress of fighting, of being off balance, of being unhappy. Well worth the money."

"Your house? Your business?"

"The money will make all that secure. It's money well spent." He pulled her closer. "I love you."

"Oh Beau, can it really be over?"

"The marriage is over," he said. "How Pamela takes it? That's something I can't do anything about."

"What do we do now?" she asked.

"Tomorrow I'm going to the bank to borrow some money, then I'll deliver a check to her lawyer's office, then I'm going to decide what to pack for our long weekend in Victoria." He covered her mouth in a passionate kiss that lasted forever. "I hope we have time to see the flowers," he whispered against her mouth.

"We'll manage," she said.

"Is Sylvie going to give you that time off?"

She nodded and smiled. "I told her about it the first day. Since I already had the tickets, she was very understanding. We're getting a schedule of events together so I don't miss anything in the future. And you have no idea how many things the Emersons have going on!"

He rubbed a knuckle along her cheek. "Is this a good move for you?"

"All my moves have been good ones since I met you," she said.

Their visit to Victoria was magical. The gardens seemed to be celebrating Valentine's Day, but that wasn't even the most charming thing. It was the dead of winter and yet pots of colorful flowers stood and hung all over town. The average temperatures in Victoria were milder than most of the country. It was a little like Alameda—a special place just a bit balmier than the rest of the world.

And their time there was a little like a honeymoon, relaxed and satisfying.

Despite the romance of getting away alone together, they were both anxious to get back. After the stress of the past year, having an ordinary life filled with ordinary joys felt like such a gift. Beau's home was fast becoming hers. The days following the mediation had been a little rocky for Michael and Drew, but then things settled into a routine and Lauren and Beau got together with the boys a few times. That's when she realized the kids needed this legal wrangling to be over as much as Beau and Lauren did.

She made a point to reach out to Lacey more often to make sure she was settled with the idea that her parents were not going to reconcile, but there was no such reassurance from her daughter.

"Have you seen your father?" she asked Lacey.

"Not that I want to, but I've seen him. He's making it really hard. I think he might be going a little crazy."

Lauren's jaw clenched. "Why do you say that?"

"The way he talks," she said. "The things he says. Since Christmas… Since Thanksgiving, really, he hasn't looked healthy. He's lost weight, he has bags under his eyes, sometimes he chews Tums like they're breath mints. I can't even ask him if he feels okay because he says, 'No. I'm sixty and my wife of twenty-five years left me for a younger man.'"

"Listen, seeing him is up to you, honey. He's always had some serious anger issues and I think staying with him for so long masked those problems from you girls. Beau is three years younger than I am, not exactly a younger man. Beware,

Lacey. If he's making you uncomfortable, you can just be too busy. You're over twenty-one. If you don't want to talk to me, talk to Cassie."

Lacey laughed. "And she really is too busy. Unlike me, Cassie has a life!"

"Aunt Beth will certainly make time for you," Lauren said. "Don't try to go through this alone, honey."

Lauren missed Cassie like crazy, but the great news was that Cassie had never been happier. She was overworked, sleep-deprived, deep in debt and completely happy. Jeremy was a good partner; law school, while horrifyingly difficult, was a challenge she was up to and she was doing just fine. She had new friends.

And Lauren had old friends. She met her coworkers from Merriweather and they caught up on all the latest news, including the news that Stu Lonigan had left the company.

Lauren was frustrated by the length of time it was taking for her divorce to become final. It seemed Brad's attorney had one delay tactic after another. And Brad was gathering fines for contempt, for not paying support, for failing to appear. Beau said, "It doesn't matter. The law will catch up with him eventually but in the meantime, we're fine. We're together and we have plenty to eat."

Her life was so good in spite of divorce, in spite of un-settled finances. When she went to Sylvie's house to work she was filled with gratitude. Ruth Ann was executing her move to a warmer, less expensive part of the country, though still available by phone. What files and records she kept for Sylvie were paperless and Sylvie's office was right down the hall. There were weeks that Sylvie and Andy were traveling and Lauren was alone there, holding down the fort. The job made her feel empowered. It was a great pleasure to support worthy causes even if the money was not hers.

While Erica Slade could not seem to hasten Lauren's divorce, she was able to settle with Merriweather. Lauren was given a generous settlement to avoid court, a settlement she immediately deposited in a trust and offered to share with Cassie. She was feeling downright lucky.

Beau was just thinking of quitting for the day when he received a phone call from a man who identified himself as Detective Craig Moore. It was the call he'd been waiting for, even though he had no hope of recouping his loss on the truck.

"Mr. Magellan, we have been interviewing a suspect and would like you to come in to talk with us. We'd like to know if there's any connection between the two of you."

"What's his name?" Beau asked reflexively. But his thoughts ran wild. Did the police think he orchestrated the bombing of his own truck? Impossible. First of all, he lost money on the damage—the truck was totaled for the blue book value and he'd bought it for far more. Drive it off the lot and it depreciates by thousands.

"If you wouldn't mind, sir. There's quite a lot to explain about the incident and I think maybe you can help."

"All right," he said, confused but eager to be helpful. "Give me a half hour. I was just leaving work."

"Take your time," Detective Moore said. "I'll be here."

Beau took the time to text Lauren and tell her he'd just gotten a call from the police and they wanted him to stop by the station because they had a suspect, so he'd be running a little late.

No worries, she texted back. I'll stop for groceries and start dinner.

Just like every other time he so much as thought about Lauren, his heart was full. He said a little prayer of thanks and hoped all the drama of their lives could come to an end. Living with her, depending on her, being her other half made him so happy. Every day his feelings for her grew. Lying beside her at night, waking up with her in the morning were miracles he never thought he could have in his life. And from the way she responded to him, she felt the same way. Sometimes they just held each other close, held on for dear life. She was everything to him.

He walked into the police department and thought, *maybe this will be the end of it.* He asked for Detective Moore and the man came to escort him inside to his desk.

"Thank you for coming," the detective said. "I'd like you to look at some pictures to start with. Have a seat right here."

"Sure," Beau said. The detective spread out a collection of eight mug shots and asked Beau if he recognized anyone. Beau shook his head. "No. Should I?"

"I'd like you to look at a brief video," Detective Moore said. He opened up his laptop, keyed in a command and turned the screen toward Beau. "Anything familiar about this?"

"Yeah," Beau said, watching a man approach his truck, carefully place something in the bed and run away. "That's my truck. Is that the guy? The guy who put a bomb in my truck?"

"We identified some materials and a partial print from a piece of shrapnel. To be honest, the print was terrible and we might not have made a match, but the guy is known for this kind of mischief—"

"Mischief? That was a seventy-thousand-dollar truck!"

"Oh, it's worse than that," Detective Moore said. "Recognize the background on that video?"

Beau squinted. He shook his head.

"You were at a wedding. You parked about a block away, across from a convenience store. They had security cameras in front and back and sides of the store as well as inside. They used to have a lot of robberies."

Beau ran a hand through his hair. "Did you catch him?"

"Yes, sir, we brought him in. We showed him this little movie. He admitted he made the bomb. Not very well, as it turns out. But pipe bombs are very unstable. He expected it to go off when you started driving. A little bouncing in the bed of the truck should have done the trick."

"Why, in God's name would he put a bomb in my truck? And why did it explode in the middle of the night? When the truck wasn't moving? Was it hooked up to some kind of timer or something?"

The detective shook his head. "Like I said, pipe bombs are real unstable. They've been known to blow up in a mailbox hours after being put there. I'm guessing, since he won't admit to this part, but I think the bomb was very peaceful in the grooves in the truck bed and you didn't have any fast starts or sudden stops, didn't hit any big bumps... It could have spontaneously exploded—that has been known to happen. But we also found pawprints around the truck. Probably a large, domestic cat."

"What did he admit?" Beau asked.

"He's a repeat offender. He was paid to make the bomb and put it in your truck and the location was disclosed to him. Plain and simple, it was a hit, Mr. Magellan. You and your girlfriend were targets. Our suspect fell apart like a cheap watch, gave us everything to keep his sentence down. He'll testify."

"My God, was it Lauren's husband?" Beau asked.

"No, Mr. Magellan. It was your wife."

He was stunned for a second. "Pamela?"

"You seem really shocked."

"Yeah, I'm shocked. How would she even know someone who would do something like that? I mean, she's a loose cannon... She's kind of self-centered and angry, but..."

"Self-centered, angry people are sometimes very resourceful. Has she created trouble before?"

"Not trouble like trying to kill people!" he said. "She blames people for her problems, manipulates, she can be very selfish…"

"She's going to be prosecuted," Detective Moore said. "Are you in an ongoing relationship with her?"

He shook his head. "Our divorce will be final very soon—everything is done but the filing. When that bomb was put in my truck, that was my best friend's wedding, way before we signed the final papers. I was with the woman I've been seeing for a few months. The woman had nothing to do with the divorce. Pamela left me well over a year ago. Once I said we'll call it quits, she wanted to patch things up." He shook his head in frustration. "I thought she was a little crazy…"

"Maybe more than a little," the detective said.

"Are you absolutely sure she wanted to kill me?" Beau asked.

"I'm sure. She hasn't confessed to that but the bomb maker said he agreed to do it for seven thousand dollars. He…um… recorded the meeting and took a picture of the money with his iPhone. He's a real up-market assassin."

"God," Beau said. "This is going to crush her sons."

"Do they have a good relationship with you?" Detective Moore asked.

"Yes. I try to be there for them. They're eighteen and twenty-one. Grown up but… But not, you know?"

"I know," the detective said. "Maybe you should get some professional help with this?"

"I don't know," he said. "I just sat through a day-long settlement mediation with her, agreed to give her a lot of money and she never even twitched. God, if I'd just tried to kill someone, I'd have been a little nervous during a property settlement conference, during a divorce. Wouldn't you?"

"I don't know, Mr. Magellan," he said. "I never ordered a hit on anyone."

"Who does something like that?" Beau asked, still in shock.

"You'd be surprised. The big difference here is she almost made it happen. Most of our suspects try to make their deal with a cop and they go down before it gets too scary. This was a little close. You were very lucky."

A door opened with a squeak, closed with a click. Beau looked to the back of the office. Two plainclothed officers were escorting Pamela out of the office. Her hands were handcuffed behind her back. She wore her amazingly sexy business attire—jacket with a tight waist, slit in the skirt, four-inch heels, lots of cleavage, pretty blond hair, long scary nails. He stared at her and tried to remember the small, pretty, vulnerable girl in the torn jeans and the oversize man's shirt, her brown hair pulled back in a ponytail, a couple of little boys on her lap, begging for ice cream…

She met his eyes, frowned and turned away.

"When did she get so cold?" he asked.

"I don't know, buddy. But she'll make bail. You might want to be real cautious."

Beau said he would, but the question about Pam's coldness, he was asking himself.

"I have to go home," Beau said. "I have to tell Lauren, who I love. I have to tell my boys, who I love as if they were my blood sons. This sucks so bad. How could she?"

"What could you have done different?" the cop asked.

He did a memory check in a matter of seconds. The little boys. Their poor abandoned mom, all the times she left and he was all they had. He remembered her temper, her selfishness. He would have taken the boys as a single dad but she never would have let that happen.

"I don't know."

During what is usually one of the most beautiful months of the year in the Bay Area, there was darkness at Lauren's and Beau's door. Just when Lauren thought it couldn't get any worse, Beau came home from his meeting with the police wearing an expression of anger that she'd never seen before.

"Good Lord, what is it?" she asked.

"The bomb in the truck? It was Pamela."

Lauren was stunned. "She made a *bomb*?"

"She didn't make it," he said. "She hired someone to do it."

"To destroy your truck?" Lauren asked, shaking her head.

He pulled her into his arms and held her tightly. "To kill us," he said in a whisper. "It's a miracle it didn't explode while we were both in the truck. I still don't know how she knew it would be just us. What if the boys were there? Was she willing to kill them, too? God," he said, a catch in his throat.

"My God," she said. "Who would do that?"

He didn't answer. He just held on to her. After a long while, he said, "She's been arrested. She'll be prosecuted. But I was warned she'll probably make bail." He ran his fingers through her hair, tucking it back behind her ear. "Maybe my house isn't the safest place for you to be. Maybe you should go to Beth's. Or Sylvie's."

She kept her hands on his shoulders and shook her head. "Now? I don't think so. We've come so far and we don't know how far we have yet to go. What do the boys say about this?"

He shook his head. "I don't know what they know. I have to call them. If they knew this was going to happen and said nothing to warn us, then I don't know anything about them."

Of course Drew and Michael didn't know what their mother had done and it went down hard. Michael nearly collapsed in an emotional outburst, crying like a five-year-old. Drew was more stoic. He was angry. "I'm through," he said.

"Listen, we're going to get some counseling," Beau said.

"Do you still have to give her a million dollars?" Drew asked.

"I'm pretty sure I do," he said. "I'll check with the lawyer, but I don't think one thing has anything to do with the other."

"I don't think you should," Drew said.

While Drew let his anger spill out, Michael buried his face in his arm and sobbed, probably as much from shame and humiliation as disappointment and fear.

"I don't know how it got to this," Beau said. "When I met your mother, she was just a sad, poor girl. I have a lot of experience with being poor. Poor doesn't mean bad or stupid or criminal. It just means worn-out jeans and lean meals. I grew up poor and my parents were good, God-fearing, law-abiding, hardworking people. We laughed a lot, we all pitched in. Your mom was always so angry, I could never figure out how she could stand to live with that anger. And I think she had a pretty good life. Maybe not when she was a kid, but she got a pretty good education even if she didn't finish her degree. She had a good job, a decent home, plenty of everything. And she's beautiful. I can't explain why all that was never enough."

"I think it was me," Michael said through his running nose and teary eyes. "I told her about Tim, about him getting married. I told her I was going to the wedding, that you were the best man. I told her where it was."

"It wasn't your fault," Beau said. "If not there, she'd have found another place. It wasn't because of anything you said."

"You're the only person who ever stuck with us," Michael said.

"We're going to get help with this," Beau said.

Lauren sat across the room at the breakfast bar, just listening.

"Lauren, I'm sorry," Michael said.

"Oh darling, it wasn't you. It was us. It was Beau and me. We married people who are selfish and controlling. We had to move on from that, of course. And divorcing them was not going to be tidy. I don't think either of us imagined it would be this dangerous but at the end of the day, we're not very surprised. I ended up in an emergency room. Beau was so lucky to only lose a truck. Divorce can be a terrible ordeal. We're the ones who are sorry. You shouldn't have to go through this."

Early the next morning, Beau spent about a half hour on the phone with Tim. His best friend asked him if he could afford some good counseling. "I'll manage even if I have to sell body parts," Beau said.

"Ask at a domestic violence shelter," Tim suggested. "Or maybe the DV unit at the police department."

"This is the kind of thing you see on the news," Beau said. "Not the kind of thing ordinary people have to deal with!"

"It's a crazy, cracked world, my friend. It never hurts to also pray. I'm kind of partial to prayer."

"Buddy, I never prayed so much in my life," Beau said.

CHAPTER EIGHTEEN

Pamela spent very little time in jail. She hired an excellent attorney, was out on bail in less than forty-eight hours, but her passport was taken away and she was immediately served with an order of protection to stay away from her ex-husband and sons. She called them all repeatedly, making excuses and denying the charges and so went back to jail for twenty-four hours, which seemed to quiet her down. At least temporarily.

Beau delivered the divorce settlement money to Pamela's lawyer so that his business would be cleared and was counseled by his lawyer that he was definitely entitled to a civil suit against his ex-wife to recoup some of his monetary losses. But Beau was exhausted. More lawyers and courts and lawsuits held zero appeal. He decided all he wanted was his freedom, at any price.

"That's dangerous thinking," Sonja told him. "Please don't say that out loud."

"Think she can find a way to make me pay more? More than sleepless nights for me and for Lauren and the boys?"

Deep in the dark of night Beau and Lauren whispered about it. They had thought their marriages were difficult and heartbreaking, not life-threatening. They had assumed their spouses would be selfish and greedy, not physically dangerous. Neither of them thought of themselves as cagey enough to get half of what they'd accrued in the marriage; neither was capable of really hurting someone for revenge or material wealth.

Beau just wanted to make the world beautiful. Lauren just wanted to live in peace and protect her family.

Beau found a way to make things better. At least once every week, depending on Lauren's schedule, he stopped by the Emerson home and took her to a favorite park or garden for lunch. He knew the best hidden rooftop gardens, the most beautifully landscaped parks, the most delicious hideaways. They would eat a takeout lunch and talk like they used to in the gardens of Divine Redeemer.

Slowly, the tension seemed to ease, probably because his business was growing as it did in the spring every year. He had several designs in the works and planting yards and rooftops had begun because the weather was heavenly. An architectural magazine featured three of his rooftop gardens, the article went viral and he thought he was going to have to hire an answering service to take the additional calls that were coming in. Michael and Drew seemed to be getting along all right, thanks to some counseling, and Beau's home life was better than it ever had been even with the danger they had experienced.

But, he looked in the truck bed and under the truck before getting inside every time he had to drive somewhere. It was a little like OCD but he decided if that was the worst thing that came of his mis-marriage and severely problematic divorce, he'd live through it. When he wondered if he'd manage another day through the stress, he just took Lauren into his arms, felt her mold herself to him in sweet affection, and he'd know he was finally where he wanted to be.

In April Lauren let her rental house go and even though her lease was for a year, the owner was very decent about it all. He probably didn't want the domestic disturbances she'd been having to wear on the neighborhood any further. It left Beau's home as her only home. It was not only where she wanted to be, it was also where she needed to be. They relied on each other now, after what had happened.

Beau and Lauren also enlarged Beau's garden and updated the backyard because the weather was wonderful and Lauren had never loved being outdoors more. When she had lived in Brad's house, she found her backyard to be too sterile and manicured, too artificial. In Beau's yard and garden, there were things to watch growing and it was exciting. First there were little sprouts, then full thick stems then the start of fruits and flowers. Every morning, still in her robe, she wandered through the yard and garden, pulling a weed here or there, deadheading a bud or flowers, and before long Beau would join her, grooming the plants.

She had hardly any time to worry about her divorce, though she did check with Erica regularly. Brad was clearly stalling. Erica thought he'd rather pay fines and additional court costs than pay her, even though that wasn't going to work out for him. It would all catch up with him eventually. Lauren's job for Sylvie's foundation was so rewarding, so busy, her schedule packed with meetings and planning sessions, she didn't have a lot of time to worry about Brad. She and Beau were getting along just fine. The job had empowered her, made her feel vital again. She met with event planners, consultants, lawyers, account managers and sat in on the foundation board meetings.

Lauren talked to Lacey a couple of times a week and saw her for lunch or dinner about once a week. Sylvie had even hosted them at her house one day for lunch. Lauren wasn't quite as worried about her daughter. Lacey seemed to be getting her footing, which probably had a lot to do with spending more time with Lauren at Beau's house. She might be spoiled and a bit shallow, but she was growing more fond of Beau by the day. And she was seeing Brad less. Brad had, in his lifetime, driven a lot of people crazy.

In truth, Lauren hardly cared about her divorce anymore. Brad signing off on the marriage, even giving her a big check, could not possibly make her any happier than she was. She tried to explain that to Lacey. "I live in a stable environment with a very good man and his boys treat me kindly, with respect. I have a great job, good friends, my girls are in good health and while I'm not able to contribute much, I'm still able to help both of you."

"But what am I going to do after I get my master's? In less than six months? Teach junior high? I'll have to give up everything! The salaries are so low!"

"I don't know, kiddo. You might have to find a different kind of job. You're welcome to stay with me and Beau if you want to. You might have to start over like a lot of us have had to do."

"But start over doing what?" Lacey asked.

Lauren shrugged sympathetically. "Some choices are very hard to make. God knows I've put off the hard choices and regretted it, but once I dared to start over I've been so happy. Just finish your degree for now, then keep an open mind. I don't have a lot of money to give you but I'll cover your head and feed you." Then she laughed and said, "Wait till you see the garden in Beau's backyard."

And Lacey said, "I don't think his garden is going to get me as excited as it gets you."

★ ★ ★

Brad asked Lacey regularly what her mother was doing for work, for fun, for getting along financially and Lacey just said, "We'll get along so much better if I don't talk about you with Mom or about Mom with you."

But Brad knew. He couldn't get near her—there was that restraining order, something he believed she'd done for show and leverage. It didn't help her in any way that he could see. He knew she'd lost her job before Christmas, that his buddy Stu had resigned because of it, and that she was seeing a younger man. Some blue-collar type. A landscaper. A damn gardener. What was her problem? Was the pool boy all tied up? The landscaper probably supported her on his tips.

And he knew the gardener's ex-wife had tried to have them killed. Once the police had interviewed him and explained why, he began following that story obsessively. The woman had been arrested and indicted and would stand trial. He wondered how smart Lauren thought she was now. Had that been a wiser choice than saving her marriage? But then Lauren wasn't that bright, was she?

He knew Lauren was talking to Cassie and must be barely talking to Lacey; Lacey was deep in her studies and didn't even always take his calls. He wasn't sure how Cassie was affording law school but he did know she'd chosen that wimpy Jeremy who would probably never amount to much over her own family. Cassie had written him off over that misunderstanding— Lauren's black eye. That could all be explained. He couldn't help it that no one believed him. He was set up. It wasn't him.

He knew he still had control of the family money and wasn't going to part with it gracefully.

Things weren't going well at home. He had the same yard crew, house cleaners, window washers, but there was no one to pull it all together. When the housekeeper washed his pants instead of taking them to the cleaners, there was no one to grab them, take them in for appropriate pressing. All the details fell through the cracks and it made him furious. He had immediately hired an assistant, someone to run his errands and handle any other details for him. He found out that domestic assistants didn't weather him "correcting" them, pointing out the right way to do things, as well as a wife. He was now on his fifth in nine months and he couldn't stand her. He never mentioned this to his daughter because he didn't want Lauren to know.

He was having trouble at the hospital. He was always in a bad mood, sidetracked by his failing marriage, or was that pending divorce? He was driven out of his mind by the idea that his beautiful wife was getting shagged by a younger man. Never mind Brad had had his share of much younger women, he had once had such wonderful control over Lauren. The thing that drove him craziest was, he never saw this coming. Even though she had threatened many times, he never thought it would happen.

He hated Lauren and he wanted to punish her, but his lawyer had warned him over and over that any kind of physical violence was going to cost him big. It would put him away. And felonies that included violence and assault might cost him his license.

He'd had a couple of complaints filed with the hospital. A resident and an OR tech had both accused him of abuse. He was under a lot of pressure; maybe he was a little terse. He dropped an instrument and a nurse said he threw it. They both needed to get spines. Limp dicks. Complaining babies. They should have worked for important surgeons like he had. He had never been coddled. And he hadn't complained. Filing complaints? What was this world coming to?

Then came the straw that broke the camel's back. He was tortured by the money this divorce was going to cost him, he hated that he'd lost one daughter to Lauren and was barely hanging on to the other, he was furious that she had implied to some people that he was *abusive* and swore out a legal order of protection... But he reached his breaking point when he learned that she was working for the Emerson Foundation. Those were *his* friends! He'd been Andy's friend for years!

It was a simple accident. He called Andy and asked him when he was free for a round of golf at Pebble Beach. Andy said he'd have to check his calendar. Then he asked when the golf tournament for Andy's kids was coming up and Andy said, again, he'd have to check his calendar. Brad's hackles rose and he said, "What's going on? Are you avoiding me for some reason?"

"Not at all, Brad! I'm sure we'll continue to have a very amicable friendship and we appreciate all your support. We'll find a good day to get together when it's not awkward."

Brad had laughed and said, "Why would it be awkward? You don't like the color of my money? You managed to get your hands on plenty of it—if you don't kick my ass on the golf course, you eat it up at the charity events!"

Andy chuckled and said, "I love your money. I just don't want to put any further strain on you and your ex-wife. Sylvie depends on her. Best assistant Sylvie has ever had. It's a good relationship."

"How's that?" Brad said, after a long pause.

"I was just referring to the fact that Lauren is Sylvie's administrative assistant and director of the foundation, and that's working out very well. For Sylvie and for me. So we want to keep it like that. Don't we?"

Brad was stunned, but he said, "No problem there. Now take a look at the calendar and let me know when you're free. It's been a long time."

"Absolutely!" Andy said.

Brad hung up on his friend and thought, *fuck golf!* He

seethed. Had she moved into his circle of friends? And left them wondering if they should socialize with him?

He called Lacey. "So, I've asked you a couple of times now. What is your mother doing for work?"

"Well, she was offered her job back at Merriweather, but she got something else. And I've told you before, it just keeps things nicer if we don't talk about Mom..."

"I heard she's working for the Emersons," Brad said.

"You heard that? Where did you hear that?"

"From the Emersons, that's who! You might have told me! They're my friends, not hers! She obviously used my friendship with them to get a job!"

"I don't think so, Dad," Lacey said.

He hung up on her. He called Lauren. To his surprise, she answered.

"It's been nine fucking months!" he said angrily. "Don't you think enough is enough? You've turned everyone against me, tried to wrench everything I've earned away from me and now you're fucking some yard boy! You promised me life! If you end this cruelty right now, I'll put the house in your name. I'll pay for law school for Cassie. You can negotiate your own terms! This can't go on!"

She hung up on him. She blocked his number—he tried to call her back and was informed by a tinny mechanical voice that a call from his number wouldn't go through.

He threw things for a while, not caring. Housekeeping could clean it up when they serviced the house.

He had trouble sleeping, so he drank. Not too much, just a few. The next day was just a clinic day. The cleaning lady called his cell phone and asked, "Dr. Delaney, there's broken things in the dining room! Like an earthquake!"

"Oh yeah. Sorry about that. Mrs. Delaney was at the house having a little tantrum, throwing things. I meant to sweep up, but I had to get to the hospital."

"*Mrs.* Delaney?" she asked.

"That's what I said!"

He hung up and she called back. "You want to save any pieces?" she asked in her heavily accented English.

"No! Toss it!"

A few days later he had to cancel a surgery because he hadn't been sleeping, he was exhausted and noticed a slight tremor in his hands. Low blood sugar, maybe. He checked his blood pressure and it was high, which he assumed must be Lauren's fault. He prescribed himself something that should bring it down.

The lawyer called and informed him that a bench warrant would be issued, demanding his presence in court. "Let 'em try," Brad said.

"Listen to me, Brad. They can arrest you. They can lock you up. They can leave you in jail until you cooperate with the process."

"You said they don't do that!" Brad argued.

"Judges would much rather see the two parties negotiate a settlement and get on with their lives, but if you refuse to negotiate, if you refuse to appear, there's nothing I can do to help you."

"Then I'll get another lawyer!" he said.

"Doctor, you're losing control. Can I recommend someone for you to talk to? I know a judge, retired judge, who is counseling now. He really helps disgruntled clients pull it together, get control—"

Brad disconnected.

A warrant was delivered to his office, demanding he appear in court. He didn't. A few days later, he was arrested and taken to jail. He missed several surgeries. It took him a couple of days to untangle everything. He was visited at his office by the chief of surgery to whom he said, "Do you have any idea how vindictive a woman can be?"

"Maybe you should take a couple of weeks off and get this straightened out," the doctor in charge said. "It hasn't gone unnoticed that you're getting more agitated by the day and frankly, you could put the hospital at risk."

Brad told the chief of surgery to go fuck himself. And for that his privileges at the hospital were suspended.

Lauren was returning from the store with several bags of groceries. She brought the first two into the house through the back door and left two more bags in the trunk. It was going to be a big night. Both of Beau's boys were coming over as well as Lacey. There could also be a girlfriend or two, depending on who had to work. The weather was perfect for grilling and sitting out on the patio. It was the middle of May, Cassie and Jeremy would be coming home in a few weeks. Jeremy for a visit, Cassie for a longer visit as law school was on summer break, but Jeremy didn't want to interrupt his research for too long.

She put groceries in the refrigerator and left the nonperishables on the counter as she moved toward the back door to get another load.

"Hello, Lauren," she heard.

She nearly jumped out of her skin and actually grabbed her chest in shock. It took her just a second to catch her breath and reach for the phone. Brad was sitting on the sectional in Beau's great room.

"Don't do that," he said. "Please."

That request was not polite or solicitous, but commanding as usual and so she ignored it and dialed 911. She rattled off her information as calmly and quickly as possible. "My husband is here, in the house, and I have a restraining order because I'm afraid for my life. Please come. Please help." Then she put the phone on the counter, leaving the line open, so she would have two hands free to fight him off, if necessary. "How did you get in here?" she asked him.

"I followed you right in," he said. "If you're serious about keeping me away, I would expect you to be careful, but you've always been such a ditz."

"What's your plan?" she asked him.

"I thought we'd talk. If you'll just tell me what it's going to take we can get this behind us."

She frowned and nearly laughed. "What it's going to take?" she echoed.

"I'll forgive you and take you back. I'll even give you something for security if that's important. But you have nearly ruined my life, my career, my relationship with my daughters and friends, and I think you've got your revenge by now. Let's get this over with. It's been nearly a year. What are you holding out for?"

She shook her head. "I just want to be divorced," she said. "Let the lawyers work out the details." She strained to listen, hoping to hear sirens.

"I've been suspended from hospital privileges because of you," he said. "My closest friends are now your friends. And employers—they're your friends and employers. I can't even imagine what kind of lies you had to tell to make all that happen, but I give up. I just want my life back. What's it going to cost me?"

She squinted at him. Was he truly crazy? She shook her head a little wildly. "I never did anything to you," she said in an urgent whisper. "I only want to get away from you! You're mean and dangerous and you should go now. Go before the police get here."

"I've spent days in jail because of you," he said. "My partners think I'm unstable because of you when all along you were the unstable one. But I can deal with all that if you'll just give me my life back. Give me my kids and friends and life."

"How am I supposed to do that, Brad?" she asked.

"I will do whatever it takes to put it back the way it was, back when I had some control and could make things work. It was difficult, you've always been difficult, but once I figured it out, everything was fine. It's not anymore."

"It wasn't fine," she said. "It was terrible. We slept in separate rooms. We were both so unhappy. I have never understood why you didn't ask for a divorce first!"

"Because it worked," he said. "It wasn't perfect, but it worked. I took such good care of you. You always had the best of everything and I didn't ask for much in return. It worked."

"*Worked*? Was that the life you wanted?" she asked with a shake of her head.

He grimaced and suddenly pulled a small, silver handgun out of his pocket. "The alternative is much worse," he said. "I need my life back. I can't function like this. That's all I'm after. It was just fine."

"Brad, don't be rash—you'll find someone better. You'll find a woman who suits you better, who likes things the way you like them. You're so popular with your patients and co-workers…it won't be long before—"

He waved the gun around. He stood and he looked so tired, so worn. "I told you what my plan is. You never listen. We have to go home and end this craziness. I don't have anything more to lose. Because of you changing your mind, I'm losing everything."

"But that's not true," she said. "You have the house. You chose it. I never even looked at it, it was always your house. You have a successful practice. You have had other women— we both know that. You have two daughters and if you'd only tell them you care about them, they'd be there for you. What more do you need?"

"I need you to come home, Lauren. I don't want to be alone anymore. There's no one to talk to."

"But… But you never talked to me," she said.

"Of course I did," he said. "I called and texted every day. I talked to you after work every day. I talked to you on the weekend. We went out to a nice restaurant every week. Twice a week. We traveled and made friends…"

"You shoved me, pinched me, yelled at me! We did only what you wanted to do, went where you wanted to go! *We* didn't talk—*you* talked! And if I said anything—" He scowled and pointed the gun at her. "Please," she said. "Please don't."

The back door opened with a crash as Beau came in. He carried two bags of groceries, then kicked the door closed with his foot. He grinned at Lauren. "Get a little distracted, honey?" he asked. Then he noticed Brad. "Whoa!" he yelled, dropping the groceries on the floor and leaping to place himself in front of Lauren.

Brad slowly raised the muzzle of the gun to his right temple.

"No!" Beau shouted, flying the few long steps across the great room to tackle Brad, knocking the gun away from his temple. They wrestled for control of the gun for a moment and then there was a loud pop. A full two seconds passed as Beau and Brad struggled. Then Beau slid to the floor, a growing river of blood running from the left side of his chest. His eyes were open in shock, his lips parted in a soundless cry.

"Beau!" Lauren screamed, running to him. She knelt on the floor and lifted Beau's shoulders, holding him in her arms.

Brad, still hovering over them, just looked down at them.

"Help him! Brad! Help him!"

Brad just stood there, watching. A dazed look on his face.

Lauren pressed down on the wound with her hand as she stared up at Brad. She finally heard sirens, but they weren't close enough. "Brad," she said calmly. "If you help him, I will come home. We can put it back the way it was."

Brad went to the kitchen, came back with a towel. He

knelt on Beau's other side, pressing the towel to Beau's upper chest. The gun lay on the carpet and Brad went into his clinical mode. The police kicked the door and rushed in, weapons drawn. "We need medical," Brad shouted. "We've had a shooting accident. He's losing blood but he's still conscious. Bullet to the upper left quadrant. It's still in there."

"How did this—" one of the officers attempted.

"I'm a surgeon," Brad said. "We can get ahead of this. I'll call ahead for a surgery setup."

Lauren leaned over Beau, grateful to feel his breath on her face. "Stay with me," she whispered. "It's going to be all right."

Paramedics arrived less than two minutes later, the police confiscated the gun from the floor. Then there was a great deal of commotion while the medics started an IV, packed the wound, applied a bandage and got him on the gurney. "I'm going with him," Lauren said to the paramedics. "My ex-husband isn't a practicing surgeon—take this man to the nearest suitable hospital."

"We're going to Alameda," one of them said. "Go, go, go."

"Wait," Brad yelled. "Lauren! You're coming with me!"

She stopped and turned to stare at him. Her clothes were stained with Beau's blood. "God have mercy on your soul," she said to Brad. "He's the shooter," she said to the police. Then she turned and jogged after the gurney.

"Wait!" Brad called. "Hey, what are you doing?" he asked the police. "Hey, Lauren! Tell them it wasn't my fault!"

But Lauren got into the ambulance with Beau. She leaned her forehead against his and her tears fell on his face.

"Hey," he said. "Hey, don't be scared. I'm okay."

"I think we're okay, ma'am," the paramedic said. "Missed his heart, lung and vital artery. Some worry about the condition of his shoulder..."

"You have to be okay," she said.

★ ★ ★

Lauren had been aware of the gun, but ironically it had never interfered in her life or in her conflicts with Brad. Their house was burglarized years ago and Brad decided he wanted a gun for protection, but he had little interest in it. He was not a gun lover. He was not a shooting enthusiast. In fact, he probably hadn't cleaned or fired the weapon in years. She found that to be a slight miracle.

Brad was not arrested immediately. The police interviewed Lauren while she was at the hospital waiting for Beau's surgery to be completed, but they had the dispatcher's tape of her 911 call. Since she'd left the line open the conversation between Brad and Lauren was recorded. After the completion of Beau's surgery, Beau told them that it was true, he had intervened in Brad's suicide attempt. "Because I didn't even think," Beau said. "You don't want anyone to do that to himself, right? I just reacted."

"If I'd lost you, I think it would have killed me," she said.

"But you didn't and I have no regrets. Since I met you, I'm even more aware of how precious life is."

Brad was arrested and booked. The charges were murky because the worst thing he had done was violate an order of protection and point the gun at Lauren. In a split second, the result of that could have been catastrophic. But it was clear that Brad had snapped. Lauren learned that as they booked him he kept carrying on about being a surgeon, a well-known surgeon with many friends in high places. The routine medical examination given to new inmates was brief. His blood pressure was noted as high but it wasn't surprising as he'd just been arrested and brought to jail.

But that first night in jail, Brad had a stroke. He was assumed to be asleep but when the guards realized something was wrong he was rushed to the hospital and was operated on. It was as if sixty years of rage exploded in his brain and he was not going to make a full recovery. It left him mentally and physically handicapped.

It took a few weeks of emergency legal intervention but Lauren helped Lacey assume the role of legal guardian and obtain a power of attorney so that Brad's own money could cover the bills for his care. Grandma Delaney at eighty-five was not able to help much. In fact, she was growing more fragile by the day and her only son's infirmity didn't help her condition.

Brad didn't seem to remember what had happened to him and while his limitations frustrated him, he was receiving top-of-the-line care in one of the best rehab and extended care facilities in the Bay Area. His right side was paralyzed and he was mostly helpless.

And it gave Lacey a purpose. She quickly began to develop an interest in estate management and long-term care administration. Lacey started talking about studying business or even law.

This certainly wasn't the purpose Lacey had envisioned for herself, but for once she was in complete control, at least as long as she had the counsel of her mother. Brad was not his usual blustering, abusive self but rather dependent and very emotional. He cried a lot; he asked for Lauren and sometimes he thought Lacey was his wife, though his speech was barely understandable. He was a bit like a child and his neediness touched his daughter.

The family court, with the help of the attorneys and mediator, were going to be able to finalize Lauren's divorce, money could finally be moved, the big house could be put on the market, and the last chapter on their troubled marriage could be written at last. Cassie visited and saw her father and he seemed pleased to have his daughters near again, though the most he could do was squeeze a hand.

Lauren did not visit him, though she did have some pity

for him. She made herself available to Lacey and the administrator at the extended care facility where Brad lived, tried to speed up the funding for his care by helping Lacey work with the attorney, and consulted with medical personnel, but had decided on the day the bullet pierced Beau's chest, she had ended her personal involvement with her ex-husband. Brad would never operate again, but with any luck and great rehab therapy, he might walk and feed himself without spilling all his food. Would he be able to read? Follow the plot of a television program? Have a meaningful conversation? Only time would tell. The damage from the stroke was significant.

But at the end of the day, she was very proud of her daughters. Maybe she hadn't failed them after all. Lacey managed her father's estate and his care and because Cassie spent a couple of months of summer in Alameda, helping her and renewing their relationship, it felt as though they could be a family once again. While Cassie was on the West Coast, gatherings with Lauren, Beth, Cassie and Lacey were sparked with laughter and love. They were a family again.

A family with a great many branches and some very sturdy roots.

EPILOGUE

It was August. They'd had quite a year. Beau was officially divorced, as was Lauren. Pamela was in the wind, fleeing prosecution and prison. When she'd been indicted, she immediately lost her job. She could have used her settlement money from Beau to hire a good lawyer to defend herself but instead she used it to abandon everything, including her sons, and run. She could turn up again, like a bad penny, but he really didn't expect her to show her face around Alameda again. Beau knew he couldn't control how the boys dealt with their mother, but he was definitely through with her. But the good news was Pamela wouldn't gain anything by trying to kill him now. Her one attempt at that, before their divorce, would have made her a widow and she would have inherited the full estate. Now, all that was due to her was some equity in Beau's house and in order to collect it, she'd have to come back to Alameda. If she did that, she'd be arrested and there would be no bail. Her one attempt had been an expensive failure.

Beau had been in a sling for three months, since his first surgery in May, the one that immediately followed the gunshot wound to the shoulder. That bullet, that small bullet, made a mess of things. He had a second surgery to try to improve on his pain and mobility and it seemed to be working. At least that's what the physical therapist said. And Beau's pain management was fine; he was comfortable most of the time and gaining strength in his left arm. Enough strength to pick and pluck in the garden and bring it into the kitchen for Lauren.

He was doing just that when his cell phone chimed and he looked at the text. He laughed. Then he laughed again.

Lauren was in the kitchen and tonight would bring their kids together, something they enjoyed so much. They did a lot of cooking when the kids came. It would be Cassie's last night with the family before going back to law school, so Beth and her family were coming, too. Beau came into the kitchen through the back door, gave her his basket from the garden but was holding his phone with the hand in the sling. He was grinning like a fool.

"I have good news," he said. He gave her a kiss before turning the phone toward her. "Look at this."

The message said, We're coming back to CA in a month and will be staying awhile. The picture showed Angela leaning back against Tim, his arms around her, his hands cradling a large, pregnant belly. Surprise.

"Only good surprises from now on," Beau said.

"Oh! Look! I had no idea they hoped to start a family! Aren't they cute?" Lauren said. She smiled at Beau. "It's been a wild ride but it appears that everyone came out of it in a better place."

Beau slid his good arm around her waist and pulled her against him. "I'd go through all of it again if it meant you loved me at the end of the craziness."

"I'm yours," she said. "And you're mine."

"Good. I'm glad that's settled."

"It's settled. And final," she said.

★ ★ ★ ★ ★